"NO ONE WRITES A BETTER THRILLER THAN BRAD THOR."

—*The Washington Times*

#1 *New York Times* bestselling author Brad Thor's "unforgettable debut"★ *THE LIONS OF LUCERNE* is . . .

"A hot read for a winter night."

—*People*

"Well-written, fast-paced, great characters, fascinating plot, and a climax that will give the reader a case of vertigo."

—Nelson DeMille★

"Fast-paced and exciting."

—*Minneapolis Star Tribune*

"Nonstop action, relentless suspense."

—*Library Journal*

More acclaim for Brad Thor and Scot Harvath, "the perfect all-American hero for the post–September 11th world" (Nelson DeMille)

Praise for *Backlash*

"As close to perfect as a thriller can be."

—*Providence Journal*

"*Backlash* is a triumph."

—BookReporter.com

"*Backlash* is the best thing Thor has ever written."

—The Real Book Spy

Praise for *Spymaster*

"A modern Cold War 2.0 thriller . . . impossible to put down."

—*National Review*

"Thor convincingly portrays Russia as a reborn Cold War–era evil empire hell-bent on reconquering its former territory."

—*The Washington Post*

"A master of action and pacing, Thor continues channeling the likes of John le Carré in crafting a thinking-man's thriller packed with as much brains as brawn, making *Spymaster* a must-read."

—*The Providence Journal*

"A terrific, terrific read."

—KKTX

Praise for *Use of Force*

"No one writes a better thriller than Brad Thor—and *Use of Force* . . . will be viewed by many as his very best."

—*The Washington Times*

"Pure thriller gold . . . well conceived, perfectly timed . . . elegantly paced, harking back to the best of masters like Alistair MacLean and David Morrell."

—*The Providence Journal*

"A gripping thriller!"

—Jake Tapper

"His best book yet. Powerful and reads like the news of what is going on today."

—Glenn Beck

ALSO BY BRAD THOR

Path of the Assassin
State of the Union
Blowback
Takedown
The First Commandment
The Last Patriot
The Apostle
Foreign Influence
The Athena Project
Full Black
Black List
Hidden Order
Act of War
Code of Conduct
Foreign Agent
Use of Force
Spymaster
Backlash

BRAD THOR

THE LIONS OF LUCERNE

A THRILLER

EMILY BESTLER BOOKS

ATRIA

New York London Toronto Sydney New Delhi

EMILY BESTLER BOOKS

ATRIA

An Imprint of Simon & Schuster, Inc.
1230 Avenue of the Americas
New York, NY 10020

This book is a work of fiction. Any references to historical events, real people, or real places are used fictitiously. Other names, characters, places, and events are products of the author's imagination, and any resemblance to actual events or places or persons, living or dead, is entirely coincidental.

First Emily Bestler Books/Atria Paperback edition June 2020

EMILY BESTLER BOOKS / ATRIA PAPERBACKS and colophon are trademarks of Simon & Schuster, Inc.

For information about special discounts for bulk purchases, please contact Simon & Schuster Special Sales at 1-866-506-1949 or business@simonandschuster.com.

The Simon & Schuster Speakers Bureau can bring authors to your live event. For more information, or to book an event, contact the Simon & Schuster Speakers Bureau at 1-866-248-3049 or visit our website at www.simonspeakers.com.

Manufactured in the United States of America

19 20

Library of Congress Cataloging-in-Publication Data is available.

ISBN 978-1-9821-4816-4
ISBN 978-0-7434-8329-2 (ebook)

This book is for my beautiful wife, Trish—
my life, my love, and my best friend.

For reasons of national security, certain names, places, and tactical procedures have been changed within this novel.

Fortes Fortuna Adjuvat.

Fortune favors the brave.

THE LIONS OF LUCERNE

PROLOGUE

"Senators," said Fawcett as he strode across the polished floor in his monogrammed Stubbs and Wootton opera slippers, "I'm so very pleased you could make it."

The study was lined from floor to ceiling with beautiful leather-bound books, most of them first editions. Velvet draperies were drawn tight against the windows, obscuring from view the frigid waters of southern Wisconsin's famed Lake Geneva. The industrialist's eagerly awaited guests sat in two leather club chairs by the fireplace.

Senator Russell Rolander was the first to stand. "Donald, good to see you." The senator stuck out his beefy paw and pumped Fawcett's hand. Rolander and Fawcett had been roommates together at the University of Illinois. The senator had been a college football star and continued his notoriety through many years with the Chicago Bears before going into Illinois politics. Long known as one of Washington, D.C.'s biggest power brokers, Rolander was a ranking member of the U.S. Senate, held a coveted position on the Appropriations Committee, and owned a weekend home down the road from Fawcett's.

Slower to rise was New York senator David Snyder. Snyder shook Fawcett's hand only after it had been offered. Described as a sneaky little son of a bitch by his adversaries, Snyder had scaled the rocky heights of the American political landscape by adhering to a simple mantra: *Do unto others before they do unto you.* He was a master of dirty tricks, and there were few in Washington who had dared cross Snyder's path. Those who had, hadn't survived long politically.

Snyder, a slight man of wiry build and soft features, was the mirror opposite of the large, rugged, blond-haired Rolander. However, what Senator David Snyder lacked in physical stature, he more than made up in brainpower. That intelligence, coupled with a genius for strategy, had landed him an all but permanent spot on the Senate Intelligence Committee. There wasn't a covert operation conducted in the last seven years that didn't somehow or other have Snyder's fingerprints on it.

Fawcett, always the showman, picked up a remote from the inlaid Egyptian box on his desk and pointed it at a wall of books to the right of the fireplace. The false wall slid back to reveal the entryway to a smaller room, about fifteen by fifteen feet. The white walls were decorated with rococo trim and were lined with more leather-bound books. The entire space was permeated with the smell of honey. The wood floor was covered by a large oriental rug. A small fireplace, trimmed in marble, stood in the southwest corner. It utilized the same chimney system as the fireplace in the large study, which helped keep this room a secret to outsiders. Several gilded mirrors hung on the walls and reflected the room's centerpiece, an enormous antique rolltop desk. A plush couch, with handsomely carved legs, sat opposite the desk. Fawcett waved his guests into the adjoining room. Once all three were together, he tapped a button on his remote and the wall slid shut behind them. With only minimal pressure from Fawcett's fingertips, a set of faux book spines sprang forward from one of the bookshelves, revealing a set of crystal decanters.

"Brandy anyone?" said Fawcett as he removed a large snifter and a decanter filled with the amber-colored liquor.

"I'll take one," replied Rolander.

"Scotch rocks, if you've got it," said Snyder.

As Fawcett began pouring the drinks, he motioned for the men to take a seat on the couch. Rolander, very much at ease with himself, plopped right down onto the antique sofa. Snyder lingered, wandering around the small room for a few seconds pretending to admire the decor. The high-tech surveillance sweeper, disguised as a beeper on his hip, had vibrated uncontrollably as he and Rolander were led down the long hallways of Fawcett's palatial home toward the study. An adept student of security and surveillance systems, Snyder had noticed many of Fawcett's obvious safety measures and had guessed at the ones he couldn't see. No doubt Fawcett had the best money could buy. An extremely cautious man, he never left anything to chance. Snyder knew that much about him and that was one of the reasons he'd agreed to become this deeply involved.

The sweeper hadn't vibrated at all since he had entered the secret room, and for the moment, Snyder was satisfied their conversation wasn't being monitored. He took his three fingers of scotch from Fawcett and sat down on the sofa next to Rolander.

"You know, Donald, we should have all of our meetings in this room," said Rolander. "I like it. In fact, this has got to be one of my favorite rooms in the whole house."

"What's that smell?" broke in Snyder. He vaguely recognized the scent, but couldn't exactly place it, nor why it was arousing him. "It's strangely familiar. Smells like some kind of powder."

"It's honey," said Fawcett. "Technically, it's beeswax. The wood floors in here are polished with it."

The minute Fawcett said the word *honey,* Snyder knew why the smell was so familiar and so arousing.

• • •

Mitchell Conti, or Mitch, as everyone was fond of calling him, had joined Senator Snyder's staff two summers ago. He was a strikingly handsome twenty-three-year-old who quickly became very popular on the Hill. He cut a wide swath, dating numerous female aides and pages. To any outside eyes, Mitch Conti was into women only, but David Snyder knew better and so did Mitch. There had been constant electricity between David and Mitch from the moment they met, and one weekend when Mitch brought papers over to the senator's town house for his signature, long looks over drinks led them straight to the bedroom.

Mitch had been fond of a product known as Kama Sutra Honey Dust that he'd found at an adult novelty store. The dust was really a fine powder that smelled and tasted like honey. Mitch would brush it all over Snyder's body with a small feather duster and then lick it off. Not only had David liked it, but so had the many women who'd shared his bed between visits from Mitch.

The half-empty canister of honey dust under the bathroom sink was Snyder's only reminder of his twenty-three-year-old lover. Several months into their affair, Snyder had discovered that Mitch not only had been seeing another man on the side, but also had plans to blackmail *him,* David Snyder, one of the most powerful senators in New York history. Snyder had come too far to have it all come crashing down over something like that.

Two weeks later, Mitch and the other man were the victims of yet another D.C. drive-by shooting. The politicians were up in arms that this sort of thing could happen again, and this time to someone from the Hill. But the anger quickly subsided. The deaths became, as David Snyder knew they would, just another unfortunate statistic on the D.C. crime blotter.

• • •

"The entire room, including the beeswax polish, is an exact copy of Louis XV's secret study at Versailles," said Fawcett. "As a matter of fact, this rolltop desk," he said, sweeping his hand over the smooth wood, "is Louis's original desk. The first rolltop ever made. The one at Versailles is just a copy, though those putzes have the balls to try and pass it off as the real thing.

"I told you how we got it, didn't I?" Fawcett said to Senator Rolander.

"Yeah, you used to have it in your place in Chicago."

"Well, Senator Snyder here hasn't heard the story." Fawcett looked at Snyder and raised an eyebrow as if to say, *You're not going to believe this.* "When the palace of Versailles was stormed by the people of France, they saved the paintings and sold off the furniture. Those prissy academics who run Versailles now have been scouring the world trying to buy back all of the original furniture.

"They made it perfectly clear that they believed the desk was a national treasure and that they would go to any lengths to get it back. They claim that they were dealing directly with the owner, but that's a load of bullshit. The owner was a savvy old bird who used Sotheby's on the sly to mount a very discreet bidding war. I had one of my lawyers from Amsterdam represent me as an anonymous buyer. The French bid high right from the get-go, and we followed them straight up. There was no way I was going to let them get it. Bill Gates was hovering around the fringes of the bidding, and I thought I was really going to have some trouble out of him, but he lost interest after a while. When the other players fell out of the running and we were neck and neck with the French, we let them win the bid."

Snyder leaned forward surprised. "If you let them win the bid, how'd you end up with the desk?"

"I'll tell you how," said Fawcett, "and if I do say so myself, it's brilliant. We had a girl inside who handled the banking. For their deals, especially one of this size, Sotheby's has very strict rules. They don't care if you're Charlie de Gaulle or Charlie Potatoes, if you can't come up with the payment, you lose your place in line. They came back to us when the French money didn't show and asked if we would match the bid. Meanwhile, the Frogs were going batshit trying to figure out what went wrong. It was beautiful. Our girl had worked it so she was spotless. It looked like the bank in France screwed things up. We were able to get the rolltop for a fraction of what it would have cost if there'd been an all-out bidding war. And let me tell you this, it felt good to stick it to the Frenchies."

Rolander had heard the story before, but the guile of his old college roommate made him smile nonetheless. Rolander was amazed at how far sheer force of will and personality had carried Fawcett. He sometimes wondered where he would be if he'd been as ruthless. Being a senator wasn't bad by a long shot and Russ Rolander hadn't got to where he was by sitting around, but what would it be like to have Fawcett's money and power? What would it be like for him to support all of his vices with his own money, rather than depending on the steady stream of Fawcett deposits to his Caribbean bank account?

Well, if you were going to be in a pocket, Rolander reasoned, *it might as well be a deep one.*

Snyder's reaction wasn't much different. He was also amazed at the lengths to which Fawcett would go to get what he wanted. Snyder felt a bizarre sense of camaraderie with the man. Both he and Fawcett knew no limit to their passions, nor to the depths to which they would descend to force the world to give them what they wanted. As much as they had in common, though, there was one thing that Snyder knew for sure, he was smarter than Donald Fawcett would ever be.

"So," continued Fawcett, "that's how my little Louis XV room came to be. How much do you want to bet that he banged Marie Antoinette right on that couch you're sitting on?"

Snyder tried to suppress it, but a slight smile crept across his lips. Fawcett might have monkey loads of money, but he didn't know shit when it came to history. Marie Antoinette wasn't married to Louis XV, she was married to Louis XVI.

"I get what I want. Don't I, Russ?"

"That's right," Rolander managed between coughs, as Fawcett, who had been walking behind the couch, had smacked him hard on the back mid-swig of his brandy.

Snyder didn't like the way Fawcett circled the room like a buzzard looking for a wounded animal, and was glad when he finally sat down behind the desk.

"Enough small talk," said Fawcett, looking into his snifter as he swirled his brandy, releasing the sweet, metallic vapor. "Where do we stand?"

Rolander sat up straighter, his imposing size dominating the couch, and cleared his throat. "As you know, Donald, the deal has been moving along smoothly. We have our foreign assets in place, and the advance information we have received fits the equation perfectly . . . as we knew it would. In an undertaking such as this, the CYA, or cover-your-ass factor, cannot be stressed greatly enough—"

Fawcett interrupted Senator Rolander. "That's what I never did like about politicians, always worrying about covering their asses when they should be worrying about doing their jobs."

"Listen, Donald," said Rolander, "don't you fucking patronize me. This is one serious deal, and if you think I'm not covering my flanks, you are sorely mistaken."

"There's nothing wrong with covering your flanks, Russ. Just don't spend so much time watching your ass that you miss what's right in front of you. Understand?"

"Yeah, I understand, all right. I just hope you do. This isn't shooting fish in a barrel. This is serious business. The smallest detail could turn this into a major clusterfuck and send us all running for cover . . . or worse."

"Spare me the lecture, Russ. I know this is serious business. I've got billions riding on it. Jesus, with all of the power problems in California alone, you'd think we'd be developing our fossil fuel capabilities further, not scaling back. What the fuck are they thinking? Alternative energy sources? Not only are they dangerous and unreliable, they're just too much of a hard sell to the American public."

"But, you forget about the greenhouse gases and global warming," broke in Rolander.

"Fuck the greenhouse gases, fuck the Kyoto Protocol, and fuck global warming," spat Fawcett. "That's all a bunch of inconclusive bullshit. I have invested tens of millions of dollars trying to get you and your colleagues back east to see the light on this one. God, if I never see another lobbyist or politician with his hand out again, it'll be too soon. But, after all is said and spent, where'd my money get me? Nowhere, that's where. If this fossil fuel rollback happens, I don't even want to think about how much money I'll lose. It's bad enough the government has forced us into selling power to states like California at fire-sale prices, but now they want to go further and whittle away our market. I have gone at this thing every way I can, and now the buck stops here."

"Which brings me right back to what I was saying, Donald. To avoid this thing hitting the fan, we've got to have a flawless strategy," said Rolander.

"Relax, Russ. I told you already that I have the details all worked out. You think I want this deal to go sour? Besides, the trail goes so cold before it reaches either of your doors that even Rudolph the fucking Red Nosed Reindeer couldn't follow it. Got me?"

"I gotcha," said Rolander, "but you get me, Donald. I don't care how much money you've put into this deal and I don't care how much you stand to lose. No more changes. This thing goes off as planned. You of all people should appreciate the value of what I'm saying. Our offshore associates are not happy with how you've pushed up the closing."

"You let me worry about them," said Fawcett. "In fact, as I've said before, let me worry about everything. All of the players are being extremely well compensated for their participation. There is no reason for anyone to be getting jumpy. The closing was moved up because the closing had to be moved up. That's the nature of the business. We're all professionals here, so let's get our acts together and get on with the deal. Now"—Fawcett rubbed his hands together in anticipation and leaned forward over his desk—"what's the word from Star Gazer?" Two sets of eyes fell upon Senator Snyder and awaited his report.

Snyder took a deep breath and, smoothing the crease in his left trouser leg, began to speak. "As we expected, he has agreed to become a player in the deal, but he did have some reservations."

"He didn't have any objections other than those we forecasted, is that correct?"

"That is correct," said Snyder.

This was the part of the game that Fawcett loved, the psychology. He had known exactly how Star Gazer would react. He would be indignant at first, considering the proposal out of the question. Then the stroke and sting, as Fawcett liked to call them, would begin. First his ego would be stroked and then his fears would be stung. It was an age-old tactic, but it worked every single time. The more self-absorbed the personality, the greater the success. Star Gazer was about as self-absorbed as they came, although he hid it very, very well. This camouflage ability was Star Gazer's greatest strength. Seeing people for exactly who they were, knowing what motivated them and how to turn those motivations to his advantage, was Donald Fawcett's.

"What are you two talking about?" demanded Rolander.

"What we're talking about," answered Snyder, "is that Mr. Fawcett read Star Gazer like an open book. He accurately forecasted what Star Gazer's objections and areas of concern would be. He knew which cards should be played, and in which order, to successfully bring him on board. Star Gazer has left us with a brief list of 'demands,' our full agreement with which being the only way he will participate. The list is exactly as Mr. Fawcett predicted."

Rolander looked at Fawcett, impressed. "He agreed to come aboard?"

"Indeed he did," replied Snyder. "Now, as to his conditions."

Fawcett leaned back in his chair and smiled.

"Condition number one: After the deal is closed, the president is to be returned to his office"—Snyder paused before finishing his sentence—"alive."

CHAPTER 1

The exterior ice chime sounded, warning of potential ice on the roadway, and Gerhard Miner gripped the leather steering wheel of his black Audi A6 a little tighter. His Gucci-clad foot pressed down harder on the accelerator. The sun was setting over Lake Lucerne, and a chill wind, blowing since lunch, began to pick up. *Ah, what a lunch that was today,* Miner thought to himself as the sleek black sedan hugged the shores of the choppy Swiss lake. *It was absolutely exquisite.*

Claudia Mueller, an investigator from the Federal Attorney's Office, had been pressing Miner for a face-to-face meeting to discuss a cache of armaments missing from a military base outside of Basel. Crates of special night-vision goggles, flash bang grenades, Swiss SWAT assault rifles, antitank missiles, plastique, and a couple of next-generation nonlethal weapons known as glare guns had all mysteriously disappeared.

Though Claudia had insisted her questions were just routine, Miner had been putting her off for over two months. He claimed his caseload didn't provide a single extra moment to meet with her. Surely the security of Switzerland, which Miner was charged with, overrode the necessity of asking him a few "routine" questions.

He half expected her to go away, but she didn't. Claudia wanted badly to talk with Miner and for good reason.

Five years ago, he had commanded a special division of Swiss intelligence that tested the security of military bases and weapons installations throughout the tiny country. Miner had been so successful at breaching security at the bases that his unit was shut down for fear of further embarrassment to the military establishment, and he was transferred to a different department of Swiss intelligence.

Not only had Miner commanded the special division, he had also created it. The idea for the division—known as *Der Nebel* or, most appropriately, *The Fog,* in English—stemmed from training Miner had received while on U.S.–Swiss cross-training exercises in Little Creek, Virginia. Little Creek was where the U.S. Navy SEAL teams involved in Atlantic, Latin American, and European operations were assigned. It was also home to the Navy's Special Warfare Development Group, not to be confused with "Dev Group," the Navy's elite counterterrorist unit formerly known as SEAL Team Six, which was based in Dam Neck, Virginia. The Special Warfare Development Group was a SEAL think tank where new weapons, equipment, communications systems, and tactics were developed.

The investigative affairs agent's long list of boring questions had been the last thing Miner was interested in sitting through, but curiosity eventually got the better of him and he ordered a copy of Claudia Mueller's personnel file. In his position as one of the Swiss government's highest-ranking intelligence officers, he did not find the file hard to get, nor did his request seem at all out of the ordinary.

Miner flipped through Mueller's file with only minimal interest. As he reached the back, he slowed. The backs of files were always the most interesting part. Included were her service photo, her most recent passport photo, and best of all, a magazine photo from a climbing competition in which she had taken first prize. In sharp contrast to the serious service and passport photos, this picture showed a proud and energetic woman. Here, her ruddy face was flushed with adrenaline and the excitement of competition. She was gorgeous. There was no need to put Claudia Mueller off any longer. At that moment, Miner not only knew he had to meet her, but he had to have her.

An hour and fifteen minutes away in Bern at the Federal Attorney's Office, known as the Bundesanwaltschaft, Claudia Mueller was studying the file of Gerhard Miner for the thousandth time. Out of all the people she had spoken with during the course of her investigation, Miner had been the toughest to nail down. Sure, Miner had his reasons for being unavailable, and they all checked out when Claudia leaned on her boss to speak with his contacts at the Ministry of Defense, but something bothered her. Call it her Swiss fetish for organization. Something about Miner just didn't jibe.

Miner was fifty-three years old and never married. He was a handsome man, tall, about six foot two, and extremely fit. His gray hair was perfect, as were his expensive custom-made Italian suits. In almost any woman's opinion, Gerhard Miner would be quite a juicy catch. She was studying the photos of him yet again, glued to his deep brown eyes, when the phone rang.

"Hello?" Claudia answered, still staring at the file in front of her.

"Fräulein Mueller, this is Gerhard Miner of the SND." *Strategischer Nachrichtendienst,* in Swiss German, translated to the deceptively benign sounding "Strategic Information Service." The highly secretive Nachrichtendienst was a division of the Ministry of Defense and responsible for counterespionage for Switzerland. Not much beyond that was known about it, not even by the most enlightened and connected of Swiss citizens.

Instantly, Claudia's attention shifted from the pictures in front of her to the voice on the other end of the phone. "Well, Herr Miner, to what do I owe this unexpected pleasure?" Claudia asked pleasantly, masking her eagerness. After leaving messages and being dodged by Miner for the last two months, she was excited to finally have the man himself on the phone.

Miner leaned back in his chair and wondered what Claudia might be wearing. He pictured her in a highly provocative outfit, completely unlike what a woman of her position actually wore to the office. His mind continued to wander as he answered smoothly, as if on automatic pilot, "I should say the pleasure is all mine. I can't remember the last time a woman pursued me as aggressively as you have."

"I hardly believe my repeated requests for information in a formal investigation to be in the same category as you are imagining, Herr Miner."

"Of course not. I apologize. I'll tell you what, I have time available tomorrow to meet with you if you still want, but after that I will be quite busy with an ongoing assignment."

"Done," replied Claudia. "I'll meet you at your office say—"

"Oh, I'm quite sorry once again."

"Why?"

"I won't be in my office tomorrow. I'm taking a little time off and will be at my home in Lucerne."

It wasn't unusual for government officials to keep a small apartment in the capital and then commute home on the weekends. The Swiss were extremely loyal to their cantons and ancestral homes. Claudia herself spent many weekends with her family back in Grindelwald in the house that would one day pass to her when her parents were gone.

She paused to figure out how long it would take her to get from Bern to Lucerne and whether she should go by car or by train.

"I'll tell you what," began Miner.

Again with "I'll tell you what," Claudia thought. After being dodged for two months, Claudia was ready to jump down Miner's throat, but she knew she had to be careful. She had recently applied for a new position within her organization, and stepping on the toes of one of the Ministry of Defense's most respected officers wouldn't help her move any quicker up the ladder.

Life at the Bundesanwaltschaft had grown to be extremely tedious for Claudia. She had taken the job with the Federal Attorney's Office right out of law school. She was fluent in all four official languages of Switzerland: German, Italian, French, and even the rarely spoken Romansch. She was also fluent in English. Her enviable ability with languages, tenacious manner, and keen eye for detail made Claudia a shoo-in for the Bundespolizei, the investigative affairs division of the Bundesanwaltschaft. As much as Claudia had enjoyed her job in civil intelligence at the outset, she longed for the promotion that would take her out of the mundane business of being a glorified detective and put her on cases that were much more exciting and that she could actually prosecute.

But no matter how badly Claudia wanted to switch to another department, she would not for a moment compromise an ongoing investigation. Worse than stepping on a few Ministry of Defense toes would be not solving this case. And if she couldn't solve this one, she was sure she would end up staying exactly where she was, or worse, she would get demoted, or possibly even fired.

Claudia's boss, Arianne Küess, had been handpicked to be head prosecutor for the war crimes tribunal at the United Nations Court. This meant that the missing weapons case was being led by the very disagreeable Deputy Federal Attorney, Urs Schnell. This was Schnell's first case and he wanted it wrapped up with a ribbon ASAP. He had placed a very high priority on this, and the weight rode chafingly on Claudia's shoulders. The problem was that she had not made any progress and was quickly running out of leads.

"Let's meet for lunch here. Is that convenient for you?" Without even waiting for a reply, Miner continued, "We'll meet at the restaurant in the Hotel des Balances in the Old Town. Say, twelve-thirty?"

No, it wouldn't be convenient for her to travel to Lucerne, but Claudia needed to speak with Miner, so she agreed and hung up the phone. That evening, she agonized over what to wear. She wanted to appear professional, but knowing Miner's penchant for women, she couldn't help but want to play her good looks for all they were worth. She was scraping the bottom of the ethical barrel and she knew it, but she was desperate. She chose an attractive, tight-fitting navy blue skirt that rode just above the knee and a form-fitting navy blue blazer with a funky silver blouse. She left one button undone and then undid the second upon entering the lobby of the hotel at twelve-twenty-five the following day.

Miner had been considerate enough to select one of the restaurant's quieter tables. The booth was framed at one end by a window facing onto the Reuss River. Beyond a clutch of empty iron patio tables, a group of Lucerne's swans paddled slowly past the city's historic, covered Kapellbrücke bridge. Miner appeared to be watching them as they up-ended their snow white tails, plumbing the depths of the quickly flowing current in search of food. In reality, he was using the reflection of the window to observe Investigative Affairs Agent Mueller's entrance, as well as the rest of the lunch patrons who had entered the restaurant in the last twenty minutes. Miner watched Claudia walk almost the length of the dining room, then feigned surprise when she finally reached the table.

"Herr Miner, good afternoon. Sorry to startle you." Claudia leaned over to shake his hand, certain that he had seen her entrance.

The game was on.

• • •

Two hours later, dissatisfied and angry, she left the Hotel des Balances. She needed to walk a little and clear her head. Claudia made her way up the hotel's short cobblestone driveway toward the Weinmarkt, in Lucerne's Old Town.

The Old Town, on Lucerne's right bank, was a pedestrianized area of aging cobblestone streets and buildings from the sixteenth through the eighteenth centuries. Many of the facades were decorated with frescoes depicting Swiss life. The ground floors of the buildings housed boutiques, restaurants, and small shops. One couldn't walk two meters in this part of town without seeing displays of watches or cuckoo clocks. There was no question that it was geared heavily toward tourists, but its beauty always had a soothing effect on Claudia.

She wandered aimlessly past the shops along the Kapellgasse trying to make some sense of her meeting with Miner. He had been cordial, but cordial to the point of condescension. It hadn't taken Claudia long to realize that Miner wasn't going to reveal anything, at least not willingly. He was extremely uncooperative, choosing to shroud himself in the cloak of national security whenever Claudia put a direct question to him.

"Where were you on the night the weapons were stolen?"

"On assignment."

"On assignment where and for what?"

"I cannot say."

"Can't say where, or can't say for what?"

"Neither."

"And why can't you say?"

"It is a matter of national security."

"And a large amount of sensitive weaponry missing from a Swiss defense depot isn't a matter of national security?"

"All I can say is, it is not my matter. It's yours."

"Herr Miner, is it that you can't tell me your whereabouts on the night in question, or is it that you just won't?"

"It is both," Miner replied. "I won't tell you because I can't."

"Are you aware, Herr Miner, that I can get a court order to compel you to answer my questions?"

"Yes."

"So, why don't you make it easier on both of us: answer my questions and I will go back to Bern to pursue my investigation from there."

"Fräulein Mueller, I am not in the business of making your job easy. I serve the Federal Republic of Switzerland. I'm not at liberty to answer the questions you're asking. Should you wish to attempt to compel me to answer, I assure you your efforts will be met with much resistance. I do a job for the people of Switzerland that is, shall we say, *delicate.* I have done this job for more years than you have even been alive. My position does not require me to answer your questions. I have told you I would be of no value to your investigation, yet you pursued me nonetheless."

Claudia was determined to get something out of him and, so, changed course. "Perhaps, then, as you are an expert on the security of Swiss military installations, maybe you could suggest to me how such a theft would be possible and where such weaponry might be secreted or sold, if that was the intent."

"Fräulein Mueller, I have learned that there are many ways to enter one of our bases undetected. A person or persons could have done so with or without assistance from someone inside. Were there any signs of a forced entry?"

"Not according to our investigation."

"Were the security measures functioning properly at the time the theft was assumed to have taken place?"

"Yes, they were."

"You of course questioned the entire base staff to see if anyone saw or heard anything unusual during the time in question?"

"Naturally."

"And?"

"And, no, nothing unusual was seen or heard."

"Fine, then, that brings us to your next question. As far as where such merchandise could be hidden, the answer is, anywhere. And, as far as where such merchandise could be sold, my answer again is, *anywhere.* You simply do not have enough evidence to even begin to formulate a hypothesis as to what happened. You are chasing ghosts, and I frankly do not see much hope for a successful outcome to your investigation. But, your day is not a complete loss. Since you have come all the way from Bern, you can at least enjoy your lunch and perhaps we can take a stroll together afterward."

Claudia spent the rest of their lunch probing for answers while Miner deftly parried each question. Miner also had the indecency to try to seduce her. He found Claudia attractive, and, in all fairness, she had attempted to use her wiles to goad a little more information out of him. Instead of coughing up some information, though, he had come on to her even more strongly. Claudia felt she should have known better. Though everything about him indicated he had a passion for women, passion did not necessarily equal weakness, and gambling that it might had been Claudia's mistake.

The end of their lunch was no less frustrating than its beginning. Without even consulting her, Miner ordered dessert for the two of them. This was a liberty that sent Claudia's already boiling blood over onto the stove. Number one, he ordered liquor, which Claudia didn't touch while working, and number two, he went on to lecture Claudia on her poor taste for turning down a fabulous dessert wine that the hotel Food & Beverage manager kept specially in the cellar for him. *No doubt,* Claudia thought to herself, *Miner had something good on the F&B manager to rate such treatment.* She made a mental note to check the manager out when she got back to Bern.

It wasn't enough that he let her know the wine was a special delicacy the hotel reserved solely for him. No, Miner had to go on and make sure that uneducated little Claudia knew exactly what she was missing. In a tone that was entirely haughty, and which entirely suited Gerhard Miner, he launched into what sounded like a rote recitation of a wine club's tasting notes.

Vin de Constance was a dessert wine from the Constantia estate in South Africa. It was a favorite of Napoléon Bonaparte, who had thirty bottles a month shipped to Elba to ease the misery of his banishment. The king of Prussia as well as Louis XVI loved Vin de Constance. Dickens celebrated it in *Edwin Drood,* and Baudelaire said, "only the lips of a lover surpassed it in heavenly sweetness." Only twelve thousand bottles were produced annually, with almost all of them accounted for before they hit the market. An American colleague who had introduced Miner to the stuff helped arrange for a case to be sent to Switzerland. No small feat, as Vin de Constance was one of the most coveted wines in the world.

Throughout this ridiculous speech, Claudia developed a pretty good plan for where Miner could put his wine if the hotel's cellar ever got overcrowded. Though she had already politely declined Miner's offer, he poured the expensive liquid into her glass anyway. A faint sneer developed at the corner of Miner's mouth when Claudia grabbed the neck of the bottle and repeated, "I said, no thank you." The sneer, which Miner quickly masked with a false smile, proved to Claudia that the man was not completely impenetrable. She counted this as one small victory in the series of sharp defeats that had been their lunch.

Claudia had so strongly insisted on questioning Miner because he was her last possible lead. She had exhausted everything else. Claudia had gone back and questioned the military base staff again and again. She had monitored their bank accounts and purchasing patterns, hoping that if there was someone involved on the inside, he or she would slip up and make a large deposit or a large purchase that couldn't be explained away. To date, nothing had come to light. Nothing had turned up in Switzerland, and nothing had turned up on the black markets abroad.

The Vin de Constance lecture notwithstanding, Claudia felt as if she didn't know any more today than she had yesterday and that her whole trip to Lucerne had been a waste of time. As far as the missing weapons were concerned, Miner did have better means than anyone else in all of Switzerland to steal them. Claudia was dead-on. But just because Miner had once been involved in government-sanctioned exercises testing the security of Swiss military establishments didn't mean that he had anything to do with her theft.

Miner was also right about something. Any attempt to try to get a judge to compel him to answer her questions would be met with resistance from the highest ranks of the Swiss government. Lacking any evidence whatsoever against Miner, there was no way anyone would force him to cooperate.

With Miner refusing to cooperate, Claudia didn't even have straws to grasp at. All she had was air. Her investigation had been marked by failure after failure. Though her gut told her one thing, her mind told her it was a million-to-one shot that she could have turned Miner into a bona fide suspect. Now Claudia Mueller's investigation and her career were at a complete standstill.

• • •

As Gerhard Miner pulled into the long-term parking lot at Zurich International Airport, he was no longer thinking about Claudia; his mind was back on his mission. The sudden schedule change had bothered him, but such was the nature of his business. Heads of state often shortened trips or changed plans altogether at the last minute.

As this trip was set to coincide with the birthday of the American president's fifteen-year-old daughter, Miner had been certain that, barring any international incident, the president would spend as much time as he could on his ski trip. The fact that the president was now planning to cut it short by a couple of days was inconvenient, but it didn't make the mission impossible.

Miner entered the empty first-class line and presented his ticket and passport. He went out of his way to be extra flirtatious with the female desk staff, who wondered why such a handsome man did not have an attractive woman traveling with him to Athens.

While waiting in the Swissair lounge for his flight to board, he changed tack and acted enraged when a young waitress spilled a glass of cabernet all over his trousers. The poor young girl thought it was her fault, when, in fact, Miner had leaned his shoulder forward and nudged her tray as she was placing a cocktail napkin on the table. His explosion earned him an effusive apology that lasted from the first-class lounge all the way to the gate from a Swissair airport services manager. Once Miner had been seated on the plane, the manager again apologized and asked the chief first-class flight attendant to take especially good care of this long-suffering passenger. Miner had achieved exactly what he wanted. At least five people would be able to vouch that he had boarded the Swissair flight to Greece.

He spent the next week and a half in the popular ports of Paros and Mykonos, spending too much money entertaining new friends and repairing repeated "mechanical problems" on his rented sailboat. He overtipped waiters, barmen, and harbormasters. Not only would Miner be remembered, but many would be anxiously awaiting the return of the man and his easy-flowing money next season.

Secure that his alibi was well established, Miner sailed to the uninhabited island of Despotiko, about three hours southwest of Mykonos. Waiting there for Miner, just as planned, was his cousin from the Swiss town of Hochdorf, a carpenter who bore an incredible likeness to him.

Happy to have a free vacation and knowing the sensitivity of his cousin's occupation, the carpenter from Hochdorf never asked any questions. The plan was for him to continue sailing south to Santorini and then Crete, where he would leave the rented yacht, citing a string of mechanical problems as the reason. The carpenter would then make his way to the western port of Patras, where a first-class cabin was booked on a Minoan Line cruise ship to Venice.

His cousin would be traveling on Miner's passport and Visa credit card. Knowing that cabin stewards present first-class passengers' passports for them to customs officials as a courtesy, Miner was not worried about his cousin or his passport receiving any undue scrutiny. The carpenter was to spend a week in northern Italy before proceeding via train to France.

Miner had booked his cousin on an overnight train in a first-class compartment. As the train would be crossing the French border while passengers were sleeping, the steward would gather passports as passengers boarded, present them to border officials sometime during the night, and then return them with breakfast in the morning.

After a week in France, the carpenter would take a final overnight train back to Switzerland, where the customary passport collection by the steward would once again be conducted. When the steward delivered the passport with breakfast the next morning, the carpenter was to place it in a thick, manila envelope with the canceled train tickets, credit card receipts, and other odds and ends he had been told to accumulate during his wonderful vacation. The envelope was addressed to a post office box in Lucerne and stamped with more than enough postage. When the train arrived in Bern, the carpenter would mail the envelope from the train station post box before catching his connecting train back to Hochdorf.

With eyewitnesses, customs records, and a credit card trail that would lead through three European countries all but guaranteed, Miner entered Turkey from Greece with a false Maltese passport as part of a tour group, feeling quite confident that his alibi, if ever needed, would be airtight.

Twenty-four hours later, the people seated in the airline's waiting area paid no attention to the rumpled western European businessman who sat reading a day old copy of *The International Herald Tribune.* Disguised with blond hair, a full beard, blue contacts, and padding that made him appear twenty kilos overweight, Miner was now traveling on a Dutch passport as Henk Van DenHuevel of Utrecht.

He sat reading an article he had found quite by chance. It dealt with the upcoming ski vacation United States president Jack Rutledge was to take with his daughter, Amanda, and what it would cost American taxpayers.

As first-class passengers were welcomed aboard flight 7440 from Istanbul to New York, Miner folded the newspaper under his arm and made his way toward the gate thinking, *They have absolutely no idea what this trip is going to cost.*

CHAPTER 2

"You guys having an awesome day or what?" asked the young liftie as Scot Harvath and Amanda Rutledge shuffled up to get on the next chairlift. He was referring to the snow that had been falling all day.

"Light's kinda flat," replied Amanda.

Scot had to laugh. Amanda was relatively new to skiing, but she was picking up the lingo and the idiosyncrasies of a spoiled skier pretty quickly.

"What's so funny?" she said as the lift gently hit them in the back of the knees and they sat down, beginning the ride up to Deer Valley's Squaw Peak.

"You, that's what's so funny."

"Me? What do you mean?"

"Don't get me wrong, Mandie; your skiing's come a long way, but you've skied, what, maybe five or six times in your life?"

"Yeah, so?"

"And it's always been that East Coast garbage. All ice, right?"

"And?"

"Well, it's just funny to hear you complaining about the light when you are skiing on snow people would kill for."

"I guess it is kind of funny, but you've got to admit that it's tough to see anything in this weather."

On that point, Amanda Rutledge was one hundred percent correct. The snow had been falling steadily for a week. Hoping to indulge his passion for astronomy, Scot had brought his telescope on this trip. The lights back home in D.C. made it impossible to see anything in the night sky. Unfortunately, the weather in Park City had so far refused to cooperate. Today, in particular, it was really coming down. Visibility was extremely low, and the conditions worried Scot enough that he suggested the president and his daughter take the day off and wait to see what tomorrow brought. Regardless of what the head of his advance team had to say, though, the president made it clear that he and Amanda had come to ski and that's exactly what they were going to do.

Unfortunately for his ski plans, the coalition the president had cobbled together to get his fossil-fuel reduction bill—the bill that signaled a financially devastating blow for the major oil companies, but would breathe long overdue life into America's alternative-energy sectors—through Congress was starting to crack. The president's constant hand-holding of key "swing" voters was absolutely necessary if he was to see his legislation through. The predicted turnover in the upcoming congressional election spelled doom for the president's pet project. The simple fact was that this bill could pass only in this session.

Even though he had already shortened the length of his vacation before leaving D.C., the president was thinking about returning even earlier now. Scot understood the man's desire to get in as much skiing and quality time with his daughter as possible before returning to the capital.

"Are you dating anyone now?" asked Amanda.

The sudden change of subject caught Scot off guard and pulled his mind back from the president's problems and the weather.

"Am I dating anyone? Who wants to know?" he teased.

Blushing, Amanda turned away from his gaze, but kept speaking. "I do. I mean, you never seem to talk about anybody."

Scot started to smile again, but didn't let her see. He thought she must have been building up her courage all day to ask him.

Amanda had had a crush on Scot ever since he'd become part of daily life at the White House, and everybody knew it. More than once, the president had had to reprimand his daughter and remind her not to distract Scot while he was on duty. Amanda, or Mandie, as Scot called her, was a good kid. Despite having lost her mother to breast cancer only a couple of years ago, she seemed as normal as any other child her age. She was smart, athletic, and would someday grow into a beautiful woman. Scot decided to change the subject.

"That was one heck of a birthday party last night," he offered.

"It was pretty cool. Thanks again for the CDs. You didn't have to get me anything."

"Hey, it was your birthday. The big sixteen. I wanted to get you a car, but your dad's national security advisor thought that behind the wheel of your own machine, you might be too dangerous for the country. So, the Ferrari will just have to sit in my garage until we can change his mind."

Amanda laughed. "Not only were the CDs sweet, but I really appreciate the lessons today."

Before joining the SEALs and subsequently being recruited into the Secret Service, Scot had been quite an accomplished skier and had won a spot on the U.S. freestyle team. Against the wishes of his father, Scot had chosen to postpone college to pursue skiing. He had spent several years on the team, which trained right there in Park City, Utah. He did extremely well on the World Cup circuit and had been favored to medal in the upcoming Olympics. When Scot's father, an instructor at the Navy SEAL training facility in their hometown of Coronado, California, died in a training accident, Scot had been devastated. Try as he might, after losing his father, he hadn't been able to get his head back into competitive skiing. Instead, he chose to follow in his father's footsteps. After graduating college cum laude, he joined the SEALs and was tasked to Team Two, known as the cold-weather specialists, or Polar SEALs.

Scot knew that it was not only his familiarity with Park City, but also his background and experience that were key factors in his being selected to lead this presidential advance team. He also knew that was why President Rutledge had agreed to indulge his daughter's request for Scot to ski on her protective detail today and give her pointers.

Amanda had been overjoyed, and despite the "flat light," she felt the day had been perfect.

"You're an excellent student, so the lessons are my pleasure." Scot's radio crackled, interrupting their conversation. He held up his hand to let her know he was listening to his earpiece. Amanda remained quiet.

"Norseman, this is Sound. Over," came the scratchy voice via Scot's Motorola. *Norseman* was the call sign Scot had picked up in the SEALs, which had remained with him ever since. At five feet ten and a muscular one hundred sixty pounds, with brown hair and ice blue eyes, the handsome Scot Harvath looked more German than Scandinavian. In fact the call sign didn't derive from his looks, but rather from a string of Scandinavian flight attendants he had dated while in the SEALs.

The voice on the other end of Scot's Motorola identified as *Sound,* was the head of the president's protective detail, Sam Harper. Harper had taken Scot under his wing when he joined the team at the White House. The head White House Secret Service agent, whom Harper and Scot reported to, was William Shaw—call sign *Fury*. When you put Harper together with Shaw, you got "The Sound and The Fury," and anyone who had ever screwed up on their watch knew exactly how appropriate that title was.

Communications had been fine over the past week, but for some reason the radios had been cutting in and out today. *Maybe it was the weather.*

"This is Norseman, go ahead Sound. Over," said Scot via his throat mike.

"Norseman, Hat Trick wants to know how Goldilocks is doing. Over."

"Mandie," said Scot, turning to Amanda, "your dad wants to know how you're holding up."

When then Vice President Rutledge came into office after having three times been named one of D.C.'s sexiest politicians, the hockey-inspired nickname Hat Trick, meaning three goals, became an inside joke among the people who knew him. Though Jack Rutledge found the media's focus on his looks somewhat embarrassing, he didn't object to the nickname, and so, via the Department of Defense, which issues the presidential and vice presidential code names, it stuck. After the president's wife passed away, word quietly spread among White House staffers that the president would not seek to return to Pennsylvania Avenue for a fourth time. The code name had turned out to be aptly prophetic.

Amanda's code name, on the other hand, was an obvious call. With her long, curly blond hair, she had been called Goldilocks for as long as anyone in the White House could remember.

"I'm a little hungry, but other than that pretty good," she said.

"Sound, Goldilocks is shipshape, though she'd like to get into the galley sometime in the near future. Over."

"Roger that, Norseman. The lifts close to the public at sixteen-thirty; that's twenty minutes from now. Hat Trick wants to know if Goldilocks wants to keep going, or if we should wrap it up. Over."

Scot turned to Amanda, "Your dad wants to know if you want to have them keep the lift open for us, or if you want to make this the last run and we'll ski back to the house?"

"My toes are getting kind of cold. I think I've had enough skiing for today. Let's make this the last run."

"Sound, Goldilocks wants to little piggy. Over." "Little piggy" referred to the children's nursery rhyme where the fifth little piggy went *wee, wee, wee, all the way home.*

"Roger that, Norseman. Hat Trick concurs. Let's meet at the last lap. Over."

"Last lap, roger that, Sound. Norseman out."

• • •

When Scot, Amanda, and their security detail reached the meeting point known as the last lap, the president, Sam Harper, and the rest of the team were already waiting for them.

"Hi, sweetheart," said the president as his daughter skied up, and he gave her a hug. "How's your skiing coming along? Notice any difference now that you're sixteen?"

"Sixteen doesn't make any difference, Dad. But I have gotten better."

"Is that so?" replied the president, glancing at Scot.

"Yes, sir, Mr. President. Amanda has come a long way this afternoon. I think she could take us all down Death Chute if she wanted to," said Scot.

"Death Chute?" said Amanda. "You've gotta be nuts. I wouldn't even snowplow down that thing!"

Several of the Secret Service agents laughed nervously. Death Chute was one of the most difficult of the off-piste chutes that fed back to the area where the presidential party was staying. The home the president was using was located in the ultraexclusive ski-in, ski-out Deer Valley community known as Snow Haven.

The Secret Service agents' nervousness was well founded. Death Chute required a tremendous amount of skill to navigate and would have been a nerve-racking challenge for even the best of them. Not only were there lots of rocks and steep vertical drops, but as the piste began to flatten out before dropping off again, there was a wide plateau filled with trees.

Quite an accomplished skier, the president loved tackling a new chute each day on his way back to the house. He skied easy runs with his daughter in the mornings, and then they split up after lunch so he could ski the more difficult trails. The superchallenging, end-of-the-day chutes he had to choose from were technically known as backcountry and not part of Deer Valley's marked and maintained trail system. Therefore, the chutes had not required a lot of work for the Secret Service to secure. All of the routes feeding into them were simply made off-limits to any other skiers.

As the president's confidence grew, so did his desire to tackle harder chutes. The "rush" he got was a rewarding way to end the day. All of the chutes he had tried up to this point were grouped in one area. Death Chute stood alone, a bit further to the east, and the Secret Service knew it was only a matter of time before the president decided he wanted to give it a whirl.

The only person who could possibly have given him a run for his money on Death Chute was Scot, and he was skiing with Amanda's detail today. Amanda would take the long, easy way down, as she had all week. That was okay. The last thing the president wanted was for his daughter to get hurt.

"So, honey," began the president, "what do you think? You take the high road and I'll take the low road, and I'll be sippin' hot chocolate afore ye?"

"I might beat you yet!" yelled Amanda as she gave herself a push and started shooting down the longer, yet safer of the two routes. Scot and the rest of his team smiled at the president's group and took off, quickly catching up with Amanda. She seemed hell-bent on beating her father back to the house, an impossibility unless she dropped over the rim of the bowl and shot straight down. Even with her growing skill and confidence, Scot knew she wasn't ready to tackle something that serious yet.

Amanda used her poles to push herself forward and picked up more speed. One of the agents skiing to the right of Scot shot him a look suggesting, *Somebody's cruisin' for a bruisin'*— and before Scot could return the look, Amanda caught an edge and tumbled down hard. First she lost a pole and then a ski, then the other pole and the other ski.

When she finally came to a stop, her gear was scattered across thirty feet of snow uphill from where she lay. Scot caught up to her as she stopped sliding.

"Impressive! If you're gonna go, go big. That's what I always say."

Amanda was on the verge of tears, her pride hurting more than anything else.

"That's not funny," she said, sniffling.

"I'm sorry. You're right; it's not funny. Are you okay?"

"What do you care?" she said, wiping the snow from her face.

Scot started to laugh.

"It's not funny, Scot. Cut it out!"

"I know, I know. I'm sorry, Mandie. You were really flying, though. You looked good. Right up until the point you biffed. You know, we should have tagged your gear before you decided to have a yard sale."

"Stop it!" Amanda managed before breaking into a fit of laughter.

"Oh, so that was a mistake? There wasn't supposed to be a yard sale today? Whoa, then I better gather up the merchandise before we upset any of the neighbors."

He told Amanda to sit still and joined Secret Service agent Maxwell, who was uphill gathering her equipment. When Scot reached Maxwell, he saw that he was staring into the distance at the presidential party making their way down Death Chute.

"Glad I'm not on that detail," said Maxwell as he handed Scot one of Amanda's skis.

Scot dusted the snow out of the binding, checking for damage as he waited for the next ski. "Maxwell, the reason you're not on that detail is that when it comes to skiing, you suck."

"Fuck you, Harvath," said Maxwell as he shoved the other ski at him, confident he was out of Amanda's earshot.

"No, seriously. I heard that Warren Miller was looking to shoot a little footage of you for his next ski film. It's going to be a spin-off of that movie *Beastmaster,* only worse. He's going to call it *Biffmaster.* Nothing but your wipeouts—"

"Fuck you."

"I'm not kidding. Nothing but three hours of wall-to-wall Maxwell face down in the snow."

"Fuck you."

"There'll be some of those trademark Maxwell-fully-geared somersaults, some awesome face plants . . . I think you could be up for an Oscar, my friend."

"Harvath, which part of *fuck you* do you not understand? I mean, I'm good to go on explaining either of the two words to you—"

Scot laughed as Maxwell lost his balance reaching over to pick up one of Amanda's ski poles.

Looking off toward Death Chute, Scot, too, could see the president and his detail still making their way down. The detail was doing a good job of keeping up with him. Everybody was right on the money. As he turned to take Amanda's gear back to her, he glanced once more at Death Chute, just in time to see the president's group near the trees and two Secret Service agents wipe out.

Maxwell had already recovered and gone down to Amanda. He was handing over her poles when Scot skied up.

"Well, Maxwell, it looks like the heat will be off your skiing at dinner tonight."

"What do you mean?" he asked.

"I think I just saw Ahern and Houchins bite it going into that part of the chute with the trees. But, with all the snow falling, it's hard to tell."

"At least I'm not the only one who bought it this afternoon," said Amanda as she got to her feet and dusted the remaining snow off her jacket.

"I told you," said Scot, " the end of the day is when most wipeouts happen. You're more tired than you think, and some people push it a little too hard."

Agent Maxwell took the skis from Scot and let Amanda lean on his shoulder for balance as she put them on. "I hope nobody hit a tree," he said.

"That's a good point," responded Scot as he engaged his throat mike. "Sound, this is Norseman. Do we need to send the Saint Bernards and schnapps down for Ahern and Houchins? Over."

Scot's radio hissed and crackled. There was no response. He tried again.

"If either of them blew their knees, I've got a buddy here who's a great surgeon. Tell Ahern and Houchins I'll split the commission with them if they use my guy. Over."

He waited longer this time, but there was still nothing but static.

"Sound, this is Norseman; we saw two agents go down. Can you give us a sit rep. Over?"

Sit rep was short for "situation report." The president had probably pushed his guys just a little too far and just a little too fast for the end of the day. This really was the most common time for wipeouts. Ahern and Houchins were probably all right, but as head of the advance team, Scot felt responsible for every agent and wanted to know for sure.

"Sound, this is Norseman. Let's have that sit rep. Over."

Nothing.

Scot decided to change frequencies to the direct channel with the Secret Service command post. The blowing snow was beginning to pick up again. "Birdhouse, this is Norseman, come in. Over."

"Scot, I'm getting cold," said Amanda as she snapped into her bindings.

"Quiet a sec, Mandie."

Scot pressed the earpiece further into his ear, but all he got was crackling static.

"Birdhouse, repeat, this is Norseman, come in. Over." Scot waited.

"Birdhouse, repeat, this is Norseman. Can you read me? Over."

More static.

Agent Maxwell looked at Scot, who shook his head to indicate he hadn't made any contact.

"What do you think?" said Maxwell.

"I don't know, and I don't want to cry wolf to the rest of Goldilocks's detail just yet. I'll try my Deer Valley radio. If that doesn't work, then we harden up." *Harden up* was the Secret Service term for immediately closing ranks and body-shielding their assignment from any potential threat.

Scot tried three times to raise Deer Valley's ski patrol and then tried Deer Valley's operations station. There was no response. All of the radios were completely down. Scot let out a loud whistle, catching the attention of the rest of the detail agents, and gave the harden up command by waving his gloved index finger in a high *circle the wagons* motion above his head.

In a matter of seconds, Amanda's protective detail had her completely surrounded. There was an incredible array of weaponry drawn, from Heckler & Koch MP5s to SIG-Sauer semiautomatics, and even a modified Benelli M1 tactical shotgun. The men's eyes never stopped surveying the area as Scot explained that he had seen two of the president's detail agents go down and all radio communication was dark.

There probably was a simple explanation. Ahern and Houchins could just have wiped out, and the radios *had* been acting up all day, with the weather the most likely culprit, but that was not how the Secret Service was trained to think.

Operating procedure dictated that they take the fastest and safest route back to the command center immediately. With the loss of radio contact, Birdhouse would already have scrambled intercept teams to recover both details as quickly as possible. But they were still a long way off. It was time to move.

Amanda saw her chance to break in and asked, "Scot, what's going on?"

"Probably nothing, Mandie, but we need to get you back down to the house as quickly as possible," said Scot. "You've done an awesome job today. I'm really proud of you. Your skiing is red-hot. Now, the normal way we go home would take us a bit too long. If we ski through the bowl, I can have you sipping hot chocolate by the fire with your dad in fifteen minutes. What do you say?"

"This is about him, isn't it? Has something happened? Is he okay?"

"I'm sure he is, and the quicker we get back, the quicker you'll see for yourself. Do you think you can do the bowl with me? I'll be right next to you."

"I don't know. I think I can handle it."

"Good girl."

Scot smiled reassuringly at Amanda and gave the order to move out. The detail dropped over the icy lip into the steep bowl. The wind grew more fierce and sent sharp blasts of snow into their faces. Amanda was slow, but at least she was moving forward. It was terrifying for her, but to her credit, she was doing everything Scot had taught her—weight on the downhill ski in the turns, leaning forward into her boots, and keeping her hands out in front as if she were holding on to a tray.

Even though Amanda's cautious skiing slowed them down, it looked as if they were going to make it without incident.

Then the detail heard what sounded like the crack of a rifle, followed by the low rumble of a thunderhead. Scot had been around mountains too long not to recognize that sound.

Avalanche.

CHAPTER 3

Despite his formfitting winter assault fatigues lined with a revolutionary new weatherproof thermal composite, Hassan Useff lay in his coffin of snow and shivered. He had been one of the toughest kids growing up in his balmy, south Lebanon village and was now one of the Middle East's finest snipers, but the cold and being buried alive beneath two feet of snow were beginning to get to him. When the hideous repetition of his own raspy breathing was finally interrupted by two squelch clicks over his earpiece, the fear and cold immediately disappeared, replaced by a rush of adrenaline surging through his stiff body.

Useff tensed and released his muscles several times to relieve some of the stiffness in his joints. Cradling the high-tech glare gun in his gloved hands, he heard an almost imperceptible whine as he powered the weapon up.

Two more clicks over the earpiece and he readied himself to spring from his snowy grave.

Buried completely from view in several more snowy crypts nearby, Gerhard Miner and five more of his "Lions" were about to undertake the most daring mission of their lives.

• • •

"Son of a bitch," cursed Sam Harper to himself as his ski clipped the edge of another rock. He loved skiing, but hated having to follow the president down Death Chute. He had fallen a little bit behind and was glad that several of the younger guys on the detail were able to keep up with the commander in chief.

The biggest consolation of all was that Ahern and Houchins were behind him. At least he wouldn't be the last one to ski up when the party rested in the flat area among the trees before tackling the final vertical drop.

When Harper reached the beginning of the trees, everything began to happen in what, had he survived, he would have described as a split-second flash.

Three final squelch clicks came over Hassan Useff's earpiece, signaling that the last members of the president's Secret Service detail were entering the heavily treed area. Springing from his icy hideaway, Useff began pulsing his glare gun as his fellow team member, Klaus Dryer, did the same twenty meters away.

The results were exactly as planned. Even with their UV-protective ski goggles, the entire protective detail, as well as the president, was *dazzled.*

The glare guns were Russian copies of the nonlethal weapon developed by the American Air Force's Phillips Laboratory. First brought into action in Somalia in 1995, the purpose of the high-tech laser weapon was to temporarily blind and disorient an enemy.

Temporarily was all Miner's team needed.

Useff and Dryer's cross-pulsing in the narrow alley formed by the trees created a blinding laser funnel that the president's team couldn't escape. This included the members of the Secret Service countersniper unit, known as JAR, or Just Another Rifle, who were posted strategically throughout the trees along this leg of the president's run.

Completely blinded and disoriented, several agents lost their balance and wiped out before they even had a chance to come to a complete stop. Those agents who had already been in the process of slowing down and could stop, instinctively drew their weapons, but they had one major problem. They couldn't see a thing.

Not knowing where their fellow agents were or, more important, where the president was, every single agent, weapon drawn or not, had been rendered not only totally useless, but helpless as well.

Useff gave the go command over his lip mike as he shouldered the glare gun and switched off the safety of his silenced German-manufactured Heckler & Koch MP5 submachine gun. The pleasure of being able to freely kill so many agents of the Great Satan was almost unbearable. He had already shot two Secret Service agents before the rest of the team had fully sprung from their hiding places.

As the Lions' silenced machine gun rounds drummed into the bodies of the defenseless Secret Service agents, Miner made his way toward where the president had fallen.

"Harp, Harp," mumbled the president from where he lay in the snow, still blind and disoriented but alert enough to call out for the head of his protective detail as he tried to raise himself into a seated position.

Miner dropped to his knees next to him and removed the president's gloves and jacket. As he helped him sit up, he placed a copy of the *Salt Lake Tribune* on his chest, pulling the president's hands in so he could feel it. Instinctively, the president grabbed hold of it. Miner shot several quick Polaroids and slipped the slowly developing pictures into his pocket. Then he took the paper away and, with a pair of trauma scissors, began to cut through the left sleeves of the president's sweater and turtleneck.

"Toboggan! Where is that toboggan?" Miner yelled.

"Harper? What's happening?" repeated the president.

"There's been an accident, Mr. President," responded Miner in perfectly American accented English. "You need to lie back now and remain still, while we start an IV."

"Who are you? Where's Harper? What's happened to my eyes? I can't see."

"Please, Mr. President. You need to be completely quiet and completely still. My team is attending to the others. There you go. Let's just lie back. Good." Miner knew the effects of the glare gun would be wearing off soon. From his pack, he withdrew an insulated medical pouch, unzipped it, pulled out a bag of saline solution, and began an IV on the president, who continued to call for members of his protective detail and complain about his eyes.

Once the IV was in place, Miner filled a syringe with a strong sedative called Versed and piggybacked it into the IV line. The effect was almost instantaneous. The president's eyes rolled back, closed, and his body went limp.

As one of Miner's men rushed past, towing an all-white ski-patrol-style transport toboggan, Dryer made his way over to Hassan Useff.

Without even turning, Useff began speaking, knowing Dryer was behind him. "This is Sam Harper, head of the president's protective detail, is it not?"

Though Harper was badly injured from his fall and couldn't see who was standing above him speaking, he knew the Middle Eastern accent didn't belong to anyone on his team. "Yeah, I'm Sam Harper, and whoever you are, you are in a lot of trouble. Give yourself up."

"Typical American arrogance. Even in the face of death," said Useff.

"Fuck you," snarled Harper as he attempted to draw his weapon.

"Once again, typical. Is nothing original in this country?" asked Useff as he squeezed off a three-round burst into the career Secret Service agent and father of two's head.

Ever since Dryer had recruited Useff for this assignment, he had marveled at the man's hatred for the United States. That hate, coupled with the Lebanese man's intense religious fervor, made him perfect for this job. Hassan Useff was the only non-Swiss on the team.

As he began walking away, Useff said, "Protecting the president, he should have been the best. A pity he won't be remembered that way. The pathetic coward never even fired a shot."

When Useff had his back completely turned, Dryer withdrew an empty Evian bottle from the pack he was carrying and picked up Harper's SIG-Sauer P229. "I think the Americans might beg to differ," were the last words Hassan Useff heard before the .357 bullet, effectively muffled by being shot through the plastic bottle, ripped through the back of his skull, killing him instantly.

Dryer placed the SIG-Sauer in Harper's dead hand. He then withdrew a model 68 Skorpion machine pistol with a silencer and fired indiscriminately into the bodies of the dead Secret Service agents lying around him. He blew through two more twenty-round magazines before placing the Skorpion on the ground next to Useff and shouldering the dead Muslim's glare gun and H&K.

The waters were now sufficiently chummed.

CHAPTER 4

"Sound, this is Birdhouse. Do you copy? Over. Norseman, this is Birdhouse, do *you* copy? Over."

Secret Service agent Tom Hollenbeck, head of the command center for the president's ski trip, had been trying to reach both details for the last seven minutes.

Communications had been sporadic throughout most of the day. The mountainous terrain, the secluded location of the command center just outside the home the president was staying in, and the terrible on-again, off-again weather, made things extremely difficult.

Hollenbeck called out to his assistant, Chris Longo. "Hey, Longo. Can't we do anything at all to pump this up?"

"For *Chrissake,* Tom. What do you think I've been doing for the last five minutes?"

"All right, all right. No need to get pissy. Just fix it."

"Hollenbeck, if I knew what was wrong, I would have fixed it already."

"Hold on a second. We've got the Deer Valley radios. Have we tried those?"

"Yes. I already thought of that."

"And?"

"They've also been having trouble."

"What kind of trouble?"

"Same as us. The radios just aren't working."

"Is that normal?"

"It happens, but not often."

"Damn it. How about the Smocks, then? They transmit on a different frequency than our radios, don't they?"

The Smock, or Doc Smock, as it was officially known, was a new piece of technology made for monitoring soldiers in battle. It was a skintight vest with sensors, worn under the clothes, that transmitted the wearer's vital signs, via a small unit in a fanny pack. It could also indicate if the vest had been breached.

Even though the technology was still experimental, two duty agents on each detail were wearing one.

"Yeah," said Longo, "the Smocks are on a different frequency."

"Well, see if you can punch them up."

"See if I can punch them up? Do you want me to work on boosting our Motorolas or do you want me working on the Smock signals?"

"No, you work on the radios and reaching the teams. Who's watching the Smocks now?"

"Palmer is."

"Fine. Palmer!" yelled Hollenbeck as Longo went back to trying to raise the two details.

"Yes, sir?" responded an attractive, young female agent from a corner of the Secret Service command center.

"Can you give me a full sit rep on all four Smocks?"

"Not really."

"Why not?"

"They've been off and on all day."

"What do you mean?"

"I mean sometimes they seem to transmit and sometimes they don't."

"Why?"

"I don't know. Could be the weather. Could be some sort of interference. For all I know it could be that the Nintendo in the break room is messing with them. This is still experimental technology."

"How were they operating yesterday?"

"Clear as a bell. I've even got the printouts of vitals broken down over fifteen-minute intervals. Do you want to see them?"

No, Agent Tom Hollenbeck did not want to see them. What he wanted to see was the president, his daughter, and the rest of the detail agents skiing up to the front door joking about who had eaten the most snow today.

"What's the longest amount of time you have been without a Smock signal?"

Agent Palmer looked down at her watch. "Up till now the longest interval without a signal was just about three minutes. Now we're going on eight."

The same amount of time the radios had been out of commission.

"Palmer, how would you say the weather was yesterday compared to today?"

"A little better, but not much."

"Longo!" yelled Hollenbeck.

"What now?" asked Longo.

"Do we have any rovers with a visual?"

Rovers were the teams of snowmobiles and Sno-Cats that followed the two details as closely as possible. They were loaded with what the Secret Service referred to as CATs, or Counter Assault Teams. The

CATs were heavily armed and armored agents whose sole job was to lend the protective details fire support.

"The last rover report came in as the teams split for their final run from the last-lap rendezvous position, right before the radios went down. Goldilocks took the low road, and Hat Trick opted for the high road," replied Longo.

"Which high road?" asked Hollenbeck.

"Death Chute."

"It would have to be that one, wouldn't it? What's the next potential rover or JAR visual contact for Hat Trick?"

"There's a JAR unit among the trees in the middle of Death Chute."

"I know about that one. I haven't been able to raise them. What about the next rover?"

"There's no access for a rover team until about half a mile down from the treed plateau on Death Chute."

Hollenbeck didn't need to confirm where the next visual was for Amanda's detail. She had taken the same route home every day. There was normally a pretty good line of sight directly from the command center, but today wasn't normal. The snow was blowing harder, reducing visibility to next to nothing, and Birdhouse had lost all radio contact with any agents more than one hundred yards from the command center.

"So," began Hollenbeck, "we have had no visual, nor radio contact with the details for the last eight minutes?"

"That's right, boss," answered Longo.

"Okay, that settles it."

Hollenbeck stood up from his chair and called for everyone's attention. He slung his lip mike back over his head and toggled the transmit switch to get the attention of the agents on patrol outside the command center. For some reason, transmissions close to the command center were not interrupted.

All eyes in the room, and ears outside, were now trained on Hollenbeck.

"Everybody, listen up. We have a potential hostile situation."

CHAPTER 5

Miner gave rapid orders to Anton Schebel when he arrived with the toboggan. "Crack the blanket and help me lean him forward to get this sweater the rest of the way off."

Schebel did as he was told. In quick succession, he pounded the pockets of hot packs lining the toboggan's body bag with the butt of his semiautomatic. Before he had finished with the hot packs, Dryer rejoined Miner and was taking over.

"Useff?" inquired Miner as they removed the president's sweater, careful not disturb the IV.

"He left early. Cocktails with Allah. Everything is on schedule," said Dryer as they worked the president's turtleneck off.

"Good. Get the bag over here and lay it next to him."

Dryer laid the body bag out lengthwise next to the president.

"Everything else off now. Pants, socks, boots, ring, watch, even the underwear." Miner wasn't leaving anything to chance. He knew the president wore at least one homing device and that it was cleverly hidden. The fact that he might be surgically implanted with another one was unlikely, but Miner had brought the special body bag along just in case. If the president was surgically implanted with any additional homing devices, the signal would never breach Miner's clever Kevlar-like design. The bag had been constructed so that as they zipped it shut, the IV could be hung on a special rail at the rear of the toboggan and the tube would still be feeding through the bag into the president's arm.

Dryer and Schebel placed him in the warmed bag and loaded him into the toboggan. With the lining of hot pockets, at least he wouldn't freeze. Miner's plan certainly didn't entail dressing the president in new clothes. At least not yet.

When the bag was belted to the toboggan, Miner spoke into his lip mike. "Two minutes."

Gerhard Miner, Klaus Dryer, Anton Schebel, and the other team members clicked into their hybrid cross-country, downhill telemark skis. The incredibly strong men quickly began powering their precious cargo into the trees.

"Ninety seconds."

Dryer led the way, wearing special night-vision-style goggles. Eight days before, he had marked some of these same trees with a special paint that upon contact with air, oxidized and became invisible to the human eye. The goggles now allowed Dryer to pick up the paint's unique chemical signature and follow the escape route he had marked through the maze of trees.

Finally, the flat ground grew steeper and they picked up more speed. Klaus knew they would be out of the woods in only a few more seconds.

Miner had taught his men that the plan depended on absolutely perfect timing. If the toboggan flipped over, or one of them stumbled, all would be lost. There was no margin for error.

"Thirty seconds."

The team, now out of the trees, rapidly cut a diagonal path across the dangerously steep mountain face.

Gravity and the toboggan's smooth round bottom began causing it to slide downhill, instead of across the face. Schebel, an experienced sled-dog driver, put his weight on the up-mountain side of the toboggan to help it stay on course.

Snow and ice screamed from the back of the rig as it dug into the mountain and fought against the unnatural course it was being forced to take. If Schebel lost it now, both he and the president would be hurled into the valley.

The toboggan continued to edge out of Schebel's control. He leaned harder into the yoke and tried to right the toboggan's course. He cursed Dryer for not computing the grade of the mountain better and Miner for not outfitting the toboggan with a sharp set of runners like a bobsled.

Schebel was the biggest and strongest of the group, and that's why he had been chosen to pull the toboggan. It looked as if he wasn't strong enough, though. Everything they had trained for and risked was going to be lost.

Schebel tried again to put all of his weight on his uphill ski. The result was disastrous. The toboggan careened wildly out of control so that it faced straight down the mountain. It began to pull Schebel backward. He cursed again, sure he was going to be killed. Schebel and the president slid rapidly down the mountain instead of across it.

In a last-ditch attempt to get control of the sled, Schebel threw all of his considerable bulk onto his opposite ski. For what felt like an eternity, nothing happened. The toboggan pitched hard, as if it was going to flip over and carry Schebel with it. Then, a miracle occurred.

As the toboggan was close to capsizing, its upper seam caught in the frozen snow and acted like the edge of a ski, putting it and Schebel back on course. He was downhill from the rest of the team, but he saw Dryer change direction and make his way down toward an outcropping of rock. As long as the toboggan cooperated and stayed on this new course, Schebel would be okay.

While Miner resumed the final seconds of his countdown, Dryer saw two enormous boulders looming in front of them. The boulders, which looked impassable from this distance, marked the head of a small, incredibly steep and dangerous chute.

Compared to this one, Death Chute was child's play, but for six of the world's top mercenaries who had spent their entire lives challenging the world's most unforgiving mountains, it would not pose a problem.

When Dryer was within meters of the small passageway, Miner reached for something strapped to his chest. It was a small black transmitter with a strip of red electrical tape wrapped around its rubber antenna. When Miner had a hold of it, he depressed its only button.

A sound like the crack of a rifle, followed by the roar of a thunderhead, reverberated from far above them as they began their arduous descent.

CHAPTER 6

The icy snow whipped against the Secret Service's mobile command center, and every agent inside was looking directly at their chief of operations, Tom Hollenbeck.

"We have had no visual or radio contact with either protective detail going on nine minutes. Visibility is also severely impaired. I am upgrading the current situation to Hostile 2 until further notice. I want the president's residence locked down and all duty agents that are raisable to report in. The perimeter is to be locked and lit. I want the backup tactical units on deck and ready to deploy. The rest of you know your jobs, so let's move."

Hollenbeck finished issuing orders and then turned his attention to the window as he tried to peer through the sea of snow. A group of counterassault agents waited outside for their orders, which they knew would be next to come.

For some reason, the radios within a hundred yards of the command center still worked, so Hollenbeck didn't need to go outside to address the waiting agents. "I want both Hat Trick's and Goldilocks's intercept teams to mobilize immediately. You are to assess the situation and report back in person ASAP to Birdhouse unless radio contact can be reestablished. Until then, you are to assume that we are operating dark under a hostile scenario. Your objective is to compile a sit rep and get it to me as quickly as possible. This is not an escort service. I repeat, not an escort service. As soon as you know anything, I want you back here. Don't waste any time. Any questions?" asked Hollenbeck sternly.

"Negative. Teams One and Two, understood. Out," came the response from the intercept leader outside the command center. Within seconds, the two four-man teams of Secret Service agents clad in insulated Nomex jumpsuits and medium-weight body armor had their Polaris snowmobiles fired up and were heading to intercept their respective "packages."

"Can we get anything aloft in this?" asked Hollenbeck of one of his operational assistants.

"From here, no. It looks as if things are supposed to be getting worse. We've got the president's Marine Corps White Top at the bottom of the hill, but even as good as those pilots are, this weather is impossible and their helicopters aren't made for it. The best we could do is scramble a Black Hawk from Hill Air Force Base."

"How long would it take?"

"Ten minutes to get it up and twenty to thirty more to get on site, but there isn't much they can do searchwise with the visibility cut down to less than nothing."

"Call Hill and have them put one on standby. I want those rotors spinning until I say otherwise."

The operational assistant turned away from Hollenbeck and patched through on the com link to Hill Air Force Base to order up the bird.

"Longo," barked Hollenbeck, growing tenser by the moment, "are we green yet on those Motorolas?"

"We are still no go. Situation dark on all communications."

"Palmer?"

"Sorry, sir. Still nothing on the Smocks either."

Just when Agent Hollenbeck thought things couldn't possibly get any worse, he heard the resort's avalanche sirens begin their low, mournful wail.

CHAPTER 7

There wasn't time for him to think, only to react. For most, reacting without thinking could be a dangerous thing, but not when you were trained to make life-or-death decisions in milliseconds.

Based on where the sound of the avalanche came from, Scot instinctively knew that they were right in its path. The job of a protective detail in a threat situation was to immediately cover and evacuate their protectee. Evacuation in this case was impossible, at least for the time being, but maybe, just maybe, Scot had a chance of covering the president's daughter. It would take every ounce of skill and strength he had in his body.

He managed to yell, "Avalanche," he hoped loudly enough for the other agents to hear, and then voiced a quiet, "Oh, shit," to himself. There wasn't time to tell the other Secret Service agents what he was planning to do.

Amanda apparently didn't hear his cry of "Avalanche" or know what the loud noise was, because she kept slowly skiing down the bowl. Scot pulled up short on his downhill ski and, squatting deeply like a weight lifter getting ready to deadlift, positioned himself behind Amanda. This had one chance of working.

The tidal wave of snow was already barreling down on top of them. Assuming the radios were still out of commission, Scot yelled for the other agents to follow him. With the roar of the avalanche filling his ears, he couldn't be sure if anyone had heard him.

"Don't move! Just let me take you," yelled Scot as he grabbed all one hundred and ten pounds of Amanda Rutledge around the waist and lifted her up off her skis. Startled, she screamed, but didn't fight him. The severe downhill angle and their combined mass sent them rocketing down the slope. With the diminished visibility, Scot couldn't be sure if he had calculated right. He *had* to be dead-on. If they undershot what he'd seen, they would be dead. If they overshot it, they would be dead. And if the blinding snow had played a trick on his eyes and what he thought would be there wasn't, that also could result only in their death.

While Amanda was by no means heavy for a girl of her age and Scot Harvath was in incredible shape, carrying her as they raced downhill ripped and tore at every fiber of his tightly muscled body. His entire back was on fire, and his thighs felt as if there were red-hot coils wrapped around them. Every primal instinct within him shouted for him to let her go and save himself, but he had been trained to be a master of not only his body but his mind, which meant that fear and pain would serve him, not the other way around.

Amanda must have known what was going on, at least on some level, because the minute Scot picked her up, she went as limp as a kitten lifted by the scruff of the neck.

He'd known when he heard the sound of the avalanche that outrunning it would be impossible. He didn't even dare venture another look back. The slightest wasted movement could immediately put the two of them on the losing side of this equation.

The freezing ice and blowing snow tore into Scot's face like shards of broken glass. He and Amanda picked up more speed as they traversed the face of the bowl. This was where the simple physics of Scot's plan was working severely against them. In an avalanche, the heavy snow chooses the fastest path available to it. Drawn by gravity, this path is always straight down, tearing apart anything in its way. Instead of going straight down, Scot and Amanda were going almost straight across the mountain. With each foot they gained in going across, the avalanche gained fifty coming down. There was absolutely no room for slipups.

Scot had no idea if his fellow agents had heard him yell, if they had interpreted the sound of the avalanche for what it was, or how they had reacted. For now at least, there was no way to find out. He could only hope that they had taken his lead and were following right behind.

The roar had become deafening, and it reverberated throughout Scot's entire body, shaking him as he held Amanda. It seemed as if they had been traveling forever, even though it had been only a matter of seconds. *Where are those goddamn rocks?* he screamed to himself.

As it turned out, Scot had dangerously undershot his target. Through the blizzard of blowing snow, he could just make out the outcropping, further across the face and significantly below where they were now. *Damn it!* he thought.

Knowing this was his last chance, Scot pointed his skis, himself, and Amanda straight for the bottom.

They picked up speed at a terrifying rate. Scot's knees pistoned up and down like jackhammers as he absorbed not only his weight but also Amanda's. He fought with all of his might to keep control of his skis, which were furiously slapping the packed snow like a pair of loose dock planks in a hurricane.

He and Amanda were going way too fast. One bump in their path and it would all be over. There was no way that any skier, even one of Scot Harvath's caliber, could keep this up.

Then, he saw it. The outcropping of rock was racing up to meet them as quickly as the avalanche was racing down to swallow them.

Harvath put the distance at twenty yards and closing. His mind raced through the trillion calculations necessary to gauge the successful achievement of the next step in his plan: *stopping.*

The logical answer he received to his seemingly illogical request was simply, *"Three . . . two . . . one . . . Now!"*

Scot wrapped his arms tightly around Amanda and threw all of their collective weight over his left ski. He covered her as best he could with his body, acting as a human air bag to protect her from injury, as they brutally spun and pounded out of control toward the rocks below.

Over and over again they somersaulted with furious speed, each time crashing down hard on one or the other of Scot's shoulders. Between the white snow of the bowl and the blowing white of the blizzard, Harvath fought hard to keep focused on which way was up and where their target was. It was impossible. They continued to flip wildly out of control. The sound of the avalanche was so loud now he couldn't even think.

As quickly as they had been rolling, they were immediately stopped by slamming into a sheer wall of rock. Scot cried out in pain and held on to consciousness just long enough to see a torrent of wet snow pour over them and Amanda's limp body lying motionless beside him.

CHAPTER 8

The first thing he noticed when he regained consciousness was the eerie silence. The absence of noise was deafening. They had barely made it to the rock overhang in time. The plan had just worked. They were positioned beneath a narrow stone ledge that had formed a partial barrier to the avalanche. The claustrophobic box they were in was about eleven feet long, three-and-a-half feet wide, and four feet high. They were amazingly fortunate. Where there wasn't rock, they found themselves surrounded by snow, but there was at least some room to move around—as if they were in a small cave. Scot hoped the other Secret Service agents had been as fortunate, but he doubted they had.

In the dark, Harvath began to slowly make an overall assessment of his condition. His ankles felt okay, shins were fine, knees were sore but probably would bear weight. His thighs felt like mush and were bruised, but didn't seem like a problem as long as he was lying down. He carefully fished his Mag-Lite out of his pocket and turned it on. Next, he struggled to bring his knees up to raise himself into a sitting position, and that's when the pain started shooting through every inch of his upper body. He gave up immediately.

Covering Amanda during their fall, Scot had taken most of the beating along his back and shoulders. From his waist up, *everything* hurt, and he couldn't tell what might be broken. At least there were no apparent open fractures, and he was only bleeding slightly from an abrasion on his forehead, so for that he gave thanks.

From where he was lying, he could see the outline of Amanda's left leg. He needed to get to her and knew it was going to hurt like hell, but he pushed the thought from his mind. With all the strength he could summon, Scot rocked his body slowly from right to left until he got up enough momentum to roll all the way over. He was right. Rolling over did hurt like hell, but it was nothing compared to what came next.

When he'd been on his back, he could look straight down past his ski boots and make out Amanda's leg as she lay on her side. Now that he was on his stomach, he couldn't see her, because she was behind him. Scot summoned up another surge of strength and, banishing the pain from his mind, managed to lift himself onto his elbows. This change of position sent searing, red-hot spikes of pain up his arms and into his battered shoulders. He began turning his body around upon the cold, rock-strewn snow so he could face Amanda. His legs refused to cooperate, and for a moment he was afraid he might be paralyzed. Eventually, he felt his ski boots move.

Scot's incredibly weakened legs were not of much use, so he went back to dragging himself in Amanda's direction while the incredible pain in his arms, shoulders, and back threatened to slam him back into unconsciousness.

It took the resilient Secret Service agent over fifteen minutes to crawl ten feet. Even though he didn't want to, Scot was forced to stop every couple of seconds to catch his breath. He probably had cracked one, if not several, ribs in the tumble down the mountain. Nevertheless, he was alive, and if Amanda was too, then they both had won, so far.

As he drew closer, he could see Amanda's chest slowly heaving up and down in the beam of his small flashlight. Thank God, she was breathing. At least she was alive. Harvath tried feebly to call out to her, but all he could manage was a hoarse whisper. He would need to get a lot closer to communicate.

He continued his pattern of crawl, rest, crawl, rest, until his face was even with the back of Amanda's head. With her face turned away toward the sheer rock wall of the overhang that had saved their lives, he couldn't tell if she was conscious.

Scanning the top and back of her head, he didn't see any injuries, but that didn't mean there weren't any. Scot knew that attempting to reposition her head could worsen any spinal trauma that might already be present. He would have to carefully support her head, neck, and shoulders, and at this point he didn't have the strength to do it.

"Amanda?" he whispered in his hoarse, dry voice. "Can you hear me? Mandie sweetheart, it's Scot. We're alive. We made it, but I need you to talk to me. I need to know if you're okay. C'mon, honey, just a couple of words. Let me know if you can hear what I am saying."

Amanda didn't respond, and Scot didn't have the energy to keep talking. He had resisted for as long as he could the syrupy blanket of unconsciousness that had been threatening to overtake him. It was no use. As hard as he tried, he just couldn't fight it. All he wanted now was to sleep. Peaceful sleep. *I'm so sorry, Amanda.*

CHAPTER 9

"Palmer!" yelled Hollenbeck to the nearest Secret Service agent in the command center. "Get on the horn to Deer Valley and find out if those avalanche sirens are legit. I want to know why they're sounding and if there has been an avalanche. I want a full, and I mean *full* report!"

"Yes, sir," replied Palmer, who immediately contacted the resort's emergency services department.

"Longo! One question. Are we green?"

"Negative. We are still dark."

Tom Hollenbeck had been standing for the last nine minutes. He couldn't think of sitting down. He needed to pace. His crew knew him well enough to steer clear.

He walked over to one of the windows and watched the whipping snow outside, racking his brain for what his next move should be. The president's life, his daughter's, and the lives of no less than thirty Secret Service agents were in his hands.

"Sir!" cried Palmer as she came running up to Hollenbeck with her notepad. "Deer Valley says that there was an avalanche."

"Shit! Give me the *w's,"* said Hollenbeck, which was Service slang for "who, what, where, when, and how many."

Palmer looked down at her pad and began reading off her list of facts. "Apparently, this was a pretty big one. Several ski patrollers heard it and, knowing what it was, called it in to their base as a potential. Only two patrols actually got a visual and confirmed it."

"Why only two?"

"Look at the way it's snowing outside. With weather this bad, you'd have to be practically on top of anything to see it."

"All right, so several patrols heard what sounded like an avalanche and called it in as a potential, while only two could actually give a positive visual on it. And they also called it in?"

"Correct, sir."

"How? I thought their radios were down."

"Yes, they are."

"Then how did they do it?"

"Apparently, they used a citizen's band radio inside one of their ski patrol huts."

"A CB?"

"The call came through loud and clear."

"Why do you suppose a CB would work, but not our gear and not Deer Valley's regular radios?"

"Apples and oranges."

"What do you mean, 'apples and oranges'?"

"The CB uses a different frequency than those used by the Secret Service or Deer Valley. The weird thing is that our gear is much more sophisticated. Everyone else should be having problems, not us."

Hollenbeck agreed and tucked that nugget away for later while he proceeded with the matter at hand. "Okay, Palmer. Now for the ten-thousand-dollar question. Where did the avalanche begin?"

"According to the ski patrol, it began at Squaw Peak."

Hollenbeck's hand shot through a stack of papers and laminated charts on his desk, pulling out the topographical map the Secret Service's TAT, or Threat Assessment Team, had prepared. It detailed all of the president's known and potential ski routes, along with rotating postings for the JAR and CAT teams. Hollenbeck had a photographic memory and knew exactly where Squaw Peak was, but hoped in his heart of hearts that he was wrong. He wasn't.

Squaw Peak was the highest peak of Deer Valley, and it fed directly into the basin the president and his daughter were skiing through.

In anticipation of Hollenbeck's next question, Palmer said, "The slide was on this side of the mountain and would have funneled a wall of snow, ice, and debris directly along the routes of Hat Trick and Goldilocks."

For the first time in ten minutes, Hollenbeck sat back down in his chair.

CHAPTER 10

With almost a straight vertical drop and so much that could have gone wrong with the descent, Miner's Lions had done an exceptional job. His men deserved their sobriquet. They certainly had the hearts of lions. In assembling the best-trained force-for-hire in the world, Miner had revived Switzerland's illustrious mercenary tradition. It seemed only fitting that his men should carry a name that honored their predecessors.

Not far from the heart of the city of Lucerne was a majestic monument carved into a sheer rock face. It depicted a lion resting on a shield bearing the Swiss coat of arms and paid tribute to the 786 members of the Swiss Guard who died defending King Louis and Marie Antoinette during an attack on the Tuileries in 1792. Even the American author Mark Twain had called it the most "moving" piece of rock in the world. Upon Miner's suggestion, his men had taken the name and had been his band of courageous and deadly *Lions* ever since.

It took the Lions ten minutes to make their descent. When they emerged from the icy crevice, the lead skiers took off their skis and began removing a series of snow-white tarps that hid three Ski-Doo snowmobiles.

No words were spoken, as time was still a critical element. Dryer helped Schebel attach the toboggan to the back of one of the snowmobiles, and Miner unzipped the bag carrying the president to make sure his IV was still firmly in place.

The rest of the crew snapped out of their bindings and placed their skis into the specially fitted tubes on the sides of their snowmobiles. There were two riders on each machine, one to drive and another to lay down fire if need be, though Miner knew it wouldn't be necessary.

He climbed onto the back of the snowmobile driven by Dryer, which would pull the toboggan, and gave the signal to fire up the machines and move out.

CHAPTER 11

Scot Harvath's eyes snapped open as a searing bolt of pain spat him back into consciousness. His entire body ached. The sensation ebbed away, and then another wave came crashing back in.

He had known pain of this magnitude before, as well as soul-chilling cold, during his SEAL training. That training had taught Scot that what the mind believes, the body will achieve. He and his fellow teammates had joked that in SEAL training they had known the most horrific torture ever conceived of by the civilized world, but every single ounce of it had been designed to prepare him for situations just like this. SEALs absolutely, positively never give up. The SEAL motto was, "The only easy day was yesterday," and even though Scot Harvath's paychecks now came from the Secret Service, he would always be a SEAL.

Scot moved just a fraction and had to suppress the urge to cry out. It didn't matter. One of the benefits of the pain, if you could look at it that way, was that his head was clearing and he was regaining control. His body would have no choice but to cooperate with him. Passing out again was not an option. It couldn't be an option. Scot was acutely aware that with each ten minutes that passed, avalanche survival rates for those buried beneath the snow dropped like a stone.

Harvath painfully pulled himself into a sitting position and wiggled his way over so that he was sitting directly above Amanda Rutledge's head. He set the Mag-Lite next to him and turned his palms upward. Carefully, he slid both of his hands beneath her back, supporting her head, neck, and shoulders as he rolled her over. She made no sound and continued to breathe in slow, shallow breaths.

"Mandie? It's Scot. Can you wake up for me? Say something, honey. C'mon."

Scot removed his small backpack, placed it on the ground next to him, and retrieved his flashlight. He opened Amanda's eyes, expertly shining the light into each one. Her pupils didn't constrict. That was a bad sign. He focused his thoughts on getting them to safety.

There was no way to tell how deeply they were buried. In an avalanche, the heavy snow could set up like wet concrete, making it nearly impossible to dig your way out.

Scot remembered his radios and gave them both another try. "Mayday, Mayday. Birdhouse, this is Norseman. We need assistance. Over.

"Deer Valley, Deer Valley, do you copy? Over."

Nothing but the crackle of static came back. Scot decided to conserve his energy and his oxygen. There were more important things to think about now. Number one, he had to keep Amanda warm and try to stabilize her. Number two, he had to get them both out of this situation alive.

So far he was batting a thousand on the staying-alive part, but their fight was only fifty percent complete. Without any radio contact or anybody knowing where they were trapped, there was no telling how long a search party would take to find them. With the weather the way it was, efforts were going to be severely hampered.

Harvath had opted against having the detail agents carry the avalanche-safety transmitter-receivers so popular with backcountry skiers. The avalanche transmitter-receiver was about the size of a small walkie-talkie and was constantly set on *transmit,* broadcasting a low-frequency signal, so that if someone were ever trapped in an avalanche, like now, other people in the party could set theirs to *receive* and start homing in on that person's location to rescue him or her. Scot was completely against this equipment for several reasons.

One, an unfriendly source could potentially lock in on these signals, and two, with JAR and CAT teams strategically interspersed along their routes, help would always be immediately available via radio contact, if not visually. All things considered, he thought the choice not to outfit agents with the avalanche transmitter-receivers was still the right one. However, Scot had never anticipated that their radios would go out.

As if they didn't already have enough problems, Scot looked at his watch and realized it was nearing 4:45 P.M. The sun would be setting soon, and as it went down, so would the temperature. If they didn't get themselves out and to someplace warm, they'd be Popsicles by morning.

CHAPTER 12

Harvath slid out of his jacket and placed it over Amanda to help keep her warm. She was lying on snow-covered ground, so the gesture was more symbolic than anything else. Amanda would have been better served with the jacket placed beneath her, but he'd already moved her once and didn't want to risk it again.

Her pupils not constricting was a sign of abnormal brain function. Despite all of Scot's efforts to cushion Amanda, she'd probably hit her head during the fall down the mountain. Only a doctor would be able to know for sure what her prognosis was, and that made their situation all the more dire.

As Scot's head continued to clear, he realized they probably had a little more air available to them than he'd originally thought. He needed to begin the dangerous process of extricating himself and Amanda from their snowy dungeon. He crawled back down toward Amanda's feet, dragging his backpack with him.

Confident that he was far enough away that a minor cave-in of snow or ice wouldn't land on Amanda, Scot reached into his pack and withdrew what looked like a telescoping ski pole. The pole was known as an avalanche probe and was used by search parties to feel for avalanche victims beneath the snow. As Scot began extending the device, he breathed a sigh of gratitude that he had been safety conscious enough to bring it along.

He picked an angle that looked to be the safest and easiest to dig out from and began feeding the pole through, careful not to disturb any unstable snow. The pole fed out for what felt like a million miles. They had survived a major avalanche.

Shrugging off the fatigue that leaned on him like a heavy boulder, Harvath assembled his collapsible snow shovel and prayed he wouldn't bring the icy roof crumbling down on top of them.

Bending his knees and putting one foot against the rock wall behind him for leverage, Scot began the delicate process of digging out. The last thing he wanted to do was to cause a cave-in.

When he felt he had tunneled a sufficient distance forward, he began scraping the snow along the ceiling in front of him. It created an ice spray that rained down on his face and hands. The process was agonizingly slow. Time and again, Scot backed out of the tunnel, pulling the recently shoveled snow toward him, and deposited it within their frigid cave.

On his eleventh grueling trip back into the tunnel, Scot felt the shovel break the surface. He let the crisp plates of frozen snow fall down on him as he dug an exit wide enough to crawl through.

A chill wind howled as he pulled himself through, and the snow was falling harder and blowing faster than before. The sun was completely gone, and Scot couldn't make out anything below them in the terrible conditions. He sat on the rim with his heavily booted feet resting within the tunnel and took two seconds to catch his breath. It was biting cold, but at this moment he didn't feel it.

Now that they had a way out, Scot was faced with an even bigger problem. With Amanda unconscious and unable to help him assess her injuries, moving her might cause permanent damage. On the other hand, it was equally, if not more dangerous to stay where they were. There was a very good chance they might freeze to death, or even worse, be reburied in a secondary slide. Though he was certain a massive rescue effort was now under way, there was no way the rescuers could have known that he and Amanda had traveled so far across the face of the mountain. It would take them days before they started looking in this area. He thought about using his flashlight to signal for help, but realized it wasn't powerful enough to reach any significant distance in this weather. Scot had to risk moving her, and the sooner, the better.

Sliding back down on his stomach, Scot reentered the cave. With his Mag-Lite, he checked Amanda again, only to find that her condition had not changed. Her pulse felt weak and her breathing was still slow and shallow.

Scot used his mini-shovel to move all of the snow away from the entrance of the tunnel so he would have less trouble getting her out. After that was done, he took off his ski boots and removed his bib-style ski pants. Underneath his ski pants, he wore tight-fitting Lycra biking pants, which he prayed would be enough to keep him from suffering from exposure.

As much as he hated to do it, Scot knew he had to move Amanda to prep her and get her out. With his knife, he cut the padded straps from his backpack and fashioned a crude C-collar, which he fastened around Amanda's neck to keep it from moving. He used the supporting plastic shell from inside his pack as a short back board. He then cut the straps off Amanda's bib ski pants and gently put her already jacketed arms and upper body into his ski coat. Next, he removed her boots and slid her into his ski pants, carefully threading the bib straps underneath her back.

The knife came in handy again as Scot fashioned two primitive booties out of the large zippered compartments of his pack. Hopefully, they would help keep Amanda's feet somewhat dry. Taking her down the mountain with her heavy boots on was not an option. Not only would the added weight be difficult for Scot to bear, but it could also exacerbate any trauma she might have already suffered. He put the nylon booties over her boot liners and pushed her feet gently into them.

Knowing he could never clomp all the way back in his own heavy, uncomfortable ski boots, Scot pulled out his liners to keep his feet warm and then used what was left of his pack to fashion his own booties from the waterproof nylon. Feeling like a postapocalyptic caveman, Scot was now ready to drag Amanda out of their hole and hopefully down to safety.

As he readied himself to go, Scot realized he had made a critical mistake. In an effort to protect Amanda from any falling snow or ice, he had dug the entrance to the escape tunnel at her feet. Amanda was wearing his bib pants so that Scot could pull her by the excess length of the straps dangling next to her shoulders, which meant she was pointed in the wrong direction to be dragged from the cave.

It was bad enough that Scot was going to drag her anywhere without knowing how injured she was, but now, to get her out, he was going to have to turn her around. The cave was only three-and-a-half feet wide, so he would also have to bend Amanda's legs to do it. *Could this get any worse?*

Ever so gently he bent her knees up. Next, he placed his hands beneath her shoulder blades and began maneuvering her upper body toward their only way out. Scot knew all too well that if Amanda had suffered any damage to her back, he could be making it permanent. She was such a good kid with such energy. The thought that she could end up paralyzed because of his effort made him sick, but he knew that he couldn't allow his emotions to control his thinking. It ran counter to his training. He tried to filter the thoughts from his mind, but not before he heard a sickening *pop.*

Harvath froze in his tracks. *Please, God. Please tell me that wasn't something in Amanda's back,* he said to himself. When he looked down, he saw her ski jacket had caught and chipped off a piece of ice on the cave floor. Scot breathed a sigh of relief and then another when he had Amanda fully turned around and at the mouth of the tunnel.

It was as if he'd had to go into a cold, dark womb, turn a breech baby, and now had to pull it through the birth canal into the world. With his ski gloves back on and the loose straps of the bib ski pants in his hands, Scot moved backward two feet and then pulled Amanda slowly forward for one. The journey out of the icy cave seemed to take forever. At this point, it was nothing but Scot's sheer force of will that kept them moving.

To pull Amanda's limp body through the final vertical portion of the tunnel, Scot had to summon every ounce of strength his reserves had to offer. It didn't matter how tired he was or how much pain he was in. The only thing that mattered, and the only outcome Scot Harvath was willing to accept, was complete and total success in extricating Amanda Rutledge, the president's daughter and one-day-old member of the sweet-sixteen club, from that icy cave and getting her back home to safety.

After he slid Amanda onto the snow next to the mouth of the tunnel, he sat for a moment to catch his breath and quiet the symphony of screaming muscles throughout his body. He removed his flashlight and checked Amanda's eyes again. They were still dilated. He took off a glove and checked her pulse. It had grown weaker. He had to get moving, now.

Careful not to disturb her neck, Scot unfurled the hood from beneath the collar of his jacket and velcroed it shut as best he could around Amanda's face. With the wind and snow blowing so hard, he wanted to keep her as warm and dry as possible.

He stood, wrapped his hands around the straps of Amanda's makeshift stretcher, and slowly began easing her down the mountain.

The going was brutally difficult. Scot continually sank down into snow up to his knees, sometimes even to his thighs. There was no way to tell which snow was firm and which would give way. And every time Scot sank into one of these unexpected patches, the added weight of Amanda's stretcher-borne body dangerously threatened to topple him over and send them both hurtling down the face of the mountain.

The wind bit into Scot with a piercing cold against which neither his exertion nor the tepid fumes from his emptying tank of adrenaline could warm him. The razor-sharp crystals of snow tore in sheets across his exposed face like sandpaper.

Harvath fought back against the storm and commanded himself to go forward, one step at a time. Hampering his already slow movement was the knowledge that he had to proceed with a gem cutter's precision, so as to shield Amanda from any added trauma whatsoever. *One foot in front of the other,* thought Scot. *Failure is not an option. We will make it!*

He pressed forward through the hellish wind and cold. He had now lost all sense of time and space. All that mattered was getting Amanda back home. Scot was vaguely aware that his body had stopped shivering in its feeble attempt to keep warm. *At least my legs are still moving.* But what Scot mistook for his legs moving of his own volition was actually a stumble in slow motion. In truth, his legs had given up three yards ago, and it was only through an amazing effort that he kept moving down the mountain without losing complete control.

Finally, he fell forward into the snow. Like the old brainteaser about a tree falling in the woods with no one to hear it, Scot wondered, would his fall make any sound, or any difference? After all, they were completely alone. Or so he thought.

Two hundred yards away, wearing next-generation infrared goggles, the leader of Amanda's Secret Service intercept team picked up the heat signature of two forms, prone in the snow. In a breakout maneuver that would have made the best F-18 pilot envious, the agent gunned his Polaris snowmobile in their direction.

Within seconds, the snowmobile's miles-per-hour gauge showed the needle well over one hundred, and he quickly closed the gap with Scot and Amanda. The rest of the intercept team was hot on his trail.

The leader pulled up next to Scot and Amanda, while the rest of the team surrounded the two bodies lying in the snow and used their goggles to continue searching the immediate area.

As an agent carefully rolled him over, Scot let out a low moan.

"It's Norseman! He's alive!" shouted the team leader to the other intercept members. He then moved over to Amanda and felt for a pulse. It was weak, but at least her heart was beating. "He's got Goldilocks too! They're both alive, but in bad shape."

The team leader engaged his throat mike in an attempt to raise the command center. "Birdhouse, this is Hermes, do you read? Over." There was no response, which is what he had expected. His original orders had been not to escort anyone back, but the game had changed. Every Secret Service agent was selected on the basis of a wide variety of criteria. One of the most highly prized was intelligence, along with the ability to make the right decisions in a life-or-death situation.

Hermes addressed his men. "I want two pop toboggans inflated. I will transport Goldilocks on mine and Archimedes will transport Norseman. I am changing our status to medevac under Hostile 2. Hammer 4 and Hammer 5 will take the GPS coordinates so we can return to this location to search for the rest of the party. Let's move. Go! Go!"

Harvath was only faintly aware of the hissing air and of being strapped into an emergency inflatable pop-up toboggan. As soon as the intercept team swung the snowmobiles around to speed them all back to the command center, he once again slipped into unconsciousness.

CHAPTER 13

By the time the Lions reached the farmhouse of Joseph and Mary Maddux, they were seven minutes ahead of schedule. Miner was pleased.

The farmhouse had been selected because of its remote location. It was on the outskirts of the small town of Midway, which bordered Deer Valley. The nearest neighbor was three miles away. The only access was via either a terribly potholed dirt road or the narrow canyon behind the west side of the farm, which, during this time of year, was only navigable by experienced snowmobile operators or cross-country skiers.

Joe and Mary Maddux had spent their Sunday the same way as always. Even though their large extended Mormon family saw them as retired, the word didn't exist in their vocabulary, and who could be with twenty-two grandchildren and eleven great-grandchildren? If anything, the Madduxes had become even busier in their golden years.

The morning had started with the elderly couple getting up before the sun. While their faith prohibited labor on the Sabbath, there were some exceptions, such as tending to animals, which Joe and Mary did before having breakfast and heading off to their ward for Sunday services.

The bishop spoke of the success of four local Mormon boys on mission in Asia and the tragedy of two others who had been killed in the past week in an Atlanta ghetto while they were spreading the good news of the Mormon Church. Joe's mind wandered, as it did more and more these days during the almost five-hour Sunday services. Mary, ever the devout follower, listened intently as the bishop spoke about the role of a good Mormon wife and reminded his flock that it was only through a husband's proclamation that a wife would be accepted into the celestial kingdom. Mary smiled at Joe, knowing that after fifty-seven years of marriage to her best friend, he was certainly going to bring her into the celestial kingdom with him. She was absolutely correct. What she didn't know was how soon she would be dispatched.

For the last week, Joe had been feeling a bit under the weather, and so he and Mary decided to forgo the traditional Sunday family supper at their oldest daughter's home. Instead, they decided they would have a light meal and relax at the farmhouse without the distraction of children, grandchildren, and great-grandchildren. Had they chosen to attend supper at their daughter's house, it would have saved their lives.

• • •

At two in the afternoon, no one really paid attention to the eighteen-wheeler truck that rolled down Sweetwater Road toward the Maddux farmhouse. Its driver cursed the minefield of potholes he was forced to navigate. The truck was emblazoned with the Mormon Church's trademark seagulls and the logo of Deseret Industries so it would appear as if it were headed out to a farm to pick up a charitable donation of furniture, farm supplies, or canned goods, or to deliver a contribution to a deserving family. Although the Church never did anything on Sundays, Miner had anticipated correctly that anyone who saw the truck would just assume the Church's business was a rare exception to Sabbath abstinence.

Miner's groundsman turned up the long, snow-covered lane of the Maddux farm, convinced that he had not drawn any undue attention to himself. The idea of painting the semi truck and trailer with the Mormon seagulls and Deseret Industries logo had been brilliant. In a state where Mormons were raised not to question the actions of their church and where non-Mormons didn't pay much attention to Mormon goings-on, nothing would seem out of place, and therefore the truck was the perfect cover. Miner had also informed the groundsman that to the trained eye of someone like a state trooper, the truck would obviously appear overloaded, but even troopers wouldn't pull it over for fear of the tangled web of hassles it might create in this heavily Mormon state.

The lane opened into a wide courtyard, which was bordered by the farmhouse, a large white barn, two grain silos, and several outbuildings. The groundsman turned the truck around so that it was facing the way it came, with the trailer doors pointed toward the barn. It was parked at a slight angle so that any passing motorists who might be curious would see that the truck was from the Church.

Having observed the Madduxes for the last several weeks, the groundsman had their routine down pat and knew they would not be home from their daughter's before six-thirty at the earliest, and by then the Lions would be long gone. He unlocked the rear trailer doors and extended a long skid plate ramp. He then slid open the barn door and disappeared into the semitrailer. As he was about to unload the first of his cargo, he stopped and cocked his head in the direction of the driveway, thinking he heard something. The man's keen hearing hadn't deceived him. Faintly, in the distance was the low rumble of Joe Maddux's truck turning up the snow-covered driveway.

Quickly, the groundsman jumped out of the back of the trailer, closed its metal doors, and slid the ramp back into place. A million questions should have raced through his mind, but he was trained to react, not waste time. He managed to slide the huge barn door closed before the Maddux's truck came into full view.

In his blue-and-white Deseret Industries coveralls, he knew he looked the part. He struck a casual pose by the side of the semi and even managed a small grin. He waved to Joe and Mary Maddux as they pulled into the courtyard.

"Good afternoon, Elder Maddux," said the groundsman with a slight Utah lax on the consonants of his perfect American English when Joe Maddux stepped down from his pickup truck. "And good afternoon to you as well, sister."

"Good afternoon," replied the couple in unison. Mary climbed out of the passenger side to get a better look at the enormous truck parked in their driveway.

"I'm sorry I'm a little bit late for our appointment," said the groundsman as he walked toward the couple, his right hand outstretched.

"Our appointment?" replied a confused Joe Maddux, who shook the groundsman's hand and then watched Mary do the same.

"Yeah, I got caught up in traffic on 215, and then with this weather and all, I almost couldn't get up the canyon. But, being a soldier for the Lord doing the Church's good work, I think He was looking out for me."

The logos on the truck and the uniform of the groundsman impressed Joe Maddux. Ever mindful of pleasing the Church, he replied, "I owe you an apology. I didn't know we had an appointment. I feel a bit embarrassed. Can you tell me what this is all about?"

"Oh, no. Don't tell me. You folks didn't hear about this either? Well, if this isn't the third surprise stop I've made today. And on a Sunday to boot. I'm gonna have to get on the phone and give someone a good talking to," said the groundsman, smiling.

This time it was Mrs. Maddux who spoke. "We don't know what this is all about, but if it involves the Church, I'm sure they do. It's cold out here. Why don't we go inside, and you can use our phone to get to the bottom of this."

"You are both too kind."

The Madduxes led the groundsman across the snowy drive and toward the farmhouse. They climbed the flight of concrete stairs, and Mr. Maddux opened the glass storm door covered with the sun-faded stickers of his grandchildren. Joe then opened the unlocked front door, seemingly unconcerned that he was revealing his lack of security. It didn't matter. The groundsman already knew that the Madduxes habitually left their home unlocked. As a matter of fact, he had been inside on several different occasions, both when they were out and when they were home asleep. He probably knew the house and the property better than the doddering old couple did themselves.

"So, how can we help, Mr. . . ." began Joe Maddux.

"Baker. Brian Baker, sir," replied the groundsman. "I am here to pick up some old farm equipment that you offered to donate for some of the Church projects in Mexico."

"Hmmm . . ." said Maddux as his wife took his coat and hung it in the hall closet. "I can't say that I remember offering to donate any farm equipment. I mean we have in the past, but now all we really have is the tractor for the light bit of cropping we do, and we need that. I don't know what to tell you. Must have been some sort of mistake somewhere."

"There probably was. Like I said, you folks aren't the first ones today who were an incorrect pickup for me. Would you mind if I made a quick call to the dispatch at Deseret to let them know?"

"Of course you can," replied Mrs. Maddux. "You can use the phone in the kitchen. Just follow me."

"Thank you, ma'am."

"Not at all."

Mrs. Maddux led the groundsman to a canary yellow rotary dial phone that looked as if it had been mounted on the wall in the mid-seventies.

"I haven't seen one of these in years," marveled the groundsman. "I didn't even know folks still used rotary phones." He laughed.

Mrs. Maddux smiled. "We have a simple rule around here: 'If it ain't broke, don't fix it.' "

"I hear you. Too many folks spending too much money on things they just don't need."

"Amen to that," came the voice of Mr. Maddux from the other room, where he had turned on the old color television set.

"Ma'am, I don't want to be a bother, but we've got one of those tricky phone mail systems down at the dispatch—"

"Oh, I can't stand those," broke in Mrs. Maddux.

"Well, that makes two of us," responded the groundsman with his warmest smile, "but you see I need to use a push-button phone if I want to bypass the system and get through to the dispatch man. Seeing how it's Sunday, all we've got is a skeleton crew down in Salt Lake. There's no operator on duty. You wouldn't happen to have a push-button phone, would you?"

The groundsman knew perfectly well that they did and where it was located.

"Yes, we do have one upstairs. But I think our service is just rotary. Would that still cause a problem for you?"

"No, ma'am," lied the groundsman.

"Okay, then. Follow me and I'll show you where it is."

Halfway up, he stopped and asked Mrs. Maddux, "Ma'am, do you suppose your husband would mind coming up, just in case I need him to confirm anything to the dispatcher?"

"Of course not," said Mary Maddux, who leaned over the banister and called to her husband.

"Okay, I'm coming!" yelled back Mr. Maddux, who didn't like being pulled away from his TV, even if it was for the Church.

Mary led the groundsman into the master bedroom. On the nightstand was a touch-tone phone with oversized glow-in-the-dark buttons. It was preprogrammed with the names of the Madduxes' children and had special speed dial buttons for *Police, Fire,* and *Ambulance.*

The groundsman moved toward the right side of the bed next to the phone and unzipped the top of his coveralls. He pretended to fumble in his breast pocket for something.

"I've got that invoice in here somewhere. Probably ought to get a clipboard one of these days."

Mrs. Maddux smiled politely and inwardly hoped that this misunderstanding would not put her and Joe in bad standing with the Church.

The groundsman heard the footsteps of Mr. Maddux as he came down the green shag carpeted hallway. He stopped fumbling in his coveralls when he found the true item he was looking for. His hand tightened around the butt of a cold Walther P4. The nine millimeter was fitted with a silencer, and despite its extended length, he drew it from his coveralls in less than the blink of an eye.

This was the part that he enjoyed the most, the expressions on his victims' faces when they knew death was only seconds away, but this couple had no telling expressions whatsoever. They were in utter shock, and their faces were blank. This kind of thing never happened in Midway, never even happened in Utah. It was utterly beyond their ability to comprehend. Not even a sniffle from the missus. They just stood there as if they were watching it happen to someone else on television.

Then, the dam broke. Mrs. Maddux let out a wail; the tears welled up in her eyes and began to roll down her cheeks as the reality of the situation hit her full force. They were going to die. The mister, on the other hand, still had no clue. His instinct was to comfort his wife, and as he reached out for her, the groundsman shot him twice in the forehead.

Spatters of blood, mingled with slivers of bone and pulpy gray matter, sprayed across Mary's face, and she began a repetitive mumble through her sobbing. All she could manage was, "Oh, God. Oh, God. Oh, God . . ."

"Good thing you went to church this morning, eh, Mary?" hissed the groundsman, his English now accented with his Swiss-German tongue. "In your next life, when the kids invite you to dinner, I suggest you accept."

He pointed the suppressed Walther at Mary Maddux and pulled the trigger. Anticipating the end, Mary turned her head at the last moment. The bullet tore away a huge piece of flesh and the underlying cartilage from the bridge of her nose. She fell to the floor screaming. Angrily, the groundsman fired his remaining rounds into her neck, chest, face, and head as she writhed in agony on the bedroom floor. Soon, her movements ceased, and she was still.

Mr. Maddux, unlike his wife, the groundsman mused, had been cooperative enough to fall back onto the bed. The groundsman lifted the man's feet and placed them on top of the chenille bedspread. Except for the bullet holes in his head, it looked as if he had just lain down to take a nap.

The groundsman then dragged Mrs. Maddux across the floor to the other side of the bed and hefted her up and onto it. When she landed, her arms were upright above her head. He toyed with the idea of stripping the old couple and leaving them in a sexually suggestive pose, wondering what the Mormon relatives would think, but there was other work to be done.

After he washed his hands in the small guest bathroom down the hall, careful not to leave any fingerprints, he went outside to finish unloading the contents of the semi into the barn.

With the truck unloaded, there was nothing for him to do but come inside and wait for Miner and his fellow Lions.

The small family room was warm, and its large window provided the groundsman as good a view as was possible through the blowing snow of anyone coming up the driveway. The television was still on, tuned to a station with an American football game.

Halfway through the third quarter and a pack of cigarettes later, the groundsman began to feel the telltale signs of his low blood-sugar level. Healthy as a horse since a child, he had made his doctor in Zurich explain three times how diabetes could have chosen him when no one in his family had ever had it. The doctor explained that there was no specific reason but that it was quite manageable, provided he took the right precautions. Of course the first precaution he took was never to let Miner know about his condition.

From a pocket in his coveralls, he withdrew a Nestlé's chocolate bar and broke it into perfect little squares, calculating how many he might need to keep his blood sugar up for the rest of the day. He lay the silver foil, with its purple-and-white wrapper, on his lap and put a piece of the creamy milk chocolate into his mouth. He sucked on it slowly, savoring it as he closed his eyes.

Then, from out of nowhere, came the sound of breaking glass from upstairs. The groundsman leapt from his chair and grabbed the German-made pistol from the end table beside him. Cautiously, he moved forward toward the stairs, crept up them and then down the hallway's green shag carpet. He inched toward the master bedroom, which was where he believed the sound had come from. He gripped the pistol tighter, grateful that he had replaced its spent magazine. As he neared the bedroom door, he inhaled deeply, applied slight pressure to the trigger, and spun into the open doorframe.

In an instant, he had not only surveyed the room, but also the condition of the two bodies lying atop the bed. The source of the noise was apparent at once.

He had left the woman's arms above her head and now noticed that one arm was splayed across the nightstand and the glass frame of a picture of seven small children lay broken on the floor. *Post-mortem reflex.*

The groundsman lowered his pistol and laughed out loud. As quickly as he started, he stopped. His ears had picked up the high-pitched whine of snowmobiles. He looked at his watch. Miner and the men were ahead of schedule.

He took the stairs three at a time and landed with a large thud in the downstairs hallway. As he bounded into the family room, he found his chocolate wrapper and bent down to gather up the pieces that had fallen on the floor. Not wanting Miner to find him away from his assigned post, the groundsman folded the wrapper around the chocolate and shoved it back into his coverall pocket. He used his handkerchief to grasp the half-filled water glass he had been using to ash his cigarettes in and flushed the contents down the hall toilet. He rinsed the glass with rusty brown water from the kitchen tap and returned it to a drying rack next to the sink.

He made it outside just in time to pick out the first glimmer of snowmobile headlights. Through the swirling and blowing snow, he could see them speeding toward him at the rear of the farmhouse.

CHAPTER 14

With Sam Harper, the Secret Service's number one man on-site, missing in action, Tom Hollenbeck was now in charge. When word reached him that Agent Harvath and the president's daughter had been recovered and brought in unconscious, he left instructions that he was to be notified immediately when either one came to.

The storm was making it impossible to coordinate search-and-rescue efforts. Even so, Hollenbeck contacted Hill Air Force Base's commanding officer and requested that they locate the two closest choppers with advanced heat-seeking FLIR, or forward-looking infrared, units and have them flown to Deer Valley as soon as humanly possible. Hollenbeck hoped that by the time they got there, there would be no need for them, but contingency plans always had to be made.

All the officers the Secret Service had available were sent out to try and locate the president and his team. As Longo was still having no luck getting the Service's Motorola radios to work, Palmer had taken it upon herself to get hold of Deer Valley's resort manager and have him send over as many portable CB radios as he could scrounge. Communications wouldn't be secure, but at this point that was the least of the Secret Service's worries.

Every available ski patroller and search-and-rescue volunteer from the surrounding three counties had been called in to help with the search. At risk were not only the president and the protective details, but the countless number of civilians who had been skiing on runs affected by the avalanche.

Hollenbeck sent Palmer out with a civilian team to comb the area where Agent Harvath and Amanda had been found. The remaining Secret Service agents took two of the best search-and-rescue people from Deer Valley's team and as many local law enforcement personnel as they could muster to help coordinate their search for the president. As much as he hated it, Hollenbeck knew that his job was to stay behind and run the operation from the command center.

When the call came that Agent Harvath was regaining consciousness, Hollenbeck grabbed a microcassette recorder, his parka, and flew out the door.

• • •

The soft, orange glow of a bedside lamp was the first thing Scot noticed as he began to come to. As his eyes opened further, he saw the boards of knotty pine that paneled the ceiling and below that a wallpaper border that ran the length of the room and depicted moose and deer in a wooded area. The blanket on top of him was heavy. It felt as if he had on more than one, but the one he could see was red and gray wool with white snowflakes. As Scot looked further down toward his feet, he noticed the footboard was carved from rough-hewn logs. He then realized he was in one of the guest rooms of the president's chalet and it was still night.

"Well, it looks like the wee lad is finally waking up," came a voice with a mock Scottish accent.

Scot's reflexes kicked in, and he tried to sit up. "Amanda! Where's—"

"Whoa!" came the voice again. This time the funny accent was gone and the man spoke in his normal Texas drawl. "She's here, Scot. Just across the hall. Dr. Paulos is taking care of her."

"How is she?"

"To tell you the truth, I don't know. My main concern is you right now, so let's relax and let me take a look." The doctor removed a penlight from the bag next to him and shined it in both of Scot's eyes.

"I want to see her."

"First I am going to complete my exam; then we are going to get an update from Dr. Paulos, and then if he says it's okay, you can see her."

The voice, bad accent and all, belonged to Dr. Skip Trawick. He and John Paulos had been friends of Scot's since his ski team days. Scot was a pretty good mimic, but the Scottish accent was one he just couldn't get down, so Skip always used it as his funny way of saying hello.

As head of the advance team for the trip to Park City, Scot had recommended both Skip and Dr. Paulos as the on-site medical pros. Now he wondered if that had been such a good idea.

"Damn it, Skip. Who the hell do you think got you and John these gigs as docs for the presidential party? Let me up; I have to see her."

"You, my friend, haven't changed a bit. You know that? Still as haggis-headed as ever."

"Cut the crap."

"It would be my pleasure, but first the exam. Now, how many fingers do you see?"

"None, you haven't poured anything yet."

"So far I'm going to say your neurological function is the same as it always was, low to subpar."

"Yuk, yuk, yuk. C'mon, Skip. I want to peek in on her. I have to know how she is."

"As soon as I am finished. Any areas of severe pain?"

"Yeah, right in my ass. I'm going to give you to the count of three to help me out of this bed, or I'm going to shove you off and do it myself. One—"

"Alive and kicking. That's a good sign, isn't it, Dr. Trawick?" asked Tom Hollenbeck as he threw his parka on a chair next to the door and made his way over to the bed.

"Maybe. The patient, though, claims to have a pain in the ass," replied Dr. Trawick.

"The patient *is* a pain in the ass," said Hollenbeck. "What's the story? Anything broken, concussion?"

"I haven't been able to complete my examination, as of yet. The patient is not being compliant."

"Not compliant? Skip, you son of a—I'll give you noncompliant."

"And a wee bit aggressive," said Skip, the Scottish accent back again.

"Jesus, Skip. You're on duty. Could you at least pretend to be a professional for a few minutes? On second thought, fuck this. I'm getting up," said Scot.

"Hold on there, Harvath," Hollenbeck said sternly. "I want you to cooperate. None of this tough-guy stuff. You just lie there and let the doc take a look at you."

"Fine. Go ahead, Skip. The sooner you're finished, the sooner I can get over to Amanda."

"You're not going anywhere until I get a full statement from you. Just settle down, would ya? My God, Scot. We've got a very serious situation on our hands right now, so get focused," said Hollenbeck.

"I'm sorry, Tom. You're right. If the good doctor would unplug me from this IV, I'd be happy to get started."

"No way, José. The IV stays in. You came in severely dehydrated. I want to get some more fluids into you first," said Dr. Trawick as he continued to examine Scot from head to toe.

"I brought a tape recorder with me. We'll take your statement verbally," said Hollenbeck.

"Verbally? But what about him?" said Scot as he motioned to Dr. Trawick.

"What about me? I'm still on nonoperational Special Forces duty, Scot."

"Oh, so that's what you call shagging kegs when members of your old unit come to town," said Harvath.

"Listen, as one of the 'Quiet Professionals,' I know how to keep my mouth shut."

"Oh, yeah? Coulda' fooled me, 'cause it's always open."

Hollenbeck hated to break up the lovefest, but he had bigger concerns. "Dr. Trawick, I don't have time for you to sign a National Security Non-Disclosure Document. I am aware of your status as a Special Forces operative, and I know that you've maintained your top secret clearance. In the interest of tending to your patient and the ongoing emergency, I want to make sure you understand that nothing said within this room is to be repeated."

"No problem, Agent Hollenbeck. You have my word."

"Can you also get his word that he'll shut up and not repeat that lame-ass story of how he served his country by treating an elephant in the Kuwaiti zoo during Desert Storm?"

"Now who's the comedian? Why don't you try to sit up? I want to listen to your heart and check your ribs."

Harvath stifled a groan as Dr. Trawick helped him sit up. The agents who brought him in had cut away his sweater and turtleneck, as well as his Lycra pants, placing him in a hospital-style gown before putting him into bed. As Harvath leaned forward, his gown was open in back and Hollenbeck saw what looked like a topographical map of green, blue, and yellow islands, bruises that covered his back and shoulders.

"Holy shit. Are you sure you're up to this?" asked Hollenbeck.

Trawick said, "I'm going to shoot some adrenaline into your IV, and that should help give you a little more strength. You want anything for the pain?"

"No, let's get this over with, and then I want you to clear me for the hot tub downstairs so I can soak this out."

"Scot, this isn't some post-ski-competition session. You walloped yourself quite a few times back in those days, and God knows you scared the bejesus outta me more than once, but your body has suffered some serious trauma here. So far it doesn't look like anything is broken. If there's no blood in your urine, I might postpone having you go to the hospital for further tests, but if I do, you're gonna stay right here in this bed for several days at least. Now shut up for a second and take a deep breath."

Scot did as he was told, and Hollenbeck waited until the doctor had removed the stethoscope from his ears before he launched into a series of questions and recorded everything on tape for later transcription.

Scot ran down the list—seeing the president, Harper, and the rest of the team at the last lap, Amanda's wipeout and the communications outage, the decision to take her through the bowl to get back to the house, the avalanche, getting to the outcropping, being buried, digging out, and trying to get Amanda's unconscious body back to the house.

Occasionally, Dr. Trawick broke in with questions that pushed Scot to reach a little further back. Long-term memory questions like, *What's your address, your telephone and driver's license numbers?* were easy for him to answer, but he had problems with some short-term memory questions such as *What hotel are you staying in, what airline did you fly to Utah on, and when was your last visit to the White House?*

When he was finished recounting his tale, the room was completely silent. After a moment, Dr. Trawick let out a long whistle.

"You know how lucky you are to be alive, boy?" he asked.

"Yeah, I know."

"I worry, though, about the short-term memory loss. I don't know how much is gone."

"Like you said, Skip. It's just like the old days. I got whacked in the head and I'm a little fuzzy . . . on some utterly unimportant stuff, I might add, but it'll come back."

"I'm sure it will, but at some point I am going to need to run some tests on you, nonetheless."

Scot ignored Skip and turned to Hollenbeck and asked, "What's the status on the others? The president, Harp, Maxwell?"

Hollenbeck inhaled deeply before he responded. "At this point, there is no status. The radios are still down, and you and Amanda are the only ones we have recovered."

Scot couldn't believe his ears. "No status? That's ridiculous. Nothing from the CAT or JAR teams? Nothing off the Smocks? You can't even get his five cents' worth?" *Five cents' worth* referred to the homing device that every president was provided with by the Secret Service. It was an Indian head nickel containing a transmitter that operated on a special frequency that could deliver GPS coordinates. The president always carried this coin on his person and referred to it as his "good luck piece." Although tonight, it didn't seem to be bringing anyone any good luck.

"The Motorolas, the Smocks, everything was intermittent throughout the day. Because it was across the entire communications platform, we wrote it off to weather or mountain shadow anomalies. It wasn't until we were down for several minutes that we raised the alarm. So, in answer to your question, we have no status."

"What about search-and-rescue?"

"All available agents have been sent to Death Chute with some of the ski patrol and sheriff's department S-and-R guys. Agent Palmer is leading a civilian team back where we picked you and Goldilocks up. I think Palmer's team is going to have better luck."

"Why do you say that?"

"You were picked up in the bowl. The bowl is easily accessible. We've already got some construction lamps and related equipment en route. I must have personally spoken with every construction company within a hundred-mile radius. Any and all heavy earth-moving equipment that exists is trying to make its way there right now."

"But what about the president and Sam?"

"You tell me, Scot. You've skied Death Chute. You were the one who was in charge of securing it. What kind of equipment do you think we could get onto a nearly vertical drop face?"

"Choppers."

"Grounded."

"Not our stuff. Not those Marine pilots."

"Yes, even our stuff and even our guys. When you feel up to it, take a peek out the window. You can't even see your hand in front of your face. It's a complete whiteout. What's more, we can't get lights up where we need them, and we certainly can't get any cranes or bulldozers in there because the area is so inaccessible."

As the severity of the situation began to sink in, Harvath pressed his palms against his forehead.

"What we do have going for us," Hollenbeck continued, "is that you saw the president's detail make it to the first plateau around the treed area. The CAT team waiting at the bottom never saw them come out, so we have a general idea of where they might be."

"But that snow came roaring down the mountain. They could have been totally swept past the CAT team."

"I don't think so. If you really did see Ahern and Houchins wipe out by the trees, then the rest of the detail would have held up for them. I am going to assume that they heard and interpreted the avalanche the same way you did and went into the trees. We've got over fifty people up there right now with dogs. We have to hope for the best. The mushers will work the pups, and the rest will link and sink." *Link and sink* was a search-and-rescue technique in which a line of people moved forward side by side, as if linked by an invisible chain, sinking long aluminum poles into the snow every foot, in an effort to feel something or someone underneath.

Scot looked up at Hollenbeck. "Have you called Washington yet?"

"Yeah. They told me we're authorized for anything we need."

Dr. Trawick cleared his throat, indicating that he was through with his examination. Scot and Agent Hollenbeck both turned to look at him.

"There's no question that you took quite a beating. I am still amazed that, all things considered, you didn't break anything. In light of what happened, your injuries are relatively minor."

"Good, then I can—"

"Hold on a second. I'm not finished. When I say your injuries are minor, that doesn't mean they aren't serious. While nothing appears to be broken, you may have a few cracked ribs. I want to wrap you with an Ace, ice the bruised areas, and then get you into my office for some X rays and probably a CT scan. Until then, you are to stay in bed. I am going to keep you on the IV for another twelve hours and monitor you. What I am most concerned about is your head trauma. So, for the time being, you are staying put."

"Thanks all the same, Doc, but I plan on going back out there to help in the search. They need every live body they can get."

"You're welcome all the same, but you're not going anywhere. Your body is of no use to anyone in this condition. You go out there like this and they'll end up having to waste time carrying you right back in again."

"I doubt that—"

"And, beyond the total fatigue and exhaustion you have suffered, there's also some frostbite and mild hypothermia. Any average person probably would have died out there. Your survival says a lot about your training and will to live. I repeat, you are one lucky S.O.B."

"Are you finished now, because I've got stuff I've gotta do?" said Scot as he tried to raise himself off the bed.

"Lie down," barked Hollenbeck. "That's an order! Harvath, why do you insist on being such a jackass sometimes?"

"Tom, with all due respect, I was head of the advance team. The safety of the presidential party as well as my fellow agents was and is my responsibility. You need my help."

"Not in this condition I don't. Forget it."

"I'm not going to debate this with you, Tom."

"You're damn right you're not. You are staying in that bed until Dr. Trawick or Dr. Paulos says otherwise. You got me?"

"C'mon, Tom. Be realistic."

A crackle, followed by Hollenbeck's call sign over the CB radio clipped to his belt, prevented him from arguing any further with Scot, and he raised his hand for silence.

"This is Birdhouse. Over."

"Birdhouse, this is Hermes. We've got something. Over."

"Copy, Hermes. What's the situation? Over."

Despite the effort, Scot sat straight up to listen to the exchange.

"Birdhouse, it appears as if we have recovered two agents from Hat Trick's detail. They are extricating them as we speak."

Thank God, Hollenbeck thought to himself. "What's their condition? Over."

"Still extracting, hold on a sec . . . I'm moving over to get a better view."

"Roger that. Birdhouse is holding."

Several seconds passed.

"Birdhouse! Birdhouse! Hat Trick's agents are down! Unnatural causes. I repeat, unnatural causes."

Hollenbeck couldn't believe what he was hearing. Scot strained forward to take in every piece of information. He knew that there was absolute pandemonium on the face of Death Chute right now. All of the agents would have their guns drawn, feeling vulnerable in the dark, not knowing if the threat was still present or long since gone.

"Hermes, this is Birdhouse. Tell your team to sweep and reap. I repeat, your team is to sweep and reap. Do you copy? Over." *Sweep and reap* was the command to scour the immediate area for hostile targets. If any were encountered, the threat was to be neutralized by taking the perpetrators into custody or by punching their tickets as quickly as possible.

"Roger, Birdhouse. Hermes's team will sweep and reap. Over."

Hollenbeck had four CAT teams outside, and he got on the radio and mobilized them next. Two headed off toward Death Chute, and the other two took defensive positions around the house. As he completed his commands, he turned back to see Scot trying to get out of bed. This was more than he needed to handle. He turned to Dr. Trawick. "Sedate him. Now."

"We can't do that. Not in his condition."

"Fine. I want a guard on this door tonight. He doesn't leave."

Harvath was only able to squeeze out a couple words of protest before Hollenbeck grabbed his parka and ran out of the room, slamming the door behind him. Scot knew he was licked, at least for now.

CHAPTER 15

Miner once again looked at his watch. Everything was still going according to schedule. Every phase of the operation brought with it new challenges and potential pitfalls. The greatest risk Miner and his team were running right now was in transporting their precious cargo, but even in that, he had plotted for every eventuality.

Wasatch Front Ambulance Service had a fleet of fifteen vehicles that, in one of the fastest growing counties in America, were always in demand. Drivers performed routine inspections of their rigs, as they called them, before each shift. With them driving so many steeply graded mountain passes every week, their brakes were of the utmost importance to them. When the driver of ambulance 17 had come on duty yesterday and found brake fluid pooled on the ground beneath his rig, he immediately notified the dispatcher.

As Wasatch's mechanic was overwhelmed with a string of mysterious problems on four other rigs, the dispatcher called to have the rig towed to a local garage, where it could be repaired by an outside mechanic.

When the tow truck arrived and picked up ambulance 17, the

groundsman had been waiting across the street in a nondescript gold Ford Taurus to take down the name, address, and telephone number of the mechanic's shop stenciled in bright green letters on the side of the tow truck. A simple call from his cell phone to Grunnah Automotive verified what Miner had told him to expect in the land of Utah. After closing early on Saturday, the garage would not open again until Monday.

The alarm system at Grunnah Automotive was more for show than anything else. The groundsman had it deactivated in no time. He spent the next half hour repairing the ambulance and helping himself to Cokes from the refrigerator in Mr. Grunnah's office. He then slipped into dark blue trousers and a dark blue shirt with official-looking patches on it, drove the ambulance out of the garage, being careful to close the roll-down door behind him, and rendezvoused with the Deseret Industries eighteen-wheeler, into which he loaded the ambulance.

Eighteen hours later, as the stolen ambulance rocketed down Provo Canyon, passing the Sundance Resort, Miner phoned the pilot of his chartered MediJet plane.

He spoke with the urgency of a doctor transporting a patient in very serious condition. The wail of the sirens and the clipped British accent he affected dovetailed perfectly with what the MediJet crew had been led to believe was their assignment.

The refinery fire in Magna, Utah, two weeks prior had been one of the worst the industry had ever seen. The blaze had burned uncontrollably for several days, and the smoke had been so thick that it had shut down all but two runways at Salt Lake City International Airport. Before the flames had been extinguished, environmentalists from several groups had flocked to the scene with their banners, decrying the continued pollution of the environment by big business, particularly the oil and gas industries. Several media outlets had run stories about the mounting toll oil and gas disasters were taking on the planet. On television, scenes of the Kuwaiti oil fields aflame during the Gulf War competed for time alongside images of dead oil-soaked seabirds being plucked from the shores of Alaska following the *Exxon Valdez* disaster. The Magna refinery fire was worldwide news.

"And we will be able to take off?" Miner asked into his cell phone from inside the bumpy ambulance.

"Yes, sir, Doctor. As far as we can tell from the weather reports and our information from the tower, this window should hold for about forty-five more minutes."

"Good, and you have informed the tower of our need for priority slotting for takeoff?"

"Yes, sir. From the looks of it now, we're the only ones that'll be leaving, but as a medical emergency we have priority anyway."

"Good. How is the air traffic in general throughout the area?"

"This is typical mountain weather. The snow and wind have tapered off some down here in the valley, but it's pounding the higher elevations up in the mountains. Salt Lake International is experiencing stack-ups both in and out. Even with a medical emergency, we still would have had our work cut out for us getting off the ground out of SLC."

Miner had arranged for the MediJet to await his team at the Provo Municipal Airport in Orem, forty miles south of Salt Lake City, for precisely these very reasons. First, he could count on the weather being less severe at the lower-elevation airport than at the one up by Deer Valley, and second, with a medical emergency out of Provo Municipal, Miner knew that he could call all of the shots. The runway would be plowed and the jet de-iced by the time he got there. All he needed to do was load his "patient" and they would immediately be cleared for takeoff.

The fact that the private airfield would ask few questions and their security was lax to nonexistent had been another plus.

The pilot spoke again over Miner's cell phone. "What is the patient's condition?"

"He's stable but still critical."

"Confirmed. Per your instructions, Doctor, we have added the extra equipment you asked for."

"Excellent. And you are sure that there will be no problem with the stretcher and its oxygen tent fitting in the plane?"

"Absolutely not. Normally, we would transfer the patient from the ambulance stretcher to our own, but when you explained that the tent's seal couldn't be breached because of the risk of infection, we just off-loaded our stretcher. As long as yours has the dimensions you indicated, our clamps will be able to secure it in place. I just hope he'll be comfortable. It's quite a long flight to Stansted."

"I appreciate your concern. He's pretty heavily sedated, as you can imagine."

"I would imagine. It is such a tragedy. I think everyone was moved by the Magna fire."

"Indeed, this gentleman is lucky to be alive, but we're just not sure for how much longer. Have you made the arrangements for us with British customs?"

"Yes, just as you asked. I have alerted our London office, and they have been in contact with the authorities at Stansted Airport. If you provide me with all of your passports on the plane, including the patient's, we'll have you cleared before you have him in your transport."

"And your office is aware of the severity of this man's injuries? Third-degree burns over ninety-five percent of his body, including his face?"

"Yes, Doctor. The authorities will also be made aware of that fact, as well as the issue of the tent not being breached. To tell you the truth, I don't think you are going to run into any problems at all. Like I said, there doesn't seem to be anyone who wasn't touched by this story. Plus, the patient is British, correct?"

"Yes, he is."

"Well, I've found that always helps. I mean here this poor—what was his occupation?"

"A chemist for Fawcett Petroleum."

"Right, a chemist. Here this poor chemist is burned in a terrible fire, and all he wants to do is be repatriated so he can die on his own soil surrounded by his family. If there is even the slightest hiccup with the immigration folks at Stansted, they're going to have to deal with me, personally."

"Thank you, Captain. I am counting on that. Our ETA is fifteen minutes. Please contact the tower for your clearance and have the jet ready for takeoff."

"Roger."

As Miner pushed the *end* button on his cell phone, he turned to the groundsman working next to him. "How are we doing?"

The groundsman, not only a master assassin but also a master of disguise, sat back and invited Miner to admire his handiwork.

"Excellent," commented Miner as they sealed the oxygen tent above the stretcher.

Through an ingenious use of latex and special-effects makeup, the president of the United States had been hideously transformed. One look at him, along with a mention of the Magna refinery fire, would be all they needed to turn even the most difficult and hard-hearted customs official to jelly. The unbreachable oxygen tent, complete with a patient who in no way could match his photo in the false passport Miner carried for him, would get them waved right through the security of Stansted Airport. Of that Miner was sure. The officials might even offer him a motorcade, which of course, he would be forced to decline.

CHAPTER 16

When Harvath awoke, he had no idea how long he'd been sleeping. His eyes focused and he saw he was in the same room he had been brought to last night. At least he hoped it had been last night. It must have been. There was no way he could have been out for more than six hours, eight tops.

Even though the curtains were drawn, he could tell that it was early morning. The snow was still falling, but not as hard as before. He decided from the pressure on his bladder that he had gotten more than enough fluids, and so he reached over and pulled the IV from his arm.

Across the room to his left was the open door to a bathroom. Dr. Skip would be pissed, no pun intended, that he hadn't saved his urine for him to examine, but that was life.

Scot's stomach muscles contracted as he crunched painfully upward and used his arms as buttresses to keep himself from falling backward onto his pillow. The pain not only was still in his back and shoulders, but had found new places to set up shop.

Halfway there, Scot thought to himself. He shifted his weight onto his left arm and with his right, reached out and threw back the covers. Breathing a little harder than just getting out of bed warranted, he inhaled deeply and in one motion swung his feet out from under the blankets, pivoting his body so that he now sat on the edge of the bed.

With the weight off his arms, he was now able to stretch. His range of motion was severely limited. He had taken some beatings before, but this one was definitely Academy Award material. Nothing, though, that a long, hot shower couldn't help.

Harvath eased his feet to the floor and slowly stood up from the bed. His legs were weak, but with a concerted effort he propelled himself forward to the bathroom.

Taking the gown off was the hard part. With the straps tied behind him and his arms so stiff, he couldn't reach around to untie them. He walked toward the toilet, lifted the bottom half of the gown like a skirt, and began to relieve himself. Then, ever so slowly, Scot inched the gown over his head until it came all the way off. He reached inside the shower and turned the control all the way to *hot.* As he did, he caught a glimpse of his back in the mirror. He wouldn't win any beauty pageants, that was for sure, but it would heal.

God bless the president for having friends that can afford houses like this, Scot thought as he sat on the marble bench in the ornate shower and let the hot water beat down on him. After what he figured had been a good fifteen minutes, he flipped the lever that activated the steam shower and closed his eyes. As he breathed in the searing moisture, he replayed the events of the past twenty-four hours in his mind. The avalanche didn't make any sense. There had been a lot of snow falling, but both the Utah Avalanche Forecast Center and Deer Valley's avalanche-control team had assured him that the risks were minimal. Scot himself had even made the trip up to Squaw Peak to test the conditions that very morning.

Could more snow have fallen than he thought? Even though the UAFC had rated the risks minimal, there still had been risks. The weight of responsibility rested heavily upon Scot's battered shoulders. He sat in the shower in a trance and replayed everything over and over in his mind. Then, with a jolt, he sat upright. He had completely forgotten about Hollenbeck's conversation with Hermes right before his exhaustion overtook him, *Two agents down . . . unnatural causes.*

Scot threw the lever back to *shower* and twisted the knob all the way to *cold.* He had learned this trick in a massage club in Hong Kong. A hot bath followed by a cold plunge was better than four cups of coffee any day.

The shock to his system had the desired effect, and Scot climbed out of the shower feeling alive, his senses keen, even if his body was still in pain. He promised himself no sedatives or pain medication, no matter what Hollenbeck or Dr. Trawick said. He hated how those things could cloud his mind, and his mind was his most important weapon. Gumming up the works was just asking for trouble.

Not seeing his clothes lying around, and figuring they had probably been cut off him, Scot was relieved to find a terry cloth bathrobe in the bedroom's cedar closet. He put it on and headed for the door.

When he stepped into the hallway, he noticed the door across from his was wide open and the room's bed was made. He searched his brain for what Dr. Trawick had said about Amanda. Hadn't he said she was across the hall? If she had been, she had been moved, and Scot added her whereabouts to the list of questions he had.

There were no detail agents in the hall as he made his way toward the stairway, but he did hear voices coming from below.

Walking in a straight line across a level surface was one thing. Walking down stairs was another. Scot leaned heavily on the pine banister as he forced his knees to bend and accommodate. He let out a small thanks that none of the agents in the enormous, picture-windowed living room had seen his struggle. After three shuffling steps at the bottom of the landing, he was spotted by Agent Palmer.

"What are you doing up, Scot?"

"I'm not paid to sleep, and I want to know what's going on."

"It's bad. Real bad."

"I heard Birdhouse talking with Hermes about finding two agents down last night."

"From what I heard, you took a real beating. Are you okay?"

"I'm fine," Scot growled with a little more venom than Agent Palmer deserved. "Would somebody just tell me what's going on?"

"Have you eaten?"

"Palmer, damn it. I want to know what's happening."

"Listen to me, Scot, just relax. A lot has happened, and I mean *a lot.* I'll be more than happy to fill you in. Why don't we get you some breakfast, and I'll tell you everything. You're gonna need to sit down for this."

Palmer walked away for a moment toward the front door and returned carrying a blue duffel bag with a Secret Service emblem on the side.

"They had to cut you out of your clothes last night. Hollenbeck figured you might need some things, so he had one of the agents get this stuff from your hotel."

"He's all heart." *My hotel.* Scot still couldn't remember its name.

"There's a bathroom just down the hall there. Why don't you get dressed and meet me in the kitchen? I'll put some coffee on and see what I can rustle up foodwise."

"Thanks, Palmer."

"No prob."

• • •

Twenty minutes later, shaved and past the painful ordeal of getting dressed, Scot appeared in the kitchen wearing jeans, a sweatshirt, and a pair of Timberland boots. Palmer was sitting on a stool at a granite-topped cooking island reviewing paperwork.

She looked up from her reading and saw Scot standing in the doorway. "How are you doing?"

"Enough about me. Let's have some answers."

"You know, Harvath, I'm willing to cut you some slack for what you went through, but you're getting dangerously close to the limit."

"I know," Scot said as he took the stool next to her, glad that it had a soft cushion he could rest his body against. "I'm sorry. I just want to know what the big picture is."

"Fine. I can understand that. There's a lot to go over, so why don't I pour us each a cup of coffee and we'll get started. I hunted up a microwave breakfast. One of those eggs-and-bacon things. Probably doesn't taste too good—"

"Sold. I'll take it."

With a cup of steaming hot coffee and a bland microwave breakfast to keep his mouth busy, he listened as Palmer explained what the Secret Service knew so far.

"At sixteen-ten yesterday afternoon you relayed Goldilocks's desire to call it a day. You met Hat Trick's detail at the last lap, from which he proceeded with his detail toward Death Chute and your detail accompanied Goldilocks toward her usual route back here. At approximately sixteen-twenty-five your report states that Goldilocks wiped out and while you were retrieving her gear, you thought you noticed Ahern and Houchins fall going into the treed area of Death Chute. It was at this point that you noticed communications—"

"Palmer," said Scot between bites of hash browns, "can you please skip ahead to the stuff I don't know? Give me the abridged version."

"You know, I could just let you sift through the reports."

"Don't give me a hard time. Give me the facts."

"All right, all right. Your team didn't make it."

"None of them?"

"We've recovered five members of your detail already and are looking for the others, who are now presumed dead. The five we've got were killed by the avalanche."

Scot hung his head and pinched the bridge of his nose, trying to fight off the headache and emotion he felt coming on. "And Goldilocks? What's her condition?" he asked without looking up.

"She suffered some severe head and neck trauma, frostbite, and hypothermia. Had you not gotten her out of the snow and the intercept team not found you when they did, she never would have made it. Her condition is guarded, but stable. She has some damaged vertebrae, but they believe they can be fixed."

"Will she be able to walk? Is there any permanent damage?"

"According to Dr. Paulos, there shouldn't be any permanent damage. It looks like she's going to pull through."

"Thank God for that. What about Hat Trick?"

"That's where it gets really bad. Every member of Hat Trick's detail is dead."

"Dead, how?"

"Nine millimeter, best we can tell."

Scot couldn't believe what he was hearing and sat up ramrod straight. "What? They were all taken out?"

"All of them." Palmer paused for a moment to let it sink in before continuing. "We had several JARs, as you know, in the trees along that part of Death Chute, and they were sanctioned as well."

"What about Hat Trick?"

"We don't know."

"What do you mean, you don't know?"

"We haven't been able to recover his body."

"Holy shit." Despite the anger and sadness he felt, his years of training had taught him that when the time came, he would be able to grieve privately, but that for now, he needed to filter his emotions. What mattered was not how he felt, but how he *thought.*

"So," Scot continued with amazing composure, "the entire detail and the JAR team was sanctioned. There is no sign of Hat Trick. I can't believe this. Somebody must have grabbed him."

"We're not positive, but—"

"You found all of the other bodies, sanctioned, but not his. Sounds like he was grabbed to me. Have there been any demands?"

"Hold on. You are getting way ahead of things here."

"Palmer, how am I getting ahead? You found all the detail agents, but not Hat Trick. They normally stick pretty close to him."

"Yes, but this was an avalanche. He could have been swept in any direction."

"Don't give me that. You know how this looks. If it was just an avalanche, that would be one thing, but his detail was terminated."

"Scot, we're all in shock. Never in the history of the Secret Service have we lost so many agents protecting the president. Nor has anyone ever succeeded in a kidnapping, which *is* how we're playing this."

"So, you do agree."

"Yes."

"Jesus, I can't believe this."

"We do have one lead, though."

"What kind of lead?"

"Harper managed to get off a shot and kill one of the people we believe were responsible for the attack."

Good ol' Harp, Scot thought to himself. "They left the body behind? Who was it? What can you tell me?"

"We're waiting for confirmation on the identity. We've had to wire the prints and picture off to CIA station chiefs in the Mideast."

"Sand Land? You're telling me the job was carried out by a bunch of Bedouin Bobs? That's impossible! The only thing they know about snow is that it's spelled with two different letters than *sand.*"

"What I'm telling you is that we've got upward of thirty dead Secret Service agents, a missing president, and one deceased male of Mideastern descent found at the scene of the crime with a bullet in the back of his head that I'm betting dollars to doughnuts was fired from Sam Harper's SIG."

Scot put his elbows on the cold granite countertop and rested his head in his hands. He had to be dreaming. Soon he would wake up and this nightmare would be over.

As he sat there with the microwave breakfast and coffee going sour in his stomach, the pieces began falling into place. "The failure in our communication systems wasn't caused by the weather, then, was it?"

"We still don't know."

"So, what's the status of our investigation? Are they gridding Death Chute and going through it millimeter by millimeter?"

"No."

"No?" Scot asked incredulously. "What do you mean *no?*"

"Scot, you put the pieces together just as fast as everyone else did. The president has been kidnapped or worse, and that now makes this an FBI matter. We have been instructed to secure the area."

"And that's it?"

"Yeah, that's it."

"Who gave those orders?"

"It came from D.C. after Hollenbeck spoke with the director of the Secret Service. Agents from the Salt Lake FBI field office are already on-site waiting for the special agent in charge who is going to handle the investigation. He's due in about an hour."

Scot groaned, knowing who it would be. "Let me guess, the SAC is Gary Lawlor, right?"

"Yeah, the FBI's deputy director himself. Makes sense. The director is gonna have no choice but to stay in D.C. and coordinate. This is going to be one hell of a firestorm."

CHAPTER 17

Harvath needed to clear his head. The information Palmer had relayed was overwhelming. Upward of thirty agents dead and the president missing, presumed kidnapped. It was too much to grasp.

Scot grabbed a blue-and-white Secret Service parka hanging by the back door of the kitchen and walked outside. Three agents taking a cigarette break looked in his direction, but didn't say anything. What could be said?

Harvath walked into the woods alongside the house, and when he felt he was out of sight of the other agents, leaned against one of the tall trees and closed his eyes. A million questions raced through his mind. *What happened? How could I not have seen this coming? Did I overlook something during the advance?*

Every whacko in a four-hundred-mile radius had been accounted for, the more dangerous of them locked up for the few days the president would be here. There hadn't been any pings on U.S. Immigration hot sheets, and there had been no new threats from any extremist groups that had even hinted at this.

He breathed deeply, letting the chilly air fill his lungs, and held it until it burned. Slowly, he let the air escape in a long hiss. He repeated the process again, trying to get a handle on what was going on.

Upward of thirty agents killed and the president missing. Scot began second-guessing himself, convinced that there had been some sort of warning sign that he'd missed. There were still agents out there trapped under the snow, but Palmer had been right. The chances that they were alive were slim to none. Scot fought back a surge of guilt. Many of those men had been his friends, and they all had been *his* responsibility. *Not now,* a voice inside him said. *Turn and let it burn.* But it was so hard. Even though he was trained to be a master of his mind and emotions, he was still human. He had lost comrades before, but it had been on missions to faraway places where he had been striking at threats to domestic or international security. Those men had fallen in battle, but this, this wasn't the same. These Secret Service agents never had a chance, never saw what was coming. And they had been hit on home turf.

The thought of foreign insurgents executing this attack on American soil and then scooting back to wherever they came from, especially if it was Sand Land, really pissed Scot off. Deep breathing out in the woods wasn't the road to the answers he wanted. Besides, his ribs were killing him. The answers would be found where the action was, up on Death Chute. Until Gary Lawlor got here, the crime scene still belonged to the Secret Service, and as the leader of the presidential advance team, Scot felt he had not only a right, but a duty to examine every inch of it.

• • •

"What, are you nuts?" said a young FBI agent from the Salt Lake field office when Harvath ducked under the tape and started making his way to the scene.

Scot had hitched a ride up with a Sno-Cat that was hauling equipment as close as it could get to the plateau, where a combination of Secret Service and FBI agents were acting as Sherpas, walking the gear the rest of the way to the crime scene.

"Listen, Agent"—Scot looked at the identification tag hanging around the man's muscled neck—"Zuschnitt. I need to get in there and take a look around." The man had about three inches and a good seventy-five pounds on Scot, but Scot had messed with bigger guys and come out on top.

The FBI agent was in no mood to deal with Harvath. His orders were to let no one in until Lawlor got there, and he intended to make sure those orders were carried out. "This is a crime scene under the jurisdiction of the FBI. No one goes in there except FBI. *Capisce?*"

Capisce? *Where did a Salt Lake Fed with a name like Zuschnitt pick up* capisce? Scot wondered. His need to get answers turned the flame up on his anger a couple of notches. "My name's Scot Harvath, Secret Service. I was head of the advance team—"

"Boy, are you going to have some explaining to do. I wouldn't want to be in your shoes," snapped Agent Zuschnitt.

This guy is a real asshole. I thought this shitty treatment was reserved for muscling in on local law enforcement jurisdictions or when the FBI got one-upped by the CIA. Most of the FBI guys Scot had met in his career had been pretty decent. The Secret Service and the FBI normally got along quite well. This guy, though, was asking for it.

"Agent Zuschnitt, I know you're doing your job, and I'm just trying to do mine."

"If you'd done yours, the FBI wouldn't have to be here cleaning up your mess."

"What's your fucking problem?"

"I don't have one. What's yours?"

Harvath's *pissed-off* meter was now well into the red zone, but he fought to stay in control and keep his cool.

"Over two dozen men probably have died on my watch—"

"And you want me to let you in here to contaminate this crime scene? Somehow that's going to make everything all right? Guess again, buddy."

"You know," said Harvath, backing down, "you're right. You've got a job to do, a post to stand. I can appreciate that. If you couldn't keep one lowly Secret Service agent out, it'd probably make you look like a pretty big ass."

A smile spread across the lips of the beefy FBI agent as he smelled victory and saw Harvath turn to walk away. The smile disappeared when Harvath quickly spun around and delivered a blow to Zuschnitt's sternum. It felt like a red-hot ingot of lead that had been fired at him from a cannon. As the air rushed from his lungs and the agent doubled over in pain, Harvath placed his palms on Zuschnitt's shoulder blades and drove his knee up into the man's mouth, splitting his lip open and knocking him unconscious.

"So much for professional courtesy," said Harvath as he ducked under the tape and walked up the hill to where several small flags had been placed in the snow.

Blue tarps were pitched over the bodies to protect against further snow accumulation. Sealing the scene was the right thing to do, but there was no reason that Scot shouldn't have been allowed in. The scene was already greatly disturbed because of the rescue efforts. Snow was one of the biggest pains in the ass to try to gather evidence in. This case was no exception. As a matter of fact, the difficulty had been compounded by the avalanche, which Harvath now knew was no accident.

Scot moved from tarp to tarp, looking beneath each one, recognizing every face. The eyes of many of the bodies were still open, staring right through him. The pattern of precise head shots on all of the bodies coupled with random bullet wounds on some didn't make sense. He had a feeling that before this was over, he would be running across a lot of things that didn't make sense.

Scot was trying to process the information as he walked over to one of the final tarps, under which lay the body of Sam Harper. He lifted the sheet of blue plastic and saw the body with the SIG-Sauer clasped in Sam's right hand. A flood of memories poured through Scot's mind, and it was almost impossible to push them out.

• • •

Whenever a president made an appearance on or near water, the Navy SEALs were called upon to provide support. Harvath had transferred to Dev Group after several years with Team Two and was part of a contingent of SEALs that assisted several such protective details for a former president who loved to race his Cigarette boats off the coast of Maine. Scot had proven himself to be extremely talented on many occasions, but when he discovered and defused a small explosive device meant to disrupt one of the president's outings, Secret Service agent Sam Harper stood up and took notice. Harper had been looking for someone just like Scot to help improve the Secret Service's protection of the president.

He pursued Harvath back to Little Creek, Virginia, where Scot was an active part of the SEAL think tank. It took some doing, but Harper eventually succeeded in wooing Scot on board the Secret Service team. After Harvath completed his courses at the Secret Service advanced-training facility in Beltsville, Maryland, he joined Harper at the White House. Not only did Sam Harper show him the ropes, but he made him a part of his family. Scot had lost track a long time ago of how many barbecues and holiday dinners he had eaten with Sam, his wife, Sharon, and their two daughters. The thought of how they would take this news tore right through his heart.

• • •

"What the hell are you doing?" came the voice of a very angry Tom Hollenbeck.

Without turning around, Harvath walked toward the last and final tarp, which he knew must be covering the man Harper had shot.

"Harvath, I asked you a question!"

Scot lifted the tarp and stared at the bloody body. Half of the back of its skull had been blown away.

"What the hell's the matter with you? Assaulting an FBI officer? Damn it, Harvath, look at me."

It took him almost a full minute to tear himself away from the body of the Middle Easterner. Silently, Scot was making a promise to Harper. He would personally deliver the bullets that would take out every last one of the fuckers responsible for this tragedy.

"Skorpion," said Harvath so quietly that Hollenbeck almost didn't hear him.

"What?"

"The machine pistol, it's a Skorpion," said Scot, turning to face Hollenbeck.

"What about it?"

"They're manufactured by the Czechs, but are the darlings of every Middle Eastern group with a bone to pick."

"Speaking of bones, my friend, I've got a big one to pick with you. I know what kind of weapon that is, but I've got a couple of other questions. Just what the hell were you thinking when you coldcocked that FBI agent?"

Scot shook off the melancholy trance that had descended on him when he had seen Sam Harper's body. "He was asking for it."

"Asking for it? He was doing his job maintaining the integrity of this crime scene. You know damn well that in a situation like this it becomes the FBI's purview."

"Yeah, when we call them in."

"And we have called them in, so therefore you've gotta back off. Our job now is to function in a support capacity."

"Doesn't that piss you off, Hollenbeck? Whoever did this breached our security, killed our men, and took the president."

"We can't be sure that he was taken."

"Not you too. Come on."

"Of course it pisses me off, but that doesn't change the fact that the law is the law."

"We're supposed to be the best protective force in the world, none better. And yet, someone was able to just fly in here, wipe out our team, and then take off with the president."

"Scot, we're all in shock over this. None of us can believe it happened. *You* saved Goldilocks, though, and you should be extremely proud of that. We are all proud of that."

"But, Tom, they took the president. Our president. Not only are our reputations and the reputation of the Secret Service at stake here, but so is his life. We can't just sit back and do nothing."

"Scot, the cold reality is that he might already be dead. We have no idea either way. They could dig four feet in another direction and come up with him . . . though I doubt it. I actually agree with you. I think he's been grabbed, which is all the more reason for us to cooperate and play the parts we've been assigned. Now, let's get you out of here. I'm gonna have to do some fast talking to keep your bacon out of the fire, and I need a few minutes to think."

"Thinking is only going to waste time we already don't have. We need to act."

CHAPTER 18

Senator David Snyder picked up the phone on the first ring, just as he had when it had softly rung hours earlier around midnight. Outside, a steady rain drummed against the windows of his Georgetown town house.

Looking carefully to see if the figure next to him showed any signs of stirring, he spoke quietly into the phone. "Yes?"

"Senator, it's Zuschnitt. I—"

"Zuschnitt? Jesus Christ. Hold on a second. I can't take this call here."

Senator Snyder pressed the hold button of the black Sony phone on the oriental nightstand next to his bed. Very carefully, he slid out of bed. He put on a white Turkish bathrobe, a pair of Dunhill slippers, and made sure to close the bedroom door behind him as he left the room.

Snyder tapped the switch of the ornate chandelier that illuminated the gently curving staircase. Heavy clouds and steadily falling rain made the morning darker than it normally would be.

At the bottom of the stairs, he crossed a marble entry hall and opened the front door to retrieve his morning papers. Wrapped in plastic were copies of *The Wall Street Journal, The Washington Post, The New York Times, USA Today,* and *The International Herald Tribune.* Even though his aides would clip any relevant articles for him at the office, he liked to get a jump on the day's news while he was still at home.

Shuffling into his study, he could make out the headlines on several of the papers through the plastic sleeves. They all said more or less the same thing: "Utah Avalanche. President Missing. Feared Dead." Snyder turned on the bank of television monitors in his office, which showed studio newscasters in suits speaking to reporters in the field who were garbed in heavy winter parkas with the brightly colored logos of their respective networks prominently displayed. The sets were muted, yet Snyder could tell the reports were coming from the site of the president's ski vacation and the avalanche. It was the biggest story in the country, if not the world.

He dropped his cord of newspapers on the couch next to the fireplace and pushed the *on* switch of the Heat-N-Glo remote. The fireplace crackled to life. If D.C. wasn't wrapped within a damp, bone-chilling cold, it was ninety-five degrees with one hundred percent humidity. There never seemed to be a happy medium in this town, for anything.

Snyder moved around to the back of his desk and lit a cigarette. He didn't care if he kept Zuschnitt waiting.

Salt Lake City was one of the largest FBI field offices in the country. This was due to the fact that at weapons facilities across Utah, America was honoring its nuclear reduction and disarmament treaties with the former Soviet Union. In the political chess game that had raged between the two countries for decades, neither had yet grown to trust the other, and consequently, the Russians had a large number of their people in Salt Lake monitoring our dismantling-and-disposal progress, just as we had a large number of people in different sites throughout Russia for the same reason.

With all of those Russians running around, the U.S. government felt it was a good idea to keep as close an eye on them as possible, and the job fell to the FBI. Always relying on his own "inside" sources, Snyder had cultivated many contacts in domestic and foreign intelligence-gathering communities. While Zuschnitt might not have been the brightest bulb in the box, he had a nasty streak that Snyder liked, and the man had been easy to buy. Snyder now questioned whether giving him his secure home phone number had been such a good idea, but he reasoned it was better than having Zuschnitt call him at the office.

"You're late," said a gruff Senator Snyder as he picked up the phone and dragged on his cigarette.

"I know, but—"

"Shut up and listen to me first. Where are you calling from?"

"I'm calling from the Salt Lake field office on the phone we use to route communications through from suspected fugitives and felons. It's the one that records all outgoing and incoming calls . . . Where the hell do you think I'm calling from? You don't think I'm smart enough to use a secure line? I'm calling from a pay phone at the resort."

Controlling his anger at the man's insolence, Snyder responded, "Where at the resort?"

"Near the medical facility, but don't worry. There are no other government staff around here. I'm the only one, and in my condition, I fit right in."

"In your *condition?* What do you mean?"

"I got sucker punched by a loose cannon on the Secret Service. Some prick named Harvath. I guess he was head of the president's advance team."

"Not only head of the advance team, but he was also a member of the president's detail. You mean he's still alive?"

"Yeah, I guess he transferred over to the president's daughter's detail yesterday morning before the avalanche."

"Who else survived?"

"As far as we can tell, only Harvath and the president's daughter."

"Any clues as to the whereabouts of the president?"

"At this point, nothing. The Secret Service uncovered the body of a towel head with a machine pistol, put two and three together and got seven, then called us in. The director of the FBI has Gary Lawlor on his way out here. They are treating this as a kidnapping."

"And the media?"

"For now, they're being kept back from the scene. They've been able to piece together that several agents and civilians were killed in the avalanche and that the president has not been recovered, but other than that, they don't know anything."

"Back to your getting *sucker punched.* What happened?"

"That asshole Harvath wanted to get in and take a look around where the president and his detail went down. The Salt Lake field office had directions to take over the crime scene and secure it until Lawlor arrived. Nobody was to get in, including Secret Service. Shit, you should see how bad they had already trampled it. Anyway, Harvath insisted, and I told him no. When I wasn't looking, he sucker punched me. That was a real pussy move."

"Yes, but he managed to get the better of you, didn't he?" Snyder didn't expect Zuschnitt to respond. He refiled Scot Harvath's name in the back of his mind and returned to questioning the FBI man. "Anything further to report?"

"Besides the fact that I took three stitches in my lip, my face is swollen up like a balloon, and I'm lucky he didn't break my jaw? No, I guess there's nothing further to report."

"Then I guess that's all we have to talk about. I expect your next report to be on time, whether you have managed to get yourself bitch-slapped again or not. Am I understood?"

"Yeah, I hear you."

"Good."

"What do you want me to do about the press?"

"Let me think." For a moment Snyder pondered when the right time would be for Zuschnitt to leak that the president wasn't buried beneath the snow, but had actually been kidnapped. "You're still wearing your pager, aren't you?"

"Of course, all of the agents are."

"When it's time for you to share our little story with the press about what has truly befallen the president, I'll page you and tell you how I want you to handle it. Understood?"

"Yes."

"Good." Snyder hung up the phone before the man could say anything else. Simultaneously, the black Sony phone in the master bedroom upstairs was hung up by an extremely intrigued lover who hadn't been sleeping since the first covert call had come in around midnight.

CHAPTER 19

Within seconds of meeting David Snyder, he could see why Mitch had found him so irresistible.

The idea of his boyfriend sleeping with his boss to get ahead had never appealed to André, but Mitch had assured him it would only be temporary and that it was just how things sometimes had to be done in Washington.

André had sat by and watched what was supposed to be a onetime thing blossom into a full-blown affair between the senator and his junior staffer. To say it bothered him deeply would have been the understatement of the millennium, but André was in love with Mitch and in love with the life Mitch promised the two of them would have together.

The fact that Mitch had dated a lot of women on the Hill was no secret, and André had accepted that as part of their cover, but Mitch's deep involvement with Senator Snyder began to bother him greatly, especially when Mitch disappeared for entire weekends or when the senator called in the middle of the night and ordered Mitch to "hightail his little ass" over to Snyder's town house.

It had finally got to the point where André couldn't take any more. If he couldn't have Mitch all to himself, he didn't want to be in a relationship with him. It was bad enough that André had to hide the fact that he was gay, both at the D.C. law firm where he worked, as well as with his family, but to have to hide to the rest of the world the deep love he felt for Mitch was just too much. André Martin eventually reached his limit. He was through with living in secret, and he delivered Mitch an ultimatum. For the rest of his life, André knew, he would have mixed feelings about how he handled the response.

Mitch explained that he'd been trying to unwind himself from the affair for the past couple of weeks. The more he tried, the odder the senator became; distant and cold at times, downright inquisitorial at others. The senator's temper had begun to flare, something Mitch had never seen before, only heard about. Sex with the senator became rougher, almost as if the man wanted to hurt him both physically and emotionally. Even through all of this, it was important, Mitch said, for him to have an amicable parting with the senator if he was to preserve his job. André felt *he* should be more important to Mitch than any job, and so to make his point, he moved out of the condo they shared. André knew he had done the right thing, but he was still racked with guilt.

Mitch told André again and again how much he loved him and that he wanted more than anything in the world to be with him. He stated that he was sure the senator was going to let him go soon; the treatment had become so bad that he couldn't imagine that the senator would want him around any longer anyway. Mitch even said he would give it just one more week and if the senator hadn't ended it, he would. He promised André with all of his heart that he would do it and asked him to hang on just until the end of the following week.

In his heart of hearts, André believed Mitch. His spirits began to lift, and he decided that if the relationship was in fact ended by the following weekend, he would move back in with Mitch. André went so far as to make late reservations for that Saturday night for the two of them at their favorite restaurant, Monroe's in Alexandria.

When Saturday arrived, André sat by himself waiting for Mitch, and while he consumed three lonely glasses of chardonnay, he did a lot of soul-searching. Realizing Mitch wasn't going to show, he paid the check and left Monroe's, convinced everything had been a lie. Mitch's job and his affair with the senator were more important to him in the end than André.

He walked back to the Holiday Inn where he'd been staying since leaving Mitch and convinced the bartender, who was closing up, to give him a final nightcap. André slugged back the vodka and tonic, almost spitting it out when the partially astute bartender said, "Whatever she did, you'll get over it, pal."

After draining a third of the tiny bottles in his makeshift minibar and cursing himself for falling in love with someone who didn't really care about him, André fell into a deep and dreamless sleep.

When he awoke the next morning, his head was pounding, but at least that distracted him from the aching in his heart. He went into the bathroom, peeled the plastic sheet from around one of the cups, filled it with water, and chased down two Advil.

Reaching outside his door, he collected his complimentary *USA Today* and *The Washington Post.* He threw the two papers onto the bed and returned to the bathroom, hoping that brushing his teeth would make him feel a little bit more human.

After brushing his teeth, André crossed the room and sat on the edge of the bed. He quickly scanned the room service menu and picked up the phone to order breakfast. He didn't have the heart or the stomach to walk to one of the local cafés.

"Good morning, Mr. Martin, this is Tabatha. May I take your order, please?"

"I don't know how good the morning is, Tabatha, but you may certainly take my order." He began reciting what he wanted, half looking at the room service menu and half skimming the *Post*'s cover stories. "I would like a pot of coffee. Two eggs and— oh, Jesus, no."

André had gotten to the small article regarding a drive-by shooting the previous night that had killed Mitchell Conti, aide to Senator David Snyder, and an as yet unidentified man believed to have been a friend of Mr. Conti's.

"Mr. Martin, are you okay?" asked the room service operator.

"Cancel my order," was all André Martin could manage before rushing to the bathroom to throw up.

• • •

Through some very low-key questions to close mutual friends, André tried to piece together Mitch's movements before the shooting. Everyone said that Mitch had been very down lately because of his job difficulties and because of losing André. Apparently, Mitch had been out with his friend Simon, looking for a gift for André, when the drive-by shooting occurred.

The police assumed that it was just a classic case of "wrong place, wrong time" for Mitch and Simon when they were caught in a hail of bullets. But what the police failed to dig up was who the shooters were and who the assumed target was. Despite the initial public outcry, Mitch and Simon became just another statistic. But not to André Martin. Something was rotten in the capital of democracy.

The whole thing smelled funny. There were conflicting accounts about the shooters, their vehicle, and nothing solid about the intended victims. The more André looked at it, the more he was convinced the drive-by was not an accident.

He continuously replayed in his mind the things Mitch had told him about Senator Snyder, how he never lost and no one ever stood in his way. André also remembered the final message Mitch had left for him at the Holiday Inn saying that he thought he knew of a way whereby the senator would have to cut him loose from the affair but still allow him to keep his job. Mitch had bragged he might even get a promotion out of it, and then they both could celebrate getting their lives back to normal.

Had Mitch been foolish enough to think that he could blackmail the senator? Had he thought the senator would end the affair and yet still allow Mitch to keep his job and maybe even go so far as to give him a promotion? It sounded like something Mitch might try. He'd always thought he was smarter than everyone else. On more than one occasion, André had told him he was too smart for his own good. No matter what Mitch might have thought he had on the senator, any way he came up against him, he would have lost. The more André thought about it, the more the drive-by shooting made sense if you assumed Mitch had been the intended victim. And the more the drive-by shooting made sense, the more André was determined to avenge the death of Mitch Conti.

• • •

Even though it hadn't been easy getting close to the senator, André had eventually succeeded. While he didn't have the political network that Mitch'd had, he was an excellent fact finder and quickly assembled his own dossier on the New York senator and the causes closest to his cold heart. Several months later, through a partner's wife at his firm, André was able to wrangle an invitation to the Gold Circle Ball of the International Diplomats' Forum.

At the black-tie affair, André was every bit as striking in his tuxedo as Mitch would have been. He came to the event bolstered by a couple of martinis, convinced he would be able to seduce the senator. The senator had indeed noticed André, but it took "coincidentally" bumping into him at several more important functions before the two had a real conversation.

Once they had their first "date," André wisely played hard to get, acting unimpressed with the senator's lifestyle and power, which only served to set the hook deeper. Snyder was soon thoroughly taken with André and couldn't get enough of him. Jealous and insecure, he wanted André with him every moment.

Lately, though, Snyder had seemed tense. None of the signs would have been visible to a casual observer, but André had been studying him long enough to know when something was afoot, and whatever it was, it was very big.

All of his experience as a lawyer told André that he could be in a lot of trouble snooping around in the life of one of the country's most powerful senators, but he wasn't after state secrets. He wanted personal secrets, and André knew the man was dirty. He knew he was responsible for the deaths of Mitch and Simon, and André wanted to hang him with that, if not something equally damning. He also knew that if Snyder ever caught on to him, an accident would happen just as easily to him as it had to Mitch and Simon.

When Snyder had sneaked out of the house shortly after receiving the first strange phone call around midnight, André had known something important was happening. He'd let himself out a side door and caught the senator getting into a cab half a block down the street. The rain made it difficult to see, but André managed to get the cab's number and soon thereafter caught one himself.

The senator was in a hurry and didn't take many precautions against being followed. André had no trouble staying with him. A half hour later when the cab turned onto a posh residential street in McLean, Virginia, André knew where his quarry was headed. He told his cab to stop and watched the senator's driver say something into an intercom at the large iron gates of a brick Georgian Revival. Moments later, the gates swung open and Snyder's taxi drove through. Satisfied, André instructed his cabbie to take him back to the town house in Georgetown. He lay in bed awake for the rest of the evening, pretending to be asleep when the senator came home. He didn't stir until Snyder got out of bed to take the second phone call.

Now, in the overcast light of a rainy morning, André hung up the black Sony phone and rolled over to his side of the bed, contemplating the implications of what he had just heard. It was time to get up, and he thought a hot shower might steady his nerves.

He walked into the bathroom and didn't even feel the radiant heat from the tiled floor on the soles of his feet. He turned the shower control to *hot* and climbed in, scrubbing himself with a lemon beeswax soap, one of the many bath products the senator liked to indulge himself with. His mind racing, he was so preoccupied he didn't notice his lover had entered the bathroom until the shower door swung open.

"André, I think you and I need to have a little chat."

CHAPTER 20

When Harvath and Hollenbeck had hiked to the bottom of Death Chute, there was a Sno-Cat waiting to take them back to the command center. Once they were seated inside and were under way, Hollenbeck pulled a stack of Polaroids out of his parka and handed them to Harvath.

"Ever seen one of these back in your SEAL days?"

Harvath looked intently at the first picture. It was a box, painted white, about the size of the average surround-sound subwoofer. By its appearance in the picture, it had been found buried in the snow. Scot flipped through the shots, which were taken from different angles. In some, the box was partially obscured by the branches of a pine tree it was under.

"I don't know. It looks like a white box," Harvath said, handing the photos back to Hollenbeck.

"When our guys found it, we had no idea what it was either. Our gut said it might be an explosive device, so we got the bomb tech guys up there right away."

"Where? Up there?" Scot asked, gesturing over his shoulder back toward Death Chute. "I thought this was an FBI investigation now."

"It is, but we were operating outside the secured crime scene under the pretext of discovering if any of our agents might have survived the slide."

"But you said they were all accounted for."

"Now they are. But we hadn't released that information to the FBI at that point. Listen, I don't want to split hairs with you. I busted your ass up there because that's my job. I've heard about that guy, Zuschnitt. He's got a reputation with the FBI for being a real prick. That's probably why he got stuck posting the crime scene. Think about it. That's a pretty long rotation to be standing with your thumb up your ass in the freezing cold."

Harvath laughed at the image. It was the first time he had laughed all morning. "I guess you're right."

"Damn straight I'm right. Now I want you to look at these," he said as he pulled another group of Polaroids from his pocket. "Once we determined the device was not an explosive, we were able to discover that it was encased in panels and that the panels could be removed."

Scot flipped through this set of pictures with greater interest. Each displayed a different exposed section of the box's interior, which contained densely packed electronics.

"It looks like an air-sick bag for a supercomputer that had a really bad lunch. There must be at least a hundred circuit boards crammed in there. There could never be enough air circulation in there to keep whatever this thing is from overheating. Unless—"

"It was placed in the snow?" responded Hollenbeck, who'd already come to that conclusion. He pulled some more photos from his parka and narrated as he flipped through them. "The alloy construction of the box probably helped circulate the cold. There are also fans and a set of tubes with screened vents, which we think acted as a cooling system. Any guesses yet as to what its purpose is?"

"Judging from this picture," said Scot, pointing to the one Hollenbeck had just revealed, "I'd say that little device there is a low-profile antenna. If you have your guys look up into the tree above where you found the box, at the very top you'll probably find a camouflaged transmitter with a booster."

"Yup, that's exactly what we found."

"So, this device is a transmitter of some sort. I'd be willing to bet you may have found the source of our communications problems."

"It was. We shut it down, and the radios and everything else came back on line clear as a bell. What do you make of this?" said Hollenbeck as he removed a final Polaroid from the stack and handed it to him.

Harvath studied it carefully. "The writing looks Korean. By the sophistication of the equipment, I'm going to guess this is something from our friends in the north. Most of the components will probably turn out to be Taiwanese, but the overall design and assembly is probably North Korean."

"I had our communications guy look at it, and then I slipped Jim Bates and some of his White House Communications Agency people up to take a peek. They've never seen anything like it, but they're all guessing it's a very sophisticated jamming system."

"But why'd it jam our communications and not the CB radios?"

"It could be that proximity-wise they weren't close enough, or—"

"Tom, proximity had nothing to do with it. Our radios were cutting in and out when we were on Deer Valley's main runs. If this was an overall jam, the CBs would have been affected as well."

"The other possibility Bates and his WHCA guys are kicking around is that the device can be tuned to jam specific frequencies and at different intervals."

"On for a minute, off for twenty," Scot said, more for his own benefit than Hollenbeck's. "It got us used to the on-again, off-again status of the radios. Made us think it was some sort of natural anomaly."

"Yup."

"But for that, you'd have to already know at least what frequencies the Secret Service was using, and that's a closely guarded secret."

"Exactly. So, whoever was jamming had to have an inside line on the frequencies of not only our radios, but also Deer Valley's and the Smocks."

"Deer Valley's wouldn't be hard to get, but ours? Are you suggesting a leak? No way. Not possible."

"I want you to stay quiet about this, Scot. Understand? I don't want to start a witch hunt."

"I wouldn't worry about starting it. Pandora's box is going to open all by itself. I'd be more worried about how you're going to close it."

CHAPTER 21

A million things swirled through Scot's mind as he and Hollenbeck made the rest of the ride to the command center in silence. He felt like that painting *The Scream.* The phrase, *You're only as strong as your weakest link* kept piercing the chaotic jumble of his mind. The idea that someone on his team had leaked information to anyone, much less a source with hostile intentions, was unfathomable. *Maybe the information wasn't leaked,* Scot tried to tell himself. The problem was, once it has been suggested that you have a leak, you become focused on it. It becomes hard to concentrate on any other possibilities.

When the Sno-Cat came to a halt, Harvath and Hollenbeck didn't wait for the driver to get out of his cab and come around back to open their compartment. They were on the ground and on their way to the command center before the man got halfway around the machine.

"Tom, can I get my SIG back?" said Harvath, who figured someone on the team must have secured his sidearm for him when he was brought in unconscious last night.

"As long as you promise not to use it on any FBI agents. It's in the lockdown cabinet in the command center. I left Longo in charge, so you can sign it out with him."

Scot made his way to the extra large Winnebago that had been brought in from the federal garage in Las Vegas to act as the primary communications and command center for the president's visit. While the house the president was staying in, just fifty feet away, was also loaded with agents and electronics equipment, this was the nerve center of the operation.

Scot found Longo in back bent over a laptop, clicking away at the keys.

"Hollenbeck told me I could grab my SIG back from you."

"Your what?" said Longo, distracted by the report he was working on. Written reports were the one thing Scot hadn't ever been able to get used to. The Secret Service loved their paperwork.

"My SIG-Sauer. It's about this long," Harvath said, showing him with his hands, "blackish gray, and fires these things we call bullets when you pull on the trigger. If you want to find an apple you think might fit on your head, I'll give you a little demonstration of how it works."

"Very funny. Glad to see your accident didn't damage your sense of humor. I'm sorry, the WHCAs have been crawling all over me about how the radios went down, and I've got to document every single thing. The report's got me hung up."

"Since when does the White House Communications Agency give the Secret Service orders?"

"Those guys are Department of Defense, just in civilian clothes. Hollenbeck said to cooperate with everyone. He's really worried about how the Service is going to . . . hell, who am I kidding? He's worried about how the Secret Service *already* looks on this one. We lost the president. I still can't believe it. Now the FBI's got their top pit bull coming in, and he's bringing the Hostage Rescue Team with him. The special agents in charge of both the FBI and Secret Service Salt Lake field offices have been on the warpath around here, and I'm just trying to keep my head low so it doesn't roll."

"Listen, Chris, you're not going to lose your head."

"You don't think so? Harvath, I hate to break it to you, but over two dozen agents are dead and/or missing, the president is gone, and we've got next to nothing lead-wise. Heads are definitely going to roll. You know I like you, but as head of the advance team on this one, it looks like you might be married to King Henry." Being "married to King Henry" was an inside joke that referred to the British king who beheaded several of his wives after he had grown tired of them.

Chris hadn't needed to say it. That thought was one of many flying around Harvath's head, as well as a sense of crushing responsibility for the deaths of his fellow agents. Scot's only hope of getting out of this one with his career intact was to be part of some significant breakthrough.

"Here's your weapon," said Longo as he turned from the cabinet, setting the pistol on the table and handing Harvath a clipboard. "Sign right there."

Scot strapped on his holster, handed the signed clipboard back to Longo, and walked toward the door.

"You know where the term *severance pay* comes from, Scot?" said Longo as he hung the clipboard on a peg inside the cabinet and locked it again.

"No, but you're going to tell me, right?"

Ignoring Harvath's sarcasm, Longo continued. "It's also from England. When prisoners were going to be beheaded, they offered the axeman a little extra money to make sure he chopped their heads off with one, clean blow."

"Thanks. I'll be sure to remember that," said Scot as he held the door to the Winnebago open a little longer than he should have, eliciting moans and shouts from the cold agents inside.

Crossing the compound toward the main house, Scot replayed the conversation with Longo in his mind. He knew that the other agents didn't blame him. Scot Harvath had been single-handedly responsible for ushering in some of the most significant improvements in Secret Service training and tactical procedure in years. But he also knew that as head of the advance team, he had to bear a tremendous amount of the responsibility for what had happened.

Looking up at the sky and the still falling snow, Harvath felt that the agents not yet recovered by the search-and-rescue teams were a lost cause. The president, though, was a different story. He was probably still alive, and it was only a matter of time before demands for his ransom would be made.

Scot thought about Amanda lying in a hospital bed in Salt Lake, glad she would make a full recovery. He didn't dare think about what conditions the president might be languishing in at this moment.

There was no question that Scot's career was probably finished, at least with the Secret Service. He would be transferred to a less "sensitive" posting and would most likely be relegated to protecting third world delegates on visits to the United States . . . if even. He definitely would never be allowed to head up an advance team again or, for that matter, work another presidential protective detail.

He could return to the SEALs. His teammates had always thought Scot was better suited to offensive operations than defensive anyway, but he was too proud. He couldn't go crawling back. Everyone would know that he had been responsible for the security arrangements for the president's ski trip. The SEALs were an honorable operation and not something you ran back to with your tail between your legs when you failed someplace else. *Failed*—the word tasted bitter in his mouth.

Had he failed? And if so, by whose definition? As a SEAL, failure meant giving up, not acting, throwing in the towel. The Secret Service might begrudgingly accept a sidelined position while the FBI came in to run the investigation, but that didn't mean he had to. The more Scot considered his options, the less he could see he had to lose.

The Senate inquiry, which was bound to come down eventually, would tie him to a stake and roast him. There would probably be other sacrificial lambs, but he knew that back in Washington they were already engraving his invitation to the party. Even if he resigned from the Secret Service before then, he would still be forced to testify at the hearing and be roasted nonetheless. They would need someone to blame. It was part of the pathological makeup of politicians.

The other thing gnawing at him was the oath he had taken to protect and serve his country and the president. As good as the FBI was, it would take them a hell of a long time to get everything coordinated. By then, evidence would be lost, and the kidnappers would be even farther away. The FBI would have to wait for demands to be made. They would continue to go through the motions of looking for evidence, and if they were lucky, they might turn up a lead, but Scot wasn't holding out a lot of hope the FBI would catch a break. There was no question in his mind that the president was still alive. If the intent had been to assassinate him, his body would have been found along with those of the rest of his detail.

There was a lot to be said for a collective effort, but when that effort was not quickly coordinated and executed, nine out of ten times it ended in disaster. The FBI and the Secret Service were playing defense. Every cell in Scot's body had been trained for offense, and offense called for action. Besides, he thought again, what did he have to lose?

CHAPTER 22

Scot found Vance Boyson and Nick Slattery at the edge of the perimeter, leaning against the flatbed of a Deer Valley avalanche-control truck checking their equipment. Vance had been a friend of Scot's from his days on the freestyle ski team, as well as an important contact during Scot's sweeps of Deer Valley for the president's visit.

Vance noticed him approaching and dropped what he was doing to greet him. "Hey, Scot, how you feeling, man?"

"I've been better, fellas," replied Scot.

"We heard you really took a good spill down the mountain."

"It wasn't anything worse than I've ever eaten off a jump."

Nick stopped his equipment check and turned to join the conversation. "Is there any word yet? There must be a thousand ambulances up here, but we haven't seen any of them go down. That's not a good sign."

"No, it's not good," said Scot. "Listen, I need a favor. Now that the weather's a little better, can we get your bird up?"

Vance looked at Nick before responding. "Sure, where do you need to go?"

"I want to go up top on Squaw Peak to get a better look at where the avalanche started."

Nick sucked in a big breath of air between his teeth. "The sheriff has told us that area is off-limits until further notice."

"I'll take full responsibility. The sheriff doesn't even have to know. If he says anything, you inform him you have been directed by the Secret Service to lift one of their agents up there for further investigation."

"Agent Harvath, you're a cool guy and everything, but I don't—"

Nick was interrupted by Vance. "Of course you don't want to interfere with a federal investigation. If Scot says he needs to get up to that peak, then he needs to get up there. We were told from the beginning to provide the Secret Service with any and all assistance they required. Well, this agent needs assistance and he's going to get it." Vance winked at Scot and said, "Get in the truck."

• • •

Deer Valley's chopper was primed and ready for takeoff when they arrived at the helipad off the main access road. Scot and Vance spent the short drive talking about the equipment they would need when they got up to the peak. Most of it was standard gear that the chopper already carried, but when they came to a stop near the pad, Vance shouted instructions to Nick above the roar of the rotors.

The chopper rose rapidly and looking down, Scot could make out the flurry of activity below. Because of the route they took to get to the helipad, they had bypassed most of the chaos. Now, though, Scot could clearly make out the battalions of rescue vehicles and news trucks parked pell-mell along the roads.

As the chopper continued to rise, Scot discussed with Vance the details of the avalanche while he slid into a pair of Deer Valley yellow-and-green ski pants Nick had brought from the truck.

Everyone had been kept away from the peak, so even the Utah Avalanche Forecast Center experts hadn't been able to get up there to conduct any examinations yet. All they had been able to do was make assumptions. A lot of snow had fallen, and avalanches were part of the natural order of things. Only so much snow can build up on the face of a mountain before it crumbles under its own weight and falls in the only direction it can, straight down.

"It really isn't that unusual," replied Nick via the microphone attached to his headset.

"It's not the act itself that bothers me, it's the timing and ferocity," said Scot, who noticed the peak looming up in front of them. "Can the pilot get close enough to give me a good look at the face?"

"No can do. We don't know how unstable it is, and the rotor wash could trigger another slide. There's a small plateau in back, near the top. He can set it down there, and we can work our way around on foot." Vance turned around in the copilot's seat so he could see Scot's face as he asked his next question. "You think you're up to it?"

"Don't worry about me. You just get us there."

• • •

The hike to the face hadn't been as easy as Scot had hoped. The wind was blowing four times stronger at this elevation, and the chopper pilot needed three attempts before he was able to put down on the small plateau. Harvath was losing the feeling in his fingers from the cold, and the pain in his muscles was increasing with each passing minute.

As the wind grew stronger, Nick suggested they rope up for safety. While Vance was handing the end of the rope to Scot, he asked, "What exactly are we looking for up here?"

"Pornography," Scot replied.

Both Nick and Vance stopped what they were doing to look at him. *"Pornography?"*

"It's an expression. I can't give you a good definition of pornography, but I know it when I see it. I'll know what we're looking for when I see it."

The group rounded the narrow ridge trail and began closing on the face of Squaw Peak. Vance led, with Scot next, followed by Nick. Harvath kept looking high and low, searching for anything that was out of the ordinary. He held up his hand and called out for Vance to stop. His climbing partners closed the gap and stood on either side of him.

"You see that?" said Scot, motioning to a small crevice that had a pocket of chipped stone just above their heads.

"Sure do," said Nick.

"It looks like someone has been up here doing a little climbing, and it looks relatively recent," replied Vance.

"This area is technically off-limits, isn't it?" asked Scot.

Vance was the first to respond. "It always is. Especially during the winter and even more so with the president's visit. Heck, you were the one calling the shots. None of our guys were even allowed up here unless one of your men was with us."

"And did any of your guys come up here?"

"They would have needed to be cleared by either me or Nick, and as far as I know, there were no requests, so neither of us cleared anyone."

Scot turned to Nick for confirmation, who nodded his head in agreement.

Fifty feet below them, Scot could see the shelf of snow and ice from which the avalanche had broken off. It wasn't hard to distinguish, as the levels of snow above and below were so dramatically different. Vance saw what Scot was looking at and immediately spoke. "Lemme guess."

"Yeah, I need to take a closer look."

Knowing he would be outvoted no matter what he said, Nick unshouldered his pack and began laying out the coils of rope they had brought along, leaving Vance to, hopefully, talk some sense into Agent Harvath as they untied their safety line.

"Scot, we have no idea how stable or unstable that shelf is down there."

"All the more reason I have to get down to it now."

"Can you explain to me what you hope to find down there?"

"I can't go into great detail, Vance, but I don't think that avalanche started on its own. I think somebody helped it."

"What? You think somebody triggered that avalanche on purpose? Why would somebody do that?"

"I don't have all the answers, but I'm starting to put together a picture. See that?" Scot gestured toward where Nick had wisely chosen a new location in the rock crevice in which to drive a piton, so as not to disturb the area Harvath had pointed out earlier. "I think somebody was up here, not too long ago, who hammered in one or several pitons, depending on how much support they needed, and belayed down the face."

"But that's nuts. No amateur backcountry climber would have done that."

"Who said anything about amateurs? These people were extremely professional."

"Even so, how do you know that their climbing caused the avalanche?"

"I don't think the climbing caused it. As a matter of fact, I think whoever was responsible for the avalanche was long gone from here by the time it started. Are we ready up there, Nick?"

Nick gave the thumbs-up. He had placed a couple of extra pitons just to be sure and threw Harvath a new length of rope on which he would be belayed.

"Take this," said Harvath, throwing Nick an orange wax crayon he had removed from the command center. "I want you to draw an *X* next to each one of the pitons you've placed, so that the investigative team can tell the difference between your work and what was here before we got here. Nick nodded and began marking off his piton locations.

Scot looped the rope through the metal ring in his harness and threw the coil of rope in his right hand over the ridge and down the face of Squaw Peak. Vance tied off a safety line to the harness and began giving Scot instructions.

"You look like you know what you're doing, so I am going to assume you've rappelled before."

"More times and from more different objects than you can possibly imagine." Scot grinned.

"Well, this is going to be a little bit different. Because we have no idea how stable the snow is, you can't bounce down; you've got to walk back very slowly. Place your feet with extreme caution and listen very carefully for any cracking sounds that might indicate the shelf is moving or might be ready to break away. You got it?"

"Yeah, I got it," said Scot as he turned his back to the ridge and the valley far below. Looking over at Nick he asked, "On belay?"

"Belay on," Nick replied.

"Climbing," said Scot.

Which was followed by the mountaineer's response from Nick, "Climb on."

Ever so slowly, Scot leaned back into his harness and allowed himself to take baby steps over the lip of the ridge until he was standing on the icy face itself. He gave each of his balled fists a couple of quick squeezes to try and warm up his fingers before slowly letting out the slack in his rope.

As Scot moved backward down the face, choosing each step with care, Nick released the necessary amounts of slack from the line.

Harvath noticed divot-like depressions in the snow that could have been footprints or merely small, windblown craters. It was hard to tell.

The descent seemed to take forever as he moved step by step, always stopping to listen before lightly putting his weight on the next foot behind him. Scot's aching body was cooperating so far, but just barely. A small smile crossed his lips as he thought of what Dr. Trawick would have said had Scot asked permission to go climb a mountain. He probably would have certified him insane right there.

Throughout the climb, Scot paid close attention to the strange pockmarks he was seeing in the snow about three feet off to his left. He realized they were too uniform to be a naturally occurring phenomenon. What prevented him from believing they could be footprints was their small size. Then it hit him.

Scot looked up at his own marks made scaling down the face. His prints were about half the size of regular prints, and for good reason. When they had gotten out of the helicopter, Vance had handed him a pair of crampons. The sharp metal teeth strapped to his boots were the same devices that would have been worn by any climber, even a half-wit amateur, when trying to tackle a surface covered with snow and ice. Whoever left the tracks off to Scot's left did so knowing that by the time they were discovered, the person who made them would be hundreds, if not thousands of miles away.

Scot was nearing the edge of the shelf where the avalanche had broken away. He glanced again at the tracks left by the previous phantom climber and noticed they had begun to veer away from him. He steadied himself on the rope and carefully lifted his right hand to depress the talk button on the Deer Valley radio strapped to his chest.

"Vance, do you read me? Over."

"Yeah, I got ya. What's up?"

"We were right. Making my way down, I can see there's been somebody here recently with crampons."

"Are you sure?"

"Sure enough. Listen, the trail diverges off to my left and then over the lip. I'm going to need to push off and swing over to where the tracks end. I'll need some slack. Give me about twenty more feet."

"We'll let out the slack; just be careful you don't touch off another slide, okay?"

"I am being careful, and believe me, if you've got another way to do this, I'm all ears. At some point I have to swing out over the lip, so I'd rather get it over with. Out."

Scot waited until he saw a sufficient amount of the line slide down the face and dangle beneath him. He calculated how much thrust he would need to push himself off the snow to reach his target and hoped that using that much force wouldn't crack the shelf beneath him and send it tumbling into the valley below. There were a lot of rescue personnel and many of his fellow agents still combing the area down there for survivors. Scot was convinced the first slide had been no accident, but there was no telling what instabilities were left behind.

Testing the strength in his legs, Scot bent painfully at the knees several times to get the momentum going to launch him in the right direction. Above on the ridge, Vance and Nick could only hope Scot knew what he was doing, because they were operating completely blind.

On the count of three, Scot once again told himself. *One . . . two . . . three!*

The push sent him backward into the air, away from the steep peak face and hurling toward the area beneath the shelf where the crampon tracks disappeared.

Knees bent, ready to absorb the impact, Scot's body came back hard and fast toward its target. Judging by his speed, he thought that he had pushed off with a little too much force and consequently was coming back in too fast. He braced himself for the impact.

When the shark-teeth-like crampons dug into the ice, the jolt raced up his legs, past where it should have been absorbed by his knees. Scot had misjudged his own strength. His knees had not yet fully forgiven him for the punishment they had suffered over the past twenty-four hours, and they failed to take the brunt of the shock. His legs buckled, and his whole upper body slammed into the sheer face. Scot didn't dare take either of his hands from the rope.

Snow and ice began showering down on top of him. He could hear Vance calling frantically over the radio. The snow was beginning to fall faster, and Harvath knew he didn't have much time.

Through the shower of snow, he quickly looked above him along the ridge as best he could, then looked down. Both above and below him there were marks consistent with the detonation of some sort of explosive device. From the little he could see, it had not been the type of device fired by avalanche-control cannons from the valley. The spread and pattern were completely different.

When Scot let out a little more slack to drop closer to the area beneath him, he was hit from above by a sheet of ice that felt as if it weighed at least one hundred pounds, and he was knocked right off the face.

He tightened his grip frantically on his rope, knowing that it only had a finite amount of feet before it ran out. He cursed himself for being taken off guard by the ice sheet and loosening his grip in the first place. Scot fell with sickening speed, all the while fighting to regain control. He bumped his head several times, and then, with a loud snap, everything came to a halt.

With the blood rushing to his head, Scot realized that he was hanging upside down by his safety line. He made a mental note to kiss Nick and Vance right after he punched both of their lights out for letting him fall so far. About ten feet above him, he could see where his primary rope had come to its end.

Knowing, or actually hoping, Nick and Vance would be doing their best to pull him back up to the ridge, Scot summoned what strength he could and tried to right himself. His body was weak and sore, but it complied. As he swung back into the face and dug in with his crampons, Scot promised himself that very soon he'd take that long overdue vacation.

CHAPTER 23

Back in the helicopter, Scot accepted Vance and Nick's excuse for letting so much slack on the safety line escape. He also decided not to punch both of their lights out.

As Vance explained it to Scot while he lay exhausted yet safely supine back upon the ridge, Scot's slam into the face of Squaw Peak had caused what they all feared, a secondary avalanche. It was small and came to a stop well before it could cause harm to anyone below in the valley, but Scot had acted like a magnet for the falling snow and ice, which piled on top of him and exponentially increased his weight upon the rope.

Pitons were popping left and right, and both Vance and Nick thought for sure they would be yanked over the edge. Neither of them ever even considered letting go; that just simply wasn't an option. They were able to finally dig in and get control of Scot's fall at the very last minute. The burn marks in their gloves attested to their courage and Scot's extremely good fortune. He wanted to kiss the guys, but before he could, a voice from the Deer Valley helipad came over the headset. It instructed the pilot to return to the pad to shuttle an FBI team to a crime scene in nearby Midway.

"Midway?" Scot leaned forward and said while tapping Vance on the shoulder. "That's just the other side of the mountain, isn't it? What do you suppose is going on over there?"

Vance was reading Scot's mind. He radioed back to Deer Valley asking where the FBI team was to be taken. As the information was relayed across the headsets, the pilot nodded that he knew where it was, and Vance pointed for the pilot to go in that direction.

"Lemme guess. You're going to take responsibility for this one too?" queried Nick.

Scot only smiled and asked the pilot if there was a pass or anything like that connecting the area around Death Chute to the farm they were headed toward in Midway.

"There are a couple, but only one that could be considered a pass in the sense that it can be completely traversed," replied the pilot.

"Do me a favor and follow it," said Scot.

Vance turned in the copilot's seat and asked, "What are you thinking?"

"Just a hunch."

"Great," said Nick, leaning his head against the window of the chopper and staring up at the ceiling, "another hunch. Let's see if we can get fired on this hunch, or better yet, maybe we can actually get killed this time."

"Not a chance," said Scot as he placed a thankful and reassuring hand on Nick's shoulder. "When the helicopter touches down, I'm getting out and you're going back to Deer Valley."

"Too bad," said Vance, turning back around in his seat to look out the front. "This was just starting to get interesting."

• • •

Before jumping out of the helicopter, Harvath thanked his friends and asked the pilot to do him a favor and make sure the FBI got to enjoy some of the Wasatch Mountains' scenic beauty on their way over. The pilot laughed and gave him the thumbs-up.

Scot straightened up once he was sure he had cleared the rotor blades and walked over toward the three Wasatch County Sheriff's Department Suburbans parked in front of the Madduxes' farmhouse.

"FBI?" said a deputy sheriff as Harvath approached, digging his credentials from his pocket.

"Secret Service. I'm Agent Harvath, head of—"

"The president's advance team. I remember reading your name on the memo that came around about the visit. I'm Ben MacIntyre, deputy sheriff. You working with the FBI on this?"

"Yeah. Whenever the president is involved or we think there may be some sort of connection, we tackle these things together," lied Harvath right through his teeth. "Why don't you fill me in on what you've got."

Deputy MacIntyre removed a small notebook from the breast pocket of his coat and started reading: "About seven-thirty this morning we got a call from the daughter of the old couple that lives here, Joseph and Mary Maddux. Apparently, after church yesterday, they passed up on the normal Sunday dinner at the daughter's house because the father wasn't feeling well. The daughter tried to check in with them a couple of times last night and couldn't get ahold of anyone. She thought maybe they'd turned in early and, being older folks, just didn't hear the phone.

"So, this morning she tries again, several times, and there's still no answer. Worried that they might have been in an accident or something, she called our office and asked if we'd swing by."

"Your office?" asked Harvath. "Why didn't she come herself?"

"She lives down in Orem," said the deputy, referring back to his notes. "It's a pretty long drive up here, especially with the weather. Plus she works and didn't think the boss would let her. A couple of our guys know, or I should say knew, the Madduxes, so they didn't mind coming out."

"*Knew?* They're dead?"

"Yup, Mr. Maddux was shot close range to the head, and Mrs. Maddux suffered multiple gunshot wounds."

"Have you contacted your sheriff?"

"Yes, sir. He's been over with your people in Deer Valley working that avalanche, but now he's on his way back here with the FBI. We also have our medical examiner on the way as well as a homicide team coming up from Salt Lake County. The highway patrol and the state park rangers are buttoning down all the roads around here."

"Well done, Deputy. You did everything by the book. As I was already in the air, I was routed here first. Has anyone touched anything inside?"

"Nope, the first officer on the scene had his winter gloves on and only took them off to check for a pulse on each of the victims. He tracked a little snow inside, but we've laid down some plastic, so that ought to lessen contamination of the scene."

"Good job. I trust your sheriff told you no one else was to be allowed in until he arrived with the FBI?"

"He certainly did."

"Good. Make sure you send them in to me when they get here."

"Sir, my orders are that no one gets in until the sheriff and the FBI get here."

"Deputy, when do you think the sheriff called me?"

"He called you, sir?"

"When do you think he called me? Before he talked to you or after?"

"He didn't know about anything till I called him, so it would have to be after."

"Exactly, so when the sheriff told you to keep the scene secure until he got here, that was before he knew I was already airborne and could get here faster."

"Uh, huh."

"Deputy, I don't need to draw you a picture. You're a smart man. By now you've figured out that if the sheriff is coming all the way over with the FBI and the head of the president's advance team is already here, this is some pretty serious stuff."

"Yes, sir."

"Listen, I've done a lot of advance work in some very out-of-the-way places. Most of the county sheriffs we work with would make Gomer Pyle look like an astrophysicist. I'm not blowing smoke up your ass. Your department does a damn good job. I don't want you to get in any hot water with your boss, but I have my own boss to think about, and he's the president of the United States. Now, if you'll cut me a little slack, I can get started and have a preliminary report for the FBI guys when they get here. What do you say?"

"I guess so. We were told to cooperate with the Secret Service with anything they needed."

"Good man. Where are the victims?"

"Master bedroom. Second floor, down the hall on the left. Do me a favor and wear these. We want to keep the crime scene as uncontaminated as possible," said the deputy, pulling out a pair of paper surgical booties from a box in the backseat of his truck.

"Thanks," said Scot, accepting the paper booties and a pair of latex surgical gloves while walking up the steps of the house. "I meant what I said. You guys are pretty impressive."

A piece of plastic had been laid in front of the storm door, and Scot stood on it while he took his Timberlands off and slipped on the booties. Snapping on the rubber gloves, he opened the double doors.

As a nonsmoker, Scot immediately detected the lingering odors of cigarette smoke. The smell grew stronger as Scot neared the family room. He quickly turned and walked back to the front door.

Catching the attention of one of the Wasatch County officers, he asked, "Officer, do you know if Mr. and Mrs. Maddux are Mormon—" Scot noticed a slight change in the face of the officer and, catching his *faux pas,* switched to the more politically correct term preferred these days by the Mormons. "I'm sorry. I mean were they members of the LDS church?"

Pleased that an outsider would show such respect for their faith, the officer responded, "Yes, sir. Mr. Maddux had been our bishop for a long time. He retired a ways back, but we still saw him at church and all the functions."

"I see," replied Scot. "I take it by your answer that you are a member of the Church as well?"

"Yes, I am."

"And you abide by all of the Church's covenants?"

"I certainly do."

"So you don't smoke?"

"No, sir. Never."

"How about Mr. and Mrs. Maddux. Did either of them smoke?"

"No, sir. I can tell you as sure as I am standing here that they were perfect examples of what members of the Church of Latter Day Saints should be."

Harvath turned his attention back to Deputy MacIntyre. "Ben, could there have been any of your guys smoking in here?"

"No way. Why?"

"How about near the front door at all?"

"Not a one. What are you getting at?"

Without answering, Harvath turned back inside, closing both doors behind him.

He needed to see the bodies. How they were killed and how they were placed would hopefully tell him something about the killers. The scenic route Scot had asked the Deer Valley helicopter pilot to take would delay the FBI for only so long. With his eyes wide open and all of his senses operating at their peak, he climbed the creaking stairs to the second floor.

Talk about a time warp, Scot thought as he looked down the hallway at the green shag carpeting. *At what point in the aging process do people just give up and let time pass them by?*

At the top of the stairs, he'd noticed a door ajar directly in front of him. Walking over to it, he pushed it the rest of the way open with his foot. It smelled of strongly perfumed soap, exactly the way a bathroom in a grandmother's house should smell. Everything was neatly in place, except for a towel that appeared to have been hung hastily back on the rack next to its neatly folded twin.

Scot looked into the tub, which was perfectly dry. Next he checked the washbasin, and it too was dry except for a little pool of moisture around the drain. He noticed that the faucet had a very slow drip. Scot tightened the handle and the dripping stopped. Judging from the little bit he had already seen of the place, he knew the Madduxes kept one neat and clean house. Someone other than the Madduxes had used this sink recently and had been careless both with turning off the water and with hanging the towel.

Leaving the bathroom, Scot made his way down the hall toward where the deputy had said the master bedroom was. He passed rows and rows of photographs of family vacations, picnics, weddings, and posed Kmart shots of what must have been the grandchildren. The whole array was hung in chronological order. What he assumed were pictures of Mr. and Mrs. Maddux in their youth were at the beginning of the hall, and the display transitioned into their later years as one got closer to the master bedroom. Each night they would have actually relived their lives on the way to bed. It gave Scot an eerie chill to think that the final posing of the two would be at the very end of the hallway, where they lay in death.

And *posing* was a perfect word for it. Scot entered the room and saw the couple laid out on their bed. The killer hadn't surprised them in bed, because they were both fully clothed and were lying on a white chenille bedspread now puddled with patches of rusty brown. There were also marks along the floor, undoubtedly caused when one of them had fallen and been dragged and then slung onto the bed.

The damage to Mr. Maddux was consistent with a professional hit: concise, cold, and accurate. Mrs. Maddux's injuries were anything but. With half her nose blown away and additional gunshot wounds to her neck, chest, head, and face, it looked as if someone had lost control or was in a complete and total rage. The gruesome scene was going to keep the police, the sheriff, and the FBI busy for a while.

As Scot had been flown from Deer Valley to Midway, a theory had formed in his mind. One of the biggest questions he had, outside of how the kidnappers had been able to ambush and take out the president's detail, was how they had gotten away. Everything he had seen so far served to reinforce that these people were absolute professionals. Each precise detail had been planned and probably practiced until it was perfect. Aside from assaulting a structure like the White House or Fort Knox, it was hard to think of a more daring, more dangerous, or more difficult undertaking than this. Yet, the kidnappers had succeeded.

The FBI would sweep the room for hair, fibers, and prints and would also look to see if the killer had left any other sort of clue, such as a note or a distinctive marking. Scot was positive they wouldn't find any notes. Psychos who wanted to get caught left notes, taunting the police and Feds. While Scot couldn't pass judgment on how psychotic this killer was, he knew one thing for sure—he was professional.

Scot tried to put the killings in context. If the FBI was on their way here, chances were pretty good that they were thinking the same thing he was. The kidnappers would have needed a base. The only way off Death Chute was by foot or helicopter. With the weather the way it had been yesterday, there was no way a chopper would have been able to get there. Plus, a helicopter would have made too much noise. The surrounding mountains acted as one big echo chamber. Only a craft with supersilent capabilities would have been quiet enough to get in there undetected.

Harvath thought about that for a second, not yet ready to rule it out. Flying low enough, a stealth helicopter could have evaded the radar monitored by the Secret Service agents who had been posted with the FAA in the Tower and Approach Control at Salt Lake International Airport and breached the protective "No Fly Zone" over Deer Valley. The sophistication of the jamming device Hollenbeck had found demonstrated loud and clear that the kidnappers had access to some very high-tech equipment. But the one element that didn't fit was the human element—the pilots.

Even U.S. Night Stalker pilots, the best in the world, couldn't have tackled that storm last night. In normal conditions, the downdrafts around the valley were amazingly tough to handle. As Scot thought further, assembling a mental picture of the area where the bodies of the president's detail were found, he realized there wasn't enough room to land any sort of helicopter. Scot ran down how it might have happened. What if the kidnappers were able to get their hands on a helicopter with stealth capabilities, and what if they could find a pilot crazy enough to tackle the downdrafts, and what if the pilot was good enough to do it in a raging snowstorm, and what if he could land in a heavily treed area that didn't provide enough space? Would it have been possible? *Absolutely not,* thought Scot. *That was too many "what-ifs."*

The kidnappers would have had to *ski* down the mountain along a route they were relatively confident would not allow for them to be spotted and then rendezvous with some sort of transport that would either facilitate their escape or be an intermediary step along the way.

When the Deer Valley helicopter had flown Scot over the only serviceable pass to Midway, the pilot had told him the other routes would be traversable only if you brought climbing gear, plus they switched back on themselves often and would take double, and in some cases triple, the time. When Scot had asked if a four-wheel-drive vehicle could make it through the pass, the pilot had said it was possible, but why would you use a jeep when a snowmobile would be so much faster?

• • •

Reaching the bottom landing again, his nose and the smell of cigarette smoke led Scot back into the family room. He stood for several moments with his eyes closed, trying to put himself in the mind of the killer. The Madduxes were not smokers, so it must have been the killer who had lit up, and more than once. That heavy smoke smell didn't come from just one cigarette. So, he'd had time for more than one. *Why?*

Simple. He was waiting. Scot's mind began to turn faster. *Waiting for what? His colleagues, the kidnappers, to arrive with the president. He waited right in this room and smoked. What else did he do?* Scot looked around the room; there were no books or magazines, but there was a television set. He walked over and turned it on. After a few moments, the set warmed up enough and its picture popped to life. *Where would he have sat?* Harvath looked behind him and spotted what must have been Mr. Maddux's La-Z-Boy recliner. It had *man of the house* written all over it.

Knowing he was compromising the crime scene, but needing desperately to put the pieces of the puzzle together, Scot sat down in the chair and extended the tattered leg rest by pulling on the worn handle. The old La-Z-Boy lurched backward as the footrest sprang up, placing him in a very comfortable position. *If the killer had been smoking, he would have needed an ashtray and a place to set it. He could have rested it all on his chest as he waited and watched TV, but if he had gone to this extent to make himself comfortable, why not use the end table immediately to his left?*

Scot scanned the items that sat on the end table. There was a *TV Guide* with a ring on its cover where a glass had been placed, a few knitting needles that probably belonged to Mrs. Maddux, a pair of reading glasses, and a couple of coasters. *Coasters? Why would there be a moisture ring on the* TV Guide *if there were coasters right on the end table?* That didn't seem to jibe with the fastidiousness that reigned throughout this house.

Scot mimicked smoking, imagining the killer had used a pop can or something similar for the ashes, and let his left hand trail back toward the table, where he believed the makeshift ashtray would have been. The movement was difficult. Not just because of his sore muscles, but because of the position of the end table. The killer would have needed to rotate his torso and actually look at what he was doing, or he would have missed his target. Scot thought the chances were pretty good that he had missed once or twice and jumped out of the chair to test his theory.

Examining the edges along the surface of the end table, he saw a grayish, powdery dust that could have been cigarette ash, but only a lab would have been able to tell at this point. Dropping to his knees, Scot searched along the bottom of the table and found what he was looking for. Resting in the fibers of the matted orange carpeting were indeed cigarette ashes. The killer had obviously missed.

Then something else caught his eye. The end table was between the La-Z-Boy and a long couch. Judging from the wear on the couch cushion closest to the end table, that was where Mrs. Maddux sat while Mr. Maddux occupied the La-Z-Boy and the two watched TV. Underneath the couch was something dark and square. Scot reached under and pulled it out.

He held it up to the light coming in through the window. It was a piece of chocolate, perfectly square, that had been broken off from a larger bar. It was stamped with a distinct *N,* which Scot recognized as being the monogram of Nestlé, and the almost imperceptible word *Lieber* across the *N.* Conscious of the heat in his fingers, Scot transferred the chocolate square into his palm and walked across the entry hall into the kitchen, hoping the Madduxes had some Ziploc bags. He placed the chocolate on the edge of the counter by the sink and started rummaging through the drawers underneath. In the fourth drawer he found what he was looking for.

Scot crossed to the refrigerator, took several ice cubes from the freezer, and dropped them into the larger of the two Ziploc bags. He then put the piece of chocolate into the smaller bag, zipped it, and placed it into the large bag to keep it cold. He slipped the package into his outside parka pocket and turned his attention to the garbage can under the sink.

There wasn't much garbage and nothing that could have been used to ash a cigarette into. As Scot was closing the cabinet door that hid the trash can, he heard the telltale signs of an approaching helicopter. Leaning against the sink, Scot looked out the window above it to see if he could make out the approaching FBI team. Nothing yet, but they would be here very soon. As his mind raced through what else he should be looking for, Scot looked down at the dish rack to his left with its three upturned glasses. He upended them one by one, placing his nose inside and inhaling deeply. With the second one, his hunch was confirmed. After placing the glasses back in their original positions and running back to the family room to right the La-Z-Boy, Scot closed the front doors behind him and put the paper booties in his pocket as he laced up his Timberlands.

"Looks like the gang is on approach," said Deputy MacIntyre as Scot finished tying his shoes and came down the front steps of the house toward the assorted police vehicles.

"It's about time," replied Scot.

"You learn anything while you were in there?"

"Naw, not really. Pretty much just as you called it. I know it's been snowing a bit, but did you fellas find any tire tracks or anything out here on the perimeter?"

"Yeah, some pretty big mothers."

"Really? How big?"

"Looks like maybe a big rig. Eighteen-wheeler. Came right up to the barn. There were some others like one of them big flatbed pickups that uses the doubled-up tires in back, but only singles in front. And some other single-tread tracks behind the barn, probably snowmobiles."

"That sounds like a lot of activity, Deputy."

"Well, in the winter, the farmers get a lot of snowmobilers across their property, so that might be where the ones across the back of the barn came from. The doubled-up tires could have come from any number of neighbors around here. That's Mr. Maddux's pickup over there and he's got singles, so it wasn't from him. Those eighteen-wheeler-looking tracks are a little more confusing. The way it was backed up to the barn makes me think there might have been a drop off or something."

"Or a pickup. Did you or your men look inside the barn?"

"Nope. We were going to, but that's about the time we made contact with the sheriff, and he told us to secure the area and hold off on anything further until he got here."

"Yeah, he was probably right. My guess is," said Scot, gesturing to the incoming helicopter, "that they'll want to check out the victims first, then they'll look over the house, and then they'll start their search of the other buildings. I'm gonna get the outer search started. After they've searched the house, do me a favor and send 'em over to the barn, will ya? Thanks."

Scot finished with his most engaging smile and made his way to the barn. He was walking quickly, while trying not to attract any undue attention. The roar of the chopper could be heard from just overhead. Scot knew he'd been blessed with more time on this crime scene than he should ever have had.

Thankfully, the barn wasn't locked, and he was able to slip inside and shut the door behind him just as the Deer Valley helicopter touched down outside. It took Scot's eyes a minute to adjust to the diminished light, and while he waited, he filtered through the mess of tire tracks he had seen leading to the door.

The snow made it difficult to perfectly identify what had made them, but Scot had to give the deputy from Wasatch County another ten points. His interpretation of the tracks was probably right on the money. Casts would confirm things for sure, but what Scot was trying to do now was create the best picture he could of what happened.

His eyes adjusted, and he walked around the edges of the large dirt floor, hugging what in Mr. Maddux's younger days had probably been horse and pig stalls, trying not to trample on any evidence. The floor was a maze of all sorts of different tracks. Scot could see that the snowmobile tracks led from the back door of the barn, across the floor, and stopped at a deep horizontal groove in the dirt floor. The picture was becoming clearer now. Scot knew that if the falling snow hadn't obscured them completely, he could probably open the back door of the barn and find that the tracks would lead all the way back through the pass, to a secluded spot somewhere adjacent to Death Chute.

Suddenly, the barn was awash with light. It fell across his shoulders and landed on the floor in front of him. That light, coupled with a cold wind on the back of his neck, told Scot the FBI had decided to take up their investigation of the barn more quickly than he'd thought they would. Without turning around, he knew exactly who was standing behind him.

CHAPTER 24

"Only if this farm had a woodshed would there be a more appropriate place for me to tan your hide," came the voice of the FBI's number two man, Gary Lawlor, who was standing between the open barn doors. "Just what the hell have you been doing?"

Before turning to face him, Scot slipped off the latex gloves and shoved them inside his parka.

"You can hand those goddamn gloves right over to me. That way I won't leave any fingerprints, and when they find your body, they won't be able to link it to me."

"Gary, just wait a second," began Harvath.

"First of all, this isn't a fucking social call, Agent Harvath. You address me as Deputy Director or Agent Lawlor, you understand me? And secondly, *'wait a second'?* How dare you tell me to wait a second, boy? Who the hell do you think you are?"

"Do you want me to answer that, or are you just going to run right over what I have to say?"

"Shut up."

"There's my answer."

"You know what, Scot? You're a real wiseass. That's always been your problem. You're a great operative, but your mouth gets in the way too often. It's beyond me how you ever made it through the Navy, especially the SEALs."

"I guess that recommendation from the special agent in charge of the San Diego FBI field office went a long way."

"It must have. I don't know what I was thinking when I wrote that for you."

"You did it because you knew that's where I wanted to be. You knew I had certain talents and that they could teach me things that—"

"Yeah? Really? Did the Navy teach you that it was okay to assault a federal officer? Did they teach you that it was okay to trespass on not one, not two, but three secured FBI crime scenes and, while you're on one of them, start an avalanche that not only would bury potentially critical evidence, but might also endanger the lives of hundreds of rescue workers and investigators down below? And while I'm at it, what are you, in the fucking tour business now? If it hadn't been for the sheriff knowing where we were going, that fucking helicopter pilot would have gone by way of New Jersey to get here. I *know* you had something to do with that."

"Jesus, Gary. I lost at least thirty men. Good men. All on my watch. I was responsible for each and every one of those guys. Most of them have families. What do you expect me to do?"

Lawlor's incredulous voice rose to a level that could be heard well outside the barn. "What would I expect *you* to do? I would expect you to honor the oath you took to uphold the laws of this country. That's what I would expect you to do!"

Scot stood and stared at Lawlor. Of all people, this was someone he'd thought would understand him, understand what he was doing. After Scot's SEAL instructor father was killed in a training exercise, Gary Lawlor, a longtime friend of the family, had become like a second father to him. While they didn't always see eye to eye on things, Scot felt Gary should at least cut him slack because of their history.

The problem Lawlor had right now went far beyond their relationship, though. Scot needed to be put back in line. His voice calmer, Lawlor said, "Scot, you're in a lot of trouble. Do you understand that? You've completely thrown the book out the window."

"What would you be doing in my place?"

"Damn it, Scot, are you that thick? We're not talking about me, and we're not talking about the realm of possibilities. We're talking about what you have done and the trouble you're in."

"Let me ask you a question."

"You do realize the president has been kidnapped and I have absolutely no time for this?"

"How did you nail the guys from the Scripps bombing? Did you do it by your precious book that you seem to place above everything else?"

Scot had just touched a very deep and painful nerve. Harvath was referring to a standoff at the Scripps Howard Institute in La Jolla, California, over ten years ago, when Gary was in charge of the FBI's San Diego field office. A radical group had taken over the facility and were holding several of its staff hostage. When the FBI's Hostage Rescue Team assaulted the building after a weeklong standoff, they weren't prepared for what they found inside.

The strength of the terrorist group was twice what they had expected, and the terrorists had anticipated every route the FBI would take in assaulting the building. All of those areas were rigged with charges. Men that weren't mowed down by automatic weapons fire were blown to pieces by the explosives.

Lawlor was the type who would never ask men to do anything he wouldn't do himself. He had been on the winning side of several high-profile kidnappings, raids, and assorted tougher-than-hell cases before and since the Scripps incident, but he could never shake the feeling that somehow he should have known what was waiting inside that building for the HRT team.

It had taken Lawlor three years, but he had managed to track down every single member of the radical group responsible for the planning and execution of the Scripps Disaster, as it became known. Some of the perpetrators came in peacefully, some needed to be coerced, and some went out with guns blazing, but Lawlor's bullets always found their targets first.

Several of the group's members fled the country, foolishly thinking they would be beyond the FBI's grasp, but Lawlor still found them. Money and time were no object. Lawlor had made an impassioned plea to the government that it must be a priority to bring these people to justice and that he must be in charge of doing it. Scot knew Lawlor broke more than a few laws and trampled upon more than a few civil rights along the way, but he got the job done. It was precisely that feeling of responsibility that Scot was trying to evoke in Lawlor.

Gary snapped to, realizing he had been drawn into a place in his mind he didn't want to be.

"That was a long time ago, and it has no bearing whatsoever on what is happening now," he said.

"So, do as I say, not as I do? Jesus, Gary, it's a shame you never had kids. You've got all the good parental lines down pat."

"You don't know when to quit, do you? The SAC of our Salt Lake office wants your ass bronzed and hanging above his desk for cold-cocking one of his men."

"The guy deserved it."

"That doesn't matter. You still assaulted a federal officer and it happened on my playing field in my investigation. Plus, there's all the other crap you've pulled. Not only is your behavior way out of line, but according to the medical report I read on you, you shouldn't have even gotten out of bed this morning."

"Gary, come on. You know how important this is."

"You bet I do. I'm the one who has to feed the hourly reports back to Washington so the director can brief the vice president. If nothing else, you should know the importance of being a team player."

"Yeah, but I belong on the field, not on the bench. I was responsible for those men, and I am ultimately responsible for the president. You've lost guys before, Gary. You've gotta know how that feels . . . how I feel."

Lawlor had had enough. "You know what? Trying to pull my chain is going to get you fucking nowhere, pal. Understand me? What happened at Scripps was a long time ago. How I cleaned it up was also a long time ago. I was operating under a federal directive that you don't have the clearance or the need to know anything about. I have made a lot of mistakes in my life, and one of them was thinking I could talk some sense into you and help get your ass out of the fire, but you keep on pushing me."

Scot was growing equally angry and fired right back at Lawlor, *"Pushing you?* So this is about you now? For as long as I've known you it's all been about you."

"That's not true, and you know it."

"Where do you think my life and career are going to be when the dust finally settles on this? Have you given any thought to that?"

"At this point, that's not my problem, but I can tell you that you're not making things any easier on yourself with all of this fucking around."

"That's what you think I'm doing? *'Fucking around'?* What's *'fucking around'* is sitting on our asses for hours, burning precious time waiting for you to get here so the investigation can be carried forward. That was a colossal fuck around."

"You know what? You've just stepped on my very last nerve. You don't know when someone is trying to give you a hand, do you? I'm going to spell it out for you, and you damn well better listen. We are effective because we are organized. I don't care how many movies you watch. The rogue cowboy never helps get anything done. He screws up the entire works. It is through cooperation, specialization, and division of the investigative labors that any investigation succeeds. It is not the efforts of one man that count, but of hundreds, sometimes thousands. When you go off half-cocked because you don't like how things are going, you not only screw things up, as in any evidence we might have been able to uncover on Squaw Peak, but you are turning your back on your team.

"When you turn your back on your team, you forgo the rights and associations thereto. Now, I can understand how you're feeling, but that does not, for one single moment, excuse your behavior. You have broken the law, and, on top of your other problems, you might have to face the music on some serious charges. You think you were fucked before? Well, any compassion that might have been available to you because of your heroic efforts in saving the president's daughter have been thrown right out the window, by none other than you yourself.

"I can see your mind working, and I'm going to tell you right now, Scot, to keep your big mouth shut. I'm telling you for your own good. You might still have a career that's salvageable, but if you step out of line one more time, I guarantee you I will personally see that you get every single thing that's coming to you. Do you get me? And don't open your mouth to say yes. You just nod your head."

Anger burned within every pore in his body like acid, but slowly, reluctantly, Harvath nodded his head.

"Good," said Lawlor, who turned and walked out of the barn. Waving to get the attention of Deputy MacIntyre, he yelled, "I need one of your men to drive Agent Harvath back to the Secret Service command center at Snow Haven. I have had about all the investigative help from him that I can stand. And, while I'm thinking of it, absolutely no stopping for *anything.*"

• • •

Back in Deer Valley, FBI Agent Zuschnitt, feeling the vibration of his pager, looked at the display and then fished in his pocket for quarters. He could have used his cell phone, but this was yet another call he didn't want traced back to him.

CHAPTER 25

Scot fumed all the way back to the command center. The hypocritical bullshit Lawlor was shoveling was too much. He knew damn well that Lawlor probably bowed, bent, and broke every rule in the book during his search for the people responsible for killing his fellow FBI agents. Nobody blamed him at all, and knowing Lawlor, nobody probably even dared to stand in his way.

In all fairness to Gary, Scot understood that there was a chain of command and a way things needed to be done for the sake of effectiveness. He'd been in the Navy, after all. But, the unassailable fact here was that Scot had lost at least thirty men and the president was missing. No matter what Lawlor said, Scot's career was in his own hands and the only thing that would turn the tide in his favor was if he stumbled upon something that broke the investigation wide open.

He'd assembled a few clues, but nothing earth-shattering. Lawlor wouldn't listen to him at this point anyway, so he was back where he'd started—on his own.

Harvath hopped out of Deputy MacIntyre's Suburban before it had even come to a stop and, flashing his credentials at the gate, was shown through. He made his way to the Winnebago and bounded up the stairs, hoping to find Palmer inside. She was in back, working at the same table Longo had been at earlier.

Glancing up from her laptop, she saw Scot coming down the narrow hallway. "Well, someone's been a busy boy today."

"Very funny."

"Who's being funny?"

"Yuk, yuk, yuk . . . Any news?"

"We got a couple of breaks."

"I'm all ears."

"Well, we got a confirmation back on the Middle Easterner. Name's Hassan Useff. The Mossad ID'd him. He was a freelance sniper who worked for many of the pro-Palestinian-liberation groups, in particular some of the more radical splinter factions of the PLO. He had been tied to several high-profile assassinations in Israel."

"Hmmm," said Scot. "Well, that does and doesn't make sense."

"What do you mean?"

"The weapon he was found with was a Skorpion. It makes sense in that the Skorpion is one of the preferred weapons of the PLO, but it's predominantly a defensive weapon. The long-range accuracy isn't that good. And because it's so small, on fully automatic it's more of an S and P."

"S and P?"

"Sorry, it's a term from my past. *S and P* means 'spray and pray.' The Skorpion cuts a wide swath when it's set to full auto, and the shooter just sprays bullets and prays he hits his target. You know, a room broom."

"But what if it wasn't set on fully auto?"

"Well, it can hold a ten-to-twenty-round magazine, but why wouldn't a sniper use a more accurate and dependable weapon?"

"Maybe he had one and his buddies took it with them."

"And, what, left him with a weapon that screams PLO? It doesn't make sense." Scot took a seat next to Agent Palmer as his eyes glazed over in thought.

"When you were in the SEALs, didn't you ever carry any American-made weaponry?"

His mind half on what Palmer had said and half somewhere else, Scot answered, "It depended on the mission, but we would never leave one of our men or any of our equipment behind. In and out without trace was our M.O."

"You know, I once dated a SEAL, and if he had applied the same policies to my bathroom, instead of leaving behind a minefield of wet towels and toilet seats in the up position, we might still be together." Palmer laughed, trying to help lift the intense mood Scot had slipped into, but it didn't work.

"You like chocolate, right?"

"Show me a woman who doesn't," answered Palmer.

"And all that stuff you brought back from your trip to Europe last year—"

"You mean the chocolate that I brought back and left in the duty room at the White House that you piglets wolfed down and didn't even leave me a piece of?"

"Yeah, that would be the chocolate I'm talking about."

"What about it?"

"Where'd you get it? I mean, did you buy it at the duty free, or did you go to specialty shops?"

"Let me see. I kind of bought it all over. I was traveling by train on one of those Eurail passes, and it was nice to have it to snack on. I just picked it up here and there."

"Any place in particular?"

Palmer tried to jog her memory. "I started my trip in Belgium, and since they're really known for their chocolate, I think I bought a good supply at a shop across the street from the train station. That lasted me through France, and when I got to Austria, I picked up some Mozart's Balls."

"'Mozart's Balls'?"

"When you say it in German, it's not as dirty."

"And, after Austria?"

"Ah, let me think, after Austria . . . Oh, yeah. After Austria, I went to Switzerland. They are really famous for chocolate, but I think it's more like milk chocolate they're famous for. The Belgians do lots of fancy things with chocolate, but not so much the Swiss. The Belgians would put chocolate on a cheeseburger and try to sell it, while the Swiss really seem to like milk chocolate bars. Next, I went to Italy and they had those awesome Baci Balls—"

"Sorry, back up a sec."

"What?"

"About the Swiss. Nestlé is a Swiss chocolate maker, right?"

"Yeah. They make Nestlé Crunch bars and I think that Coffee-mate creamer stuff."

"Right, those are a couple of the products we have here in the States, but what about in Europe?"

"In Switzerland, they make tons of different products. They make chocolate, but they also make things like baby food."

"Let's stick with the chocolate."

"Fine, from what I saw in Switzerland, there were lots of different varieties of Nestlé chocolate."

"And if they were going to import, or try a particular brand here in the U.S., they would probably give the chocolate a name in English, right?"

"Maybe, maybe not."

"Why do you say that?"

"Take something like Toblerone or Baci, neither of them changed their names when they exported to the U.S. from Europe. But those are one of those deals where the European company has built its entire identity around that one brand. The identity *is* the name of the chocolate, so they don't change it. If there were a Nestlé product that was kind of known in Switzerland, but not super famous, I think they would have their marketing people here come up with a new name for it. Let's face it, the U.S. market for fine chocolate with foreign-sounding names has got to be a lot smaller than the market for something like Snickers."

"That's a good point."

"Hey, I didn't get to where I am by being stupid," said Palmer with another warm smile. "I'm beginning to worry about you, though. Let's get off this chocolate subject. I'm sure Nestlé has a web site. It'll either be a dot-com or a dot-Ch, for Switzerland."

"Thanks, Palmer. I appreciate it," said Scot, standing to leave.

"Where are you going?"

"I haven't had anything to eat since that wonderful breakfast you cooked me this morning. I was thinking about walking down to the restaurant at the Silver Lake Lodge to grab a bowl of chili."

"Want some company? I could probably take my break a little early."

"No, thanks anyway. I need to be alone and get some things straight."

"I understand. Stick your head in when you get back."

"Okay."

Scot quickly shut the door of the Winnebago behind him, so as not to let too much cold air in and piss off the other agents inside. As he reached the bottom step, he heard the door open behind him.

Palmer peeked her head around the door. "There was one other thing. There might not be a connection, but an ambulance was found abandoned on the west side of the valley over by the Kennecot Copper Mine."

"Really? Had it been reported stolen?"

"No, the report didn't come in until after it was discovered."

"Where was it stolen from?"

Responding to the shouts of the agents inside, Palmer closed the door behind her and walked down the stairs to where Scot was standing.

"It was stolen from a mechanic's shop called Grunnah Automotive. Apparently, Mr. Grunnah had towed the ambulance in on Saturday—"

"Towed? What was wrong with it?"

"There was a problem with the brake line, so Mr. Grunnah towed it into his garage Saturday afternoon and told the ambulance company he wouldn't be able to get to it until Monday. He was closed Sunday and claims that it must have been stolen between when he closed Saturday night and when he opened up again this morning."

"How does somebody drive an ambulance that was in such bad shape it had to be towed to the mechanic's in the first place?"

"Mr. Grunnah says it was fixed."

"Fixed? I thought you said Grunnah told the ambulance company he couldn't get to it until Monday."

"That's exactly right. Grunnah says whoever stole it fixed it first."

"Seems like a lot of work to go through for a joyride," said Scot.

"For a joyride, yes. But, it's not a lot of work if you want a getaway vehicle that you can drive as fast as you want with no risk of being stopped by the police."

"I'm sure the FBI will come to the same conclusion. Thanks for the update."

Palmer turned and went back to the Winnebago as Scot made his way up the driveway toward the security gate and the main road down to the lodge. Passing through, he saw an ambulance parked adjacent to the driveway. Scot had never noticed before, but the body of the ambulance was very similar to a truck's, with a high shell over the bed. Looking down, he saw that while the tires in front were singles, the ones in back had been doubled to bear the extra weight.

Another piece of the puzzle fell into place, but the picture was still no closer to being complete.

CHAPTER 26

Knowing that there would be a baying pack of newshounds at the bottom of the road, Scot turned into the woods where he could cut across a nearby ski slope and hopefully walk the rest of the way unassaulted.

The peace, quiet, and cold air actually did him some good. His mind had been spinning since he had awakened that morning, trying to assimilate and process each new piece of information heaped on top of the last. The break from not thinking was refreshing. He watched some of the skiers coming down the slope as he walked along its edge. Though the avalanche had claimed a handful of civilian lives, it hadn't seemed to stop most people from pursuing the rest of their vacations. Human nature never ceased to amaze him. People would ski all day as if they were a million miles away and then gather around TVs in the lodge afterward saying how terrible it was that the president still had not been located.

• • •

Cooking aromas wafted uphill from the Silver Lake Lodge and into Scot's nose, sending a signal to his stomach, which started to grumble on cue. Chili in a bread bowl with a cup of hot chocolate would probably cost eleven bucks at the midmountain resort restaurant, but so what?

Coming downhill from this angle, he could make out Nick and Vance's office on the far side of the restaurant. There was another favor they could do for him, but it could wait until after lunch.

Scot's training had become second nature, and he never entered a room without scanning it completely, as he did now in the restaurant. He noted each exit, the placement of the windows, and what was beyond them. Though the large log dining room sat hundreds of people, he scanned the faces and builds of everyone within his line of sight. It was habit, and it had saved his life and those of his charges more times than he cared to admit. Harvath would walk into the rec room of a senior center in his nineties, if he was lucky to live that long, and size up each and every potential enemy, his mind engaged in reflex threat assessment.

Grabbing a tray, Scot fell in line behind a raucous bunch of Germans who had raced to get into the food corral before him. He remembered a story one of the guys on the Swedish ski team had told when they were practicing for an event in Germany. Scot had been complaining that at the lift lines it seemed as if it was every German man, woman, and child for themselves and that more than once he had come close to punching someone out for skiing right over his skis or cutting in front of him while he waited patiently for his turn. The Swede laughed and told him that was why everyone in Sweden called the Germans the *Liftwaffa.* Scott said the word under his breath as the boisterousness of the men in front of him grew.

When he finally got to the steam table, he ordered chili in a bread bowl with onions and extra cheese. Next he ordered a hot chocolate, and when the woman pointed to a coffee bar across the room with an equally long line, he opted for a milk. That they would make you stand in a completely separate line for hot chocolate made no sense, but all Scot wanted to do was eat, so he paid his bill and wandered into the sea of tables, hoping to find a vacant one for himself.

As luck would have it, a couple was getting up as Scot approached. Arguing about some problem they hadn't been able to leave at home when they set out on their vacation, neither heard Scot thank them for the table as he sat down.

He closed his eyes and bent over the bread bowl, inhaling the scent of the chili. With spoon in hand, he shoveled out a large bite, placed it in his mouth, and leaned back in the chair to savor the smoky flavor.

"Hi, there. I'm Jody Burnis. Mind if I ask you a few questions?"

It was not so much a request, as a statement. She moved fast and took Scot completely off guard. The sparkly little blond who jumped into the chair opposite him uninvited had *reporter* written all over her. "I'm from CNN, and—"

"No comment," said Scot as he took another bite of his chili.

"But I haven't even asked you any questions yet."

"But you will, and I don't care what they are. I have no comment."

"You're Scot Harvath, aren't you? Former U.S. freestyle skier turned Secret Service agent?"

"No comment."

"C'mon. I'm just trying to do my job."

"And I mine."

"You know, you guys don't own the president. The American people do."

That was the first time Scot had ever heard that one. It was patently ridiculous, and he had to struggle to keep from shooting the milk he was drinking out his nose when he laughed. "Lady—"

"Please, call me Jody."

"As I was saying, lady. No comment."

"What can you tell me about the avalanche?"

"It was made of snow and came from the top of a mountain."

"You're real cute, you know that?" she asked.

"And real hungry. Why don't you go find someone else to bother?"

"Am I really bothering you?"

"Yes."

The young reporter leaned in close to Scot with an intent look on her face and kept nodding her head as if she were listening to something.

"Do you have some sort of problem?" Scot asked her. At the same moment, out of the corner of his eye he saw the reporter flash someone a hand signal. *She must have a cameraman.*

Scot turned and, sure enough, two tables back was a man with a Betacam over his shoulder shooting the two of them talking. Noticing the lav microphone clipped to her jacket, Scot leaned over and plucked it from her.

"Hey!" she shouted.

"Zip it, lady," he told her, and then, holding the microphone as close as he could to his mouth without swallowing it, he began making strange and very loud animal calls. Behind him, he heard the cameraman yell, and Harvath turned just in time to see him swat the headphones from his head. The volume at which Scot had been making all that noise must have been extremely painful.

He turned his attention back to the reporter. "You'll probably want a release of some sort, so let me give you one. You absolutely, positively do not have my permission to use me, my name, or my likeness in any activity whatsoever. If I see my face on TV or hear my voice, I will sue your pretty little ass and your network for all it's worth. Am I clear?" He punctuated his last words by throwing the tiny microphone back at her.

"Crystal," she said, rising in a huff and going over to her cameraman. "Gene? Are you okay?"

"What's that guy's problem, man?" from the cameraman was the last thing Scot heard as the two made their way toward the exit. Unbeknownst to Scot, Agent Zuschnitt not only had witnessed the entire exchange, but had orchestrated it. And upon its completion, he quietly slipped out one of the dining room's many side doors.

• • •

Twenty minutes later, Scot had finished his chili, two large cookies, and another milk. Feeling satiated, even a little sleepy, he left the restaurant and headed over to the wing that contained the avalanche control office. The first person he saw there was Nick Slattery.

"Whoa, hold on there a second, dude. The favor bank *is closed,"* said Nick.

"Hello, pal. Whaddya know?" said Scot with a broad smile.

"What do I know? I know that I've had my ass torn off by no less than five people in the last two hours, four of whom were carrying guns at the time. I don't know you anymore, man."

"That isn't any way to treat our friend, Nick," said Vance, who pushed past Scot and entered the office carrying a cup of hot cocoa.

"Is that . . . ?" asked Scot.

"Cocoa? Yeah," replied Vance.

"How long'd you have to stand in line for it?"

"Stand in line? *Psssah.* I'm an important guy here. I don't stand in line for cocoa. Gimme a fucking break. You want one?"

"I'd love one," said Scot.

"Nick, would you mind shagging Scot a cup of cocoa? You can leave it on the desk in the outer office and then take a walk. I'm happy to help this guy because he's my friend and we've got a history, but there's no need for you to be involved any further."

"If *anybody* asks, I was getting the cocoa for *me* and then decided to take a walk to the ski patrol office," said Nick.

"Whatever you want, man. Thanks," said Vance as Nick turned and left the office.

"Did you guys get it that bad?" asked Scot once the door had closed behind Nick.

"It wasn't pretty, but I did just what you said."

"What *I* said? What'd I say?"

"To blame you."

"Hey, wait a second. I said I would take full responsibility."

"Same thing. I told Nick to keep his mouth shut, and I did all the talking."

"Do you find it funny that I'm not grateful?"

"Nick needs this job a hell of a lot more than I do, as is currently being evidenced by the fact that I am even talking to you. Now, I take it you came here for more than hot chocolate."

"Yeah, I need another favor."

"As long as it doesn't involve the helicopter."

Scot winced. "That pilot was great. How bad they give it to him?"

"He's working an oil-rig chopper in the Arctic Circle"—Vance paused for effect, looking at his watch—"starting right about, now."

"Get outta here."

"I'm just foolin'. He kept his mouth shut when the FBI guys and the sheriff chewed him out for taking the scenic route and interfering with a federal investigation. But when our boss launched into him, he told him to go screw himself."

"You're kidding."

"Nope. Technically, the guy's retired, and he does this job during the season for fun. He needs his job even less than I need mine, plus he hates the boss with a passion. He told me to thank you."

"Thank me?"

"Yeah, says it was the most fun he's had in a long time."

"Well, I was glad to be of service. Listen, about that favor I need," Scot continued.

"What can I do you for?"

"Do you have a computer in here that can access the Net?"

"Of course."

"I need to use it."

"Sure, sit right here, and be my guest," said Vance, motioning to the chair next to him.

"I need to use it alone," said Scot.

"Dude, no way. If the boss finds out that my machine has been used to surf the porno sites, then I am definitely out of here."

"I'm serious."

"All right, I can see that now is no time for levity. How long do you need it for?"

"Probably no longer than a half hour. Forty-five minutes tops."

"I can leave you alone in this office, but I've gotta stay in the outer office in case we get a call."

"Thanks, Vance. I appreciate it. Do me one more favor, would ya?"

"What?"

"Close the door behind you on the way out."

CHAPTER 27

Considering the ordeal he had been through, it was no wonder Harvath was tired. Vance could see his friend was not only exhausted, but also still in a lot of pain. When Scot came out of his office and thanked him for the use of the computer, Vance handed him his now less-than-hot hot chocolate and arranged for one of the ski patrollers to take him back up to Snow Haven via snowmobile.

Harvath had the driver go around the outside to avoid the reporters. When he arrived parallel with the compound, he thanked the patroller as two Secret Service agents waved him on through to the main house. His fatigue weighed on him. He had been trained to go for days with no sleep if necessary, but he had also been taught that sleep was a powerful weapon. Sleep helped keep your mind razor-sharp, and at this point his wasn't.

As he approached the kitchen door, he saw several agents stomping out cigarettes, cutting their break short to return inside. Knowing something must be up, Scot hastened his steps and entered the house not far behind them. Most of the agents were gathered around a large-screen TV in the AV room.

The TV was tuned to CNN, and as Scot entered, CNN's *Live Special Report* logo was just fading down and the anchor said a few words before introducing a reporter in the field. Scot's stomach tightened when he saw who it was. A bad feeling crept over him, and he let out a low moan that was overheard by several of the agents standing next to him.

"Thank you, Richard. As you know this country and the rest of the world has been holding its breath as the search for President Jack Rutledge continues amid the snow and ice from Sunday afternoon's avalanche here in Park City, where the president was enjoying a ski vacation with his sixteen-year-old daughter, Amanda. All of these efforts, though, may be in vain."

A collective intake of breath could be heard throughout the room. The images on screen went from Jody Burnis at the bottom of a ski hill with cranes and rescue equipment in the background, to the interior of the Silver Lake Lodge. The camera angle showed Jody speaking to a man whose back was to the camera and whose face was partially obscured from view. Most people watching would not know whom she was interviewing, but unfortunately, anyone who knew Scot could tell it was him.

Jody's narrative continued. "According to sources close to and within the Secret Service, CNN has learned that the avalanche that claimed the lives of over two dozen Secret Service agents and six civilians, all now confirmed dead, and which has sparked a massive search-and-rescue effort to recover any remaining survivors, including the president, apparently was no accident.

"Our sources tell us that the avalanche was created as a diversion in order to facilitate the kidnapping of the president of the United States. Of course at this point neither the Secret Service, the FBI, nor the White House will confirm or deny these reports, but we will of course keep you up to speed and bring you further information as we have it. . . ."

The chili in Scot's stomach turned, and he could taste bile. That reporter had used him, but why? Why him? If she was going to fake an interview with a source within the Secret Service, why didn't she just use a production assistant or something? If you were going to stray that far from the truth, what difference did it make? It made no sense. Had she interviewed him actually thinking he might give her something she could use and then, after their unpleasant exchange, decided to use him anyway out of spite?

Harvath walked into the kitchen and poured himself a cup of coffee. A couple of Secret Service agents who had been standing next to him in the AV room were right behind him. The expression on their faces said it all.

Scot wasn't about to let everyone think he had cooperated even for a second with CNN. "That interview was BS. I never told that reporter anything other than 'no comment,' so don't come in here looking at me like that."

"Hey, Harvath," said one of the agents, "we're not looking at you like anything. We just came in to get some coffee. That's it."

Scot shook his head in disgust and, taking his cup of coffee, walked out of the kitchen toward the front door. He needed to check the transport roster and see when the next team would be rotating out and going back to the hotels. Ever since the avalanche, all of the Secret Service vehicles had been reassigned on a priority basis. He needed to grab just a couple of hours of sleep and then he could start making sense out of things.

As he walked the snowy path toward the command center, he thought to himself that the day couldn't get much worse, but when the command center door flew open and Gary Lawlor stood staring out at him, he knew he had been sorely mistaken.

Lawlor was flanked by two large men whom Scot hadn't seen before and suspected were also FBI agents. Lawlor's face said everything. He was enraged but icy at the same time. It was a frightening juxtaposition. There was no doubt in Scot's mind that it wouldn't take much to push Lawlor into a full-on explosion. Standing here in front of all of his colleagues, the last thing Harvath wanted was to be ripped by the deputy director of the FBI, so he proceeded with extreme caution.

"It looks like you saw the CNN piece," said Scot as he walked toward him.

"Don't you move another inch!" yelled Lawlor, watching as Harvath came to an immediate stop. "Saw it? Yeah, I saw it. The whole world saw it."

"I can explain—"

"I bet you can, but at this point I don't care. You have compromised this investigation for the last time. I told you what would happen if you stepped out of line again, but you didn't listen to me. You had to do it your way."

"My way? You've gotta be kidding me. I didn't tell that reporter any—"

"I don't want to hear it."

Scot was losing his temper, and he began to raise his voice, "I don't care if you want to hear it or not; you're going to."

"Not a chance."

"Agent Lawlor, if you just get ahold of the raw tape from that reporter, you'll hear that I said nothing further than 'no comment.'"

"Agent Harvath, I don't know what you said while the camera was rolling or when it wasn't."

"But what would I stand to gain by compromising the investigation?"

"I don't know, Agent Harvath. Maybe you don't like the way the FBI is handling this and want to push things along because you think you can do better."

"I want what you do."

"You've said that several times, but you don't want to operate as a team player, and you don't want to play by the rules—"

"Play by the rules? Do you think the kidnappers played by the rules when they snatched the president?"

"Agent Harvath, I've had enough, and so have your superiors."

"My superiors? What are you talking about?"

"I have cut you more than enough slack. More than I should have. The little bit of rope you had left you just used to hang yourself with."

"Hang myself? But I told you, I had nothing to do with that CNN report."

"And I told you, I don't care. As of"—Lawlor looked at his watch—"two minutes ago, you are officially recalled to D.C."

"You had me yanked? I can't believe this."

"Believe it. Agents Patrasso and Sprecher here are to escort you back to the hotel, where you will collect your belongings and then proceed to Salt Lake City Airport. There will be a ticket at the Delta counter with your name on it. The agents will accompany you and make sure that the plane takes off with you on it. After that, you are no longer my problem."

Scot knew he was grasping at straws, but he tried anyway. "I'm sorry about what happened. You're right. This needs to be a team effort. I was just out of it, but I'll pull it together. This is your investigation, and I will respect that. I've already come up with several theories that I think are worth taking a look at, so why don't we—"

"Too late. I warned you, and *you* didn't listen. It's out of my hands."

Really reaching, Scot went for the medical angle. "I haven't gotten my CT and MRI scans yet with Dr. Trawick. We're supposed to do it tomorrow afternoon and then he can clear me to travel."

"Screw Dr. Trawick. *I'm* clearing you to travel. If you can beat the stuffing out of one of my agents, rappel down a sheer rock face, commandeer a helicopter and fly to Midway, plus give CNN interviews, then you're fine to travel."

"I told you, I didn't say anything to that reporter."

"And I told you, I don't care. Patrasso and Sprecher are going to take you to get your things, and then you are going to the airport and getting on the next plane to D.C. What you do once you're there is somebody else's problem. Now, get out of here," Lawlor said, turning and going back into the command center.

Scot looked from Patrasso to Sprecher and realized they were a pair it probably wouldn't be wise to mess with. He had a feeling Lawlor had instructed them to use any means necessary to get him on that plane. Frankly, he was too tired to try to resist.

• • •

What is the name of your hotel? had been one of Dr. Trawick's memory questions the night before. Even seeing the hotel's name now, on the big sign outside, didn't ring any bells. He really had hurt his head.

Patrasso and Sprecher accompanied him to his room, where he packed, and then took him to the airport.

The flight back to D.C. was the quickest he had ever had. Despite his headache, he slept the entire way.

CHAPTER 28

André Martin struggled against the laundry cord digging into his wrists, then let his muscles go limp. He had to stay calm. *Focus on your breathing,* he told himself. The gag in his mouth tasted like shoe polish, and a strong smell of mildew rose from the stained floor beneath him. All he wanted to do was vomit, but he knew for sure if he did, he would choke on it and die. He kept reminding himself to be calm. *There has to be a way out of this,* he thought. It had better come soon, though. The uncomfortable hog-tie position in which he was restrained threatened to drive him insane. He closed his eyes and tried to focus on what had happened.

When Senator Snyder had opened the door to the shower, André hadn't seen the hypodermic in his hand. By the time he did, it was too late. The tranquilizer worked extremely fast. Considering the difference in their sizes, deception was the only advantage Snyder had over his taller and more muscular victim.

In a strange sort of way, had he but known it, this had been André's lucky day. The senator's schedule was tightly packed, and with all the events of the last fourteen hours, he didn't have time for any diversions, especially a killing and the requisite disposal of the body. This was something he wanted time to savor. He also wanted to know how much his young lover knew.

Snyder didn't have the time to put all of the pieces together then, but lately something about André Martin had begun to bother him. Call it a feeling. Senator Snyder put a lot of stock in his intuition, especially when it was telegraphing danger signals.

Snyder had tried to rationalize his fears, thinking that as he was getting older he was getting more paranoid, but he knew this wasn't true. In fact, it was quite the opposite. The older he got, the more attuned to his senses he had become. That morning, not wanting to appear suspicious, Snyder could glance over his shoulder only so many times in the taxicab on the way to Rolander's house. Although he couldn't have proved it, he knew he was being followed.

When he returned home to Georgetown, the entry hall was perfectly dry, but the mudroom at the rear entrance to the house was a different story. There was water there, even though someone had done their best to mop up. Snyder knew that person could only have been André Martin.

Snyder was also sure André had been listening in on his phone call with Agent Zuschnitt. When he'd hung up the phone, he had done so by depressing the switch hook so he could place another call to his office. André had not been fast enough in replacing the handset in the upstairs bedroom, and Snyder had heard him hang up. Those two pieces of evidence were enough to seal Martin's fate.

From inside a false champagne split stored in the wet bar fridge of his den, Snyder removed the hypo and its potent drug. Minutes later he was at the shower door. With the thick steam and Snyder's quick moves, André never had a chance of avoiding the needle.

Like a cat playing with a mouse, Snyder couldn't deny himself the opportunity of toying with André. While he waited for the drug to take full effect, he asked him why he had followed him and why he had listened in on the phone call. To his credit, André was quite clever.

"You've been distant lately. You seem preoccupied with something or someone else," said André, his muscles growing extremely weak, his eyes showing his terror despite their heavy lids. He knew what Snyder was capable of. He struggled to gather all of his faculties to present the strongest argument he could, but the fog of the drug was pulling him down with ever increasing speed. "I thought you might be seeing someone on the side. Why else would you leave the house in the middle of the night like you did?"

"What I do, my little André," said Snyder as he yanked Martin's hair to lift his head from where it had slumped against his chest, "is my business. I am a senator, you know, and have very important business at all times of the day and night."

André tried desperately to convince him, though he knew he wasn't buying it. "I . . . I love you and I couldn't bear the thought of you with someone else. I've always been the jealous type."

"Then why didn't you confront me with it?"

"I was afraid. I wanted to be sure that you were really seeing someone else first. I didn't want to look stupid if I was wrong."

"Is that *really* it? Or do you have another reason for following me? What else have you seen?"

Snyder had turned off the water after he had injected him, and André now sat on the floor of the shower stall. The drugged man's mouth hung slack, and a silvery stream of drool ran from the left-hand corner.

The senator slapped him to get his attention. "What about the telephone call I received this morning? What do you have to say about that?"

André laughed lightly and was mumbling something quietly to himself.

Snyder slapped him again, harder this time. He had used too much of the drug. He hadn't seen it work like this before. It was no problem, though. When he returned home tonight, his victim would be willing to tell him anything. Of that he was sure.

He tried slapping André one more time. "What do you have to say?"

The mumbling continued, and the senator barked at him to speak up. When he did, Snyder was enraged.

"A little prick in the shower, that's all it was. That's all he was. A little prick from a little prick with a little prick," said André as he started laughing to himself once again.

Snyder landed a blow to the side of his head, which stopped the laughing, as André Martin fell unconscious.

CHAPTER 29

Because Scot had expected to be returning on Air Force One, he hadn't worried about how he would get home from the airport. As usual, on his departure one of the junior agents had picked him up at his apartment and driven him to Washington National, and he half expected to see another agent waiting to pick him up now. But there was nobody at the gate or outside the baggage claim. Both his beeper and his cell phone were on, but neither was vibrating to tell him he had a ride waiting. He knew this was because there was no ride.

Convinced Lawlor was somehow behind it all, Scot shouldered his bags and walked to the cab stand. After twenty minutes in line, his turn came and he hopped into a cab and headed for his apartment in Alexandria. Scrolling through his digital phone list, he found the number for Big Tony's and hit the *send* button.

The cabdriver waited while Scot went inside to pick up his pizza and a six-pack of Kirin beer. Tony's had Alexandria's best selection of imported beers and takeout pizza. The delicious smell of deep-dish pie rising through the box was a welcome change from the less-than-appetizing smell that had been rising off his cabdriver. When they reached his apartment building, Scot paid the driver and asked for a receipt. He made a mental note to put the ride on his Secret Service expenses. While he was at it, he'd throw in the bill for the beer and pizza too. What did he have to lose? Besides, even a condemned man gets a last meal.

Struggling with the bags, the pizza, and the six-pack of beer, Harvath managed to unlock the entrance door and push it the rest of the way open with his hip. The building manager had been collecting his mail for him, but it was too late to knock on her door now, so he climbed the old wooden stairs to his apartment. *The bills can wait until tomorrow.*

Reaching the third floor, Harvath turned to his apartment door on the left of the landing and looked closely at the upper-right-hand corner of the doorframe. Satisfied his apartment hadn't been entered during his absence, he balanced the pizza and beer on one knee, removed the hair from the doorframe, unlocked the door, and entered his home.

Harvath had cleared his voice mail in the cab, but now he picked up the phone and listened for the stutter dial tone just in case—nothing. A strange sense of calm descended upon him as he placed his bags in the bedroom and fell down onto the couch with the remote. He opened a bottle of the Japanese beer and grabbed a slice of pizza. Every channel, just like the airport CNN TV sets, was running the Jody Burnis story. Although careful to repeatedly state that no one had confirmed the kidnapping of the president, they pushed the fact that it hadn't been denied either. When they stated that word of the kidnapping had been from a source within the Secret Service, Scot realized he had lost his appetite and threw his half-eaten slice of pizza back into the box.

Placing the remainder of the six-pack on the floor next to him, Scot stretched out on the couch and turned to the Outdoor Life Network, which thankfully wasn't reporting anything about the president. Instead, OLN was rerunning a ski competition from Innsbruck, and he drank beer and watched it, letting his mind go blank. The last thing he remembered before falling asleep was kicking off his shoes and letting them fall onto the rug in front of the couch.

• • •

At precisely seven A.M. Scot awoke to the building manager knocking on his door. She had heard him come in last night and wanted to give him his mail. Harvath figured as long as he was up, he would put on a pot of coffee and take a shower. He skipped shaving and, after getting dressed, ate the last two Eggo waffles he had in the freezer. He was out of syrup, so he covered them with butter and honey.

Being part of the president's first team definitely had its advantages. Not only did they get a clothing allowance, because the Secret Service had to look good on TV, but they had better access to some highly sought after specialists in the D.C. area. One of those people was Dr. Sarah Helsabeck, who agreed to see Scot right away.

Harvath spent the better part of the morning being poked, prodded, quizzed, tested, and scanned. Dr. Helsabeck remarked on the incredible bruising up and down his back, saying it was amazing that the force that caused the trauma hadn't broken any bones or done any internal damage. Actually, what she really said was, "I would ask you if you got the license numbers of the trucks that hit you, but if you just tell me what color they were, a fleet this size shouldn't be too hard to track down." As she continued her examination and reviewed his test results, Dr. Helsabeck commented, "Doesn't look like anything snapped, crackled, or popped, and there don't seem to be any signs of leaking."

"So, it's all pretty good then, right?" asked Scot.

"I'm most concerned about the knocks you took to your head. The brain is a very complicated mechanism. Your films don't show any bleeding, but I'm still concerned."

"Why?"

"Well, for starters, there's your psychometrics. When you joined the Secret Service, they ran a battery of tests to establish a baseline for your performance. They charted things like your memory, concentration, and reaction time. All of which, compared to the tests we ran today, I can see are impaired."

"But, Dr. Trawick said—"

"No offense to Dr. Trawick, but his was an extremely subjective diagnosis. Without the baseline that I have, he was taking shots in the dark."

"C'mon, Dr. Helsabeck. I've hit my head before and I've been fine."

"This time, we don't know for sure. You've suffered a significant loss of short-term memory—"

"Doc, I appreciate your seeing me so quickly and running all these tests, but can you just give me the bottom line?"

"The bottom line is this: When you fell, you probably hit your head on something extremely hard, like a rock, and suffered a concussion. While you haven't forgotten who you are, there seems to be some low-grade amnesia, which is what we were talking about in terms of short-term memory loss."

"How short?"

"It's normally things that are new. You might have trouble recalling things that happened in the last month."

"Will I get it back?"

"Probably. There may be people you've met recently whom you've forgotten, or bills and bank deposits you can't recall . . . that kind of stuff."

"Are there any other potential problems?"

"You might experience difficulty with concentration, and like I said, your reaction time is down."

"What about physical side effects?"

"You may find yourself sleeping a lot more, or your sleep may be interrupted."

"Great."

"You might also continue to experience the headaches you complained to me about, as well as some nausea."

"Any other good news?"

"It's not uncommon for patients who have suffered trauma such as yours to become irritable."

"Irritable how?"

"Things beyond your control will frustrate you more than they would in normal conditions. Basically, your fuse might be a lot shorter."

Scot wondered if that was why he had decked Agent Zuschnitt, or if he would have done it regardless of his fall. After a moment of reflection, he decided he would have done it regardless. Zuschnitt had been asking for it.

"Is that it?" asked Scot.

"Pretty much. Just keep in mind that all of these symptoms I've mentioned can become more profound with physical exertion. Basically, your brain has been scrambled and you need to give it, and your body, time to repair."

Scrambled. You had to love a doctor who put things in laymen's terms. Not only did she know how to break it down, she was also a comedian. As he was leaving, Dr. Helsabeck gave him the name of a good chiropractor she knew. "You're going to need him," she said. Scot thanked her and headed out into the drizzly afternoon.

Successfully hailing a cab in D.C. in the rain is almost impossible. As a matter of fact, attempting it ought to be classified as an extreme sport. Scot was tempted to hold up his credentials and draw his gun on the next taxi he saw, but one finally stopped and he gave the driver the cross streets of a family grocery and deli near his apartment.

He walked home through the rain with grocery bags in each arm, wondering why he hadn't been called in yet by his boss. Surely, Lawlor had made a big enough fuss that people would be standing in line to chew him out. His pager and cell phone had been with him all day, but no one had tried to contact him.

It was all for the best anyway. He was in no mood to deal with anything at this point. All he wanted to do was get back to his apartment, unpack the groceries, and dig into his Reuben sandwich.

• • •

After the Reuben and a half pint of chicken soup, Harvath thought about calling Agent Palmer at the command center in Park City to see if anything new had popped up, but decided against it. He lay down on the couch to rest his eyes for a moment and quickly fell into another deep sleep.

In the darkness of sleep, he could make out what sounded like the faint drumming of jackhammers on wet cement. The thudding was soon joined by a high-pitched screeching that somewhere in his mind he knew he recognized. He lay in a trancelike state in the warm void halfway between sleeping and waking until his mind began to assemble different explanations for what he was hearing, and he felt himself being forcibly dragged upward toward the surface world of the wakeful.

His pager, cell phone, and home phone were all going off at the same time. Startled, Scot reached for the cordless phone first.

"Harvath," he said.

"Harvath, this is Shaw," said the voice on the other end of the phone.

Scot sat straight up, trying to shake the cobwebs from his head.

Reaching to silence his vibrating phone and the pager on the coffee table, he responded to the director of Secret Service Operations for the White House. "Yes, sir. What can I do for you?"

"The director wants to see you. How soon can you be ready?"

Scot looked at his watch. "I just need to grab a quick shower. I can be ready to go in twenty minutes."

"Fine," said Shaw. "There'll be a car coming to pick you up."

• • •

Twenty minutes later on the dot, Agent Harvath was showered, shaved, and wearing a perfectly pressed dark Brooks Brothers suit under his lined trench coat as he stood outside his apartment building. By the looks of it, the rain had been falling all day. Large puddles were everywhere.

Watching his warm breath rise into the cold, damp air he saw a pair of headlights turn the corner and slow as they approached him. The car Scot had been expecting to take him to his meeting would have been a typical domestic four-door, like a Crown Victoria—something that screamed *government vehicle.* Instead, a long black limousine slowed, and the rear window rolled down as it drew even with him.

"Get in," said Stan Jameson, director of the Secret Service.

The door opened, and Scot did as he was told. He had met the director on only two occasions. The man had aged incredibly since then. *The job must be taking its toll,* he thought. As soon as Scot was in and had closed the door, the heavy, armor-plated limo growled away from the curb and headed toward D.C.

"It's been a helluva couple of days," began the director.

"Yes, sir, it has," said Harvath.

A uniformed man was sitting to the director's right, and motioning toward him, the director said, "Agent Scot Harvath, I'd like you to meet General Paul Venrick, commander of the Joint Special Operations Command."

"Pleased to meet you, sir," said Scot as he shook the man's hand. With his broad shoulders, square jaw, and flattop haircut, the general was the picture of military rectitude.

"Likewise, Agent Harvath," said the general with a strong Louisiana drawl, returning Scot's grip.

"We don't have a lot of time, Agent, so I want to make this quick," said the director. "Both General Venrick and I have read your debriefing report, but something is missing, isn't it?"

Scot was confused. If he was going to get his ass chewed out and then fired, why didn't the director have him come to his office? Why do it in his limo with the JSOC commander along for the ride?

"If you're referring, sir, to what happened with the story on CNN, I was recalled before I could type up a report and—"

"Son, I wouldn't bother betting a bicycle basket full of cow chips against what any reporter has to say. Never have trusted them, never will. At this point, I'm not judging whether you said anything to her or not. Although I'd be willing to guess, after reviewing your service file, that wherever she got her story, it didn't come from you," said the general.

Before Scot could voice his thanks, the director jumped back into the conversation. "Yes, let's hold off on the discussion of where the information came from. It does seem that there is a leak somewhere inside the organization, and that in itself is very bad, but first things first. I want to hear your version of events and what you think happened."

As the armor-plated car rolled down the rain-slicked streets, Harvath recounted his story. Not knowing if the director had been informed of his exploits at Squaw Peak or the Maddux farm, he glossed over them, implicating himself as little as possible. When he had finished, the general removed a file folder from the briefcase by his feet.

"Agent Harvath, are you familiar with a terrorist organization known as the FRC?"

"You mean the Fatah RC?" asked Scot.

"Yes."

"Sure I am. FRC stands for 'Fatah—Revolutionary Council,' also known as the Abu Nidal Organization. It was classified not too long ago by the State Department as the most dangerous terrorist group in the world. They were founded in the mid-seventies by Sabri Khalil al-Banna, aka Abu Nidal, and blazed a bloody path across the Mideast, Asia, South America, and Europe throughout the 1980s. Though the organization has struck at targets of many different nationalities, if you're a high-profile PLO member and aren't aggressive enough toward Israel, you move to the top of their hit list pretty quickly.

"There was some activity up until the early nineties, but after that the organization pretty much dropped out of sight. Nidal is rumored to be very ill, if not dead already, and hiding somewhere in Libya under that country's protection—even though they deny it. For the most part, they've been quiet, and it's been said by some that they're out of business."

"That's what we thought too, until we saw this," said the general as he withdrew a newspaper clipping from *The International Herald Tribune* and handed it to Harvath. "On January fourteenth, the Austrian Police announced the arrest of a high-ranking Fatah—Revolutionary Council member, Halima Nimer. They grabbed her as she was attempting to withdraw about seven point five million dollars from a bank in Vienna."

"Where did the FRC ever get that kind of money?" asked Scot.

"They have always been extremely well financed. For a long time Iraq and Libya were two of its biggest contributors, and they have always been very judicious with their assets. That seven point five is probably only the tip of their iceberg."

"So what does this have to do with anything?"

Now it was the director's turn to speak. He cleared his throat and said, "We've received a ransom demand for the president."

Harvath was shocked. "From the FRC? What are the demands? Are you sure they're legitimate?"

"Yes," continued the director, "we're *very* sure. There's no question. Even if there were, the demands were already en route before the leak to CNN about the kidnapping. So, we know it's not a hoax."

"En route? What do you mean?" Scot looked from the director to the general, who was letting Jameson run this part of the show.

"This morning, a prepaid Airborne Express pouch arrived at my office. It had the appropriate routing codes to bypass the usual screenings and get right to me. As the Salt Lake City Field Office's address was listed as the return address and its special agent in charge as the sender, I figured the SAC had come across something that didn't make the courier flight or wasn't important enough for it. These are copies of what was inside."

He pulled three sheets from the folder that had been sitting on his lap and handed them to Scot.

As Harvath looked at the three photocopies, the director narrated for him, "Page one is, as you can see, a Polaroid photo of the president. You can't tell in the photocopy, but his eyes are very glassy and appear unfocused. In his hands is a copy of Sunday's *Salt Lake Tribune.* You notice the president is not wearing any gloves?"

Scot nodded his head.

"Well, that brings us to page two."

Scot flipped to the next page as the director continued, "This is a photocopy of the front page of that same newspaper, which the FBI lab has verified has the president's fingerprints on it. So far, they haven't come up with any other prints."

Harvath doubted if they ever would. These guys had been exceptional, right from the start.

"And finally," said the director, "a little love note from the kidnappers themselves. It also is completely clean."

When he saw the letterhead of the stationery, Scot's jaw almost hit the floor of the limo. Knowing what he was going to say, the director raised his hand to stop him. "Yeah, the Best Western, Park City. The same hotel that housed half of the Secret Service. We're checking into it. The FBI is tracking down the prepaid Airborne envelope, but I'm not holding out any high hopes for that one. I'll give you a second so you can read the note."

Harvath did.

> *Director Jameson. How small a man you must be feeling today with the shame of the country resting so heavily upon you and your men. After years of America's meddling in the affairs of other countries, its deceit and treachery has now returned home, a grown beast, to avenge the many injustices you have wreaked far and wide. Today is a great day for Islam and one which history shall remember as marking the beginning of the end for the Great Satan.*

When Scot was finished, he handed the packet back to the director. "You must have had the profilers and handwriting people already rip through this thing six million ways from Sunday. Any luck?"

"It's all inconclusive. The Middle East analysts at the CIA have taken a look at it and say that the phrasing is not consistent with what they would expect from a Middle Easterner, even if he or she had been schooled in Britain or over here."

"He or *she?*" asked Harvath.

"We can't tell. The handwriting people seem to think there are some flourishes in the script that may suggest a woman wrote it, but then they butt up against the shrinks who think the syntax is tilted strongly in favor of a male author.

"We're cross-referencing the handwriting and the word choices through the threat databases and comparing it to any and all recorded threats against the president and the U.S. over the last fifteen years. Because we believe Abu Nidal and his FRC might be involved, we've sent a copy to the Mossad for their help. Our reasoning is that the FRC was born in that part of the world and essentially remains a Palestinian organization at heart, so the Israelis might be able to shed some light on the authorship or the subtext of the message, if there is any. The problem is, though, that every move this group has made has been extremely well choreographed."

"But maybe not choreographed well enough," broke in the general.

Scot asked, "I don't understand why you tie the FRC to all of this. It could be any Middle Eastern extremist group. Why not the PLO? I understand the body in Park City was ID'd as a long gun who worked occasionally for them."

"You're right, and based on the knowledge you have so far, I'd be inclined to agree with you," said the director, "but I told you that we had received demands."

The director pulled a microcassette recorder from his inside breast pocket. "This call came into the FBI and was received at approximately eleven-thirty eastern time today. I think you'll recognize one of the voices. The other was encrypted to disguise it, and the NSA is still trying to tear it apart. What's interesting is that the caller bypassed the switchboard and got right in on a direct line."

At this point, nothing about the kidnappers was surprising Harvath.

Jameson pressed the *play* button, and after several seconds of static hiss, they heard the voice of Gary Lawlor. "Lawlor."

"Is this Deputy Director Lawlor?" came the cyborg-sounding voice.

"That's what I said. Who's this?"

A rustling sound could be heard, which Harvath assumed was Lawlor pushing himself back from his desk so he could make sure he was hitting the correct button to begin the trace on the call.

"Who we are is not important, Mr. Lawlor. Who we *have* is what is important. Do you know who we have, Mr. Lawlor?"

"I've had a lot of crackpots call me today. Why don't you enlighten me?"

He's doing a good job, thought Scot. *Keep him talking.*

"No doubt, Agent Lawlor, you are tracing this call—"

"Now, why would I do that? Traces ain't cheap, and if I traced every call that came into my—"

"Silence!" commanded the computerized voice. "We have business to discuss, and I will not have my time wasted with your pathetic FBI games."

"It's your dime, pal. You called me, remember? Why don't you cut to the chase and tell me what this is all about. I've got a lot of work to do."

"'*The chase,*' exactly. An appropriate term for what you have been burdened with. By now you have received the envelope we sent to the director of the Secret Service containing the picture of your president, the newspaper, and our letter.

"Before we do any serious bargaining for the return of your president, we would like a show of good faith from you."

"Good faith from us?" came Lawlor's voice. "What kind of good faith?"

"The United States has imprisoned two Islamic freedom fighters, Fawad Asa and Ali Ahmed Raqim. They are to be released and flown—"

"Daffy and Goofy, the Disneyland bombers? You've got to be kidding me."

"Agent Lawlor, my people do not appreciate the lack of respect you have shown these men by assigning these ridiculous nicknames—"

"Listen, buddy, we didn't assign these guys anything but prison numbers. They *earned* those nicknames. They bomb Disneyland, and then one leaves his wallet while fleeing the scene and the other is actually dumb enough to join a class-action suit against Disneyland for the damages he suffered from the bombs he himself was a party to planting."

"Agent Lawlor, I will not repeat myself. The men are to be released and placed on a plane to Tripoli in Libya. Secondly, the Egyptian government has frozen assets of the Abu Nidal Organization in cash and property worth over four million dollars U.S. These are to be released immediately. Once you have met these conditions, we will speak again."

"This could take some time. I don't have that kind of authority. Besides, how do I know that the president is alive?"

"You don't. Good-bye."

There was the sound of the kidnapper breaking the connection, and the director hit the *stop* button on the tape.

Scot looked at the two men sitting across from him. "So that's it, then. Abu Nidal's people have the president, and they are going to use him to blackmail us into helping them rebuild their organization?"

"Not according to the vice president," said the director. "He's running the show now. Once the demand came in, the president's cabinet met and the wheels were set in motion to invoke the Twenty-fifth Amendment of the Constitution transferring all powers to Vice President Marshfield until a point at which the president will hopefully be able to reclaim them."

"Marshfield didn't waste any time, did he? Has he set up shop at the White House yet?" asked Scot.

"That was one of his first executive actions," said the director.

"I bet Shaw's having a hell of a time dealing with him."

Though he was widely perceived by outsiders as a savvy political reformer, those who knew the real Adam Marshfield knew he was nothing more than a self-aggrandizing narcissist who had achieved his political success solely through manipulation of the media and public opinion. The only reason he had made it onto Jack Rutledge's ticket was that he was well liked by the majority of the uninformed general public and his presence was considered to give the party its best shot at securing Rutledge's bid for the White House.

"As of right now, Agent Harvath, as much as many don't like him, Vice President Adam Marshfield is our acting president and commander in chief of the armed forces."

Harvath thought he noticed General Venrick wince.

"And of course once word got to the FBI about the package you had received, Lawlor hightailed it back from Park City," said Scot.

"Exactly."

"Director Jameson, how do you suppose the kidnappers obtained the routing codes to get a package right to your desk and also the direct-dial number straight into Lawlor's office?" Scot asked.

"How do *you* think they did it?" the director parried back.

"Unfortunately I think we've got a leak and a big one at that. I think this same leak might have given them the frequencies we were using so they could jam our communications while they snatched the president."

"I'd be inclined to agree," said the director.

"So would I," said General Venrick. "Agent Harvath, like I said, I've reviewed your service record, and it's pretty damn impressive. I know what an asset you were at the SEAL think tank, and I can imagine how you must feel having lost so many men on your watch."

"Thank you, sir," said Scot. "I appreciate that."

"What does your gut tell you on this one?"

"Well, General, at first, when they found that Middle Eastern guy face down in the snow, my gut said there's no way a Middle Eastern group could be behind this. There's no way they could get the amount of personnel and equipment they would need into Utah without being noticed."

"Why do you say that?" asked the general.

"Sir, I saw three African-Americans the entire time I was there, and they were all fellow Secret Service agents. Utah's about as white-bread a place as you can get. The people there notice outsiders. Sure, there's a couple of growing minority communities in Salt Lake City, but Middle Easterners would stick out like a sore thumb."

"Apparently, there was at least one. We've got his body to prove it," said the director.

"Yeah, but now he bothers me even more. Here we find this guy dead with a Skorpion next to him. He's a PLO long gun, and he's found with a weapon that pretty much screams *Liberate Palestine* right from the get-go. It doesn't fit. I mean, if he's going to do that, why not have him in *'I love Yasser'* undies? Besides, I can think of a hundred better offensive firearms he could have been using, none of which would have connected him to the Middle East."

"But, Agent Harvath, if you take one look at the man and can see he's Middle Eastern, what difference does the Skorpion make?" asked the general.

"Maybe it makes no difference at all. Why would the people on his team leave him behind? They must have known we would be able to ID him quickly and be on their trail," said Harvath.

"But," interjected the director, "it did take us a while to dig his body out from the avalanche."

"It's all true and it all makes sense, but you asked me what my gut says and it says there's no way a Middle Eastern group pulled off something this complicated."

"Agent Harvath, isn't that a little prejudiced?" asked the general.

"PC or not, Middle Eastern groups, including Abu Nidal's, are not tacticians. They walk into nightclubs strapped with explosives, plant car bombs, spray crowded markets with machine-gun fire, and fly hijacked planes full of fuel into buildings. Plain and simple, they're cowards. They won't confront anyone on a one-to-one basis. They don't have the savvy or the courage to do in-your-face operations."

"Suppose, just for a moment," offered the general, "that the reason Abu Nidal and the FRC have disappeared for so long is because they have been training for this exact scenario. One of the biggest coups in the history of terrorism—something right up there with September eleventh."

"I don't buy it. Not for a second. This kind of training would have involved years of working in cold climates practicing skiing, mountaineering, and winter warfare tactics. To train and outfit a crew from the ground up on something like this would have been exorbitantly expensive."

"The FRC has a lot of money," countered the director.

"Supposedly. All I've heard is that one of their people got caught in January trying to pull out seven point five million dollars and that the Egyptians have got another four that belongs to them. So, that's eleven point five they couldn't lay their hands on.

"That Korean jamming system, the ability to get inside information, the wherewithal to pull it off . . . I think we're dealing with something and someone completely outside the realm of Middle Eastern terrorism."

"But why would the kidnappers send a note like this," said the director, waving his photocopy, "making demands for the release of two convicted Islamic bombers with suspected FRC ties and the unfreezing of Abu Nidal's assets?"

"It doesn't make any sense," acknowledged Harvath. "But if it was the FRC, how could they have recruited a known PLO sniper, even if he has been freelancing, when the FRC has killed some of the PLO's most important members? Maybe the sniper was turned—I don't know—but it creates more questions than it answers, and that makes me nervous."

"Me too," said the general. "How about you, Stan?"

After shoving the photocopy of the kidnappers' note back into his folder, Director Jameson began massaging his temples. "Yeah, I'm nervous. The neatness of some of it is what scares me. I'm beginning to think tonight might not be such a good idea."

"What might not be such a good idea?" asked Harvath.

"The FBI trace on that phone call today locked up. We got a fix on the location of the caller, but God help us if this is wrong," said the director.

"I don't understand," said Harvath.

The general took a deep breath. "Vice President Marshfield, in accordance with the United States' position of no negotiating with terrorists, has green-lighted a Special Ops team to attempt a rescue. We're on our way to the situation room at the White House. The mission will launch in less than two hours."

"But they couldn't have possibly gathered enough intel yet. They have no idea what that team will be walking into," said Harvath.

"That's exactly what we're afraid of," said the general, "aren't we, Stan?"

CHAPTER 30

The White House situation room buzzed with noise, most of which came from Vice President Marshfield's chief of staff, Edward DaFina. The VP had wasted no time moving himself and his people into the power positions in the White House, and DaFina had bullied anyone who resisted or resented the changing of the guard. He was a perfect example of a man who sought power solely to lord it over others.

Because of his background and top secret clearance, Harvath had been invited to attend a comprehensive tactical briefing with the general. He spent two hours listening to the general and his staff discuss the makeup of the JSOC team and the reliability of their intelligence. The insertion and extraction methods were reviewed, and as the team would be supported by Israeli intelligence, the makeup and components on that end were gone over as well.

Several recent security and communications enhancements at the White House made it possible to use the situation room as a command-

and-control center for the mission. Using the sit room, as it was known, meant that not only could the vice president preside at the head of the table in the high-backed leather chair reserved for the president, but all of the players would come to him. The idea of getting the Washington establishment used to seeing him in power greatly appealed to Marshfield's ego, and so he was adamant that the main command center for observing the operation be the White House.

The directors of the FBI, CIA, and Secret Service had grudgingly agreed, only with the caveat that NSA and CIA headquarters be kept available on open lines. If the satellite picture went down, the consensus among those truly in the know was that the White House's redundant backup systems were not entirely fail-safe and might not be something to count upon.

As Harvath entered the sit room behind General Venrick, he quickly glanced around, assessing those assembled. The aforementioned directors of the various agencies were present, accompanied by their aides. JSOC brass who hadn't shuttled to the Mediterranean to be on-site were in attendance. Harvath was well acquainted with several of those present, and he nodded in their direction as he caught their eyes. There were also other military and governmental personnel present whom no one bothered to introduce.

Scanning the long cherrywood table, Harvath saw Gary Lawlor and at first thought the comment that rang out from that end of the room had come from him.

"What the hell is he doing here?" asked the voice.

As Scot focused upon a group of people who were not seated, General Venrick said, "I believe Agent Harvath can be of service to us in this operation, and I have asked him to join us."

"From what I hear, the only person Agent Harvath seems to be of service to is himself, that is, when he is not being of service to CNN. And he was considered such an impediment that our own deputy director of the FBI had to have him removed from the case." The man stepped away from the group and leaned on the far end of the table. Scot could see him clearly now, Edward DaFina.

Director Jameson piped up before anyone had a chance to respond. It was obvious that there was no love lost between the two. "That is all still under investigation, DaFina, and you know it."

"Correct me if I'm wrong, but the Secret Service did succeed in losing the president, didn't it? I mean, that's why we're all here, right?"

Scot had never been one to let others fight his own battles. "Chief of Staff DaFina, I personally knew every single one of the Secret Service agents who died trying to protect the president and his daughter. As a matter of fact, from what I saw in Park City, had I not been retasked to Goldilocks's detail, there's probably no doubt she and I would be among the dead as well. So considering that you have absolutely zero idea of what the Secret Service has been through and what we go through on a daily basis, I suggest you get to the point. If you have one."

Gary Lawlor shook his head and began to massage his eyes with his thumb and forefinger. He hadn't been able to believe it when Harvath arrived with General Venrick and the Secret Service director. The kid had as many lives as a cat. Somehow, somewhere, someone had decided to cut him some more slack, but once again he was quickly hanging himself with it. Lawlor was still upset about what had transpired in Park City and was not going to stick his neck out to help defend the headstrong Secret Service agent anymore. Harvath was completely on his own as far as Lawlor was concerned.

"My point, Agent Harvath," said DaFina, warming to the challenge, "is that you and your agency were charged with a task and you failed. Failed miserably, I might add. To compound the damage, you tampered with no less than three related crime scenes and, until I am convinced otherwise, leaked sensitive information to the press. *That* is my point."

"This is a bunch of bullshit," said the general. Anyone who had sheepishly been listening to the exchange, pretending not to hear it, now turned his or her eyes toward the man who had drawn himself to his full height. "None of this has any bearing on why we're all here.

We have asked Agent Harvath to come along because of his vast antiterrorist experience and in the hopes that as one of the sole survivors of the kidnapping, he might be able to help us shed more light on what we are facing and what we will do going forward."

"Going forward?" asked DaFina. "General, you don't sound as if you believe this operation tonight will be successful. Why is that?"

"Why is that? It's because we haven't had sufficient time to gather the appropriate intelligence to mount an effective recovery."

"General, when this whole thing blew, were you or were you not involved in our strategic assessment meeting?"

"I was, but—"

"General, you were the one person who advocated moving as fast as we could as soon as we had reliable information to act upon—"

"Mr. DaFina, that's the last time you are going to interrupt me. As far as what I said, you seem to have ignored the fact that the word I used was *reliable.*"

Unfazed, DaFina continued, "General Venrick, I don't know how much more specific you need your information to be. One of the kidnappers, a freelance Middle Eastern sniper who often worked for pro-Palestinian liberation groups, was found dead at the scene. We received proof that some organization does indeed have the president, and then they asked for the release of two Islamic terrorists with suspected FRC connections who are being held in this country. When their ransom demand was phoned into the FBI, we were able to pinpoint where it came from. What more do you need?"

"What more does he need?" interjected Harvath. "For starters, how about intelligence that the phone that was used is actually in the same location the president is being held?"

"Agent Harvath," said DaFina, "I don't really care for your opinion, but I'll answer you anyway. The Israeli Mossad has assets throughout Lebanon and in particular the area we're concentrating on. The Syrian government also has its sources—"

"The Syrians?" It was now the CIA director's chance to interject. "You contacted the Syrians without consulting with my office first?"

"First of all, Director Vaile, it was Vice President Marshfield who contacted the Syrian president, and secondly, I hardly think—"

"No kidding," said Harvath.

DaFina glared at Harvath, and the CIA director took the opportunity to continue his attack. "You have absolutely no idea what you are doing. This whole operation may have been compromised."

"Director Vaile, the vice president and I are confident that the participation of the Syrians and the Israelis can only help this endeavor."

"Jesus," said Harvath. "That's it, isn't it? Not only will the vice president look good if he can get the president back, but a U.S.–Israeli operation that involves the Syrians could go a long way on the world stage in helping to begin mending their fences. You and Marshfield are going to squeeze as much political juice out of this thing as you can."

"Agent Harvath, you are way out of line," barked DaFina.

"Am I? I don't think there's a person in this room who isn't well aware that the president seriously doubts whether he will run for a second term. This whole thing stinks. This is a half-assed game to you, and you're asking good men to put their lives on the line for it."

"Agent Harvath, you sound as if you don't want the president to be recovered," continued DaFina.

"*What I want* is for the president to be recovered, but with no further American lives lost in the process."

"A commendable goal that I think we can all agree with. Good evening all," said Vice President Marshfield as he strutted in.

A chorus of "Good evening, Mr. Vice President" rang throughout the sit room. The assembled men and women took their places around the table, and as expected, the vice president sat at the head in the chair that had always been reserved for the president himself.

"Gentlemen," the vice president began, "I know we are on a tight schedule, so I think it's best if we turn this over right away to General Venrick, commander of the Joint Special Operations Command. General?"

The general stood. "Thank you, Mr. Vice President. As you all know, the intelligence we have been able to gather thus far indicates that the president was taken hostage by the Abu Nidal organization, the Fatah RC, to be ransomed in exchange for Egypt's unfreezing certain assets and the return of the Disneyland bombers. Our attempts at gaining further intel as to the health and well-being of Abu Nidal, the group's supposed leader, have been unsuccessful. What we do know is that the call the FBI received from the kidnappers was traced to a building south of Beirut outside the town of Saïda, or Sidon, as it is better known, on the Lebanese coast of the Mediterranean Sea.

"According to intelligence provided by the Israelis, this building is believed to be tied to the FRC organization, though further information than that is not available, which is troubling."

"Troubling?" said the vice president, raising his eyebrows, his hands crossed in front of him.

"Yes, sir," continued General Venrick. "The only surveillance of the building we have been able to run is via satellite, which took us longer than we would have liked due to retasking and getting it into an alternate orbit. While the Mossad does have assets in and around Sidon, there has not been proper time to conduct full-fledged surveillance."

"Correct me if I'm wrong, General, but you were the one who said we needed to strike fast if we were to have any chance of getting the president back," said the vice president. Chief of Staff DaFina leaned back in his chair with a smug look of satisfaction and stared at the general, daring him to defy the vice president.

"Yes, sir, I did say that, but—"

"Are you having second thoughts, General? I am sure you would agree with me that this is a time for action and not indecision," said the vice president.

"I do agree, sir, but going off half-cocked can result in the loss of not only lives on our recovery team, but also the president's, if he is actually in that building."

"You have doubts as to whether the president is actually there? Why didn't you bring these to my attention earlier?" said the vice president, knowing full well why the general had not been able to communicate his concerns.

"Mr. Vice President, I tried to contact you several times, but Chief of Staff DaFina told me you were busy and that he would have you get back to me."

Marshfield looked at DaFina. "Is this true?"

Feigning contrition, DaFina said, "Mr. Vice President, the past forty-eight hours have been absolute turmoil for all of us. If the general was having trouble getting through, I don't know why he didn't come to the White House to share these feelings with you in person."

Incredulous, the general answered, "Number one, I figured if I couldn't get him on the phone, I certainly wasn't going to be able to get in to see him here, and number two, I had an operation to assemble." Turning his attention back to the vice president, he continued, "Sir, even with our most sophisticated technology, the building in question has not offered even the slightest clue as to who or what might be inside."

"And this troubles you because . . . ?" asked the vice president.

"It troubles me because our men will be going in blind. They don't know how many terrorists are inside or where the president is being kept, if he's there at all."

"Are we going to go through this again?" asked DaFina, pretending to be exasperated.

The vice president silenced DaFina with a wave of his hand. "General, do you have any information that suggests that the president is not being held at this location?"

"No, sir, but by the same token we don't have enough to suggest that he is either. After lengthy discussion with my staff as well as Agent Harvath—"

"Agent Harvath?" asked the vice president. "Is he now a member of the Joint Special Operations Command?"

"No, sir, but his past experience in counterterrorism and JSOC coordinated operations I think more than qualifies him to—"

The vice president raised his hand, this time indicating that he wished for the general to be silent. "Agent Harvath, do you have something you wish to add to this, because I'm sure we would all be very interested to hear it, considering everything that has happened already."

Ignoring the vice president's sarcasm, Harvath stood as the general retook his seat. "Thank you, Mr. Vice President. I have to admit that I am in agreement with the general."

"And why is that?"

"There are a lot of pieces in this puzzle that don't make sense. We think we are making progress, when the truth is, the kidnappers are three steps ahead of us. They have anticipated every move we make and are ready for it. With the level of sophistication we have seen on their part, I find it suspicious that they allowed the ransom call to be traced."

Lawlor's head tilted almost imperceptibly to the left as he pondered the implications of what Harvath had just said.

"And you enlightened General Venrick with your wisdom?" asked the vice president.

"Everything except my opinion about the trace." Not wanting to admit that his constant headache might be affecting his judgment, Scot offered his excuse for not having come up with this insight earlier. "It wasn't until I arrived here that this piece of information fell into place. It just doesn't feel right."

"'Doesn't feel right'? You want me to forgo maybe the only chance we have to get the president back because *it doesn't feel right?* Agent Harvath, despite your feelings, do we have any information that indicates the president is anywhere else?"

"No, sir."

"And have you thought about what kind of situation we might be in if we pass up this chance tonight and the president is moved tomorrow to another location from which the kidnappers do not make any further phone calls that can be traced?"

"No, sir."

"And even if the recovery team does not find the president at this location tonight, have you thought about the intelligence we might be able to gather if we are able to take into custody any operatives of the

Fatah organization who might have some connection to the kidnapping?"

"No, sir," said Harvath for the third time. He could see exactly where the vice president was going with this reasoning. It was drastically flawed, but as he was the acting commander in chief, there was no way he could be overridden, no matter how many holes there were in his plan. The deck had been stacked against Harvath and General Venrick, but it had been used to make a house of cards. It wouldn't take much to topple it, but by that time it would be too late.

"Agent Harvath, as far as I can tell, you have not thought this mission and its consequences out in their entirety. We proceed as planned," ordered the vice president.

Choking on a response that would only have gotten him in deeper trouble and surely thrown out of the sit room, Scot sat back down. He reached for the carafe in front of him, poured a glass of water, and popped two more Tylenols. This was going to be a very long night.

CHAPTER 31

So far, the JSOC mission was going according to plan. The recovery team rendezvoused with a small fishing boat off the coast of Israel just after 2:00 A.M. The contingent of Navy SEALs had been tasked to enforce a NATO blockade in the Persian Gulf. Since speed was of the essence for this mission, code-named Rapid Return, they were the best qualified and most readily available choice for the recovery.

The dark, humid air hung over the south Lebanese coast like a wet blanket. It was stifling, yet the team members paid no attention to the heat. Their minds were focused on their assignment and the role each would need to play for it to be successful.

Back in Washington, D.C., safely tucked away in the White

House sit room, Scot Harvath knew exactly what the SEALs on that small fishing boat were feeling. Out of habit, his pulse picked up and the adrenaline began to surge as a quiet communication was relayed via satellite halfway around the world through the recessed speakers of the sit room.

"Jonah, this is Ishmael. No bites. We're headed in," said the voice of the SEAL team leader.

"Nothing on the nets either. Hope you land a big one. Happy fishing," came the response from the JSOC command center.

Even though General Venrick wore a headset that kept him continuously in the loop, he had been furious that the vice president had insisted he watch the operation from the sit room. The general trusted his people at JSOC command, but when it came right down to it, he was in charge and should have been there, rather than in the sit room as if it were a skybox at a Redskins game.

The general had explained the codes and call signs to Harvath as they waited for the mission to begin. With that information, Scot was able to translate the exchange he was hearing.

Harvath knew from experience that anywhere from one hundred to two hundred yards out, depending on the conditions, the team would slide over the sides of their inflatable and into the water. Unsheathing their knives, team members would rip holes in the craft, and its heavy outboard engine would pull it straight to the bottom. Before any wreckage could possibly be discovered, the team would be long gone.

All eyes were glued to a series of monitors strategically interspersed across the front of the sit room. There were also individual monitors recessed at each setting in the table. Internal JSOC communications from the command center drifted down from the overhead speakers. The constant narrative relayed data on the mission's progress and would be automatically interrupted any time a member of Rapid Return's recovery force broke radio silence.

Glancing around the room, Scot noticed that both the general and CIA director Vaile had laptops plugged into the White House's secure communication links. Undoubtedly, each was keeping in touch with their respective offices through private means as well. A very smart idea.

Harvath peered at the screens in the front of the room. They were considerably bigger than the monitor recessed within the table in front of him. Even though he could switch from picture to picture from where he sat, he preferred the wider panorama up front.

Each of the SEALs was outfitted with a fiber-optic night-vision wide-angle-lens camera that relayed back exactly what was in their field of view. The largest of the monitors was a flat-panel device showing images collected by an NSA spy satellite network known as Chaperone.

Chaperone was a highly sophisticated reconnaissance system designed to gather intelligence and assist in clandestine operations occurring predominantly at night. Chaperone incorporated night-vision capabilities unrivaled by any other intelligence-gathering system in existence. As it utilized several overlapping satellites, "loitering" time over a target had been greatly increased from times past.

The main flat-paneled screen at the front of the room provided a picture-in-picture view. The largest and most prominent image was of the beach that the SEAL team was swimming toward. In the lower-right-hand corner of the screen was the satellite image of what Harvath assumed was the primary objective, the FRC compound.

When the SEALs made land, they had just under a mile run inland, where a truck and two drivers would be waiting for them. Secreted in the back of the truck, the Special Ops team would be driven to within a few blocks of their target.

No one in the room spoke. The chatter of the JSOC command center and intermittent beeps, presumably from the satellites, had an eerie NASA quality to it all, as if the group were waiting for a fragile capsule to return from the dark side of the moon and report in. Scot realized that there was nothing that could be said at a moment like this. Besides, the general was still in charge and things needed to be kept absolutely quiet so he could work. He had insisted that was the one condition he would not compromise on if he was going to be at the sit room instead of JSOC command when Rapid Return went into action.

The minutes seemed like hours as the SEAL team made their way inland toward the truck. A monitor in the upper-right corner of the room showed a live picture of JSOC command. Harvath's analogy of a NASA mission hadn't been far off the mark. JSOC command looked very similar to what he had seen of Mission Control in Texas. JSOC operatives sat at long rows of computer terminals that tiered like amphitheater steps as they rose upward from the many screens covering the wall in front of them. Knowing the military's penchant for organization, Harvath assumed that the operatives would be grouped according to their skills, such as communications and satellite technology, with the most important operatives being placed in the very back near the top brass.

Each member of the SEAL team wore a special set of wide-view night-vision goggles. Recently developed for Special Operations Forces, the goggles not only improved the soldiers' field and depth of vision, but also allowed for a small computer screen to be toggled on and off in a preselected part of the goggles. On that screen, a team leader could see whatever any of his men were seeing via the fiber-optic camera attached to the top of the goggles, and it also allowed team members to view any information that their commanders wanted them to see, such as directional maps or the images coming off the Chaperone network.

Harvath stared at the intent faces of the SEALs shown in night-vision green via the cameras of their fellow soldiers sitting across from them in the truck. The detail in the pictures was astounding. The technology Scot had used as an active SEAL had been mind-boggling, but in the short amount of time he had been out, it had morphed to such an advanced degree, he almost couldn't believe it.

The narrative voice from JSOC command could be heard in the sit room once again, and everyone leaned forward into the table.

"One minute to delivery," said the voice.

The small picture-in-picture on Chaperone's screen grew, dwarfing the other as the Rapid Return team entered an area close enough to the objective that everything could be seen on one screen.

Entering a street of decaying buildings flanked by the ever-encroaching desert, the truck slowed. Having used Chaperone to try to scan the immediate area for any potentially hostile targets, JSOC command queried Israeli intelligence as to their ground assets posted at both ends of the street. The word came back all clear, and JSOC hailed the SEAL leader.

"Jonah, this is Ishmael. Time to enter the whale. Over."

"Enter the whale. Roger. Jonah out," came the response.

The team leader gave the go command. One by one, the SEALs jumped from the truck, rolled when they hit the ground, and immediately took cover.

Except for the sound of the rapidly receding truck, the street was completely silent. Knowing that police and civil defense patrols were on sporadic and unreliable schedules, the recovery team did a quick check of their equipment and moved out.

Each member of the team had memorized the satellite reconnaissance photos that showed their delivery point, objective, the extraction point, and two backup possibilities that would be used only if needed. Their silenced MP10s at the ready, Rapid Return's recovery team picked their way through the rubble-strewn alley in front of them and headed east toward their objective.

Advancing cautiously, the team froze sporadically at sounds coming from the windows above. Even though the men were disguised in the robes and headdresses of poor villagers, if any local got a good look at the heavily outfitted assault team, the alarm would surely be raised.

Dangerously close to the objective, the team, as planned, readied to split up. Although the Israelis had cross-trained with the SEALs in the past, General Venrick had insisted they be on-site only for reconnaissance and support if needed. The actual assault would be carried out by Rapid Return's American recovery team.

"Ishmael, this is Jonah. We are ready to enter the whale. Can you give us a sit rep? Over."

"Roger, Jonah. Chaperone shows you are all clear."

Too clear, Harvath thought as he looked at the screen in front of him. If the FRC was hiding the president in this location, it would be much more heavily guarded. Maybe, though, the FRC thought posting guards would attract too much attention. What was odd was that U.S. satellites had been able to show people coming in and out of the FRC building, but had not been able to penetrate to see inside. These mud-and-brick houses were nothing for the NSA's peekaboo technology, but the target building had been shielded with some sort of protective material, impervious to all the NSA's gadgetry.

As if reading Harvath's thoughts, General Venrick spoke into his lip mike. "Jonah, this is the Old Man. Are you in a position to ascertain the nature of the whale's skin?"

The fact that the satellite hadn't been able to penetrate the building had bothered Venrick as well.

Speaking quietly into his throat mike, the team leader responded, "Negative. It looks the same as all the others."

Checking Chaperone one last time, the general responded, "Jonah, you may cast your bread upon the waters. Over."

"Roger that. Jonah out."

With a flick of his fingers, the team leader sent two members scurrying around the back of the houses toward the rear of the target building. Two more were sent to the home just adjacent. Moving quickly and using the shadows for cover as much as possible, the remaining four members of the squad headed toward the ugly crimson-colored door of a house just down the street from the target building.

As arranged by the Israelis, the door was unlocked. Weapons ready, the team entered the house, sweeping the first and then the second floor. Satisfied that it was clean, they carefully made their way to the roof. Slowly, the team leader raised the trapdoor and peered out. Confident there was no immediate danger, he took off his goggles and took a pair of more powerful night-vision binoculars from his pack. From what he could see, everything was quiet. He slid from underneath the hatch and crawled along the roof to its southeast corner.

So as not to give himself away, he balanced his goggles on the parapet wall of the roof and aimed them toward the objective. The team's second in command toggled to the leader's vision screen and, not seeing anything in the vicinity of the objective, flashed the leader a thumbs-up.

The man known as Jonah retrieved his goggles, crept forward toward the corner of the roof, and gently raised himself to look over the parapet wall with his binoculars. The objective was perfectly quiet, not even anyone on its roof. These Fatah guys were either very confident or very stupid.

Crawling back to the trapdoor, Jonah put his night-vision goggles back on before signaling the team's sniper that it was all clear. Squeezing through the tight opening, the muscular and deadly accurate twenty-five-year-old rolled onto the roof and prepped his weapon.

He carried a silenced Walther WA2000 sniping rifle, which fired a .300 Winchester Magnum cartridge. Even without its Leupold night-vision scope and laser range finder, there wasn't much the sniper couldn't hit. With the specially designed barrel clamped at the front and rear, the torque from the large bullet wouldn't lift it away from its intended target. The barrel had also been fluted, further reducing the gun's vibrations on firing. With its pistol-style grip and customized butt and cheek pads, this weapon would do very nicely if anybody chose to come snooping around while operation Rapid Return was in progress.

Jonah and his two remaining team members were to make the frontal assault. Exiting the house where they'd left their sniper, the men picked their way down the deserted street, breathing a little easier knowing they were under the watchful and protective eyes of one of the best long guns the SEALs had ever trained.

The key elements of the mission were speed, surprise, and overwhelming force. As Jonah and his men neared the target building, all of its shutters were drawn. Adjusting the fine tuning on his goggles, Jonah looked up toward the flat roof and noticed that there were indeed sheets of what looked like lead protruding along the edges, covered with plaster and mud. Confident that the right people back in D.C. had seen what he had and knew what it was, he and his men carefully scanned the perimeter. There were no signs of any intrusion devices, not even dogs.

"Ishmael, this is Jonah," he whispered, his throat mike perfectly picking up every word. "It is *very* quiet. Do you detect any motion?"

"Negative, Jonah. You are all clear. Proceed when ready."

By means of the arched courtyard, two Rapid Return members were able to scale the common wall to reach the adjoining roof next door undetected.

Resisting the urge to make a joke about what a great haircut he could give the two team members who had just climbed upon the roof, the sniper kept his communication to the bare minimum and said into his throat mike, "Alpha, this is Watchdog. I have you in my sights and you are all clear."

"Affirmative," responded Alpha's leader.

Hearing that Alpha was on the next roof, Jonah said into his throat mike, "Alpha, the whale's skin may be tougher than we thought. Get over and check it out. I want an assessment ASAP."

"Roger," came Alpha's response.

Quietly, the two men picked their way across the roof of the adjoining house, wary of weak spots thanks to a training story of an operative who fell through a roof in Panama.

Jonah and his team members stayed concealed in the shadows just down from the front of the target building as the other team waited behind it.

Finally, Alpha checked back in. "Jonah, this is Alpha. It looks like the roof entry is metal, pretty thick, but the hinges are on the outside. With a little bit of give glue, I think we can breach it." *Give glue* referred to the small tubes of specially formulated acid paste that the teams carried with them on missions where doors would need to be breached and hinges couldn't simply be blown away. Once applied, it ate through almost any type of metal in only a matter of seconds.

"Hold on, Alpha," said Jonah. "Bravo, are you in position?"

"Roger. Good to go," came the voice of the Bravo leader.

"Okay then, Alpha. Start the glue, and let us know when you're ready," said Jonah.

Creeping beneath the windows of the house, Jonah and his men made their way to the old wooden front door. As he'd figured, it was locked, but it would be nothing for them.

"Watchdog, you got the door in case they don't like Avon calling?" asked Jonah.

"Knock, knock, motherfucker. Just like when we did Qaddafi. I've gotcha covered," replied Watchdog.

"Alpha, how are we doing?"

"Almost there."

"Good, listen up. Just like we planned. Fast and furious. Flash bangs first. Does everyone copy?"

"Bravo. Roger."

"Alpha. Roger . . . And it looks like we are ready to crash the party. On your command, Jonah. Over."

The men in the sit room held their breath.

"Okay. On my command. Firemen, take your positions. Pitchers, ready your flash bangs. We go in five . . . four . . . three . . . two . . . one. Now!"

In sync, Jonah's men breached their respective entry points, tossed in their flash bangs, and quickly followed once the concussions had detonated.

What Rapid Return's recovery team never had a chance to see was the white-hot blaze that moments later appeared on Chaperone's screen as the entire street, and the house they had entered, were reduced to dust. The SEALs, including their sniper, never saw it coming.

CHAPTER 32

At the same moment Chaperone showed the building exploding, the night-vision images from the SEAL battle cams disappeared and were replaced on each monitor with a chilling two-word message: *Off Line.*

The shock and silence in the sit room were quickly replaced by a frenzy of activity. Glancing up at the monitor that fed a live picture from JSOC command, Harvath noticed it was chaotic there as well.

Every phone in the sit room was being used by people trying to figure out what had happened. Scot was closest to General Venrick, and he listened as Venrick tried to get a handle on things. " . . . We were able to figure that out from here. It looks like it was a very big one. At least one to two square blocks from what Chaperone is showing us right now . . .

"First things first. Can we confirm the status of the Rapid Return team? . . . What about the Israeli assets on-site? . . . My God. Only one? Have him get in there and get a better look. . . . We have got to get confirmation. If there are injured men there, we need to get them out. . . . I agree. We began to worry about it as well, but it's a little late for that now. . . . All right. Get on the Israelis, and get back to me as soon as you get an update. In the meantime, I want you to roll back the tape on the battle cams to one minute before they went off-line and feed it back here in slow mo. . . . Negative. Until we know what the situation is, all teams are to stand by. That's it. Get going."

The general shook his head in disgust, feeling he should have pressed the vice president harder to postpone the recovery attempt until they had gathered more intelligence. Instead, a crack SEAL team had walked right into a trap. His increased dislike of the vice president was surpassed only by the shame he felt in losing men under his command. This had been a half-baked idea from the start and he should have stopped it.

As JSOC command fed back the battle cam images in slow mo, the general used his com link to give orders to freeze-frame certain images and rewind others. A team of military experts, aided by the ATF, would be poring over these pictures for months ascertaining whether there was one blast or several, where the blast or blasts originated, as well as what type of explosive device was used. But for now, the general needed to put together his *own* picture of what had happened.

The images showed that each of the assault teams was able to successfully breach its entry point and pitch in its flash bangs, hoping to stun any immediate targets with the blinding white light and concussion tremors they emitted. After the teams entered, the battle cams showed that they moved quickly and began to secure the rooms on their respective levels. The cams showed what appeared to be sleeping men in some of the rooms, but would the kidnappers actually booby-trap themselves?

Before any of the men could be secured with the plastic riot cuffs that the teams always carried, there was a bright flash and the cams went off-line. Because of the need for his vision to be unimpaired while he looked through the night-vision scope on his rifle, the sniper's battle cam wasn't of much help. His goggles had been placed on top of his pack, off to his left-hand side. His images lasted for only a few frames more than those of his teammates, who presumably were at the epicenter of the explosion. Whatever had been used was extremely powerful. Chances were low to absolutely nonexistent that any of the team had survived.

In the midst of the chaos, no one noticed that the president's direct line rang and that the vice president's chief of staff had answered it until he cupped the mouthpiece and screamed for everyone to quiet down.

The entire room was taken aback. His face was ashen. "How did you get this number?" DaFina asked.

Lawlor knew exactly who was on the phone and was the first one to react. He picked up the phone in front of him and dialed faster than he ever had in his life. When a voice answered on the other end, he gave his name, password, and location. He gave the orders to begin a trace and was floored by the response, "No can do."

"What?" Lawlor hissed into the phone. "You've got to be kidding me. This is a matter of national security. Now trace the damn call!"

Lawlor's boss, FBI director Sorce put a hand on his arm and whispered, "Gary, they can't trace any calls coming or going from the sit room. It's impossible."

"What do you mean, *impossible?*" he asked.

"When the room and equipment were updated, so were the communications. The lines had to be tap- and trace-proof. Besides, who would have ever envisioned a scenario like this where a trace would be necessary?"

Lawlor felt impotent. All he could do was sit and watch. The worst of it was that DaFina was doing all of the talking.

"He wants me to put him on speakerphone. How do I do that?" DaFina asked, once again cupping the mouthpiece.

Two button punches later and the cyborg-style voice that Lawlor remembered all too well clicked out of the overhead speakers.

"Good evening, gentlemen," the voice said.

Since the kidnappers had originally established contact with Lawlor, no one objected as he rose from his seat to walk over to the active phone. As he rounded the table, Vice President Marshfield held up a hand, stopping him in his tracks. Lawlor was stunned.

The voice continued, "I trust your vice president is present?"

DaFina slid the phone toward him. "Yes, I am here. Who is this?"

"More silly games," said the voice. "You know exactly who this is. Did you enjoy our little demonstration?"

"What are you talking about?"

"Mr. Vice President, I will say this only once. Do not play games with me."

"Where is the president?"

"He is quite comfortable, I assure you."

"How can we be sure?"

"Mr. Vice President, we have already proven that we have him and that we are capable of outthinking you and your military. The explosion was quite an unfortunate, but necessary occurrence. So many souls called to Allah, unwitting of the role they have played in the Jihad."

"Is that what this is all about, some kind of holy war?"

"I commend you, Mr. Vice President. Your knowledge of foreign affairs is greater than your critics give you credit for."

The insult raised the hairs on the back of the vice president's neck. Inwardly, almost every member in the sit room would have congratulated the kidnapper for that jibe if he hadn't been behind so much death and mayhem.

"You will not get away with this. I guarantee you," said the vice president.

"But, I already have."

"What do you want?"

"First, I want to be treated with some respect for my intelligence. Did you actually think I would not know when I called the FBI that they would start an immediate trace? Do you think after all of my careful planning I would allow this dance to be so quickly brought to an end? By underestimating me, you may be forced to pay the price twice."

"Twice?" said the vice president. "What do you mean *twice?*"

"By now you should be very well aware that your men did not survive the explosion we set. That was the first price. If we were able to slay any of the Israeli pigs that might have been working with the U.S.A. in their feeble rescue attempt, then all the better. But, the second price will come if you do not cooperate. Evidence will be produced that will link this explosion back to you and the unrecognized State of Israel. It will be seen as an act of U.S.-supported Israeli terrorism against the Palestinian people."

All eyes in the room were upon the vice president.

"Whatever evidence you might fabricate, it will never work."

"Just as a plot to kidnap your president would never work? *Tsk, tsk,* Mr. Vice President. I believe you are still underestimating me."

"You know, Mr. . . . if it is Mr. I don't even know your name," said the vice president.

"My name is not important. What is important are my demands. I want my men released immediately."

"It is the policy of the United States government not to negotiate with terrorists."

"Is it really? Is this the same no-negotiation policy that was in effect during your arms for hostages fiasco with Iran?" asked the voice.

"That was then, and this is now. We absolutely do not negotiate with terrorists. The two men you want killed scores of innocent Americans."

"In our opinion, Mr. Vice President, there is no such thing as an innocent American, and further, how many innocent people have been killed throughout the Middle East as a result of the meddling of the United States?"

Several people at the table were motioning for the vice president to shut up and discontinue his hard line with the kidnappers, but he ignored them.

"I'll make you a deal," said the vice president, pausing for effect.

"A deal? You are in no position to make demands of us! It is we who have your president, and it is we who will make the demands of you. As your show of good faith, you will release our men as we have requested and you will convince Egypt to unfreeze our assets. You will do this immediately!" said the voice, and then the line went dead.

Lawlor leaned over to his boss. "Hell of a negotiator. Where'd this asshole learn his technique?"

The FBI director didn't answer. He knew everyone else in the room was thinking the exact same thing. The vice president was completely out of his league.

CHAPTER 33

After the meeting in the sit room was adjourned, everyone quietly filed out, still in shock. They were horrified not only by the failure of Rapid Return and the loss of top-rate operatives, but also by the way the vice president had handled the kidnappers' phone call.

Director Jameson gave Scot a subtle cue to hang back with him. In a few moments the only other people still sitting at the table were the directors of the FBI and CIA, along with Gary Lawlor.

"It looks like your instincts were right," said the CIA director to Harvath.

"It didn't do those men much good, though," replied Scot.

"What could you have done?"

"I've asked myself that a million times. Not only about tonight, but Sunday too. These guys, whoever they are, really know what they're doing."

"What I want to know," said Lawlor, "is how the hell they got my direct line as well as the president's here in the sit room."

As the lock on the soundproof door of the sit room clicked and was followed by the hiss of it swinging open, the men fell silent.

"Don't you men have work to do?" asked Chief of Staff DaFina as he walked across the room to retrieve a file he had left on the table.

Vaile beat the others to the punch. "You know what, DaFina? What we're doing and how we're doing it is none of your goddamn business."

Harvath was taken by surprise. Director Vaile had a reputation for being unfailingly diplomatic. Both DaFina and his boss, the vice president, rubbed even the calmest of people the wrong way.

"I'm sure the vice president wouldn't see it that way," replied a defensive DaFina.

DaFina was all hot air, a bully. The minute someone stood up to him, he hid behind the vice president's skirts. Harvath let out an audible sigh of contempt, and DaFina turned on him.

"And you. I wasn't finished with you, Harvath," he said, turning his gaze toward Secret Service director Jameson and FBI deputy director Lawlor. "Is it or is it not true that Agent Harvath disrupted and possibly contaminated three separate crime scenes and assaulted a federal officer?"

For some reason, probably his intense dislike for the chief of staff, Lawlor changed his earlier stance and chose to come to Scot's defense. "We're looking into it."

"Looking into it? From what I hear, it was *you* that had him recalled for it!" DaFina's feigned anger was growing with each passing second, as was his satisfaction. He knew he had them on the ropes, and he grabbed at the opportunity to regain the control Vaile had taken from him. "Director Jameson, why hasn't this man been placed on leave until a full-scale investigation can be conducted?"

"I have yet to fully debrief him. This is a Secret Service matter and will be handled as such. I hardly think we need the vice president's chief of staff telling us how to do our jobs."

"Well, obviously somebody should."

"Just like somebody told you it was okay to answer the president's secure line?" fired Harvath.

Embarrassed, but not letting on, DaFina continued. "Director Jameson, like it or not, Vice President Marshfield is in charge and may be for quite some time. If, and I stress the *if,* the president does not return safely, the vice president will finish out his term. I need not remind you that your position as director of the Secret Service has already been severely jeopardized. If, and I am stressing the *if* again, the president does not return to his office, you will retain your directorship only by the consent of Vice President Marshfield. Do I make myself clear?"

Jameson was up against it. As much as he hated to admit it, DaFina was right. Before he could respond, though, DaFina continued his attempt to roll over him. "I want this man," he said, pointing at

Harvath, "suspended immediately, pending a full investigation. I don't want to see him near the White House or anywhere else for that matter. Am I clear?"

"I'll take it under advisement. In the meantime, I want to make sure you are completely clear on something. Short of a horrific constitutional crisis that would put you in the Oval Office, I am still the director of the Secret Service. I don't take orders from you. Got me?" asked Jameson.

"Director Jameson, I warn you that you are walking a very, very fine line. I can assure you that when I speak, I am speaking for the vice president, who, per the cabinet's invoking of the Twenty-fifth Amendment, is now acting president and commander in chief. Agent Harvath is to be suspended, period. Understood?"

Harvath knew he had nothing to lose and decided he wasn't going to let this pip-squeak get the last word. "You've got more to worry about than me, you know."

"You just won't disappear, will you? Of course we have more to worry about than just you," replied DaFina.

"A lot more. First, you've got a leak somewhere. Someone with some pretty substantial access. Those kidnappers had help. High-level help. And then—"

Against his better judgment, Lawlor tried to save him. "Scot, shut it."

"Agent Lawlor, with all due respect, I'm going to listen to what Agent Harvath has to say, because I guarantee you these will be the last words he ever utters in his capacity as an active Secret Service agent. So," continued DaFina as he made his way around the table so he could stand right above Harvath, "what else do you have to say? You couldn't possibly dig your grave any deeper than you have already. Or could you?"

Standing above him was an obvious power play, meant to intimidate, but Scot Harvath wasn't easily intimidated. In fact, the move pissed him off. He wasn't an idiot, and he'd been trying to couch what he was planning to say as diplomatically as possible, but his anger was building and quickly getting the better of him. He fought hard to keep it under control.

Harvath had swiveled his chair to the right as DaFina approached and leaned slightly back, assuming a relaxed, nonthreatened posture. "Mr. DaFina—"

"That's Chief of Staff DaFina to you, Harvath! Get it right. You know, it's all starting to become clear to me how this whole thing happened. Some of the people around here might be impressed with your SEAL background, but it doesn't impress me. You fucked up big time as the advance man. The whole Secret Service fucked up, and I don't give a rat's ass that you saved the president's daughter.

"The president is gone, and I don't need to go looking far and wide for somewhere to lay the blame. It's sitting right here in front of me." DaFina punctuated his next remark by poking Harvath in the shoulder with his pudgy finger. "So, if you've got something to say, then say it, because your career is finished!"

Harvath snapped. Grabbing DaFina's finger, he stood up from the chair and gave the finger a good twist, making DaFina's arm go limp, and then bent it behind him. He raised DaFina's hand upward toward the back of his neck and leaned forward to speak into his ear. "Yeah, I've got something to say. First, your mother should have taught you not to point at people, *especially* a SEAL. There's nothing that pisses me off more than when people point at me. It's not very polite. Second, you and your boss are playing a very deadly game. His *no-negotiating-with-terrorists* line doesn't fool anyone, especially me. You know what?"

DaFina winced in pain.

Harvath continued, "Your little call to the Syrians didn't fool me either. It was plain to everybody in this room. Your boss is going to milk this thing for all it's worth. And, if the president isn't returned alive, he'll have a one hundred percent approval rating when he bombs whomever you guys finger as the ones responsible. There's nothing the American people like more than an all-out bombing run. Having accomplished that, your boy will be a shoo-in for president in the next election. This whole thing stinks!"

Scot let DaFina go and turned to walk toward the door. As he did, he noticed the chief of staff cock his arm back with an open hand as if he intended to slap him. Spinning, Scot just missed DaFina's blow and brought his fist up in an uppercut to the man's jaw. With a crack, the punch landed and blood spurted from DaFina's mouth as his teeth clamped together, catching part of his lip.

Immediately, DaFina's hands flew to his face as he staggered backward. Jameson waited a beat and then fished out a handkerchief and handed it to him. When DaFina saw the blood, his rage was for real. "Harvath, if you had even a prayer of surviving before, it's gone now. You are through!"

Turning to the group, DaFina said, "Do you see what he did to me?"

This time, it was the normally quiet and reserved FBI director Sorce who spoke first. "Yeah, I saw it clear as day. You tried to strike Agent Harvath when he wasn't looking, and he turned just in time. Looked to me like he was raising his hand to protect himself and your chin got in the way. Simple case of self-defense, as I'm sure everyone in the room will agree."

"Self-defense? Self-defense! That's bullshit, and you know it. What about when he grabbed my finger and twisted my arm behind my back?"

"To tell you the truth, I didn't see that, but poking Agent Harvath is technically assault, and anything he did would have been in self-defense."

A very pissed-off DaFina glowered at the other men and said, "And I suppose you all agree with Director Sorce?"

No one said anything; they just sat stone-faced.

"All in all," continued Sorce, "your conduct is very unbecoming for a chief of staff, even a vice presidential one. I'd hate to think what the media would do with this if it got out."

"Look at my lip! I can feel it beginning to swell. What am I going to say to people?"

"Well, you can say what we used to say back in Chicago when a suspect got a little roughed up. You *slipped.*"

DaFina gathered his folder, and when he was a safe distance away and had his hand on the doorknob, he spat, "This is not over, Harvath. You are going down. I promise you."

CHAPTER 34

There was no telling how long he had been lying on the cold concrete floor of Senator Snyder's basement. What he did know was that he ached all over and couldn't stop shivering from the waves of cold that tortured his naked body.

André had always considered himself to be in very good shape. Being a junior associate D.C. lawyer who specialized in international finance didn't exactly require a hard body, but being in superlative health had always been his choice. To balance his regime of weight lifting and cardiovascular exercise, and also to give his mind something positive to focus on during the bleak D.C. winters, he had taken up yoga two years ago. It was a nice way to get his heart rate up when he couldn't get to the club or it was too dreadful outside to run. He'd never had any idea that it would one day save his life.

The hog-tie position Snyder had left him in would have immobilized most, but not André. From the beginning, his focus had been on controlling his mind and his breathing, trying not to let fear overtake him. The cords around his ankles and wrists tore into his skin, but he put the pain out of his mind and tried to focus on staying calm. The rag stuffed in his mouth threatened to gag him with every breath, but he knew, on a logical as well as a very primal level, that he couldn't give in to the urge to vomit.

With his arms drawn so tightly behind his back, any movement hurt. After struggling against his bonds several times, only to have his mind race uncontrollably ahead to what lay in store for him when the senator returned, André lay still. He assessed the situation. In his opinion, the greatest thing he had going for him, besides that he was still alive, was that he wasn't bound even more restrictively. Despite the pain, he could move if he *really* wanted to. And he did.

He realized that he didn't need his arms, legs, or his wrists to move. If he used only his pelvis and his chest, he could shuffle in a two-step inchworm process. *First, lift my chest and slide it to the right, and then lift my pelvis and follow.*

It took André almost three hours to cross the basement floor and get to the washer-and-dryer area on the other side of the room. It had been necessary to stop repeatedly to catch his breath. The exertion increased his respiration, which was already impaired by the gag and the strong odor of shoe polish that filled his nostrils whenever he tried to breathe deeply.

When he reached the laundry area, he rolled onto his side so that the cord on his wrists and ankles faced the metal leg of an old washbasin between the washer and dryer. As he couldn't stand upright, this was his only chance. He began rocking back and forth, dragging the laundry cord across the leg of the washbasin. The process was agonizingly slow.

A warm, sticky, wet feeling began to spread across his hands, and he knew that he was bleeding, but he pressed on. There was no telling when the senator would return to finish the job, and therefore nothing mattered but getting free. An animal instinct took over, and André rocked harder, sawing his wrists and ankles against the metal. All control he had over his mind had vanished. He kept thinking about wolves caught in traps who chew their own legs off to escape as he swung his body and sawed faster.

Finally there was a muffled snap and the tension on his wrists and ankles let up ever so slightly. The cord was fraying. He closed his eyes to try to shut out the pain. He resumed the fevered pitch of his rocking while he applied outward pressure on the cord from his hands and feet. Another snap. He was almost there. André rocked his body for all he was worth and was greeted finally with the sweet sensation of release. The cord ripped the rest of the way away. His feet fell backward and his arms went limp at his sides. Though he knew he needed to work on getting more circulation to his extremities, he just lay on the floor and wept for several minutes, allowing exhaustion to sweep through him. The only movement he made was to remove the gag. As he spat it out, he saw that Snyder had indeed used a shoeshine rag. He seethed with anger but was too tired to allow it to overtake him. He had won, at least so far, and he took his time savoring the small victory as he lay motionless on the floor.

After giving himself a short rest, André gathered enough momentum for the painful roll onto his back. He held his wrists in front of his face and examined the bleeding from the gashes in his raw, burned skin. Contracting his stomach muscles, he leaned upward and looked down at his ankles, which were not much better. The left side of his body looked as if he had been dragged down three miles of a highway covered in loose gravel and broken glass. It was all painful, but he would live. *What was he saying?* He wasn't out of harm's way yet.

Okay, Mr. Travolta, he said to himself, *if the key words here are "staying alive," then we need to get you out of here.* André continued to crunch upward until he was in a sitting position. He rolled his shoulders back and forth and also twisted his ankles in painful circles, helping to improve the blood flow. Stripping off the remaining cord that was clinging to him, he blessed the Lightness of Being Yoga Center for the flexibility he now enjoyed and made a mental note to make a donation when and if he was completely out of this situation.

André pulled himself to a standing position. Twisting the faucet handle, he waited for the washbasin's rusty brown water to turn clear before submerging his wrists in the cascade. The water burned at first and then felt numbingly sweet. As much as he wanted to stand and let the water run over his wrists for hours, he knew he had to get moving.

As in many of Georgetown's ritzier town homes, a laundry chute fed from the top floor of the building, where the bedrooms were, down into the basement. Not far from the washer and dryer, André saw the laundry basket used to catch whatever came down. Mingled with the senator's clothes were the brown corduroys and turtleneck sweater he had shot down the chute just yesterday. He rummaged further and found a pair of dirty sweat socks and began to get dressed.

As he finished pulling on his socks, he looked down at a bloodied piece of cord. André wasn't stupid. He knew if he brought any charges against the senator, it would be his word against Snyder's. For a good part of the time that he had lain naked, cold, and scared on the moldy concrete floor, he had wondered who would ever believe his story. Knowing the senator would do everything in his power to stop it from becoming public, André needed some sort of proof that he had been there. He looked down at the piece of bloody cord again and kicked it as hard as he could under the dryer.

He could no longer control the urge to run, and he moved quickly toward the back of the basement, where a small utility door led up a short flight of steps to the garden. Not wanting to even attempt to use the front door, for fear of bumping into Snyder, André rushed the garden door. He grabbed the cold metal handle and turned. *Locked!*

He tried again, but no luck. The door was dead-bolted with a lock that needed a key from either side. The glass was no better, as it was covered with a thick wire security mesh. A wave of nausea began to grow in the pit of his stomach. André fought to keep it down. *Think. There has got to be a way.* He knew that all of the windows in the basement were covered with the exact same security mesh. It seemed hopeless.

Looking up, as if imploring heaven for some sort of aid, he saw his salvation. Above the right-hand corner of the doorframe was a rusted nail with a key hanging from it. *Please, let this be the one.*

André took down the key and slid it into the lock, his hand trembling. It fit. But as he turned the key to the left it wouldn't budge. The same thing happened when he turned it to the right. *Shit. It's the wrong key!*

Taking a deep breath, he told himself to calm down. The senator could arrive home at any moment; André needed to keep his wits about him. He tried the key again, harder. *Careful, don't break it.* Nothing.

Remembering his own trouble with the fifth-generation key for the condo he and Mitch had shared, André applied a little English. He pulled slightly as he twisted. Joyous relief flooded his body as the key finally turned all of the way, drawing back the dead bolt and releasing the door. The moist smell of clean outside air flowed into his nose and mouth.

A steady rain was falling, and a large puddle sat at the base of the concrete steps. While trying to work the lock, he had noticed a set of gardening tools off to his right, including a pair of green Wellington boots. By the looks of them, they were Snyder's. André had bigger feet, but didn't think twice as he grabbed a pair of shears and cut the toes off of each boot. He quickly pulled them on and crept cautiously from the basement. The garden was cold and the night air was heavy with the mist of the steadily falling shower. He still had no idea what time it was and didn't care. Snyder obviously thought he could come back and finish him at any point. He had no reason to suspect André would have been able to get away.

Creeping slowly, using the large trees for cover, he made his way to the end of the garden. The stone rococo fountain gave him enough of a foothold to climb up to the top of the wall. As he pushed with his left leg to get the final thrust he needed, a stone cherub's head dislodged and clattered down with a roaring splash into the pool of water below.

It made no difference. André Martin landed effortlessly in the neighbor's yard and was off like a shot, the knowledge of what the senator would do to him if he caught up pushing him forward.

CHAPTER 35

Director Jameson saved his admonishments for the ride home, and Scot took each one of them without arguing. Had he been given a chance to get a word in edgewise, he might have admitted that some of his actions had surprised even him, but as it stood, he rode along in the director's limousine in silence.

As they pulled up to Harvath's apartment building, it was already after ten o'clock, and Director Jameson ordered him to be at the Treasury Building the next morning for a full debriefing in the presence of the secretary. Jameson also warned him that the secretary of the treasury was not a man to be fooled around with and that Harvath had better be on his best behavior.

Thanking the director, Scot closed the door of the limo, turned the collar of his trench coat up against the rain, and didn't bother to open his umbrella for the short run up the pavement to the front entrance. He ignored his mailbox and took the stairs slowly, his headache not having abated much in the past several hours. At his door, he checked that the brown hair was exactly where he had left it. It was. He took it down, removed the keys from his pocket, and let himself in.

The apartment looked exactly the same. Why he expected it to be any different, he didn't know. Sometimes he mused about how nice it would be to have someone waiting on the other side of the door when he came home, someone friendly. His lifestyle had never been conducive to long-term relationships. In the SEALs he could be mobilized at a moment's notice and be gone for months at a time without any warning. He had watched a lot of Special Operations guys go through painful and messy divorces. The simplest answer for Scot was to just avoid getting too serious with anyone. Casual relationships were a lot easier. And it had never been tough finding women who wanted to be with him—temporarily.

Several women in Scot's life had liked him enough to press him on committing to a deeper relationship. None of them ever understood why he soon thereafter broke things off or, more often, just faded away. As difficult as it was for him, he believed that was easier in the long run.

While his hectic life had calmed down a lot since retasking to the Secret Service, it was still unpredictable, and after all, old habits, especially those of the heart, really did die hard.

Scot continued to reflect on bachelorhood as he hung his trench coat and took off his suit. Putting on a dark blue sweat suit with the word *Navy* written in yellow across the chest and on the upper-left thigh, he decided a little light exercise might do him some good. He put on a pair of Nikes, exited his apartment, and headed downstairs.

With the building's history of less-than-stellar tenants and more than one break-in, the landlady was extremely glad to have Secret Service agent Scot Harvath living in one of her apartments. He had not needed to ask her twice about using a small corner of the relatively empty basement as a place to set up his exercise equipment.

The workout was slow going. Harvath spent the first twenty minutes doing some light stretching. The exercises allowed him to assess the damage that had been done to his body and how well he was healing. While he was still tremendously sore, he knew that a lot of the stiffness he felt could be relieved by working out. He wasn't foolish enough to believe that he could jump right back into his routine, so he knocked down the normal amounts he lifted to sixty percent. He remembered Dr. Helsabeck's warnings not to exacerbate his symptoms through stress or physical exertion, so he made sure not to push things too hard. His muscles burned. The familiar sensation felt good and helped take his mind off of his headache, both the one between his ears and the one that came between paychecks—his job.

Harvath finished his workout with forty-five minutes on the treadmill. The mindless repetition of jogging on the inclined belt allowed him to be lost in exercise-induced euphoria for just a little while longer. Returning to his apartment, he noticed the new-call light blinking on his caller ID box. As he crossed the living room to pick up his cordless phone, it began to ring.

"Harvath," he answered.

"Scot, thank God you're finally home. I have been trying to get ahold of you for over an hour," said an agitated female voice.

"Natalie, is that you?" asked Scot. Natalie Sperando was assistant to the social secretary of the White House and coordinated most of President Rutledge's social appearances. While Secret Service guidelines strictly forbade Service personnel from dating any executive staff, especially when assigned to White House duty, it never said anything about not being friends with them, and Scot and Natalie had become good ones during his time there.

"Yes, it's me. Scot, I need your help," she said.

"What kind of help? You sound upset. Are you okay?"

"I can't go into it over the phone. I need you to meet me."

"It sounds serious."

"Very."

"All right. I just finished working out. Let me grab a shower and—"

"I need to meet you now. Can you take the shower later?" asked Natalie.

"Nat, do you want to give me an idea what this is all about?"

"I can't. Not over the phone."

"Are you in some sort of trouble?"

"Kind of. It involves a friend of my brother's. Please, Scot. Can you just come meet me?"

"Sure. I'll bag the shower. Tell me where you are."

Natalie gave Scot the name and address, telling him to hurry. He got out of his sweats and pulled on a pair of jeans and a denim shirt. He glanced at his holstered SIG next to the bed and realized it would mean either another layer of clothing or he would have to keep his jacket on all night to conceal it. He decided against it. He wouldn't need a gun where he was going.

• • •

Harvath had the cabbie drop him at the Dupont Circle Metro stop. From there he walked down Massachusetts Avenue toward Scott Circle. He turned onto Seventeenth Street and walked to an upscale pub known as J.R.'s.

J.R.'s catered to a gay clientele that liked to refer to themselves as "guppies," or *gay urban professionals.* With its long varnished bar and stained-glass windows, had it not been for the lack of women, J.R.'s would have looked like any other D.C. watering hole. As Scot made his way through the patrons enjoying the Tuesday five-dollar all-you-can-drink special, he finally found Natalie in the back corner with a man he didn't recognize.

"Oh, Scot. I'm so glad you're here," said Natalie as she stood to give him a hug.

"Anything for you, Nat. You know that, but can you tell me what I'm doing sitting in a bar at"—he paused to look at his watch—"at twelve o'clock on a Tuesday night?"

"It's all my fault, I'm afraid. At least to a certain degree," said the man who was sitting at the table with Natalie. He looked pale and drawn. Scot noticed when he offered his hand that his wrist was crudely bandaged and some blood showed through.

Scot took the man's hand. "It's nice to meet you, Mr. . . ."

The man threw a tentative glance toward Natalie, who nodded her head that everything was okay.

"Martin. My name is André Martin. We met about a month ago when I was visiting the White House to see Natalie. It's okay, though, you must meet a lot of people in your job."

"You'll forgive me. I'm normally good with faces. What can I do for you?"

Before he could answer, a waiter who had been hovering close by came over to take their drink orders.

André ordered himself another bourbon, Natalie declined, her wineglass still half full, and Scot ordered a Heineken.

When the waiter left, André lifted his glass and finished the small bit of brownish gold liquid that remained. His hand shook.

"Okay, Nat, you said this was important and had something to do with a friend of your brother's," said Scot.

"It is and it does. André is one of Steven's friends. He—"

André cleared his throat. "Natalie, why don't I just jump in here and explain? Agent Harvath, are you familiar with the murder of Senator David Snyder's aide, Mitchell Conti, that happened almost a year ago?"

"Yeah, I think so. A drive-by, wasn't it? As I remember, the kid was pretty well liked on the Hill."

"He was," said André. "The papers billed it as a bad case of 'wrong place, wrong time,' but I never bought that."

"Why not?" asked Scot.

"Because," continued André, "they were never able to find the shooter or who the intended victim or victims were."

"Mr. Martin, I hate to say it, but unfortunately the D.C. police are only human and they have their hands full. There are lots of homicides that go unsolved every year. It's not that unusual."

"No? Well, what if I told you that Mitchell Conti was also Senator Snyder's lover?"

Scot couldn't believe his ears. He looked at Natalie, who nodded her head.

"Mr. Martin, supposing this was true, how would you be in a position to come across this piece of information? And while we're at it, what does it have to do with the drive-by, and how, in any way, does this have anything even remotely to do with me?"

"Agent Harvath, if you'll give me a second, I'll explain."

Scot sat back in his chair and was quiet as the waiter brought their drinks.

Once he was gone, André began again, "I know these things because Mitchell Conti and I were lovers. We lived together. I left him because of his relationship with Senator Snyder—"

Scot interrupted, "But I know of at least five women over the last two years that the senator is reported to have been seeing. He's known in the Beltway as quite a ladies' man."

"So was Mitch, but appearances can be deceiving. Besides, being bisexual doesn't make someone any less of a man, nor any less attractive to women."

Scot was going to have to take André's word on that one. He sipped his beer and waited for him to continue.

After a shaky sip from his new drink and a look around to make sure they weren't being overheard, André went on to tell Scot the details of Mitch's involvement with Snyder and the possible blackmail.

"It's all a very interesting story, Mr. Martin, and I'm sorry for your loss, but I still don't see what—"

"What you don't see, Agent Harvath, is that shortly thereafter Mitch was killed in the supposed drive-by shooting. I was convinced that Mitch's death was no accident and the police weren't getting anywhere, so I decided to look into matters myself."

Wonderful. This guy is a regular Dick Tracy, thought Harvath.

"I did all the research I could on Senator Snyder, and being familiar with many of his predilections via Mitch, I arranged for the two of us to meet. Of course I made it look like it was quite by chance. But little by little, I began to win his confidence and we began seeing each other—"

"Okay, Mr. Martin . . . I'm going to stop you right there. I have many gay friends. I don't want you to think for one second that this is a problem I have with someone else's lifestyle, because it isn't. But this is just a little too wild for my taste, and as far as you have explained, there's no way in the world this could have anything at all to do with me."

"But if you would let me finish."

"André, I'm going to save you the time, and please excuse me for using your first name—"

"Not at all. It's okay."

"Good, listen, I like you. You seem like a nice guy. A smart guy. If you have some concrete evidence that Senator Snyder was involved directly or indirectly with Mr. Conti's death, I suggest you take it straight to the D.C. district attorney's office. But I warn you . . . What do you do for a living?"

"I am an attorney."

"Well, then I don't need to warn you of the downside if what you know or what you think you know gets back to Senator Snyder. He is a very powerful man and has a lot of friends. He could make a lot of trouble for you."

"But, Agent Harvath, what I have to tell you isn't about Mitch's death, it's about the president's disappearance."

Natalie spoke up, but he almost didn't hear her. "See, Scot. This is the reason I called you."

Scot's attitude went from boredom and condescension to rapt interest in an instant. "If you have any information whatsoever about the president's kidnapping, I suggest you spill it right now."

CHAPTER 36

For the hundredth time in the last hour, Scot glanced warily around the room to make sure they were not being overheard. André Martin's story was absolutely incredible. Harvath now understood why Nat had brought André to him. Where else could the poor guy go? If what he was saying was true, no one would have believed him, and if Snyder wasn't out looking for him already, he was going to be very soon.

The implications of what André was saying were staggering. Harvath probed for more details, needing to paint the most accurate picture possible.

"So based on all of this, you think the senator was somehow involved in the president's kidnapping?"

"Exactly."

"I don't know, André. There's no question after what he did to you that the guy is one sick puppy, but do you really think he was going to kill you for what you overheard? I mean, from what you tell me, you don't exactly have a smoking gun," said Harvath.

"Exactly again. I didn't see or hear anything that would ever stand up in court, but he still wanted me dead."

"Are you positive he wanted to kill you and not just scare you?"

"Scot," said André, having dropped the formality of calling him Agent Harvath over half an hour ago, "I'm a lawyer, and lawyers believe that what is not said is just as important as what is. Snyder had no idea what I heard or didn't hear. All he knew was what I was saying or not saying."

"I don't follow you."

"You were right, in part, that he was trying to scare me. He scared the shit out of me and he left me in that basement to do some very hard thinking. He planned to come back and when he did, he would want answers. He would want to hear what I *hadn't been* saying. You follow me now?"

"Yeah, I do, but this is the part of your story that scares me the most," said Scot. "What you are alleging is pretty serious, and from the look and the sound of it, you can back it up. If nothing else, it would be extremely embarrassing for the senator. You're right, I don't think you were ever meant to walk out of that house alive again."

"So, you're convinced?"

"Enough to know that Natalie did the right thing in calling me."

"I knew you would help us," said Natalie.

"*Us?* As in both of you? No way, Nat. You need to let me help André alone while you stay as far away as possible. This could be extremely dangerous."

"Listen, Scot, I didn't call you up so you could sweep in here and start giving orders. André called me because he didn't know who else to turn to. Now that you've heard his story, you see why he couldn't go to the police."

"Yeah, but I'm here now, and we can help him, protect him."

"Who's 'we'? The Secret Service? From what I hear around the White House, you guys have so many leaks Vice President Marshfield is even talking about suspending Secret Service protection and using FBI bodyguards."

Scot's blood pressure began to rise. "First of all, Vice President Marshfield doesn't know his ass from a hole in the ground. The Secret Service is charged with his protection as well as the safety and security of the White House and all those within it. We're there to stay. You won't be seeing any FBI protective details; that I can assure you. As far as any leaks are concerned, we've yet to nail that down, but there isn't any reason the Service can't put André into protective custody until we get to the bottom of this. It's just going to take a little time."

"Time? But I thought you said I was in danger?" said André.

"I believe you are, but it's going to take me a couple of hours to set everything up and bring you in. While I do that, we need to get you someplace safe."

"He can come back to my apartment," said Natalie.

"Nat, I told you this could be dangerous, and I don't want you involved. You did the right thing, and now I want you to walk away."

"And I told you, Scot, that I am staying right here with André. He's been extremely kind to my brother over the years, and I'm not going to repay that kindness by ditching him in his hour of need."

Scot knew when he was licked. "Okay, have it your way, but I don't want you going home."

"Why not?"

"Because if Snyder's out looking for André and he knows the connection between you two, he might go to your apartment. How much cash do you have?"

"About a hundred bucks, I think. I hit the cash machine after work."

Harvath reached into his pocket and peeled off two hundred-dollar bills, "Now you've got three hundred dollars. I want you to get in a cab and head for Alexandria. Go to the Radisson Old Town on Fairfax and pay cash for a room for one night. Tell them you're Triple A members, but your purse and wallet were stolen and you have no ID on you, that should knock the rate in half and stop them from asking any questions. Register under the name Cashman. Once you get inside, don't call anyone. I'll call you. You got it?"

"I still think going to my place is okay."

"Nat, you asked me for a favor, and now I'm asking you for one. Go there and stay put."

"Okay, we'll do it, but make sure you hurry up."

"I'll get to you as soon as I can. Again, I don't think you are in any immediate danger; we just need to be sure."

Harvath extended his hand toward André. "We'll get to the bottom of this, don't worry."

"I hope so," said André, who stood and shook his hand. Natalie was putting on her coat. "You know, Scot, you asked me if there was anything else that seemed odd about the senator's behavior recently."

"Yes?"

"There was one other thing I forgot to mention, but it might not mean anything."

"What is it?"

"Well, it was just another inconsistency in one of Snyder's stories, but a pretty major one, I thought."

Scot raised his eyebrows as if to say, *Keep going.*

"About a month ago the senator took off on an unplanned trip. We had plans and he canceled on me. He brought me back a bottle of dessert wine. He said it was a favorite of Napoleon or Josephine or something, but it didn't make sense. The whole thing bothered me for a couple of reasons."

"Why?"

"Well, he said he was called away on a World Bank economic development conference."

"So?"

"Well, I specialize in international finance, and it wasn't difficult to find out that there were no World Bank functions at that time."

"Maybe he told you the wrong thing or you misunderstood."

"I don't misunderstand things that easily."

"You said it bothered you for a couple of reasons; what's the other?"

"He told me he had been in France for the conference, but there was a half-stripped Swiss Railways checked-luggage sticker on his suitcase."

"That could have been from a previous trip."

"I thought so too until I showed the bottle of wine to a friend of mine. He's kind of a wine snob, and I wanted to impress him. I'd never had a dessert wine from South Africa before."

"André, listen, you both need to get going."

"Just let me finish. This friend of mine had heard of the wine. It has a very high sugar content, and its import is banned in the EU."

"So?"

"So, France is part of the European Union. The senator couldn't have possibly found this in some little French wine shop like he said."

"I'm sorry, André, I still don't get it."

"Switzerland is not part of the EU, and they do allow this particular wine to be imported regardless of its sugar and alcohol levels. So, what was he doing in Switzerland that was such a big secret?"

"André, it might be something and it might not. I'll look into it. Now, both of you get going."

"What about Star Gazer?" prompted Natalie. "You said the whole thing wouldn't work without Star Gazer."

"Oh, yeah. I forgot that one."

"Who is Star Gazer?" asked Scot.

"I've got no idea. I overheard the senator mention that whatever he was doing wouldn't work without Star Gazer. Does that make any sense to you?"

"Not much of any of this makes sense. Now, seriously, you have to get going."

Harvath pushed the two toward the door and waited five minutes. He left two twenties on the table and exited J.R.'s through the back. A strange, yet all-too-familiar feeling began to creep over him in the murky D.C. night. As he turned up the collar on his trench coat once again, he wished he'd brought his pistol.

CHAPTER 37

Despite the confidence he had shown upon saying good-bye and packing Natalie and André off to the Radisson, Harvath had no idea what his next move was going to be. His credibility wasn't exactly first-rate in Washington these days, and he knew he would have to be very careful about whom he shared his newfound knowledge with. What he had was explosive and could do an incredible amount of damage whether it was true or not. The mere suggestion that a senator, possibly two, might have been involved with the kidnapping of the president of the United States was almost inconceivable.

Scot normally did his best thinking on his feet, so when he left J.R.'s he walked, ignoring the light but steady rain that fell. He moved south on Seventeenth Street, passing Farragut Square, and turned left when he reached H Street. He walked along Lafayette Square until he reached Fifteenth, sorting and resorting everything he had heard. He spun the name Star Gazer around and around, trying to get a handle on it. Who or what was Star Gazer and what did the name have to do with what Senator Snyder was up to?

At Fifteenth, without giving it any thought, he automatically turned right. A block and a half later he was standing in front of the Treasury Building. In less than eight hours he was supposed to be back at this exact site for a detailed debriefing with Director Jameson and the secretary of the treasury, Paul Feigen. He wondered if once they'd extracted from him everything they wanted, they would terminate him on the spot.

Scot remembered what he had told himself only yesterday, though it seemed like a lifetime ago. If he was going to have any hope of keeping his career intact, he would need to be part of something that helped crack the case. That something might have fallen right into his lap, thanks to Natalie Sperando. Or, so he hoped. If no one believed André's story, or if it couldn't be verified, Scot was probably as good as washed up. It would look as if he were grasping at straws, doing anything he could to save himself, no matter how ridiculous it was and no matter whose name he dragged through the mud. He had to be very careful how he handled things.

But even if André turned out to be a dead end, Harvath had taken an oath to protect the president and he had made a promise to Sam Harper. Those commitments would not disappear, no matter how tough things got. He knew he had to bring this information into the open, and he now knew exactly whom he could count on for help.

Cutting up New York Avenue, Harvath hailed a cab in front of the Presbyterian church and gave the driver an address in Arlington, Virginia. The chances that the man he was going to see would still be awake were pretty slim, but he was the only person who could help Scot and potentially . . . the president.

• • •

The front porch lights were out when Scot climbed the stairs, and he took that as a bad sign. He knew that the minute he rang the bell, not only would he wake the man inside, but the man would be pretty upset. William Shaw had a very short fuse. The Director of Secret Service Operations for the White House, and Scot's boss, hadn't come by his call sign of Fury for nothing. Scot steeled himself and reached for the glowing orange button that seemed to hover over the house's brick facade.

After several seconds, lights began turning on within the house, and eventually an exterior overhead light came on, pinning Harvath against the darkness.

"Who the hell is it?" came a gruff voice from inside.

"It's Harvath, Bill. Open up."

From inside, Scot heard a chain slide back, followed by several dead bolts. Finally, the door opened and there stood a sleepy William Shaw. He had a face of unshaved whiskers, bed head, and one hand in the pocket of his terry cloth robe, probably curled around his SIG-Sauer semiautomatic.

"Harvath, this had better be very, very good. You are just bound and determined to get on every single person's shit list, aren't you?"

"Bill, this is important. Can I come in?"

"Be my guest. Maybe I can cook up a little breakfast while you're here," said Shaw sarcastically as he closed the door behind them and relocked his dead bolts.

"Nice place," said Scot, and he meant it. The entry hall gave way to a room dominated by oxblood leather couches with brass buttons and a big-screen TV. Two walls were lined with books, and there were recessed surround-sound speakers in the ceiling. The fireplace was trimmed with an ornate mantelpiece covered with pictures of the Shaw family in silver frames. In the middle of the floor was a very large and very ornate oriental rug.

"Mrs. Shaw had good taste in everything but husbands," he said, joining Harvath at the edge of the den. Scot knew that Shaw's wife had recently divorced him and that it had been very difficult. Scot decided to change the subject and get to the point right away.

"Bill, I think I may have some new information on the president's kidnapping."

"You? How the hell would you have any? You're not even supposed to be active. I don't know why Jameson didn't grab your creds and suspend you last night. The kidnapping of the president is no longer the purview of the Secret Service anyway. End of story."

"Can we sit down? I think you'll want to hear what I have to say."

Shaw let out an exasperated sigh and waved Harvath toward one of the couches. They took seats opposite each other, and as Shaw was rubbing the remaining sleep from his eyes, Scot began his story. "I have reason to believe the kidnappers had some very high placed help."

"No shit, Sherlock. We've suspected all along that there was some sort of leak."

"I'm not talking about *the* leak, Bill. I'm talking about guys with enough power and influence to help facilitate the introduction between the kidnappers and the source of the leak."

"You know, Harvath," said Shaw, glancing at his watch, "I have to be up for work in a few hours. I am going to be able to fall right back asleep without hearing any fairy tales, so why don't you take yours and—"

"Bill, this is serious. I have reason to suspect that Senator Snyder and maybe Senator Rolander were involved somehow in the president's kidnapping."

Shaw moved forward on the couch. "Snyder and maybe Rolander? What the hell are you talking about?"

"Tonight I had a meeting with a man who claims to have been Snyder's lover—"

"Lover?"

"Let me finish and it will all become clear. I had the same reaction at first. Do you remember that aide on the Hill who was killed in a drive-by about a year ago?"

"Yeah, so what?"

"Well, the man I met with tonight, a Mr. André Martin, was involved with the aide. The aide worked for Senator Snyder and, according to Martin, was having an affair with him."

"The aide and the senator?"

"Yes. Apparently Martin got sick of the aide cheating on him and left him. The aide tried to break things off with the senator while still trying to hold on to his job and might even have tried to blackmail Snyder. Shortly thereafter the aide was killed in the drive-by."

"C'mon, Harvath. Not only is that hearsay, but it's so thin you can see through it. It sounds more like a Jackie Collins novel."

"I thought the same thing until—"

"Until what?"

"Until Martin told me that he worked his way in close to the senator and started having an affair with him himself."

"We're talking about Senator David Snyder? Confirmed bachelor and renowned ladies' man?"

"We've all got our secrets, Bill. Anyway, this Martin begins an affair with the senator, convinced he was responsible for the aide's death and determined to expose him. He watches, and more important, he listens. He listens to everything, but never lets on that he's listening. He feigns he's a heavy drinker, a sound sleeper, anything plausible that might put the senator more at ease and create an environment in which he'll slip up. Then, he does. Recently, Martin overheard some stuff the senator thinks he shouldn't . . ."

"Overheard stuff? What did he hear?"

"Well, he not only heard things relating to the president's kidnapping, but he also followed Snyder to Senator Rolander's house after

Snyder had received some suspicious phone calls in the middle of the night. By the way, remember that FBI agent I had the problem with in Park City?"

"The guy you creamed? What was his name?"

"Zuschnitt."

"Yeah, you decked him, so?"

"Well, from what Martin told me, he's been calling in regular reports from Park City to Snyder, and it seems the two of them were behind framing me as the leak to CNN."

"You've got to be kidding me."

"Nope. From what Martin says, he heard it all loud and clear when he was listening on another extension. There's no way we can prove it right now, but if I could get my hands on that Zuschnitt again, I think I could encourage him to talk."

Shaw's fingers dug into the leather arm of the couch. "What about the president?"

Harvath continued to fill his boss in on everything Martin had told him and then shared something he had not told anyone about.

"Do you remember how I went over to that Mormon farm where that couple was murdered?"

"Do I remember? Of course I do. What about it?"

"I found a piece of evidence there I didn't tell anybody about."

"Evidence?" Shaw's face was white. "What kind of evidence?"

"Well, when I entered the house, I smelled cigarette smoke. The local law enforcement guys said they hadn't been smoking in the house, and as the couple were apparently devout Mormons, I knew they weren't smokers. It wasn't a huge leap of logic to figure out that the farm had been used as some sort of a base camp for the kidnapping."

"Why did you think that?"

"The old couple was done by a professional. Shots to the head—"

"The man was, but according to the report, not the woman," said Shaw.

"Yeah, I know. I think he did the man first and the woman tried to run or something. I think he lost it and, if you'll forgive the Cagneyism, *filled her full of lead.* The president was most likely brought to the farm via snowmobile from the scene of the kidnapping and then transferred into whatever vehicle or vehicles they used from there. Nothing was amiss or stolen in the house, so that's why I think it was just used as a base."

"So, cigarette smoke is your evidence?"

"No. While the killer was waiting for the rest of the kidnappers to get back from doing the job, he was smoking and probably watching TV in the family room. I think he was eating chocolate too."

"Chocolate? Jesus, Harvath. First you tell me Senator Snyder goes both ways, then he likes to tie up and torture people who may or may not have been listening in on his phone calls and tailing him, and then your *coup de grâce* is that one of the kidnappers may have been eating candy at a scene that has yet to be determined was connected in any way with the president's kidnapping?"

"The chocolate was Swiss."

"So? There's lots of Swiss chocolate in the U.S., and around the world, for that matter. I hate to be the one to burst your bubble, but after yodeling and watches, it's probably one of the biggest things the Swiss are known for!"

"I disagree. I don't think this chocolate is an export product. At least not for the States. It had German writing on it."

"So? Maybe someone brought it back from a trip to Germany as a gift for the old couple."

"But, the couple was Mormon and caffeine is another thing that is forbidden by their religion."

"Listen, you're in enough trouble as it is. Tell me you didn't take anything from the crime scene. You left that chocolate right where you found it, right?"

Harvath couldn't tell if Shaw was trying to lead him toward the answer he wanted to hear or if he really wanted the truth. Either way, something told Scot that he should not admit to having removed the chocolate from the crime scene. "No. I left it there."

"Good. Then it's the FBI's problem and they can decide whether it's relevant or not when they find it. I think, though, that you're making a mountain out of a molehill. You're very stressed out. I haven't had a chance to read your fitness report. Did you see Dr. Helsabeck?"

"Yes."

"And?"

"And, nothing. She says I'm fine. Says my head may feel scrambled for a few more days, but that's pretty much it."

"Are you taking any medications?"

"Only Tylenol. I haven't been able to shake this headache."

Shaw was quiet for a few moments while he thought. His fingertips were pressed together in an arch in front of his nose, with his thumbs supporting his chin. Scot could hear the ticking of a grandfather clock in the hall. Finally, Shaw broke the silence. "All right, I think there's enough here to bring André Martin into protective custody while we look into this. Where is he?"

"He's with Natalie Sperando at the Radisson Old Town in Alexandria."

"Sperando?"

"She's the one who introduced Martin to me. He was a very close friend of her brother's."

"How much does she know?"

"Pretty much everything Martin does."

"Okay, so they're both at the Radisson. Is that the one on Fairfax at Montgomery?"

"Yes, about fifteen minutes down from the Metro."

"I know it. Okay, we'll send a car to pick them up and bring them in. We have a safe house not too far from there that we can use. Were you able to ascertain whether they had talked to anyone else about this?"

"No, they assured me that they hadn't. I stressed to them that anyone that they might have even hinted about this to could be in danger, and they said they were the only ones."

"Good. That makes our job a lot easier. Now, I can't promise you that this is going to help your case. At best, it's all circumstantial and it's André Martin's word against Senator Snyder's. I think he was smart to kick that piece of rope under the dryer. Forensics can place him in Snyder's house and in the basement. That kid was thinking.

"As far as you're concerned, I am going to do this quietly. You are in enough trouble as it is, and if this turns out to be a load of BS, you don't need any more problems. I am going to ask you this once, and I want you to answer me honestly. Have you spoken with anyone other than Martin and Sperando about this?"

"No."

"Are you sure that no one overheard you talking at the bar?"

"As sure as I can be."

"Okay, good. Now, is there anything else you want to tell me about what happened in Park City? If you've got anything, now is the time to get it out."

Harvath thought for a moment. "No. You know the full story."

"Do you have any idea who or what this Star Gazer might be?"

"None at all."

"For all we know," said Shaw, "with all your astronomy gear, it could be you."

"Me? What the hell do you—"

"God, calm down Harvath. I was just pulling your chain. Cripes, you're irritable."

"I'm sorry, Bill. I'm just a little on edge."

"Yeah, I can see that."

"So, what's our next move?"

"Okay, I'll get my laptop from the den for you and put a pot of coffee on. I want a full report, including any of the details you might have accidentally forgotten concerning Park City. If I am going to go to bat for you, I can't have any surprises. I want all of it while it's fresh in your mind. While you are working on that, I'll get started on bringing Martin and Sperando in. Was there an established code for calling so they would know it was you?"

"I had her register under the name Cashman."

"Fine. I'll whip up some coffee and get the laptop. In the meantime, you can use the phone on the end table there to call them."

Harvath did as he was told. He explained to Natalie that either he or Shaw would be calling back shortly with details on the pickup. He told her that they would be taken to a nearby safe house and André placed in protective custody, pending a preliminary investigation. She had done the right thing calling him, and she should be proud. They were going to be all right.

Ten minutes later, Shaw appeared with a mug of coffee and his laptop. As Scot began typing his report, Shaw headed for his den. Closing the doors behind him, he crossed the distance to the phone in three fast strides. He picked it up and dialed the number in McLean from memory.

CHAPTER 38

"Marsha?" asked Shaw, after a sleepy voice answered the number he had dialed.

"You've got the wrong number," said the voice, and the call was disconnected.

Shaw sat patiently and waited behind the thick, locked doors of his study. On a bank of monitors next to his desk, he watched an image of Agent Harvath diligently typing his report. The small hidden camera had him perfectly in frame. Three minutes later, Shaw's private line rang and he depressed the button to activate the scrambler hidden within the desk.

"It's an odd time for a phone call," said Shaw.

"This is when the rates are the lowest though," answered the voice.

Each of the parties' authentication codes completed, the conversation could now begin. They spoke freely, knowing that the lines were secure and the scramblers would prevent anyone from eavesdropping.

"You'd better have something good, Shaw, to call me this late at night. My wife and I were sound asleep."

"I do, Senator."

"Well, get on with it."

"Senator Rolander, it seems that your colleague, Senator Snyder, has been less than discreet."

"Less than discreet? Speak English, man. What do you mean?"

"I mean, Snyder allowed someone to overhear some of his more sensitive conversations."

This admission made Rolander very nervous. He gripped the handset of the telephone tighter. "What kind of conversations?"

"The worst kind. The kind that could send us all away for a very long time, if not get us executed for treason."

"First of all, I don't care how secure these lines are; I want you to watch your language, and choose your words very carefully. Do you understand me?"

"Yes, sir."

"Good, now run down what it is you're talking about and give me all the details."

Five minutes later, Shaw's story was complete. He had left out some of the details, but none of the important ones. Senator Rolander had the picture.

"That hedonistic son of a bitch," swore Rolander.

"To tell you the truth, it doesn't matter who he was sleeping with, this still could have happened."

"I agree, but what does matter is that Snyder got sloppy and now we'll have to clean up his mess. Where is Agent Harvath right now?"

"In my TV room."

"He's in your house, and you're on the phone with me? What kind of idiot are you?!"

"Relax, Senator, he's on 'candid camera.' I'm watching him on a closed-circuit monitor right now. He hasn't budged in the last ten minutes, and he can't hear us."

"What's he doing?"

"I have him writing up a full report."

"That report can never see daylight. You understand?"

"Of course. There's nothing to worry about," said Shaw as he eyeballed a set of books across the room that hid his wall safe. The report would never get out, unless he needed it to. For now, it would stay in his safe and be a nice insurance policy. Once Harvath finished it and they printed it out, Shaw would read it over, have Harvath sign it, and it would go right into the safe. "As soon as he's done, I'll destroy it. We don't need any loose ends that could cause us trouble, do we, Senator?"

Rolander didn't like the man's tone, but he let it go. "No, we don't. How long do you think it will take him to complete the report?"

"A couple of hours, based on everything I have asked for."

"Good. The last thing we want is for him to be out running around loose."

"I agree, that's why I've kept him here. Do you have any idea how lucky we are that he came to me?" asked Shaw.

"Extremely. You're sure neither he nor this Martin nor Natalie Sperando has spoken with anyone else?"

"I'm pretty certain."

"Good. I want you to keep him there until I call you back. Under no circumstances is he to leave. Is that understood?"

"Yes, sir."

Rolander took down the address of the Radisson in Alexandria and hung up.

• • •

After dialing several different numbers, Rolander finally tracked down Senator Snyder on his cell phone.

"Russell, I'd love to talk right now, but I am extremely busy," said Snyder.

Snyder could be busy with only one thing—looking for André Martin.

"Lost something, have you?" asked Rolander.

"Maybe."

"Listen, David, quit fucking around. I need to talk to you and I don't want to do it while you're on a cell phone."

"It's digital and there's no one here but us mices, so go ahead."

Senator Rolander didn't know what nobody here "but us mices" meant, but he assumed Snyder was referring to some of the contract men he sometimes hired for illegal operations.

Rolander continued, "You wouldn't be hoping, as the commercial says, to bring a little André home for the holidays, would you?"

Snyder remained silent. He was stunned.

"Are you still there?" asked Rolander.

"Yeah, I'm here. How did you know?"

"To quote an old friend, *'how I know is not as important as what I know.'* You fucked up big time. Remember how keen I was on the CYA factor? Well, my ass . . . who am I kidding?—all of our asses are out in the wind right now and it's your fault. Digital or not, I want to have this conversation over some eggs, preferably scrambled, so get back to your place and call me."

"Sorry, Russell. I still have that little lost dog, or should I say bitch, I need to find. I'll have to call you when I get around to it."

"Listen, you stupid bastard, I know where he is and will happily tell you, but arrangements need to be made quickly. Get home and call me back." Rolander hung up the phone, severing the connection.

Turning to his driver, Snyder said, "Take me back to the town house. We may have caught a break."

CHAPTER 39

The hulking, black Chevy Suburban with its darkened windows crept quietly up Washington Street through Alexandria's Old Town. This late at night, there wasn't much traffic. Even with the windows rolled up, the scent of the nearby Potomac filled the inside of the vehicle. At Pendleton Street and a sign for Oronoco Bay Park, the driver turned right. Three blocks later was Royal Street and then Fairfax. The vehicle turned left and crept northward. The glowing sign of the Radisson was soon visible. When the Suburban came parallel with the main entrance, it turned in. The driver parked directly in front of the hotel's main doors and left the engine running.

At this hour only a skeleton crew was on duty. An attractive Filipino woman, whose name tag read "Anna," looked up from her paperwork and smiled as the man approached the front desk.

"Good evening. May I help you, sir?" asked Anna in her accented English.

"Yes, you can," said the man, removing a black wallet from inside his suit coat pocket and showing her his credentials. "My name is Agent Scot Harvath, Secret Service. I am here to pick up a Mr. and Mrs. . . ." The man pulled a notepad from his other pocket, flipped a couple of pages, and pretended to come to the name. ". . . a Mr. and Mrs. Cashman. I believe you have them registered here."

The desk clerk glanced over the man's shoulder and saw the blacked-out Suburban parked in front. It looked very official, just like the ones she had seen so many times on TV. She looked back at the handsome man standing in front of her and thought that he must have the bluest eyes she had ever seen. She tore her eyes away from his and tapped some keys on her computer. "Yes, sir. They are registered guests of the hotel."

"Can you please tell me what room they are in?" asked the man.

"Is there a problem? Normally we are not supposed to give out that information," said Anna.

"I understand, and that is a very appropriate policy. This is a matter of national security, though. As I told you, my name is Agent Scot Harvath, and I am with the Secret Service. I have been instructed to pick up the Cashmans. Surely . . ." the man said, leaning in and pretending to read the clerk's name tag for the first time, "Anna, you wouldn't want to interfere with a matter of national security."

Concerned, she answered, "No, sir. Of course I wouldn't. The staff has been instructed to always assist the police and other law enforcement should they ever come to the hotel. I will need to note this in my nightly report, though."

"I understand. That's no problem. Now, would you please tell me what room they are in?"

"Let's see . . ." she said, glancing down. "Room two-fifty-seven. It appears as if they paid for the room in advance. Will they be checking out?"

"Yes," said the man. "I am going to go up and help them with their bags. Would you please call their room and let them know that Secret Service Agent Scot Harvath is on his way up?"

"Yes, I will."

"Thank you," said the man as he crossed the lobby toward the elevators.

Two minutes later, he knocked upon the door numbered 257.

"Who is it?" came a female voice from inside.

"Secret Service, ma'am. I am here to transport you and Mr. Martin."

The door did not open.

"The desk clerk said that Agent Harvath was here," said Natalie.

"She must have gotten confused. I asked her to call up to your room and tell you that a Secret Service agent sent by Agent Harvath was here to pick you up."

After a few moments of silence, the chain slid back and the door opened. Both Natalie and André had their jackets on, ready to go. They followed the man into the elevator and down to the lobby. He had instructed them that time was of the essence and that they must move quickly. As they reached the front desk, he placed their two key cards on it and kept moving.

"Thank you for staying at the Radisson Old Town. We hope to see you again," said the desk clerk as the trio exited the front door.

The man opened the side door of the Suburban. Natalie was relieved to see an agent sitting on the rear bench seat holding a shotgun. As they all climbed in and the man shut the door behind them, the vehicle, even though it was under the Radisson's brightly lit canopy, quickly darkened due to the blacked-out windows. Another man, whom Natalie figured to be an additional agent, sat in the front passenger seat. They were taking this very seriously. That was good. She and André could finally relax.

The Suburban swung out of the driveway and headed back south toward the Capital Beltway. They were on their way. For the first time since his ordeal began, André breathed a sigh of relief. "I cannot tell you how glad I am to see you guys."

"Oh, I'm sure, but not half as glad as we are to see you," said the man in the front seat. The reassuring voice put Natalie further at ease until she saw the horrified look on André's face. He was completely still.

Natalie couldn't understand why his demeanor had so suddenly changed until the passenger turned around to look at them.

The man in the front seat spoke again, and this time, Natalie knew exactly who it was. "André, I was quite upset to come home and not find you waiting for me."

CHAPTER 40

After typing out his report and making the multitude of clarifications his boss had asked for, Harvath was finally finished. It would have been done sooner, but Shaw kept interrupting him with more questions. Shaw said he was going to be present at the debriefing in the morning with Director Jameson and the treasury secretary and that he wanted to make sure Scot had all of his ducks in a row. After a final read-through of the report and Shaw's okay, Harvath printed it out and signed it. He was exhausted.

Shaw excused himself and went back to his study to make a few more phone calls. When he reemerged almost twenty minutes later, he informed Harvath that Natalie and André had been collected from the Radisson and moved to the safe house. Everything was taken care of. Shaw said that he had high hopes for Harvath's debriefing. There were some things that even Shaw couldn't help him get out of, like assaulting the FBI agent, but given the new circumstances, a lot might be forgiven and Scot might actually walk away with his job intact.

Buoyed by his boss's confidence, Scot allowed himself a moment of hope. Seeing that he was exhausted and knowing he had a big day in front of him, Shaw called Harvath a cab. While he had fought to stay awake at Shaw's, Scot allowed himself to nod off on the ride home.

When the cab pulled up in front of Harvath's Alexandria apartment building, the driver had to call to him several times before he woke up. Once he shook the fog from his head, Scot glanced at the meter and removed some cash from his wallet to pay the driver. He stumbled up the driveway, wondering why he was so groggy, and figured his head still wasn't exactly back to normal. Passing up his mailbox once again, Harvath decided he needed to get as much sleep as he could before the big meeting in a few hours. He walked up the stairs and fumbled in his pocket for his keys.

Out of habit he glanced up to see if the brown hair was still in place in the upper corner of his doorframe. Immediately, his body tensed. It wasn't there. He thought back to when he had left and wondered if he could have forgotten to do it. He had rushed out of the house for his meeting with Natalie. Had he or hadn't he? It had become second nature to him, but then again, he had been doing a lot of things lately that weren't exactly normal.

Well, either he could stand outside his front door for what was left of the night wondering, or he could go in. *Which was it going to be?* Harvath decided to go in.

He opened the door slowly and moved cautiously into the apartment, letting his eyes get adjusted to the dark. As his eyes began to focus, he noticed water on his kitchen floor. Then a sharp pain jolted the back of his head and everything went black as his body fell to the linoleum.

• • •

When Harvath awoke and slowly opened his eyes, things were blurry and out of focus. There were objects in his line of vision that were unfamiliar. He shut his eyes tightly and opened them again. As his vision cleared, the objects began to take form and make sense. He was lying on the kitchen floor looking at the bottom of his refrigerator.

His head felt as if it had been slammed in a car door. As he drew his right hand across the linoleum to help push himself up, he noticed he was surrounded by puddles of water. His ice trays were scattered not far from where he lay, as were a couple of once-frozen pizzas and a melted container of Ben & Jerry's Chunky Monkey ice cream. Looking up, he could see the freezer door was wide open.

With both hands and feet, Scot pushed himself into a sitting position and leaned against the cabinets underneath the sink. He reached up and touched the back of his head. There was a bump the size of a walnut, but there didn't seem to be any blood, dried or otherwise.

Harvath would have killed at that moment for one of his SportGel cold packs for the back of his head, but looking up once again at the freezer, he knew they would all be melted. *What was this all about? What was going on? Who had hit him, and what could someone have been looking for in his freezer?*

Scot sat on the floor, his back supported by the cabinets, until he felt he could stand. Using the counter for support, he let a wave of dizziness and nausea pass before he attempted to walk into the entry hall. He checked the front door. It was closed, but not locked. He slid along the wall in the hallway, using it to help keep him upright, and almost fell as he drew up to the living room.

He couldn't believe what he saw inside. It was an absolute shambles. The whole room had been tossed. Books, videotapes, couch cushions, everything had been scattered in someone's manic search, but for what? None of this made any sense. He carefully searched the rest of the apartment until he was confident that whoever was responsible wasn't hiding in one of his closets somewhere.

Scot knew he should call in immediately, but a wave of nausea began to sweep over him again and he decided to put off any calls until he had a long shower and was able to collect his thoughts.

In the bathroom he turned on the hot water and let it run. Before things got too foggy, Scot grabbed a small mirror from his travel kit and positioned himself with his back to the bathroom mirror. Angling the small mirror, he was able to get a good look at the damage to the back of his head. From what he could see, the skin had not been torn. It was pretty painful to the touch, but it would heal. He got into the shower, put his hands on the tile in front of him for support, and let the hot water pound against his body.

He didn't know how long he had been in the shower, but it was long enough for the hot water to start running out. Alexandria's older buildings had their charm, but they also had their drawbacks. Scot climbed out, shaved, and dried his hair. Crossing to his bedroom, he put on a light gray suit, white shirt, and blue tie. Hungry and knowing he shouldn't disturb anything in the kitchen, Scot remembered he had a box of granola bars in a hall closet. As he passed the living room, he noticed the caller ID box was lying on the floor, blinking. It showed one new call.

When he depressed the *Call List* button on the display, a number came up that Scot immediately recognized as being one at the Secret Service main office. According to the time, it had come in while he was in the shower.

By following the phone cord, he found the base station for his cordless. He hit the intercom button and was able to track down the handset, which was buried beneath one of the wayward couch cushions. Scot dialed his voice mail. It was Director Jameson. "Agent Harvath, this is the director. I have absolutely no idea what is going on or how the media got ahold of this thing so fast, but you have a lot of explaining to do. I am sending a car for you, and you'd better be there."

The media? I've got some explaining to do? What was the director talking about? Scot waded through the sea of upturned items in his living room and turned on his TV. It was tuned to a local channel, and the image of a female reporter standing in a wooded area with police, state trooper, and rescue vehicles in the background appeared on the screen.

The reporter was speaking, and Scot turned up the sound to hear what she was saying. ". . . by two joggers early this morning. Apparently the victims had both been shot in the back of the head with a large-caliber weapon. While police say they have no leads on the killer, the FBI's mobile crime lab appeared on the scene moments ago, and we will keep you informed of any developments. Back to you in the studio."

What is going on? Scot furiously switched channels until he found another live shot from the same scene. The reporter was saying, "Yes, Jean, it is indeed a tragic day for the White House, as if their problems weren't already bad enough. To compound the feelings of loss President Rutledge's staff must already be experiencing, they now must add to it the murder of the assistant to the White House social secretary, Natalie Sperando, whose body, along with that of a currently unidentified man, was found early this morning by joggers in rural Maryland. Both victims were shot once in the back of the head with what police are saying was a large-caliber weapon, most likely a handgun.

"While authorities are not speculating as to the motive for the murders, no possibilities are being ruled out at this time. Moments ago the FBI mobile crime lab arrived on the scene—"

Scot turned off the TV. The nausea was returning, and he fought it down. Two more people who had trusted him were dead, but how? And why Natalie, of all people? Scot was overwhelmed with grief. She had been such a good friend. What happened? Shaw had told him that they had made it to the safe house. *Could they have been followed? Both of them shot with a large-caliber weapon—* Before he could finish the thought, Harvath ran toward his bedroom.

This room had been tossed as well, but now Scot didn't care about preserving the scene. He needed to find his sidearm. Frantically, he tore apart the already annihilated room. *Why had he left his pistol behind last night? Why hadn't he taken it with him?*

As Scot continued to search, he caught a flash of light out of the corner of his eye. He thought it was his head playing tricks on him and tried to ignore it. He went back to searching for the gun. He was on his hands and knees now, throwing pieces of clothing over his shoulder in a mad attempt to recover the SIG. The light came back. Harvath stopped searching. He looked up at the repeating colors of red, blue, red, blue, along the wall and realized they were coming from outside.

Keeping low, he scrambled toward the window and peered out through the partially open blinds. Pulling up to the curb below were several government favorites: dark-colored Ford Crown Victorias with suited drivers, which belonged to either the FBI, the Secret Service, or both. There were also several police cars.

My God, thought Harvath, *they must think somehow that I am responsible for André's and Natalie's murders and are here to arrest me.* All things considered, Harvath was also willing to bet that the gun used to commit the crime would turn out to be his missing SIG-Sauer.

While Scot was a stand-up guy, all for telling the truth and cooperating, something told him that now wasn't the time to go gentle into that good night. He needed some answers first.

Trying to push the shock of Natalie's and André's murders from his mind, Scot grabbed his jeans from where he'd left them on the bathroom floor and transferred everything into the pockets of the trousers he was now wearing. He threw on his trench coat, stepped out, and locked the door to the apartment behind him. Turning to his left, he opened the door to the fire stairs and started down, careful not to make any noise.

CHAPTER 41

As Scot moved down the last flight of stairs and pushed open the door to the basement, he realized that a little-known feature of his building was about to pay off big time. He was glad he had done his homework.

The old apartment building Harvath lived in, as well as all of the other buildings along his block, had been owned and built by the same wealthy Virginia family. The wife had been quite the eccentric and hadn't wanted to deal with coal-truck deliveries disrupting her rather erratic sleeping patterns, so the husband had connected all of the basements by a series of passageways. The coal was delivered via the main building's chute at the north end of the block, and servants then transported it through the passageways to the boiler rooms of the other buildings.

While this system was no longer in use, the doors connecting one basement to another were still there, and Scot had long since made copies of the keys that fit the locks, just in case. It all went back to his SEAL training: a SEAL always has at least two routes of escape, because a SEAL is always prepared. Pulling his key ring from his pocket, he quickly opened the first door and then locked it behind him. Even though he thought that the basement lights were probably still functional, Harvath chose not to risk using them and drew the small Mag-Lite from his trench-coat pocket and used it to light his path.

He quickly made his way to the northernmost building, exited through the alley, and two blocks later hailed a cab. He had the driver drop him on Russell Road, just before King Street. From there, Harvath made his way to the King Street Metro stop, just next to Alexandria's Union Station.

There were still plenty of morning commuters about, and Harvath blended in with them perfectly, just another businessman on his way to work in D.C. The question was, where was he going? At the King Street Metro stop you could take either the blue line or the yellow line. *Which one?*

He decided against using his Metro Fast Pass. While he doubted it could be used to trace his movements within the Metro, he didn't trust it. Walking over to one of the automatic machines, he inserted five dollars and seconds later pulled out a One Day Pass.

After retrieving his pass and moving through the turnstile, Harvath headed for the blue line bound for Addison Road. Having ridden the underground systems in both Chicago and New York, Washington's clean, carpeted Metro system always amazed him. People never even ate on the trains, lest they get chewed out by a Metro worker or, worse still, a fellow passenger. The people who used the Metro took it very seriously, and within one visit, even tourists figured out that while you're standing on the escalator, you always stand to your right or you risk being trampled by frenzied businesspeople rushing to get their trains.

As the Metro passed through the austere beige stations, whose ceilings were lined with what looked like cough drops but were actually engineering enhancements used to reduce echoes, Harvath kept his eyes peeled for any D.C. police or the brown-capped Metro cops that might already be looking for him. So far, so good.

Harvath got off the train and exited the system at the Foggy Bottom–GWU station. The Foggy Bottom area was the neighborhood just to the west of the White House that was home to George Washington University. It was also known as the West End.

He quickly made his way down Twenty-third toward the university and G Street. Halfway to Twentieth Street was the Washington Bytes cyber café and bakery. The smell of fresh roasted coffee filled his nostrils as he walked in. They had the best bagels in town, and Scot ordered one with cream cheese and chives, along with an OJ, before sitting down at one of the terminals in the back corner.

The café was an easy walk from the White House and an occasional haunt of Harvath's when he needed to get away from the high-energy pace at work. Today, there were only a few students around, and where Scot sat no one could see him from the street.

All of the computers came equipped with a headset and web phone software. Scot reached up and disconnected the camera on top of his monitor. He allowed himself a bittersweet moment to think about Natalie once again before he took a bite of his bagel followed by a long swig of OJ and then hopped onto the web. He entered the telephone number for his home computer's dedicated modem line and swallowed two Tylenols while he waited for the connection to complete.

After two rings and some electronic cross talk between the café's computer and the one at home, Harvath was ready. He set about establishing a routing system that would bounce his call through several international servers. If the person he was about to call was tracing all of their incomings, it would take them quite a while to figure out where the call came from, and even when they unraveled the long electronic chain, all they would be left with was the appearance that the call originated from Harvath's apartment.

Ten minutes later, the trail was set and Scot was ready to make his call. He dialed the number for Bill Shaw. His secretary answered on the first ring. Harvath identified himself, and after a couple of clicks and another ring, he was put through.

"Scot, where are you?" asked Shaw.

"I don't want to talk about where I am, Bill," said Scot quietly, cautiously glancing around to make sure no one was listening. "What the hell happened?"

"Scot, I am sure there is an explanation for all of this. I promise we'll listen to you. We just need to bring you in."

"Me? Bring *me* in? What are you talking about? I didn't do anything."

"Scot, I'm here with the director—"

"You are? Why is the director in your office?" asked Scot.

"He's not. I'm in his. Your call was forwarded here. We had an appointment this morning. Don't you remember?"

"Yeah, I remember, but that's not why I'm calling. I want to know what happened to Natalie and André Martin. You said they were safe."

"*Safe?* What are you talking about?"

"Last night," said Scot, "at your house, you said you would have them picked up and put into a safe house."

"Scot, I'll admit we did talk about many things when you showed up at my home in the middle of the night, but a safe house wasn't one of them."

"What? What are you *talking* about?"

"Scot, I have explained to the director how you appeared at my house ranting in the middle of the night. I attempted to calm you down. We talked about the president's kidnapping, your feelings of guilt, your concern that you might be fingered as the inside leak. . . . I gave you my word I would do everything to help you—"

"You lying son of a bitch!" said Scot, careful to keep his voice down, but making sure the force of the emotion came through nonetheless.

"Scot, this is Director Jameson. I am ordering you to tell us where you are so we can bring you in for debriefing."

"Debriefing for what?" asked Scot.

"Twenty minutes ago a SIG-Sauer three-fifty-seven semiautomatic was found near the Sperando murder scene with a serial number that comes up positive as the sidearm issued to you. It is also covered with your fingerprints. If you are not responsible, we'll give you ample opportunity to prove your innocence."

"Prove my innocence? What about innocent until proven guilty? Sounds to me like you guys have already made up your minds on this one."

"Scot, we want to help you," said Shaw.

"You know what, Bill? I think you've helped me enough already. By the way, you don't know anything about a little redecorating job that was done at my apartment last night, do you?"

"All I know is that when you didn't answer your door this morning when our men came to pick you up, they were let in by your building manager and said the place was a complete and total mess."

"But you had nothing to do with it, nor the fact that I got whacked in the back of the head and my gun was missing when I woke up, right?"

"What would I have to do with it? You're talking crazy again, Scot."

"I'm crazy? That would be a convenient excuse, wouldn't it? I don't suppose you gave the director the statement you had me write up at your place last night either, did you?"

"Statement?" asked Shaw. "I didn't have you write up any statement. Scot, this is serious. I think your head injuries may have been graver than any of us originally thought. If you've injured your head again, we need to get you to a doctor."

"I also suppose," said Scot, ignoring Shaw's expression of concern, "that the director knows nothing of Senator Snyder's potential involvement in the kidnapping of the president."

"He knows, all right. I told him about all of the people you thought were involved, right down to the White House gardener. Scot, last night you were throwing conspiracy theories around like they were going out of style. I think this has been too much for you. We need to get you some help."

Scot was silent. Why was Shaw trying to railroad him? He was blatantly lying, but why? There could only be one answer. He was somehow involved.

"Scot, this is Director Jameson again. Listen, son. I want you to turn yourself in. Tell us where you are and we'll come get you. I promise we'll listen to everything you have to say. Just tell us where you are."

"That's a nice offer, Director, but I think I'm going to decline right now. As for Agent Shaw, I made Sam Harper a promise that I would get the people responsible for his death. You're now on that list, Bill. Have a nice day."

Harvath terminated the connection.

CHAPTER 42

If a full dragnet was not already out, it would be very soon. Refusing a direct order from his superiors to come in and answer questions about a murder investigation involving his weapon should put him at the top of every law enforcement hot sheet in the D.C. area. Which meant he didn't have much time.

As he was preparing to log off from his home computer, Harvath noticed the little flag that showed he had one message. Knowing he didn't have time for this, he still let his curiosity get the better of him, and he clicked on the *new mail* icon.

> Dear Sir:
>
> Thank you for your recent inquiry regarding Nestlé S.A. chocolate products. We are sorry to inform you that our Lieber chocolate bar is not currently available in the United States. This candy is made exclusively for the Swiss market. We would like to point out that Nestlé has a fine line of chocolates which can be purchased in the United States and other countries abroad. For a full listing of our chocolates, or for any other Nestlé products, please visit our web site at . . .

Scot logged off of his home computer and signed off from the cyber café's. He paid the earthy-crunchy chick at the coffee counter for his time on line and headed out the door.

On the pavement, he quickly scanned both directions for signs of anything that seemed out of place. Not noticing anything out of the ordinary, Scot walked down G Street to Twentieth, made a left, and headed north toward Dupont Circle. It had been less than ten hours since he had gotten out of a cab in almost the same neighborhood to meet with Natalie Sperando and André Martin. Now they were both dead and someone was trying to hang him for their murders. There could be only one reason: André had been one hundred percent on the money.

It began to rain again, and Scot popped into a small drugstore and bought an umbrella and an ugly tweed Totes hat. Using the weather to his advantage, he turned his collar up and pulled the hat down to conceal as much of his face as possible. After giving Natalie two hundred dollars last night, paying for his time and breakfast at the cyber café, the Metro pass, and now the hat and umbrella, Harvath was left with seven dollars.

He found an ATM across the street. He slid in his card and punched his code. He selected the withdraw-two-hundred-dollars option and waited. Instead of the *thack, thack, thack* sound of bills being metered out, he heard the printer printing a receipt; not a good sign. The screen flashed a benign message: *Unable to complete transaction at this time. Please try again later.*

Could they have frozen my account? Scot wondered. *There's no way they could have moved this fast.* It had to be a coincidence. He put his ATM card back in his wallet and continued to head north toward Dupont Circle. When he reached M, he hailed a cab. He had the driver hang a left on Massachusetts Avenue and go through Embassy Row past the vice presidential mansion at the U.S. Naval Observatory. Convinced he wasn't being followed, he then instructed the driver to change direction and come back along Florida Avenue to North Capitol Street and drop him at Union Station.

The fare was more than Harvath had in cash, but he had flagged a cab from a company he knew took plastic. He leaned forward through the partition to watch if his card would be accepted. It was. He had been overreacting about the cash machine. His accounts hadn't been frozen. Not yet, at least.

Even though rush hour was over, Union Station was still crowded. Harvath kept his collar up and his hat pulled down close to his eyes. He tucked the umbrella under his arm and walked with his shoulders hunched up as if he was fighting off a chill from the cold air. His hands were shoved deep into the pockets of his trench coat. His right hand played with a key André Martin had slipped him as they shook hands good-bye last night at J.R.'s. "A copy of my insurance policy," André had said. "I've always liked trains. How about you, Scot?" Those had been the last words André Martin would ever say to him.

As Harvath picked his way through the station toward the lockers, his eyes scanned the room for any surveillance. Normally, he would have hung back for a while to see if anyone was watching the locker, but there was no time for that. The longer he hung around, the better the chances were that the dragnet would swallow him.

Harvath eyeballed a couple potential exits he could sprint to if he was made and, with the small comfort that afforded, moved toward the bank of colored metal lockers. He looked at the key with its number sixty-eight and wondered if Martin had chosen it out of fondness for the old joke: "What's a sixty-eight? It's kind of like a sixty-nine except you do me and I'll owe you one." If there was anything within this locker that he could use, Harvath definitely would owe André one.

Moving down the row of lockers, Harvath stopped at number sixty-five and casually glanced away toward a set of monitors listing departures and arrivals. No one seemed to be watching him, so he moved to sixty-eight. He inserted the key and opened the locker. Inside was a manila envelope, which he withdrew and tucked inside his suit coat.

Keeping his head down, but scanning in every direction, Scot began to make his way toward the nearest exit. A crowd of noisy teenagers carrying suitcases and pillows, undoubtedly off on some school trip, cut across his path, and he had to slow his pace. When the mob passed, he noticed two men he hadn't seen before standing less than ten feet away and staring right at him. They didn't look friendly. Although they were dressed in street clothes, their eyes and their builds were not those of John Q. Public.

Scot's thoughts were interrupted when the men began moving toward him. "Sir, can we speak with you a moment?" asked one.

Harvath turned in the other direction and began walking faster. He heard the men pick up their pace. Two seconds later, there was a faint metallic click that Harvath recognized right away as the sound of a blade locking into place. Whether it was a switchblade, a stiletto, or some other type of knife, the message was perfectly clear: he was not supposed to leave the train station alive. The use of a blade, rather than a pistol with a sound suppresser, was probably to make it look as if he was the victim of another D.C. mugging. Harvath now knew that these men were professionals and didn't play for the good guys.

He could sense them getting closer. He didn't dare turn around and look. From the direction they had approached, they had forced him into an area of the station that was less populated than the rest. While there were several groups of people around, they were not close enough to witness anything. Most likely, the men would come up from behind, slide the blade between his ribs, and hold him up as if he were a friend who'd had too much to drink. They would lead him over to a bench and leave him to die. Harvath's only chance was to act fast.

Quickening his pace, he pretended he was trying to put some distance between himself and his pursuers. Just as the two men matched his stride, Harvath stumbled, his leg appearing to twist in an incredibly painful contortion. Seeing their chance, the two men moved in, but Scot was ready for them.

Just as he'd expected, the men had planned to engage in what operatives referred to as the friend-in-need scenario. As he began to fall, the first man reached out to grab him as the other man readied his blade.

In a move that seemed to defy gravity, Harvath halted his fall until he could grab hold of man number one, who was already reaching out for him. Locking his right hand around the man's wrist, with his left he pinched with searing pain into the man's elbow. He resumed his fall, dislocating his adversary's arm and sending him sprawling across the floor with a powerful thrust of his legs.

Scot rolled in classic aikido fashion and came up onto his knees, just in time to parry the attack of the man with the knife. The blade was not anything as refined as a switchblade or a stiletto; it was an extremely dangerous knuckle knife. As Harvath dodged the man's thrust, the edge of the metal knuckles caught him across the lower jaw and sent a white-hot lightning bolt of pain straight to his brain.

As the knife wielder prepared for another run, Scot noticed his accomplice with the dislocated arm was moving off toward the exit. As quickly as he made this realization, the man with the knife came at him again. This time he held it in a manner that suggested his plan was to stab in a downward motion, and Scot readied himself, still with no time to get off his knees. It was amazing that no one had seen what was happening and called for the police.

Scot focused on the blade and prepared for the way in which the man was telegraphing his attack. Then, everything changed. Suddenly, the man had another knife in his left hand, and it came slicing across from left to right. All of Scot's attention had been focused on the man's right hand. *Stupid.* He should have known better.

Harvath was able to move just in time, but the blade caught the left shoulder of his trench coat and tore it. The force of the man's attack threw him off balance, and as his assailant overextended himself, he made his left side vulnerable. That was the opening Scot needed.

Before the man could regain his balance, Scot drove his right fist up hard into his kidney. He heard a *woosh* of air along with a deep groan. The man spun with both knives, pivoting back in the other direction. Harvath ducked and repeated the same punch to the man's right side, achieving the same effect. The man groaned again, and as he prepared to come at Scot for another pass, Harvath jumped to his feet and maneuvered behind him. He landed several swift and painful blows into the man's back, as well as a kick into the back of his right knee, which sent him sprawling forward onto the polished stone floor.

Before his would-be assassin could recover, Harvath popped him twice in a very painful area beneath each shoulder blade, which caused him to involuntarily release his grip on the blades. The one in his left hand clattered onto the ground, but his right fingers were still inside the knuckle loops.

Harvath stepped on his right hand and pulled the man's head up by his hair. "Who are you?" he asked.

"Fuck you," the man sputtered.

From behind him, Harvath could hear the sound of footsteps running in his direction. He glanced back and saw two Amtrak security guards closing in fast. He decided to cut his losses.

Standing up, Harvath kicked the man hard in the ribs, knowing for sure he had broken at least three. He turned toward the approaching security guards and shouted, "You guys take him. I'm going after the other one. He got my wallet!" With that, he ran toward the door the other attacker had used.

As Harvath reached the exit, he pulled up short and carefully glanced through the glass. *It could be a trap.* He surveyed the immediate area outside the doors before he slipped outside. Everything seemed quiet. There was nothing to suggest that a man had come out only moments before holding his arm and howling in pain. Of course that hadn't happened. These guys were professionals. There was no question about that. The man would have done his best not to draw attention to himself when he exited. The main question was, *Who sent these two and why?* Whoever nailed him in the back of the head at his apartment last night could have finished him off then. *Why didn't they?*

None of the people nor any of the traffic buzzing up and down Second Street seemed to pay him any attention. Whoever the other man was, he was gone by now. Careful to make sure that he was not being followed, Harvath crossed to the other side of the street and quickly made his way toward Stanton Park. Although he had lost his umbrella in the scuffle, he had managed to retain his hat, and the rain trickled from it in small gray rivulets.

Harvath tried to repair his trench coat by tucking the torn fabric underneath the shoulder seam. It would have to do for now. He was extremely lucky that the blade had not sliced any deeper. He rubbed his jaw, and although it was sore, he quickly determined that it hadn't been broken. He would live, but he had suffered yet another blunt trauma to his head. That was twice in less than eight hours.

Cutting south on Fourth Street, Scot arrived at the Folger Shakespeare Library. He needed a place where he could catch his breath and gather his thoughts. This seemed as good a place as any. Falling in with a group of older tourists who were scurrying up the stairs to get out of the rain, Harvath blended in with them perfectly as they entered the building. The group checked their wet things and were led into a re-created Tudor gallery with dark oak panels. Everyone *oohed* and *ahhed* at the library's intricately carved Elizabethan doorways. As the group moved on, Scot found a bench and sat down, placing his trench coat next to him.

He withdrew the manila envelope from his suit coat and tore it open. Inside he found several strips of paper that he couldn't at first make out. Suddenly, he realized what they were. Apparently, André had been using a handheld Xerox scanner and the strips were meant to be put together to show a complete page. Harvath didn't have time for puzzles, so he quickly sifted through the stack. Most of it seemed to be journal entries, presumably from Senator Snyder's personal appointment book. But as Harvath continued to sift, something else caught his attention.

Two strips of paper could be placed together to form what looked like a photo negative of a note. The paper was black and the handwriting was white. The handwriting matched the entries in the senator's appointment book, but why would André have a negative of a note that the senator had written? Harvath pushed the thought aside and read:

Dear Aunt Jane,

All is well here. We are looking forward to your visit and hope that everything is ready on your end. We trust that the money we sent will cover your expenses. We expect your trip to be a roaring success. You know how to contact us if you have any questions.

Yours,
Edwin

Why would Snyder write a letter and sign it "Edwin"? Harvath kept flipping through the pieces of paper. He came across something in a totally different hand and assumed it was André Martin's.

Aunt Jane? Edwin? Switzerland? Snyder claims he has no living relatives. What's the connection?

Stapled to it was another piece of paper that listed an address for a post office box in Interlaken, Switzerland, written in the senator's hand. *Switzerland?* Scot tumbled the pieces in his mind, trying to figure out how they all fit.

What was the connection? There had to be one. Snyder had had André killed because of what he thought he had discovered. Whatever it was, it must have been explosive if Snyder would kill to protect it. Now he wanted Scot dead. Well, Senator Snyder had a little surprise coming; Scot Harvath was not that easy to get rid of.

Back outside the Folger Library, Harvath turned and headed south. Along the way he tried another ATM and got the same message as before. If he was going to figure things out, he would need a little walking-around money. He flagged a cab and had it take him to the Washington Navy Yard. He gave the driver his remaining seven dollars and got out. Checking carefully behind him, he ducked into Navy Yard Metro station and took the train one stop to Waterfront. There, he emerged again and hailed a cab for his bank on Twelfth Street, just south of Logan Circle.

• • •

The bank officer was polite and after comparing Harvath's signature to the one on his card and looking at his ID, he gestured for Scot to follow him downstairs to the vault that contained the safe deposit boxes. Scot produced his key, and in a synchronous fashion that Harvath felt sure was supposed to impress, the bank officer waited to turn his key at the same moment Scot did, as if they were about to unleash a nuclear weapon.

After the box had been withdrawn, Scot was shown to a small private room, where the door was shut behind him and he was left alone. He lifted the lid of the box and removed the normal things one would expect to find, stock certificates, bonds, legal papers . . . Once those were removed, he stared down at something he thought he would never need to use.

CHAPTER 43

As he exited the bank, Harvath carefully surveyed the street before stepping out of the doorway. All of his senses were afire, filtering the stream of input they were receiving, searching for even the slightest hint of danger. Everything looked normal, but years of training had taught him that was when attacks often happened. Half a block to his left was a red-and-white van with *Ziretta Carpet Cleaning* written across the side. A long orange hose stretched from the van across the sidewalk and into a nearby building. The generator inside the van created a tremendous amount of noise, but that wasn't unusual; carpet cleaning vans were normally loud.

As he turned to his right, he decided not to give the van a second thought. It wasn't out of place, he was. This whole morning had been out of place. Life in D.C. was not magically changing because of his experiences; the real danger for him lay in seeing threats where there weren't any. Paranoia was not going to do anything to improve his current situation.

The flip side of Scot's reassuring self-talk was that paranoia might be annoying, but a healthy dose of it served to keep you alive. No one ever got killed by being too vigilant.

Quickly, Scot made his way down the street, using the reflective storefront windows he passed to see what was happening across the street and behind him. The noise of the carpet van began to slowly fade, but it was replaced by something that sounded like a heartbeat: *boom, boom, boom.* It was faint at first, but began to increase in volume. Harvath didn't hear it so much as feel it in the middle of his chest: *boom, boom, boom.* He realized that the sound was growing louder because it was coming closer: *boom, boom, boom.*

It was the heavy bass from a pumped-up car stereo system. Without even turning to look at the vehicle, Harvath knew exactly what it would be. His colleagues at the Secret Service called them *ghettomobiles.* Cars with windows tinted in flagrant violation of city ordinances, the chassis lowered, and tires sticking out far beyond the wheel wells. The drivers of these cars didn't care that bass matured over distance and got louder and deeper as the sound waves traveled outward. All they knew was that it sounded cool. Harvath hated ghettomobiles and the *hey, look at me* machismo attitude of their drivers and occupants.

The noise was almost on top of him now, and as he listened to it approach, he couldn't be sure, but he thought the car had slowed down. He glanced ahead, but there wasn't any traffic that would have caused the car to reduce its speed. *Probably not on their way to the bank,* he thought. Drawing alongside another storefront, Harvath looked in the window just in time to see the reflection of tinted windows sliding down on the ghettomobile and a Tec 9 automatic being thrust through.

Reflexively, Harvath hit the sidewalk and rolled. Bullets tore up the concrete where he had stood. The window he'd used to covertly survey the vehicle shattered in a thousand pieces, spraying him with shards of razor-sharp glass. All the while, the stereo kept thumping its staccato beat: *boom, boom, boom.*

Harvath jammed his hand inside his trench coat and groped for his waistband. It settled on the rubberized grip of his silenced nine millimeter Glock pistol. He thought he heard one of the car doors opening, and the sudden increase in the music's volume confirmed it. From where he lay next to a parked car, the curb was too high for him to see anything in the street. With the window of the store to his left shattered, he had no idea which way the person, or persons, who had exited the car were coming.

Needing a diversion, Harvath aimed the Glock and took two well-placed shots through the rear window of the car parked in front of him. The silent spits broke the glass and sent it showering into the street. He heard one of his assailants yell, "Gun!" Harvath sprang to his feet and rolled along the trunk of the parked car that had been his cover.

A powerfully built man in black fatigues and a balaclava stood swinging his Tec 9 from side to side trying to figure out where the shots had come from. Harvath didn't waste any time. He fired twice into the man's torso because the head was snapping around too wildly to get a clean between-the-eyes kill.

The man was ripped right off his feet and thrown to the ground by the force of Harvath's weapon. As Harvath turned to fire at the occupants of the gray Nissan Maxima with the thumping stereo and polished alloy wheels, the man he'd just put down shook his head as if he had been in a daze and turned his weapon on Harvath. Scot dove out of the line of fire as bullets ripped up the side of the parked car, flattening both tires and blowing out all of the vehicle's glass.

There was no way the man could have survived two direct hits, unless he was wearing *body armor.*

To any witnesses dumb enough to still be standing on the street, this looked like one vicious drive-by, but Scot knew better. Somehow, whoever had been responsible for the attack on him at Union Station had been able to track him to his bank. While this group might look like gangbangers in commando outfits, there was no fooling Harvath; they were professional hit men. The man yelling, "Gun," had proved it.

That sealed it. Scot had absolutely no plans to turn himself in to Director Jameson until he was able to get some answers. For all he knew, by turning himself in he could be handing himself over to the very people who were trying to kill him. It was obvious Shaw was behind the deaths of Natalie Sperando and André Martin. He could be behind this as well. And if Shaw was involved, who else might be working with him? There was no telling. It could be anyone.

There was no time to figure things out now. He needed to focus on staying alive.

Scot's ears were too busy ringing from the explosion of gunfire to notice the silence that now enveloped him. The smell of gun smoke hung in the damp air, and he heard the telltale sound of boots crunching on broken glass. There was a clicking sound followed by metal scraping on metal. The shooter was reloading and coming toward him. This might be Scot's only chance.

Not knowing how many other occupants were in the car and where they had their weapons trained, Harvath raised the Glock above the level of the trunk he was hiding behind and fired wildly toward where he thought the shooter and the lowered Maxima were. He heard a loud grunt and, without looking, made a desperate leap from between the parked cars onto the sidewalk. He broke off at a run back toward the bank, staying as low as he could.

He heard the squeal of tires and the rapid fire of automatic weapons as he ran. The bullets chewed apart every car he tried to use as cover, sending glass flying everywhere. Then, as quickly as it started, the commotion stopped with the sickening slam of an impact.

Harvath cautioned a look back and saw that a furniture truck, its driver not knowing what was happening, had turned left off a side street at exactly the same time his assailants were reversing wildly down the street toward him, and the two vehicles had collided. The sound of approaching police sirens could now be heard in the distance.

As Harvath turned back toward the bank, something whispered by his right ear and tore a huge piece of stone out of the building behind him. Someone else was shooting at him! And whoever this person was, he or she was somewhere in front of him using a silenced weapon.

He hit the ground and rolled again, just as another muffled shot narrowly missed his head. Using the still intact storefront window to his left, he could see a man with a mounted rifle in the back of the Ziretta Carpet Cleaning van. Scot was pinned down. He couldn't go forward and he couldn't go back. He was trapped. Or was he?

Using the storefront image for guidance, Scot raised his pistol and fired two shots toward the red-and-white van. As soon as the shots were fired, he rolled into the street between two parked cars. *What were the chances the men in the Nissan were hanging around after crashing into the furniture truck?* Most likely, they had taken off in the car if it was drivable, or by foot if it wasn't. The vehicle was undoubtedly stolen, and with the police on their way, the men would want to put as much distance between themselves and the crime scene as possible. *Those who fight and run away live to fight another day,* Scot thought to himself.

There hadn't been any gunfire from behind him, nor any sound of someone pursuing him on foot. Chances were the men in the Maxima had fled. *One group down.*

His problem now was the shooter in the van. From where the van was parked, the shooter had a pretty good command of this length of the street. The sirens were getting closer. Both Harvath and the man in the van would have to make their moves soon.

Fours shots from the van in quick succession tore up the roof and shattered the glass of the car Scot was using for cover.

Harvath waited, but the van showed no sign of moving. They were playing a very deadly game of chicken. Show yourself and be shot; wait too long and be picked up by the police. Harvath knew the man in the van wouldn't want that and probably knew that he felt exactly the same way. He needed to make a move, and he needed to make it now.

Thinking back, Scot realized the shooter in the van hadn't begun firing at him until he had run back toward his bank, which meant that if he went in the other direction, the guy probably wouldn't have a clean shot. It was the only choice Scot had.

Harvath hadn't taken his eyes off the reflection in the glass for a second. The man still sat in the van, its doors open, with his rifle pointed in Scot's direction. He hadn't figured out that Scot could see him in the glass, or else he surely would have blown it out. Or would he? Maybe the shooter was using the glass to his advantage as well.

Fixing the position of the van in his mind, Scot turned his Glock toward the storefront and chose several spots that would allow his bullets to break the glass, but minimize the chances of hitting anyone inside. He fired and, as the glass came tumbling down, he turned his weapon toward where he remembered the van to be and began firing as he ran back up the sidewalk, away from the bank.

He managed to pin down the shooter in the van long enough to escape his line of fire. He was now safely out of range, but didn't know what would face him in just a few car lengths.

The furniture truck was still in the middle of the street. Scot kept his pistol at the ready. Sliding out into the street, he glanced back to make sure no one from the van was coming up behind him. So far, it was clear.

Harvath hugged the back of the furniture truck and moved up the passenger side. As he neared the cab, he could see the crumpled gray metal of the Maxima. It was totaled. Crouching by the truck's right front tire, Harvath held the Glock in both hands ready to swing out and search for the shooters. He took a deep breath, applied pressure to the trigger and spun, just as he heard a noise from behind.

The truck's passenger door began to swing open. An older, gray-haired black man, whose eyes were wild with fright, was attempting to climb down.

"Stay where you are," ordered Harvath. "Get back in your truck, close the door, and stay on the floor." The man did as he was told.

Scot waited a beat and then sprang forward. He swept the Glock from side to side, ready to take down any of the assailants in or around the vehicle who might still be armed. There were none. The Nissan's trunk was completely crunched against its backseat. The car's interior was filled with broken glass and brass shell casings, as was the ground around it. The men had fled. The police were almost on top of the scene, and Harvath also decided fleeing was a good idea. There was nothing to gain by hanging around.

• • •

While sifting through the contents of his safe deposit box and André Martin's envelope again, it had become obvious to Scot that his only chance to get to the bottom of things was to go to Interlaken himself. After the attack outside the bank, he knew it was the right move. *Besides,* he reasoned, *who wouldn't want a break from the goddamn D.C. weather? Rain, sleet, snow, and now bullets.* He just prayed he wouldn't be embarking on a wild-goose chase.

Three blocks away, he caught a cab that took him straight down M Street to the tony Georgetown Park mall. This time, he had cash for the driver.

For some reason, the mall's Edwardian interior, in green with brass touches, always reminded him of Harrods in London. The waterfalls, which he normally found soothing, didn't work their magic on him today. He made his way toward the J. Crew store and paid for his purchases with bills from the twenty thousand dollars in cash he had removed from his safe deposit box. He'd always kept an emergency reserve, just in case, and today he was glad he had. He didn't dare use his credit card again. He had used it for two cab rides and was sure that was how the assassins had tracked him. With plenty of cash at his disposal, he could afford to ditch the plastic.

Leaving J. Crew, he bent his credit cards back and forth until he could break them into pieces. He pocketed the pieces and made his way toward Voyageur Luggage. At Voyageur, he picked up a wheeled KIVA Designs travel bag that could be converted into a backpack. It was big enough to hold the clothing he bought, but small enough to fit into an overhead compartment. Next on his list was Crabtree & Evelyn, where an attractive woman named Leslie outfitted him with a complete men's toiletry kit and a women's Pamper Yourself gift basket. Harvath counted out the bills, thanked the clerk, and asked where the nearest men's room was.

Outside the washrooms was a bank of pay telephones. Harvath chose the one at the far end and, opening the yellow pages, looked up the eight hundred number for Swissair. Knowing the quickest way to get an operator was to select the business-and-first-class-reservation option, he pressed the appropriate button. After only a few seconds a polite agent came on the line. According to the woman, Swissair had a 5:40 P.M. flight leaving Dulles that would arrive in Zurich at 7:35 the next morning. Harvath made a reservation in the name of Hans Brauner, memorized the record-locator number, thanked the agent, and hung up the phone. Harvath had been keeping an eye on the men's room. There was very little traffic, so he decided now was as good a time as any.

Inside, he looked under each stall to make sure they were vacant and chose one toward the very end. He locked the door and placed his bags in front of him. The pain in his head made it feel as if it were cracking wide open, and his stomach churned violently with nausea. Dr. Helsabeck had been right about stress and exertion making his symptoms worse, but there was no time to coddle himself. Scot faced the toilet and forced himself to vomit. If that's what his body wanted to do, *then let's get it over with,* he reasoned.

He used some toilet paper to wipe his mouth, then removed his Crabtree & Evelyn toiletry kit and hung it from the hook on the back of the stall door. Inside was a travel toothbrush and some toothpaste. No one had come into the men's room since he'd entered, so he left his stall, did a fast tooth brushing with the water from the sink, then returned to the stall and locked the door once again.

Working quickly, Scot fished several Ziploc plastic bags out of his suit pocket. The first contained a contact lens case and the other a small white tube and what looked to be a handful of brown hair. The transformation wouldn't be huge, but Harvath had learned over the years that with disguises, the sum is often greater than its parts.

The two keys to a successful disguise were, first, to eradicate any traces of a very recognizable feature, which in Scot's case was the deep blue of his eyes, and, second, to have the disguise be as natural as possible. The more elaborate a disguise, the less chance it had of working. The final goal was not only to look like someone else, but to become someone else.

As Scot put in the brown contact lenses and used the tube of glue to apply the goatee and heavy eyebrows, he began his transformation. He pushed his hair forward and parted it in the middle. With a pair of wire-rim glasses with slightly tinted lenses and a new wardrobe in mismatched earth tones, with dark sensible shoes and a dark suede blazer, Harvath became the man whose picture and name were contained in the false passport he had also removed from his safe deposit box, Hans Brauner of Stuttgart, Germany.

During Scot's time with the SEALs, he had done a lot of cross-training exercises with some of Germany's most elite soldiers. One soldier in particular, Herman Toffle, had become quite popular with the SEALs, not only for his bravado, but also for his crazy sense of humor. Scot and *Herman the German,* as the guys called him, grew to be fast friends. When Herman left the military because of an injury, he entered the private sector and began representing a German arms manufacturer. Scot helped Herman get his weapons tested in America and also plugged him in with former SEALs around the world who were doing military or private security consulting and had a heavy say in their clients' weapons procurement.

Scot couldn't accept any commissions, but Herman felt his good friend was due something for all of the business he had helped create. Once, while Scot was on leave in Germany between SEAL training exercises, Herman led him on a cloak-and-dagger tour of Munich which, after several stops for beers, finally ended in a small apartment on the city's north side. Knowing his friend's proclivity for loose women, Harvath thought Herman had brought him to a brothel and was going to get him laid.

As it turned out, Herman had a million connections and the two men just happened to be in the apartment of one of them, a master documents forger. Herman introduced the stooped, balding man with thick glasses simply as Tinkerbell. After making Scot up with the eyebrows, goatee, glasses, and contacts, Tinkerbell had him sit in front of a tarp to have his picture taken. Two hours and five beers later, the man emerged from the back of the apartment and handed Scot his new passport. When, through the fog of beers, Scot realized what Herman had done for him, he tried to refuse the gift, but Herman said, "Men in our profession need insurance that employers can't always provide."

Harvath knew that Herman was trying, in his own way, to thank him, so he kept the passport locked safely away at his bank, not thinking he would ever need it. The passport was filled with valid entry and exit stamps from America, Canada, Europe, Asia, and South America. Trying to find the most recent stamp would drive an immigration officer crazy, Tinkerbell had said, so not to worry. The old man had also given Scot an address in Munich at which, if he dropped the passport off whenever he was in Germany, one of Tinkerbell's people would update the stamps for him. Scot knew the gift had cost Herman a lot of money, and even though he originally hadn't wanted to take it, it looked now as if it was going to come in very handy.

Harvath finished changing into the J. Crew clothes and put the rest of the new clothing into his rolling suitcase. The trench coat and suit he had been wearing went into the J. Crew bag, which he promptly tossed into a Dumpster in an alley behind the mall. Wiping his prints off the Glock, he disassembled it and threw the pieces into three different storm drains. Now all he had to do was make a phone call and he would be free to go.

CHAPTER 44

Scot Harvath, having completely taken on the persona of Hans Brauner, strolled with a certain nonchalance through the lobby of the Ritz-Carlton towing his luggage on wheels. When he'd walked through the main entrance, he'd noticed the cab line was full of taxis. In his German-accented English he told the bellman he did not need any help with his bag. Having stopped at the Georgetown American Express travel office to buy a stack of traveler's checks under his new persona, he was confident in not only the outward appearance of the disguise, but his ability to pull off the complete identity of the character.

Harvath made his way to the pay phones and, glancing at his watch, knew he would have to make this call quickly. He picked up the receiver, deposited the coins and dialed the number.

"Lawlor," said the voice that answered.

"Gary. It's Scot Harvath."

"Scot, where the hell are you?"

"C'mon, Gary, you know me better than to expect an answer to that, and don't bother tracing this call. I won't be here long enough for you to get me."

"What's this all about?" asked Lawlor.

"I was going to ask you the same thing. I had nothing to do with the deaths of André Martin and Natalie Sperando. She was a good friend. I want you to believe that. For some reason, Bill Shaw is trying to set me up."

"Bill Shaw is trying to set you up? Why would he do that?"

"I know you're trying to stall me, but I'll indulge you anyway," said Scot, looking at his watch to see how long he'd been on with Lawlor. "I think he's connected to the president's kidnapping, along with Senator Snyder and maybe Rolander as well. He's trying to paint me as a conspiracy nut."

"He doesn't need to paint you as one; you painted yourself that way."

"I did? What are you talking about?"

"I heard a recording of your call to him this morning. It didn't sound like the musings of a sane person. You're really throwing around some far-fetched notions."

"Yeah, well, if I'm so far off base with my theories, why did I get *hallmarked* today?"

"*'Hallmarked'?* What do you mean?"

"You know, *when you care enough to send the very best?"*

"Are you trying to tell me somebody tried to put a hit on you?"

"Twice. Once at Union Station and then again outside my bank on Twelfth Street not long after that. They must have been tracking my credit card because I used it to pay for cabs to both locations."

"Hit men? Tracking your cards? Scot, this is pretty serious stuff. If you come in, I promise I'll help you."

"No thanks, Gary. That's the second time I've had that offer today, and I feel a whole heck of a lot safer on my own for the time being."

"Scot, I swear I don't know anything about a hit being put out on you. That's not how we do business and *you* know it. Tell me where you are, and we'll send a car for you right away. I'll put you in protective custody while we debrief you, and then—"

"Yeah? And then what? Shaw had told me he was doing the same thing with Natalie and André Martin, and look what happened to them."

"Scot, how well did you know André Martin?"

"He was a friend of Natalie's. I just met him last night. Why?"

"When was the last time you checked your bank statements?"

Harvath looked at his watch. "You're running out of time, Gary, and you're wasting it with questions that don't make any sense."

"The Secret Service has discovered that you received several large deposits to your bank account in the past month, the most recent being the day after the president was kidnapped. The money came from an account in the Caribbean. A little digging revealed a series of shell corporations, which eventually led to André Martin, D.C. attorney and international finance specialist."

"What are you saying?"

"It's not what I'm saying, Scot; it's what everyone else is. The way it looks is that André Martin somehow used his relationship with Natalie Sperando to get to you and buy you off."

"Buy me off? What the hell for?"

"The Secret Service and the Justice Department figure you were the inside leak and helped the kidnappers in grabbing the president."

"Me? That's insane."

"Is it? Look at it from their point of view. You had the means as head of the advance team, money's as good a motivation as any, and you had the opportunity."

"You can't believe that I—"

"You were the only Secret Service agent to survive the avalanche. You then interfered with three separate crime scenes resulting in the corruption of evidence in at least one of them; you were the last person seen with Sperando and Martin alive—"

"Yeah, at a bar in D.C."

"No. A desk clerk at the Radisson in Alexandria said that Martin and Sperando were picked up by a Secret Service agent who identified himself with credentials as Scot Harvath and perfectly fit your description."

"And my gun was found near the scene of the murders. Well, someone thought of everything, didn't they?"

"Scot, if you are innocent, running is not going to help your case. Let me bring you in. I swear nothing will happen to you."

"Do you believe I'm innocent, Gary?"

"I need to hear your side first."

"I'm not coming in. Not now. Somebody has gone to a lot of work to set me up, and it looks like they're hedging their bets by trying to bump me off. I'm sorry, but I think I stand a safer chance on my own right now."

"Scot, I can help you, but this has got to be done by the book. You have to come in."

"Sorry, Gary. No way. You're not going to hear from me for a bit, but I want to leave you something to think about. If someone could put this whole elaborate plan together to silence me, what could that same person do to keep the whereabouts of the president secret? You're barking up the wrong tree with the Abu Nidal and the FRC. It's a red herring. I'm sure of it. Widen your nets. I'll be in touch."

Harvath hung up the phone, went back through the lobby, and told the doorman he was going to Union Station. Once there, he found another cab and told the driver to take him to Dulles International Airport.

CHAPTER 45

"Yah, dis is a problem ven you are a businessman, no?" said Harvath in his German-accented English.

"But it is so sweet. Your wife will be thrilled," said the Swissair ticket agent as she checked the passport of Herr Hans Brauner.

"Yah, I hope zo. I also bought her a little zomething zpecial," said Harvath, putting the women's Pamper Yourself gift basket from

Crabtree & Evelyn on the counter between himself and the agent. "Do you think she will like it?"

"I think she will love it. You are so sweet to drop everything and rush home to be with your wife when she has the baby. Some things are more important than jobs, aren't they?"

"Unfortunately, my boss doesn't approve, and I am forced to use my traveler's checks to pay for zee flight. I vas supposed to be here for another three veeks, but now vis zee baby coming early, vee do vat vee can, no?" said Harvath as he counted out almost six thousand dollars in American Express traveler's checks.

It was a risky proposition. He knew airlines were very wary of customers who paid in cash, especially for same-day reservations, but he could not use any of his Scot Harvath credit cards, even if he hadn't broken them all into pieces and flushed them back at the Georgetown Park mall, because whoever was watching would be able to track him right away. At least disguised and paying cash, he would be harder to trail. Winning the ticket agent over would definitely help him. Had she or another agent been the slightest bit suspicious, they could have created a lot of trouble for him before he even got away from the desk. It had been an expensive gamble, but it looked as if it would pay off.

Harvath continued to smile as the agent asked him the standard questions about who packed his bag and whether it had been out of his sight at any time. With a final glance at his passport, she thanked him, gave him his ticket, wished him and his wife good luck, and directed him toward the business-class lounge, where he could wait until his flight was called.

So far he had lucked out. Harvath's German was relatively limited, and he would be extremely hard-pressed to carry on more than a brief conversation with anyone, but that wasn't a problem with the American-born Swissair agent. He knew these agents would converse with him in the language he chose to use. Swissair was a thoroughly professional outfit, and that's why he had chosen to fly with them. This airline would respect his privacy. To them he was another harried businessman, torn between work and family, and trying to get back home to Europe. Because of Zurich's close proximity to the German border, there was no reason a German businessman returning home wouldn't choose to fly into Zurich rather than Munich, especially if time was of the essence and Swissair's was the next flight out.

Harvath hadn't eaten anything since his bagel and orange juice that morning. While he could have picked something up at the mall, he hadn't wanted to waste time. He was thankful for the food in the Swissair lounge and discreetly loaded up while he waited for his flight to be called.

When the 5:40 flight to Zurich was called in the lounge, Harvath stood with the rest of the businessmen and made his way to the plane. A German newspaper tucked under his arm and walking slowly, almost wearily with his bag in tow, Hans Brauner blended in with the rest of the business travelers and boarded the plane without incident.

Finding his seat, he accepted an orange juice from one flight attendant as another took his coat. He felt his muscles relax as the plane pulled away from the gate and taxied out onto the runway. When the plane's engines revved up, he felt even more of the tension drain away from his body. Placing a *Do Not Wake Me for Meals* sticker on his headrest, he slipped out of his shoes, donned the Swissair booties and eyemask from his courtesy kit, and was asleep before the plane reached its cruising altitude.

CHAPTER 46

Scot awoke in time for breakfast and enjoyed a vegetable omelet, croissant, fruit, and coffee. He made one last trip to the bathroom to make sure his disguise was still firmly in place and then watched out the window as the plane made its final approach into Zurich International.

As he walked along the never-ending moving sidewalks toward passport control, he grew convinced that the Swiss government was in cahoots with airport advertisers. Why else make passengers walk so far, if not to take in the endless stream of advertisements for Swiss watches, jewelry, pens, and chocolate?

Finally, Harvath reached passport control. It was almost eight o'clock in the morning local time, and in an uncharacteristically Swiss fashion, there was only one passport control agent on duty. Being in business class did have its advantages, one of which was getting off the plane with the first-class passengers before everyone else and being at the head of the line for passport control, but that wasn't the case today. Apparently, another flight had arrived just before Scot's, and there was already a good-sized line at passport control. The grumbling of tired, cranky passengers could be heard up and down the queue. He stood nervously in line for only a few minutes, before another passport control officer appeared at the next booth, and the line began to move faster.

Scot had decided to stay with the Hans Brauner disguise and present his German passport just in case his real one had been flagged. As the plane was landing, he went through all of the possible questions he might be asked by the German-speaking passport control officials and how he would respond. As it turned out, he didn't need any of it. Anxious to clear the backup, the passport officer just glanced at the stamps of Hans Brauner's passport and added a new one. It was a red rectangle with the corners rounded off. It had the German word for Switzerland, *Schweiz,* with the date, followed by the words *Zürich Flughafen.* As Harvath was waved through by the officer, he said a small thanks for the good fortune that had brought *Herman the German* into his life.

Harvath exited through the customs *nothing to declare* lane. Everything had gone off without a hitch, but Harvath reminded himself not to get *too* comfortable. Pretending to be slightly confused, Harvath purposely walked past the departure monitors and sign boards only to turn around and come back to them, which allowed him to check whether anyone was following him. As far as he could tell, no one was.

Following the overhead signs, he reached an information counter and picked up a small brochure that had a map of the airport and a list of shops and services. He found the establishment he was looking for and made his way toward the next concourse.

Along the way, he counted fourteen more billboards for Swiss watches, seven for pens, eleven for jewelry, and nine for chocolate. It was amazing.

Coming upon a men's room, Harvath carefully rechecked to make sure he wasn't being followed and ducked inside. He chose a stall at the end, walked in, and locked the door. Quickly he changed out of his earth-toned clothes and into a pair of baggy cargo pants, boots, and a T-shirt, which he covered with a retro seventies green sweater with red and brown racing stripes across the chest and down one sleeve. The false eyebrows, goatee, and glasses were all safely packed away. Scot was still wearing the brown contact lenses, and as he pulled on a blue knit cap, he exited the men's room. To any casual observer, Scot Harvath now appeared no different from any of the other twenty-something European or American youths who either lived in Switzerland or were vacationing there for its incredible skiing and snowboarding. This disguise, though, needed one final element to make it complete.

Harvath covered the distance to his objective in the next terminal with the slow, lackadaisical stride he imagined his new persona would have. He found the Zoom hair salon exactly where the airport services guide said it would be and went in. As the young hairstylist worked, Scot discovered she was eager to practice her English. When he told her he was in Switzerland for the snowboarding, she launched into reviews of the different places she and her friends had been throughout Switzerland, France, and Austria. He had stumbled upon a real devotee.

When she was finished, Scot paid her in the Swiss francs that he had gotten at the currency exchange in the baggage claim area before proceeding through customs. He took a final look in the mirror and gave the stylist a thumbs-up.

She had done a very good job. While anyone looking for Scot Harvath or Hans Brauner would be searching for men with brown hair, parted on the side or in the middle, Scot now sported an extremely short haircut that had been bleached a bright blond, bordering on white. While it wasn't the most inconspicuous hairstyle on the planet, it would suit Harvath's needs, and it was cold enough in Switzerland that he could always cover up with a hat if needed. Popping on a pair of dark blue wraparound SPY brand sunglasses, he strutted out of the hair salon and followed the signs to the airport train station.

• • •

The first time Scot came to Europe had been with the U.S. freestyle ski team. He smiled as he thought about how his new clothes and hairstyle would probably make him fit right in with all the members of this year's team. Scot remembered now how impressed he had been with the European rail system. Almost all of the major airports had railway terminals, as opposed to America, where the airports were on the outskirts of town and the railroad stations were right in the center, requiring some sort of transportation in between.

Reaching a schedule board near the ticket window, Scot saw that there was a train leaving soon that would get into Interlaken at 12:20.

He paid the equivalent of fifty dollars in Swiss francs and bought a second-class ticket. On the platform, he noticed a group of students and casually made his way over to them, trying to blend in. The train arrived exactly on time, and Scot boarded with them. He placed his bag, which he had converted to a backpack, on the overhead rack and sat as close to the students as possible. The train made a couple of stops within and around Zurich, then began to pick up speed as it traveled out into the countryside. Once the conductor had passed through the car and checked on people's tickets, Scot leaned back in his seat and closed his eyes.

It would take about two and a half hours to cover the 239 kilometers between Zurich and Interlaken, and by the time he arrived, he hoped to have made some sense out of the last four days.

Starting at the beginning, Scot replayed in his mind everything that had happened. It was obvious that whoever the kidnappers were, they had had inside help and it involved William Shaw somehow. Shaw was working with Senator Snyder, and the two had conspired to kill André Martin and Natalie Sperando, then pin the murders on him. They had arranged for a person or persons to steal his gun, use it to kill Natalie and André, and then leave it behind so the evidence would point directly at him. Then Lawlor had said there were deposits made to his bank account via a series of Caribbean shell companies that André Martin was somehow involved with.

Shaw had admitted that Harvath had been at his house, but denied the true reason he was there, what he did, and what they discussed. So Shaw was unquestionably covering for Senator Snyder and the two were definitely in bed together, but why? How could Shaw, a career Secret Service man, be involved with something that resulted in the deaths of so many of his own men? What was the reason? That was where it started to break down for Scot.

Why would they frame him and then turn around and try to kill him? Whoever had knocked him out in his apartment could easily have finished the job as he lay unconscious on his kitchen floor. Why not kill him right then and there? Why the cat-and-mouse game? Unless framing him would take the heat off them, and he had spoiled their plans by refusing to allow himself to be captured. How was Senator Rolander connected to all this, and who or what was Star Gazer?

As Scot tried to make the pieces fit together, other images and fragments flooded his mind that didn't seem to have a place in the puzzle. He felt his headache increase in intensity and decided to leave alone what he didn't know for the time being and focus on what he did know and why he was here.

From the outset, Harvath had never believed the kidnapping could have been conducted by Middle Easterners. Call it an ingrained bigotry he had picked up in the SEALs or a healthy understanding of what Mideast terrorist groups were and were not capable of, but an operation of this nature, carried out in snow, just couldn't have been pulled off by any group from the Mideast. Harvath had discounted the lone body found with a Skorpion as a red herring from the beginning. It bothered him that Sam Harper had managed to get a shot off, but somehow no one had ever heard it.

If Middle Easterners hadn't actually pulled off the job, could they have financed it? Yes, that was definitely a possibility, but Harvath had an even harder time believing that men like Bill Shaw and even Senator Snyder would sell their country out to foreigners. That didn't fit.

Scot's head began to throb as his mind drifted, and he struggled to again bring it back and concentrate on what he knew.

His gut told him that the people who pulled off the attack and kidnapping worked very well in snow and had a lot of experience. They had access to explosives to trigger the avalanche, money and international contacts to purchase the jammer, and came up with incredible tactical advantages that allowed them to wipe out the president's protective detail and get away leaving almost no trace at all.

Almost no trace were the key words. They had left traces at the Mormon farmhouse. There had been cigarette smoke and that piece of Swiss chocolate. He had seen mousetraps in the kitchen and in one of the bathrooms, so Harvath knew the chocolate couldn't have been there long. It had to have been dropped by whoever was watching the house, waiting for the rest of the kidnappers to return. Then there was the e-mail from Nestlé that said the chocolate was sold only in Switzerland. Had one of the kidnappers bought it on a layover on a flight from somewhere in Sand Land? Not likely. It wasn't until he read the note and saw the Interlaken post office box address in the manila envelope Martin had led him to that his hunch about Switzerland began to seem like such a good possibility.

As the train gently rocked back and forth along the tracks, Scot glanced out the window at the majestic, snow-covered Swiss mountains. A Swiss railway magazine hung from a small hook above the seat opposite him with a title in German and English: "The Eiger . . . Only for the Foolish?" Scot took down the magazine and began to skim the article. It talked about one of the country's most daunting peaks and the attempts by teams from all over the world to conquer it.

As his eyes drifted from the photos in the glossy magazine to the Swiss countryside speeding past his window, he was positive his instincts were correct. Whoever arranged to kidnap the president had put together an incredible team of soldier mountaineers. Germany, France, Italy, and Austria could also boast men potentially up to the task, but it was the smattering of clues, hints really, that narrowed Harvath's gut feeling down to Switzerland.

Scot still had the same question that every law enforcement officer in America had. *Cui bono?* It was Latin for "Who benefits?" Who would benefit from kidnapping the president? The possibilities were endless. Although all the communications received by Washington since the kidnapping seemed to point to the Fatah, Scot made up his mind to leave the *Cui bono?* question to the FBI and everybody back home.

Right now *who benefits* was not as important as *who took him and where is he?* Harvath had learned a long time ago to go with his gut. Everything that had happened, everything he had seen and felt, told him the men responsible for taking the president were from here. And as sure as he knew that, Scot also knew that he would bring the president back and bring him back alive, no matter how long it took to find him.

CHAPTER 47

The hardest thing to get used to had been the smell—the godawful smell—that and the intolerable, intermittent wailing of people being called to worship over scratchy public address systems. Then there was the sand. It was everywhere—in his clothes, in his hair, even in his food. There didn't seem to be a single crack or crevice in the president's cell that the sand hadn't made its way into. He had heard that about the desert. It would eventually overtake anything, even if it took thousands of years to do it. The sand reminded him of when he and his late wife had visited Egypt and the Pyramids many years ago. He wondered where in the world he was now.

He knew he was someplace hot. At times unbearably hot, and very dry. The calls to worship meant that he was close to an Islamic population—maybe a town, a village, or even a city of some sort. His cell had no windows, so he had no idea if it was day or night. Only the deliveries of terrible-tasting food through a sliding grate at the bottom of the cell door interrupted his isolation.

The floor was covered with straw. There was a bed with a thin mattress against one wall and a Turkish toilet in the corner—which was nothing more than a hole in the floor with two stone footrests to stand on. At first, he thought the terrible stench was wafting up from the toilet, but gradually he realized it was coming from outside and was being carried in by the ventilation system of his cell. He tried to memorize every detail, as he knew there would be a very extensive debriefing once he returned home. *If I return home,* he thought.

Of course he would return home. He couldn't let himself think otherwise. He was the president of the most powerful nation on earth. Right now in D.C. they would be doing everything they could to get him back. He knew that, and had to keep focusing on it. If the kidnappers had wanted him dead, they could have killed him already. There was no reason to keep him alive unless they intended to return him once their demands were met.

To take his mind off his confinement, the president tried to think about his daughter, but that only led to more distress. He had no idea what had happened to her. The last thing he remembered was splitting up with her detail, planning to meet back at the house for hot chocolate. As he made his way down the Death Chute, there was some sort of accident and he lost his vision. There were strange voices, and someone started an IV on him, and then he awoke in this cell dressed in a cheap and uncomfortable peasant robe bearing an Arabic logo. That was all he was really sure of.

Even though there was a huge chunk of his memory missing, it wasn't hard to figure out that his detail had been ambushed and he had been drugged, kidnapped, and then taken someplace very far away. He only hoped Amanda hadn't been harmed. He tried to convince himself that she had made it back to the house safely. Scot Harvath was on her detail, and he was one of the best. He wouldn't have let anything happen to her. She had to be all right. She *was* all right. Anything else was unthinkable. Losing his wife had been painful enough, but if anything happened to Amanda, he didn't know if he could go on living.

For now, though his body was weak and he had no sense of time, his mind was strong and he vowed to hold on. The United States would not allow its president to languish in a cell in the middle of some godforsaken desert. His salvation would come. He would be getting out, and getting out alive. This would be the only thought he would allow his mind to entertain. He had a daughter to get back to and a country to lead.

The president's interior pep talk was interrupted by the sound of the bolt sliding back from his cell door. Two large men entered wearing desert fatigues and kaffiyeh headdresses that covered their faces. One was carrying a Kalashnikov AK-47 machine gun, and the other had one hand hidden behind his back. The man with the machine gun gestured for the president to move back against the wall.

Instead of moving, Rutledge rose to his full height and said, "I demand to speak with whoever's in charge here. Now!"

For a moment, both of the men stood still, shocked into immobility by the outrageous insolence of their prisoner. The shock wore off quickly, though, and the guard with the machine gun covered the distance across the cell to the president in a fraction of a second. He raised the butt of his weapon and was preparing to strike Rutledge when the other man stopped him with what sounded to Rutledge like a quick stream of angry Arabic.

The guard lowered his weapon. The president began to breathe a sigh of relief, which immediately caught in his throat as the other man, who had been steadily moving toward him, grabbed him by the wrist and plunged a long hypodermic needle into his arm.

CHAPTER 48

At precisely 12:20, Scot Harvath's train pulled into Interlaken Ost's tiny station. Using the stairs in the center of the platform, he descended into the pedestrian tunnel and reemerged two tracks over at the main station house. He fished in his pockets for the change from the soda and bag of chips he had bought from the roaming snack cart on the train, and came up with the right amount for a locker. He placed his bag inside, deposited the money, and withdrew the key. On a counter with train schedules and tourism brochures was a customer-comment form that could be folded over and sealed. He took one and began writing in it:

If you're going to have a cocktail, you've gotta go for it. Nothing beats a full-double-full-full martini. I'll be at the one place in Interlaken that has a lot of soul.

Sealing the envelope, Harvath walked outside into the bright sunshine. Sitting among a cluster of backpacks, skis, and snowboards was a group of loud American kids. They were either travelers or exchange students off for a long weekend of fun in the Alps. The one thing that was for sure was that they were all heading to the most popular youth hostel in Interlaken, Balmer's.

"Hi there," said Harvath.

"Hi yourself," said a cute blond girl with a nose ring.

"Waiting for the Balmer's van?"

"Yeah. Lucky it's such a nice day and we can sit outside. Glad I brought my sunblock. It could be a blistering weekend if it stays this bright."

"You never know in the Alps. Listen, I was wondering if you might be able to do me a favor."

"That depends," said the girl coyly.

"Yeah, right," said Scot, smiling. "I've been split up from my friends, and I'm not sure if they are coming in on the next train or maybe got here earlier. The lady, Jackie, who runs the hostel, knows us from last year. Would you mind giving this note to one of the desk staff for her when you check in?" He handed her the sealed note.

"Sure. No problem. So you're staying at Balmer's too?"

"Yeah. We're here doing a bit of boarding. Supposed to be some really nice fresh powder coming in."

"Well, maybe I'll see you later."

"Maybe. Thanks for delivering my note."

"My pleasure."

Scot walked back into the station and waited for the Balmer's van to pick up the Americans before heading out to the main street known as the Höheweg, where he turned right and walked toward town.

Interlaken had always been one of Scot's favorite places in Europe. The name *Interlaken* meant "between the lakes" and it was exactly that, nestled between sparkling Lake Thun and Lake Brienz. Water surrounded the town in the form of deep blue lakes, bubbling fountains, rushing rivers, thundering waterfalls, and crystal-clear streams. Harvath marveled all over again as he walked by the fin de siècle palaces that stood as a reminder of Interlaken's role as a health spa mecca in the second half of the nineteenth century.

He passed the Hotel du Nord on his left and the Restaurant des Alpes just after, on his right. The next sight to greet him was the enormous expanse of park known as the Höhematte. *If I'm lucky, maybe I'll be back here in the fall, sitting in the Höhematte, sipping Sekt and enjoying the jazz festival,* Scot thought to himself.

At the far end of the park was the Jungfraustrasse and the Schuh

Café. If Jackie was in and received his note, this was where she would meet him. The name of the café and its English equivalent were pronounced the same and meant the same thing, "shoe." Knowing Jackie, she would be quick enough to make the connection between *soul* and *sole.* Full-double-full-full was a very difficult aerial ski jump and was Scot's last winner before leaving the ski team. His old friend loved martinis, and since Scot had been the one to turn her on to them, he was pretty certain she'd be able to figure out who the note was from and what it meant.

Scot entered the tourist information office directly across the street and pretended to read brochures as he watched the front door of the café. Twenty minutes later, he saw a shock of bright red hair and a face full of freckles that could belong to only one person. Waiting first to make sure she wasn't being followed, he then pocketed the brochure he was holding about Jungfrau region tours, left the information office, and crossed the busy street to the café.

Jackie Kreppler had her back to him as he entered. She was scanning the room, and he sneaked up behind her, covering her eyes with his hands.

"Quick. How do you get fifty freestylers into a shoe box?" said Harvath.

"Tell them it's going to have a sponsor!" squealed Jackie, who spun right around to hug him. "What are you doing here? This is amazing!"

"I was in the neighborhood and thought I'd drop in."

"Let me look at you," she said, pushing him away from her, but holding on to his forearms. "Nice hairdo. So you've quit government work and have gone back to the ski team?"

"Not exactly."

"I'm sure the president just loves this hairstyle. Very understated . . . very subtle. Is this some way of distracting attention away from him on assignments, because I'm sure it works. And are those brown contacts you're wearing? Why would you want to go and hide those beautiful blue eyes?"

The initial happiness Scot felt at seeing her was quickly fading under the weight of the real reason he had come to Interlaken. "Can we get a table?"

"Sure," responded Jackie, who said something to the maître d' in Swiss German that Scot couldn't understand. They were led to a small table against the far wall, away from the window. Jackie withdrew a pack of cigarettes and lit one.

"From elite, world-class athlete to smoker, who would have guessed?" said Scot.

"You try living in Europe for over ten years, married to a smoker, and not get hooked. I only have one once in a while and only when I drink. I know it's no excuse, but hey. What do you want?" said Jackie as a waiter approached their table.

"Ein grosses Bier," said Scot.

"Und einen Kir, bitte."

The waiter nodded politely and left.

They made small talk about Interlaken and how the season was going; then Jackie took a drag on her cigarette and launched into a rapid-fire series of questions. "Okay, enough chitchat. I want to know *everything* that's going on with you. What you've been doing. Who you've been dating. Why I haven't heard from you in such a long time, and most of all, how you are able to get time off during one of the biggest crises to hit the United States."

Scot saw the waiter coming back and decided to hold off on answering. The man set down their drinks along with a bowl full of heavily salted homemade potato chips and left again. Jackie dug right in.

"Where did you want me to start?" asked Scot.

"I don't know," said Jackie between bites. "Start wherever you want. What are you doing here? Vacation?"

"No, it's not a vacation. I'm in trouble and I need your help."

"Trouble? What do you mean, 'trouble'?"

Scot was quiet.

"Does this have something to do with the president's kidnapping?"

His faced must have betrayed his reaction, as she said, "Don't look so surprised. It's big news everywhere."

The fact that the kidnapping of the president was making headlines around the world was no surprise. What surprised him was Jackie's ability to put it all together so fast. She had always been able to read him so well. Even though they had been only kids when they dated on the ski team, Scot had thought she might be the one for him. When his father died, though, his life had been turned upside down. By the time he had gotten his act together, Jackie was deeply involved with a Swiss skier whom she would eventually marry. All that remained for the two of them was to be good friends. Even though Scot had the best of intentions, he seemed to keep falling out of touch, not only with Jackie, but with a lot of people who mattered to him. He always blamed his work for keeping him too busy, but as he looked across the table at Jackie, he realized he had only himself to blame for dropping the ball. She was even more beautiful now than during their days on the ski team. She was quite a woman, cigarettes notwithstanding.

"How's the hostel doing, Jackie? Every time I'm in a bookstore, I pick up guidebooks on Switzerland and there you are. The Kreppler family must have been real happy to gain such a shrewd manager cum daughter-in-law," he said.

"Let's not forget the lucky husband who got such a fabulous wife either."

"We can't forget the husband. How is old Rolf?"

"The same as ever," Jackie answered, taking a sip of her Kir. "Now, quit dancing around the subject and tell me what you mean by being 'in trouble.' Were you there when the kidnapping happened?"

"This has got to stay between you and me."

"Of course. Who do ya think you're talking to? I'm the same old Jackie. We'll make sure the tongue stays in the ol' Schuh. My lips are sealed. Besides, you're the one who came looking for me."

She was right. Scot needed her help, although only minimally. He didn't want her to get too involved. He took a deep breath and then began his story. "Yes, I was there. I was one of the only two survivors, last I heard. Most of the agents were either buried alive in the avalanche or . . ." Scot hesitated.

"Or, what? What happened?"

"Or they were shot to death."

"Shot to death? That's terrible."

"It gets worse. A woman I was good friends with and a friend of hers were killed Tuesday night, not long after I had drinks with them, and I'm now the number one suspect in their murder."

Jackie would never have succeeded at professional poker playing. Her face went from rapt attention to all-out shock. "Murder? You?" she managed.

"Yup, and it looks like my gun, which was stolen from my apartment, was used to kill them. Also, several large deposits were coincidentally made to my bank account right around the time of their murders and the kidnapping of the president."

"Are the two events connected?"

"In too many people's minds right now, *I'm* the connection. I have been framed both for the murders and for being the inside leak that helped the kidnappers take the president."

"But I thought the Secret Service thought so highly of you. The few times I heard from you, it sounded like everything was so great."

"It was great."

"Well, what about your boss? Your superiors? They know you. They should be able to vouch for what kind of a person you are. Surely they know you weren't involved with any of this."

Her vote of confidence meant more to him than she would ever know. "The problem is that my immediate supervisor, who was also my very good friend, was killed in the kidnapping and the next boss up is somehow involved in all of this on a very bad level."

"Aren't there any people higher up than him?"

"Yes, there are, but the evidence against me is pretty overwhelming. The last I spoke with them, they invited me to come in so I could prove my innocence."

"Prove your *innocence?* Whatever happened to 'innocent until proven guilty'?"

"That's why I've always liked you, Jackie. You get right to the point. Those were my feelings exactly."

"So, you fled here to Switzerland? Are you trying to avoid extradition?"

"No."

"Well, forgive me if I'm overstepping my bounds, but I think I know you well enough. If you are innocent, and I believe that you are, doesn't running only make it harder for you in the end?"

"Depends on how you look at it."

"What do you mean?"

"You see, I know I didn't do it, and so do the people who are trying to frame me."

"Okay . . ."

"Well, they seem to have changed their minds about framing me and tried twice yesterday to kill me."

Jackie drew in a sharp breath. "Are you okay? They didn't hurt you, did they?"

Scot smiled. "You know me. I'm bulletproof. They're going to have to try a lot harder than that."

"They'd better not. So what now? Do you plan on hiding out over here until things cool down? Do you need money—?"

"No, I'm okay in the money department for now, but thanks. I have a few leads I want to follow up—"

"Leads? Over here?"

They were getting into tricky territory, and Scot chose his words very carefully. "There are some people I need to track down and talk to who might be able to help me out. When the time is right, hopefully I'll have my ducks in a row and will be able to go home. In the meantime, nobody can know I'm here."

"Well, I won't say anything."

"I appreciate that. I also need to ask you a favor."

"What kind of favor?"

"I need a place to stay."

The look on her face said it all. She really wanted to help him, but what he was asking was a major imposition. Despite the camaraderie that existed between all of the freestyle skiers, even if they were from different countries, Jackie's husband had always viewed Scot as competition both on and off the hill. Rolf was extremely jealous of him and was not happy with the way Scot occasionally showed up for a visit or a letter from him would appear in the post. Scot's last visit had not gone well, and Jackie and Rolf had fought for over a week when he forbade her to ever see or speak to Scot again. Rolf would prefer that he was out of Jackie's life for good.

"You know you're not Rolf's favorite person."

"I know, and I have felt bad about it ever since I was last here. I didn't mean to upset him."

"I think it's more his problem than anything else. He's always felt threatened by you."

"I don't know why. He's a good-looking guy with a beautiful wife and both a successful business and political career. He's still active in politics here, isn't he?"

"Oh, yeah. More than ever. Listen, like I said, the whole thing between you two was always his problem more than anything else."

"Jackie, I'm sorry to put you out. If I thought there was anywhere else I could go, I would. It's just I've got some very heavy things to work out, and I need to stay somewhere safe. I don't think anyone would come looking for me at your place. I know this is a burden, but I need your help."

Chewing on her bottom lip, she swirled the raspberry-colored liquid in her wineglass. "In one sense you're lucky. First, I was around to get your message. You think you're so smart. *Full-double-full-full?* You don't think if Rolf had gotten that note he wouldn't have been suspicious?"

Scot grinned sheepishly.

"Second," said Jackie, ignoring the cute look on Scot's face, "he's in Bern for a week with his political party, so it won't be too tough to keep you hidden away."

Harvath breathed a sigh of relief as Jackie continued, "We've been rehabbing part of the *Herberge* for the summer. I can put you in one of the completed rooms, and no one should even notice. There's a lot of sawdust in the halls, you still have to use coins for hot showers, and there will be no maid service, but my guess is you're willing to accept the room under those conditions."

"You are absolutely right. I owe you big time."

"Yes, you do. Now, how do I get you the key?" wondered Jackie as she bit down once again on her pouty, strawberry pink lip. "Ah. I'll leave it with a note under one of the garbage cans in the alley behind the main building. We have about six cans, all painted bright red. One of them is smaller than the others. I'll put it under there. All I ask is that you use the back stairs and try not to draw any attention to yourself."

"Believe me, I have no intention of doing that."

"Could have fooled me with that haircut and dye job of yours."

They both laughed, and Scot reached across the table and took Jackie's soft, freckled hand. She tensed at first and then relaxed.

"I can't tell you how much I appreciate this, Jackie. I don't know who else I could have turned to."

"Well, even if Rolf was in town, we would have found a way to deal with this. You and I go back a long way."

"We certainly do."

"I just hope you can get yourself out of this mess you're in."

"I will. Don't worry."

Jackie gave his hand a squeeze and rose from the table. "I take it drinks are on you?"

"You bet. When can I look for the key?"

"The garbage was picked up this morning, so I don't think there'll be any problem if you try in about an hour. You remember the back way, round by the volleyball court?"

"You have the volleyball court going even in the cold?"

"Scot, have you forgotten the stupid stuff we used to do in the middle of winter after a couple of drinks?"

"Yes," he said, smiling.

"Liar. Anyway, I'll have you know winter volleyball happens to be a huge draw with our young clientele. I'll have the key there within the hour."

Jackie gave his hair a ruffle and let out a disapproving sigh. "You used to be such a handsome guy," she joked.

"Thanks a bunch, Jack."

"I'll see you later."

She gathered her purse and coat. Scot watched her disappear out the front door and then reappear outside the window as she made her way up the Jungfraustrasse back to Balmer's *Herberge.*

He finished his beer and decided to retrieve his bag at the station, then wander around town to kill some time before heading up to the hostel.

CHAPTER 49

The key and a note were left under the smallest red garbage can, just as promised. The little map Jackie had drawn showed that his room was in the far south end of the structure just off the main building. Despite the fact that broad daylight made it difficult not to be seen, Harvath managed to get inside and up to his floor without being noticed.

As he climbed the stairs, his nose was greeted by the sweet smell of fresh lumber. The *Herberge* itself looked like something out of an old Heidi movie. It was a typical Swiss-style chalet, wood inside and out. Painted under all of the gables were scenes of historical Swiss daily life. Flower boxes hung from every window.

Dodging assorted construction debris, Scot found his room and opened the door. Jackie had made the bed and left him several bottles of mineral water, cheese, a couple of apples, bread, a salami, an electric coffeepot with coffee, dishes, a fork, a knife, and a spoon. Next to these staples was a notepad with writing on the top sheet that read: *"By the way, none of this stuff is free. It all goes on your bill. Enjoy your stay. J."*

She hadn't changed one single bit, and thank God for that. Scot didn't know what he would have done without her. Staying at a regular hotel would have been tricky. They would have requested he leave his passport as a deposit. As it stood now, he didn't want either of the two he carried to be out of his possession.

The floor, the walls, and the gently sloping ceiling were all constructed from beautiful blond wood. The double bed had white sheets and a red checkered comforter. There was a sink off on one wall, and he figured the toilets were down the hall next to the showers he had seen. Per Jackie's suggestion, Scot had changed some of his paper money for five-franc pieces at the Interlaken post office so he could enjoy a shower with hot water in the morning. He'd also bought a couple of envelopes and some stamps. He set the coins on the counter next to the sink.

Feeling a bit warm, he opened the casement windows just a crack. They opened outward like mini French doors. In her note Jackie had mentioned that the workmen often opened them during the day but that he must remember to close them at night, or one of the staff might come up to investigate. He kicked off his shoes and sat down on the bed. From a blue plastic bag, he withdrew the purchase he had made at a shop just around the corner from the *Herberge.*

When Scot had passed a gun store called the Waffenhaus Schneider, he couldn't believe his luck. Though he wasn't a Swiss citizen and couldn't purchase a real firearm, something else sat smiling out at him from the display window.

Harvath entered and admired the wide range of weaponry. As he moved from section to section, he finally settled in front of a display by the window that read, "New from Tokyo. Airsoft!" Airsoft products were a line of authentic-looking replica firearms that fired six-millimeter plastic balls. They were so realistic that they were used in Hollywood movies and by several federal and local law enforcement agencies for training. The toy guns came in revolver models, semiautomatics, machine guns, shotguns, sniper rifles . . . you name it and Tokyo Marui made it.

Scot had finally settled on a Glock 17. It was an almost perfect copy of the exact weapon, minus the silencer, he had used to save his life just the day before. He hoped he wouldn't need to count on a toy gun to save his life in the future, no matter how realistic it looked, but until he could get his hands on a real one, this would have to do.

Sliding the cover off the box now, he removed the gun from the inner Styrofoam box. It had cost him about sixty dollars U.S., but at least now maybe he wouldn't feel so vulnerable. In a pinch, bluffing with the fake Glock would be better than having nothing at all, but the sooner he got ahold of a real weapon, the better. Rolf undoubtedly had one of the government-issued assault rifles somewhere in their house, but the Swiss didn't issue their civilian army ammunition with their rifles. That was okay; Scot didn't want to put Jackie any further out than he already had. *Besides, how the hell would he conceal an assault rifle?*

He continued to plug the little white balls into the magazine. To his surprise, they helped bring the weight of the pistol closer to what it would be in real life and didn't make any rattling noise when he twisted the gun from side to side. The best part was that it would fit neatly in his waistband without being seen. Scot set it aside and reached for the pad and pencil Jackie had left on the table with the food.

He tore off the top piece of paper with her handwriting and set the pad on the bed next to him. Fishing the manila envelope from André Martin's locker at Union Station out of his pocket, he began flipping through the papers until he found what he was looking for, the note to Aunt Jane and the address in Interlaken.

Trying to copy the senator's handwriting wouldn't be necessary. He wanted whoever read his letter to know there was a new player in the game. Putting the pencil against the pad to begin his own little note to Auntie Jane, Harvath noticed that he could see an impression of the note Jackie had written on the page before it. The realization came to him in a flash, and he felt stupid for not seeing it before. His brain really had been scrambled. It was one of the oldest tricks in the book.

The reason the note to Aunt Jane, which Scot had decided beyond a shadow of a doubt came from the senator, looked like a negative on the photocopied page was because that's essentially what it was. He had to hand it to André Martin; he'd been extremely thorough. Finding the senator's pad, André had lightly sketched with a pencil across the top page to see what had been written on the page before it. Most people wrote hard enough that their writing could be read several pages deep in a pad. Martin had known this trick and had been able to salvage the letter. It was all beginning to make sense. There was no way the senator would have engaged in his shadowy business at his office; there were too many opportunities to be found out. Instead, he worked from home, confident in his security. Based on the evidence in front of him, Harvath decided the senator was either very careless or André Martin was very clever. It was probably a combination of the two.

Scot stuck as close as he could to the language of the note contained in the manila envelope. The key was for the reader to know someone was on to him:

Dear Aunt Jane,

You have been a very bad girl. You have taken something that doesn't belong to you and many people want it back. I have no disagreement with you, but believe my silence is worth something. Why don't we meet to discuss it? I will be at the Top of Europe's Ice Palace at noon the day after you receive this.

I look forward to a mutually profitable chat.

Yours,
A friend of Edwin's

Scot read the letter several times before sealing it in the envelope he had bought. After addressing it with the Interlaken post office box, he stamped it and left for the post office.

Walking down the Centralstrasse, Harvath roamed the neighborhood, and pretended to window-shop until five minutes before the post office closed. Then, he slipped his letter into the outdoor slot, satisfied that the letter would not make it into the post office box until tomorrow morning at the earliest.

He walked back to Balmer's and ran his plan through his mind yet again. It was a long shot, and he knew it, but at this point, it was the only shot he had.

CHAPTER 50

Star Gazer hurriedly grabbed the wastebasket beneath his desk and vomited. Lying on a crumpled piece of wax paper on his desk was a man's severed finger. He knew whom it belonged to and who had sent it.

I can't believe they managed to get this into my office, he worriedly thought to himself. First, all of those Secret Service agents get killed, then the Special Ops team, and now this. This is getting way out of hand. It has to end.

Two hours later, Star Gazer sat in his study facing Senators Rolander and Snyder. Once the doors had been closed by Star Gazer's bodyguards and it was safe to talk, Rolander began, "I don't think calling this meeting was such a good idea."

"Oh, you don't?" replied Star Gazer, anger notching his voice up as he spoke. "Well, guess what? I am done listening to you! This is all totally out of control!"

"Keep your voice down!" snapped Snyder. "Now, just tell us what's got you so worked up."

"What's got me so worked up? I received a note today along with the president's finger!" he said, ignoring Snyder's request that he lower his voice.

Rolander was speechless.

"I am not going to tell you again. Calm down. What did the note say?"

"The kidnappers want fifty million dollars deposited to an account in Buenos Aries, or the next package I receive will contain President Rutledge's head."

"Our friends are getting a little greedy," said Snyder.

"They can't do this," said Rolander.

"They are doing it," replied Snyder, who turned back to Vice President Marshfield. "Are you *sure* it was Rutledge's finger?"

"Positive. It had a funny half-moon-shaped scar at the knuckle which he always bragged about getting in a sailing accident."

"What did you do with the finger?"

"What did I do with it? What do you think I did with it? I gave it to the Secret Service."

"Jesus. What about the note? You didn't show anyone the goddamn note, did you?"

"The note? Of course I did. You expect me to keep this to myself? This is all so insane. You have to stop this!" cried Star Gazer, the hysteria creeping back into his voice. "I never agreed to all of this killing, and what's more, our deal was that the president be returned *safely* to his office."

Marshfield was stepping on Snyder's last nerve. "Don't tell me what our deal was. I put it together, remember? You get your big fat war chest filled with untraceable campaign contributions and a chance to prove that you're made of the right stuff to be president. You stand tough and don't negotiate with terrorists and come out smelling like a rose. We know Rutledge doesn't plan on running for a second term, so you *sail* right into the number one position in the world. We handed you exactly what you wanted, so don't start telling me what our deal was."

"I damn well will tell you, because your whole operation is falling apart!" shot Marshfield.

"The only thing falling apart here, Mr. Vice President, is you."

"Me? You don't even have enough fingers and toes to count all the dead bodies on. And from what I hear, you let that Secret Service agent, Harvath, slip right through your grasp!"

"I'm not going to tell you again. You do your job and we'll do ours. All you have to do is to talk tough to the cameras and make sure the president's coalition for that fossil fuel reduction bill completely collapses. We want every *yes* vote so solidly *no* that even if he walked back onto the floor tomorrow morning, there'd be no resurrecting it. Do you understand me? The rest you leave to us. And for God's sake, man, pull yourself together. You certainly don't look like presidential material to me."

"I know. The pressure is just—"

"Marshfield, I'm going to say this once. I know you're a smart man and I won't have to say it more than that. If a president can disappear, think how easy it would be for a vice president to vanish . . . permanently. Get your shit together. This is the last time I am going to warn you." Snyder stood and said to Rolander, "Let's go."

• • •

Fifteen minutes later, with the privacy screen raised and knowing Snyder had his limousine swept continually for bugs, Rolander felt safe to speak. "I'm worried about Marshfield."

"There's nothing to worry about," said Snyder.

"Nothing to worry about? The man's falling apart."

"He'll be fine. Besides, he knows what will happen to him if he tries to unburden his soul. I've got a pair of eyes on him at all times."

"How deep does this thing go?"

"Deep enough to make it work. Right now, Marshfield is the least of our worries. I never should have let you talk me into concocting that plot to set up Harvath."

"There wasn't enough time to sit around and think. At the time, it made perfect sense. Killing him would have been too suspicious. Framing him solved a lot of problems in one tidy little package."

"And then it created a whole hell of a lot more. We should have terminated him in his apartment when we had the chance."

"Listen, David, there's no use crying over spilt milk. He's on the lam, and all that stunt has done is cemented Washington's belief that he's guilty."

"But he knows too much."

"Not enough. It's all circumstantial. The rantings of a nut who has suffered severe head trauma. It will never stick."

"He's managed to kill two of my best contract agents outside the bank and seriously wound three others between there and the Union Station fiasco. Harvath is not someone I'm going to underestimate again."

"From what you've told me, the two he killed were lucky shots. Your other guys, especially the one that got his arm torn out of its socket, deserved what they got for being stupid. They knew full well what kind of a background Harvath has. To try and take him up close was a mistake. One which I'm sure your people won't make again."

"No, they won't."

"Fine, now what about that ransom note Marshfield received?"

"What about it?"

"What are we going to do?"

"Nothing."

"Nothing? What do you mean, *nothing?*"

"I mean just that. I've already been through this potential scenario with Fawcett. He thought this might happen, especially considering how much money he's already paid out. It was a natural to expect our Lions to get greedy. His decision was we do nothing."

"But how can we do that?"

"Simple. If the president doesn't return alive, then Marshfield remains in the number one position to finish out Rutledge's term. A couple more well-orchestrated high-profile events while he runs down the clock for the former president and he's a shoo-in to get reelected. Then he has the potential to serve for two full terms and we'll own him all the way. It makes a lot of sense, really. We can't lose."

"Except, there's a fly buzzing around that might land in the ointment."

"Who, Harvath? For Chrissake, Russ. One minute you tell me not to worry about him and the next you're painting him as the one thing that could bring everything crashing down around us. You think I'm going to let that happen? I already have a lead on him."

"You do?"

"Surprised? You think being on the Senate Intelligence Committee doesn't have a couple of advantages? Apparently, Harvath called Lawlor at the FBI yesterday proclaiming his innocence. Ever the thorough G-man, Lawlor put a trace on the call and found it was coming from a pay phone at the Ritz. By the time his guys got there, no one fitting Harvath's description could be found, so they did the usual, questioned a bunch of staff and potential witnesses, took statements, and left."

"So they didn't nab him. What's that got to do with our problem?"

"It has everything to do with our problem. When the FBI questioned people and they said they never saw Harvath there, they were telling the truth."

"Okay . . . But I don't follow you."

"The FBI made the same mistake with Harvath that we did. They underestimated him. Do you actually think with half of D.C. looking for him he'd be wandering around without some sort of disguise?"

Senator Rolander's eyebrows arched up.

"It makes sense, doesn't it?" continued Snyder. "The Ritz is one of the city's most security conscious hotels. They have cameras everywhere. Based on the timing of the phone call to Lawlor and which bank of phones it came from, it was just a matter of rolling back the videotapes and we had him. We also had an outside camera showing him getting into a cab. The doorman remembered that he spoke English with a German-sounding accent. We got the number of the cab and showed the picture to the driver, who said he took him to Union Station."

"So he hopped on a train, but where to?" asked Rolander.

"He didn't hop on any train. He switched cabs at Union Station and probably three or more times before he got to Dulles."

"Dulles? What airline?"

"Swissair. We got ahold of the airport security tapes and quietly passed his picture around. He traveled under the name of Hans Brauner and flew to Zurich last night."

"Are you sure?"

"Yes. I saw the video myself. He was still wearing the same disguise from the Ritz."

"But Switzerland. Jesus, how did he figure out the Switzerland connection?" said Rolander, his voice taut.

"I have no idea. It must have something to do with André Martin and maybe that envelope Harvath was seen taking out of the locker at the train station."

"I knew this was going to happen. You're right, we underestimated him. Shit! What are we going to do?"

Rolander was sweating, but Snyder was as calm as ever. "I've already set the wheels in motion."

"What does that mean?"

"I sent a team over to silence Agent Harvath once and for all."

"But he could be anywhere. How are you going to find him?"

"Quietly, I flagged his passport and put both his name and the pseudonym Hans Brauner on the Swiss watch list. I've got someone manning a bogus State Department phone line and E-mail address. The directive I sent was not to try and apprehend him, only to keep him under surveillance and notify us if he shows up."

"If he shows up."

"Don't worry, he will."

"I think we should let our Lion know what's happening."

"Why?"

"What if Harvath tracks them down?"

"What if he does? He wouldn't stand a chance against them."

"I thought we weren't going to underestimate Agent Harvath anymore."

Exasperated at having to spell everything out for his fellow senator, Snyder took a deep breath before drawing the picture. "First of all, the only way I have to get in touch with them is via the post office box. It was set up that way to protect all of us. Secondly, they're trying to screw us right now by asking for more money. If we tip them off about Harvath, they might figure out a way to use him against us. It's better that we stay quiet about it. He'll pop his head up at some point and we'll be there to nail him. Don't worry. Besides, even if Harvath did locate the Lions' den, which I don't think he has a snowball's chance in hell of doing, he's no match for these guys. They'll rip him apart, and that's not an underestimation."

"But what about the president's finger? Even you've got to admit that's going too far. What if they kill him?"

"If they do, then that's just the cost of doing business."

CHAPTER 51

Harvath hated jet lag. Even though he had slept for most of the plane ride and had forced himself to stay up late last night, he still woke up early this morning. Opening his eyes, he could see that it was dark, and the only indication that anyone was up at this hour was the occasional sound of traffic from the nearby street.

He closed his eyes again and tried to force himself back to sleep, but soon realized he was up for good. The bare wood was cold under his feet. Quietly, he padded down the hall to the bathroom and then returned to his room. Scot began a slow routine of stretching, testing his muscles. Although the bruises would probably take weeks to disappear, at least the stiffness was dissipating. He chalked up his returning muscle function and mobility to the shape he'd been in before the avalanche. As he continued stretching, moving into a series of yoga postures, concentrating on his breathing, he noticed his head was still aching.

From the yoga he moved into a series of push-ups, crunches, and dips using the footboard of the bed and a chair. Covered in a light film of sweat, breathing heavily, and with a somewhat queasy stomach, Harvath grabbed his towel, toiletry kit, and a stack of coins and headed off for the shower.

When he returned, he had a breakfast of bread, cheese, fruit, and two Tylenols, followed by a cup of strong black coffee. After brushing his teeth, he dressed in another *"hey, dude"* snowboarder outfit, tucked the Glock into his waistband, put his jacket on, and crept from the hostel.

When the post office opened, Harvath was standing at the main doors with a *USA Today* newspaper tucked beneath his arm. As he walked up to the window marked *poste restante,* Scot noticed that the same woman was behind the counter as yesterday when he'd been buying envelopes and stamps.

"Good morning," he said in English, knowing the woman was fluent.

"Ah, good morning, sir. Here to see if we have received your letter yet?"

"Yes. I hope it's here. I need the money to buy my train ticket to Strasbourg."

"I will check for you. What is the name again, please?"

Harvath had not wanted to give the woman his real name yesterday and so had used the first one that popped into his head, "Sampras. Pete Sampras." He knew it was a stupid choice, but once the name had crossed his lips, he couldn't pull it back.

"Of course, like the tennis player," she said.

"Yeah, except he plays tennis better than I do and has a lot more money."

"Well, maybe we can change that. The money part, I mean," she said with a smile, writing down his name and walking to the back.

Yesterday, Harvath had completely cased the post office after his plan had come to him. Standing outside, he would never be able to tell if "Aunt Jane" or someone working for her had accessed the post office box. The only way he would be able to surveil it was from inside, but how could he sit around inside the post office all day without attracting suspicion? He remembered a con game he had seen in a movie called *House of Cards* and decided a spin on it might work.

Post offices worldwide would accept mail for you even if you didn't have a box with them, as long as the letter was addressed to you at the post office with the words *poste restante.* All you had to do was keep checking in for your mail, and when a piece arrived for you, show your passport and claim it. It was very simple.

The clerk came back shaking her head. "I'm sorry, Mr. Sampras, we still have no mail for you."

"Darn it. I was hoping to catch a morning train."

"You can check back later if you like. We have mail arriving all day here."

"That's very nice of you. You know, if it's not too much trouble, it is very cold outside this morning and I don't even have enough money to have breakfast. Would it be okay if I just sat over there and waited? I'm sure it will be here at some point today."

Harvath was pushing it. The idea of him sitting in the post office all day might not appeal to the clerk, but he had put just enough flirt into his dialogue with her that he felt she would say yes.

"I don't think it would be a problem." She smiled. "I will keep your name here, and next time I go to the back, I will check again. Maybe I'll even bring you a coffee."

"Thanks. I have my newspaper, and I will just be sitting over there."

"Very well. Next customer, please."

Scot made his way over to the wooden bench and sat down, making himself as comfortable as possible. This could be a very long wait. There was no telling how often Aunt Jane's post office box got checked, if at all. For all Scot knew, the mail might get forwarded someplace else entirely.

He positioned himself and the paper at such an angle that he could see the box, but to anyone looking in his direction, it would appear as if he were engrossed in his paper.

Ten o'clock came and went. The friendly clerk called him back over to her counter and handed him a cup of coffee, apologizing that his letter was still not there. He sat back down on the bench and waited.

At twenty past ten, a group of elderly people entered the post office en masse. Apparently, they all liked to hike down to the post office and do their business together. Several went to post office boxes, and for a moment Scot had trouble telling if the slight figure in the blue quilted jacket and brown hat was opening the box he had been watching. The group of septuagenarians milled about in front of him, blocking his view.

Through a brief opening in the crowd he saw a gloved hand close and lock a box . . . his box! Aunt Jane, or someone connected to her, had opened the box and retrieved the letter. He had purposely purchased a brightly colored envelope yesterday and could tell, even from where he sat, that the one in the gloved hand was his.

The throng of elderly Swiss moved toward him as they prepared to get into the stamp line. He politely pushed his way through the tangle of walking sticks, hiking boots, and lederhosen.

Outside on the concrete steps of the post office, Scot looked quickly to his left and caught a glimpse of a blue coat and brown cap turning the corner. He took off after it, slowing only when he got to the intersection.

A person of average height and slim build was walking just ahead of him, seemingly unaware of being followed. Harvath followed and hadn't made it fifteen feet when the figure crossed the street and looked into a pastry shop window. He knew what the person was doing. It was the same maneuver he had used on many occasions—checking the reflection in the glass to see if anyone was following. He had no choice but to look straight ahead and to continue down the block.

Luckily, streets in Interlaken for the most part were small and provided ample opportunities for ducking off. The first chance Harvath got, that's exactly what he did.

Since the person he was following had been proceeding in this direction and Harvath was confident he hadn't been noticed, he hid himself in a doorway and waited for him to walk by. Hopefully, his wait wouldn't be in vain.

Five minutes passed, then ten, then fifteen . . . nothing. Harvath had lost him. He was certain of it. Whoever he was following either had gotten spooked and doubled back or had never intended to take this route anyway. He was angry with himself for losing his quarry. Now he would have to show up for the meeting tomorrow blind, with no idea of whom to look for. That was extremely dangerous, but once more, he had no choice. The place he had set for the meeting was known as the Jungfraujoch, the Top of Europe. It was a tourist attraction carved into a glacier on the Jungfrau Mountain. The Jungfrau stood right next to the Eiger. The Jungfraujoch was a dangerous place in which to hold a clandestine meeting, but it was one of the few locations close to Interlaken that Scot felt he knew well enough and would feel safe in. The crowds of tourists would provide ample cover, it was next to impossible for a sniper to set up anywhere, and there was only one way into the Jungfraujoch—by train. Scot planned to have all of his bases covered.

As he stepped out of his hiding spot and turned up a different street to make his way back to the hotel, a pair of steely eyes in another doorway stared out from beneath the brim of a brown cap and memorized every feature of his face. The only thing that prevented Harvath from being followed was his watcher's need to discover what was inside the brightly colored envelope and return it to the post office box, before its rightful owner arrived to claim it.

CHAPTER 52

"Hey there. Where's your board?"

The voice caught Harvath completely off guard. He turned to see the group of noisy Americans he had encountered two days ago walking toward him on the platform. Leading the pack was the cute girl with the nose ring.

"You didn't forget it, did you?" she asked.

"Nope. My friends never showed up, so I'm going to have to rent my gear," Harvath replied.

"Bummer. We're heading up to Wengen. You're welcome to board with us."

"Thanks. I really appreciate it, but I bought this Good Morning Ticket thing so I'd get a cheap deal up to the Jungfraujoch."

"We did that yesterday. We took the 6:35 A.M. train. Boy, was that early. But we saved a few francs that way."

Harvath made small talk with the group until the older, greenish gray Berner Oberland-Bahnen train pulled into the station. The train had eleven cars, the front half of which would go toward Lauterbrunnen, while the back half would go toward Grindelwald. As Harvath was going to take the Grindelwald route to get to the Jungfraujoch, he said good-bye to everyone and hopped on one of the cars in back.

At precisely 7:35, the train pulled out of the station and made its way toward the first stop of Wilderswil. The steep mountains seemed to begin right at the tracks and shoot straight up. Even at this time of year the mountains gave forth with the bright hues of evergreen trees, which were made even more brilliant by the contrast of the pure white snow. As beautiful as the rugged Alpine scenery was now, Scot knew it was nothing compared to what this region was like in spring.

That was how he'd first experienced Interlaken and the Jungfrau region—mountains overflowing with a myriad of colors from all the blooming wildflowers. On the Schynige Platte alone, up and to the left of where the train was now, there were over five hundred different types of plant life visible in the spring. The waterfalls and rivers tumbled and roared into the valleys below, fed by glacier water and melting snow from high above on the surrounding peaks. As Scot continued to watch the scenery, he had to admit to himself that there really wasn't a bad time of year to visit Switzerland.

At Zweilütschinen, the back half of the train was joined to a new engine, which picked up speed and headed east toward Grindelwald. Looking out the window on the right side of the train, Scot got his first glimpse of Switzerland's famous trio of mountains: the Eiger, the Mönch, and his destination, the Jungfrau. The mountains, packed with ice and snow, were beautiful and terrifying at the same time. When he'd first visited the Jungfrau region, he had purchased a book called *The White Spider,* about several of the earliest attempts to scale the Eiger. As he looked out the window, he tried to pick out the area known as Death Bivouac, but the combination of distance and the heavy snow covering made it too difficult.

As the creaky old train rolled and squealed its way up the mountain, Harvath consulted his schedule. It was 8:03, and the train was pulling into Schwendi. One more stop and they would be in Grindelwald.

Six minutes later on the dot, the quaint village, bathed in early morning light, rose directly up in front of them. Its glitzy shops and sports stores were all modestly housed in beautiful traditional Swiss chalets of varying shapes, sizes, and colors. Early-rising Europeans garbed in brightly colored outfits clunked along the streets in heavy ski boots with skis slung casually over one shoulder. It reminded him of Park City. Scot envied them their carefree strides and the ease of the day that faced them—where to ski, followed only by where to eat. He, on the other hand, had no such luck in predicting what the day would bring.

His plan was to get up to the Jungfraujoch early and scout things out. While he could have taken the 6:35 train from Interlaken, he'd worried about being there too early and not having any crowds he could blend in with. Judging from the number of passengers on his train, he had made the right choice. A nice Saturday tourist throng would provide cover and help keep him safe. It would also be easy to disappear into if it came to that.

At Grindelwald, passengers were required to transfer to a cogwheel railway. The view of the Eiger from the station was incredible. Scot had seen some pretty crazy things in his time, but he never understood why anyone would willingly choose to climb a mountain, especially one like the Eiger.

Harvath took a last look back at the Hotel Derby and Grand Hotel Regina, which flanked the Grindelwald train station, as he crossed the platform toward the cogwheel train. It was composed entirely of second-class cars divided into smoking and nonsmoking sections. Noticing that the passengers were predominantly European and Japanese, he knew that the biggest crowd would be found in the smoking car and grudgingly climbed aboard. The honey-colored wooden seats were uncomfortable, but the incredible view of the snow-covered mountains made up for it in spades.

The cogwheel railway wove slowly in and out between houses and small farms on the outskirts of Grindelwald. As they drew even with the face of the Eiger, the train stopped at Grindelwald Grund, Grindelwald's second station, whose parking lot was filled with tour buses. The Good Morning Ticket seemed to have a lot of cost-conscious fans. As new passengers boarded, all of the remaining seats were quickly taken. Smoke filled the compartment, and Harvath was happy no one complained when he reached up for the two knobs imbedded in the glass window and pulled it down a fraction to let in some fresh air. A Japanese man, sensing Scot was not a smoker, laughed and offered him a cigarette.

The train picked up speed, and the chalets grew farther and farther apart. Harvath knew from experience that in the spring and summer the fields they were now passing would be filled with a chorus of ringing bells hanging from the necks of grazing sheep, goats, and cows. Each group of bells had a different tone so the farmer could recognize his own livestock, even in dense fog.

At Kleine Scheidegg, passengers changed to the final train that would take them all the way to the top of the Jungfrau. The red crushed-velour seats were a welcome respite from the wooden ones of the previous train. Harvath remained with his group of European and Japanese smokers, who were upset to find that for the rest of the ride there would be no smoking.

For this leg of the journey, Scot and his fellow passengers were traveling completely inside the mountain. At 9,400 feet above sea level, the train stopped for five minutes at the Eigerwand station, where windows had been carved out of the rock face so passengers could look out onto Kleine Scheidegg and the Grindelwald valley far below.

The next stop was for another five cold minutes to overlook the glacier at the Eismeer station, 10,368 feet above sea level. Harvath filed off the train and pretended to absorb the breathtaking views with the rest of the passengers.

Back on board, his heart began to beat faster, and he felt moisture forming on his palms. He leaned back in his seat, somewhat reassured by the sharp stab of the plastic Glock in his waistband.

Only moments after the train began moving, the overhead speaker began playing another tape-recorded message. It came as the others had, first in German, then French, followed by Italian, Spanish, and finally English:

"This is Jungfraujoch. The highest railway station in Europe, 3,354 meters above sea level. Please follow the direction signs to observation points and the restaurants. Thank you for your visit, and we wish you a pleasant stay on the Jungfraujoch."

Pleasant stay. As the train came into the final station and the doors opened, Harvath knew there wasn't much chance of that.

CHAPTER 53

Harvath looked at his watch. It was exactly 9:53 A.M. The Swiss were amazingly precise. Not one of the trains he had been on in the last three days had wavered one minute from its timetable. He had just over two hours to survey the area and get ready for his meeting with dear Aunt Jane.

Harvath didn't waste time. From the station, he measured how long it took him to get to the Ice Palace. Thirty meters deep within the glacier, it was a horseshoe-shaped tunnel carved completely out of the ice. Even the floor was ice. The Europeans didn't have the healthy fear of lawsuits that the Americans did. Getting any traction on the floor was next to impossible. The best one could do was a shuffle that mimicked ice-skating.

He continued on to the outdoor plateau, then back inside to check the rest rooms, shops, restaurants, and the exhibition hall. He passed the blue coin-operated luggage lockers and made his way up the long hallway to the Eiger climbing wall and the computers that let you send free E-mails from "The Top of Europe." He was tempted, but decided against it. Taking the fastest elevator in Switzerland he arrived at the Sphinx observation area and weather station. After a good look around, he descended in the elevator and headed outside to the "Adventure" area, with its dog sled rides, tobogganing, skiing, and snowboarding. The slopes were already packed.

The fact that almost the entire complex was buried deep within the icy mountain gave Scot an odd feeling of déjà vu. His mind wandered to being caught in the avalanche with Amanda. As quickly as the thought came up, Scot slammed shut an iron door to that part of himself and focused on the job at hand.

He suspected Aunt Jane and her people would show up on the 10:53 train, if they hadn't come on the 9:53 with him or arrived even earlier on the 8:53. He felt certain that they would not be coming on the one that arrived at seven minutes before noon. That would be cutting it too close and would not give them enough time to case the area and make sure it wasn't a trap.

Scot kept his eyes open the entire time he was surveying the Jungfraujoch. He looked for that same blue quilted coat and brown cap or any man that might be of the same build. He soon found that style of jacket to be quite popular with the Europeans and was frustrated on three different occasions when he thought he had spotted his prey.

For his part, he kept his wool cap pulled tight around his ears and the collar of his coat turned up. He glanced at the exhibits, picked up postcards, and looked for souvenirs while marking in his memory each nook, cranny, crevice, and exit door that could hide an enemy or provide a means of escape for him if necessary. One of the biggest advantages the Jungfraujoch had presented when he was considering it for his meeting was also its biggest disadvantage. There was only one way in or out . . . by train. Scot began to realize how stupid he might have been. Whether his head was still scrambled or he had just been too desperate to think of something else, he was quickly beginning to realize that this was not one of his all-time greatest plans. Control of the situation was everything. If he lost control, things would go very bad very fast.

As twelve o'clock grew near, Scot's hopes of swarms of tourists to use as camouflage began to diminish as many of them headed off to the restaurants for lunch. A few stragglers were still roaming about, and there were the people who probably got off the 11:53 train to look forward to, but he didn't hold out much hope for the cover he had counted on.

His nerves began to crackle and adrenaline coursed through his body as he walked down the snowy path toward one of the entrances to the Ice Palace. He figured they would expect him to enter from the main door off the elevator from the train station, and therefore chose a completely different approach. He stood outside, waiting for the right moment to start walking, having timed to the second how long it would take him to reach the halfway point. As soon as he entered the mouth of the Ice Palace, the wind that had been whipping around his face outside immediately dropped off.

He walked ahead slowly, ever aware of the slick floor beneath his boots. One hand gripped the railing as his other hand remained in his right coat pocket, where he'd transferred the Glock. Pretending to admire the sculptures carved out of the sheer ice walls, he moved from niche to niche, as if he were following the stations of the cross in an old cathedral. He was no longer picking up his feet, but rather shuffling them along the ice, getting a feel for the movement.

Up ahead, the corridor turned to the right and obstructed his view. He kept up his pace—shuffle to a sculpture, stand for a moment to appreciate it, and then shuffle to the next. He listened intently for any other sounds coming from within the cavern of ice, but heard nothing.

A wisp of a voice, from behind the iron door he had clamped down on his mind, asked him how he would know whom he was looking for and what he would do when he found them. Scot pushed the thought away and focused his energy. He would know whom he was looking for. He would be able to tell by looking in their eyes. People accustomed to killing had a very distinct look and bearing about them, just like the men at Union Station who had tried to kill him on Wednesday.

He rounded the bend in the corridor, a gust of circulating air biting at his earlobes. Before he had come in, he had removed his hat, thinking his odd appearance might fool the people he was after and thereby give him a slight advantage.

The bend behind him, Harvath now was looking at a sculpture of a large bear with a salmon captured in its jaws. Another gust of ventilation wind blew through the corridor, which glowed an eerie blue from the ice. As Harvath prepared to move along to the next sculpture, he felt a hard jab in his back and heard a woman's voice. She spoke in English, but with a Swiss accent. "We are quite fond of bears in Switzerland. It's a lovely sculpture, isn't it, Mr. Sampras? Or should I say, Mr. Harvath?"

"Sonofabitch," Scot mumbled to himself. He was taken completely by surprise. He hadn't heard her sneak up. She must have been behind one of the sculptures, waiting for him to pass before coming after him. His body tensed, ready to strike.

She could feel it. "Relax, Mr. Harvath. This is a gun I have at your back."

"You don't say. And I thought you were just happy to see me."

"I am not amused, Mr. Harvath. Please take your hand out of your pocket. Slowly."

Scot did as he was told. "How do you know my name?"

"That is not important. What is important is your interest in—"

At once, the woman's sentence was interrupted by flying pieces of ice. At first it seemed as if the statue were falling apart, but as the trajectory of the chips began changing, Scot knew all too well what was going on. Someone was shooting at them with a silenced weapon from the bend in the hallway, and they were closing fast.

The woman behind Harvath was equally distracted by the flying ice chips, quickly coming to the same conclusion he had. Without wasting a moment more, Scot drove his right elbow down hard into her stomach. He heard her gun clatter onto the ice. With a moan, she fell backward.

Scot spun, intending to pick up her weapon, but it slid in the direction of the approaching shooter and he would have had to climb over the woman to get to it. His eyes locked on her face for a brief moment. *She is amazingly beautiful* was the last thing that registered in his mind before he took off running as fast as he could down the corridor.

Because he couldn't get much traction on the ice, he wasn't able to cover much ground. He moved into an alcove to catch his breath and drew the replica Glock from his pocket. He heard more muffled spits from a suppressed weapon coupled with the tinkling of breaking ice as it shattered and hit the floor. When the noise stopped, it was replaced by a scratching noise that sounded like mice behind drywall. Now he knew how the shooter was able to move so fast—*crampons.*

The scratching sounds stopped only feet away from where Harvath now hid. There were two shooters, and they were listening for him. No one moved, and Harvath dared not even breathe.

Then one of the shooters broke the silence. *"Links?"* he asked, German for *left.* His companion didn't answer.

The man spoke again. *"Links, rechts, was?"* (Left, right, what?)

Obviously angry at his partner for talking, the other man heatedly admonished him with something that sounded like, "Chew Tea." It didn't sound like German, but Scot thought he recognized the word from somewhere.

The first man now responded with what sounded like, *"Yah beh say!"*

And the second man came right back with, *"Chutee!"*

Harvath now knew what he was hearing. During his travels on the ski team he had made it his goal to learn specific phrases in as many different languages as possible. His favorites had been the ones for *shut up* and *fuck you.* It was juvenile, he knew, but people always said, in any language you learn the bad words first. Besides, even if you knew nothing else, you could always get a guy laughing if you could say "shut up" and "fuck you" in his own language.

The "shut up" and "fuck you" he was hearing now, *chutee* and *yah beh say,* were Serbian. Why were these men speaking German first and then swearing at each other in Serbian?

Scot heard the resumed scrape of crampons along the ice. They were less than three feet from where he now stood. His hands tightened around the toy Glock. If one of them moved close enough, he could surprise him and press the pistol to his head while he ordered the other to drop his weapon. It might work. It would have to work. His ears strained, trying to judge how close they were now.

Abruptly they stopped again. They had heard something. Was it him? He hadn't even breathed and was beginning to get light-headed from holding his breath. The men began backing away. It wasn't him. They had heard something else, but what? Maybe someone else was in the hallway.

The men picked up speed, tracing back along the route they had come. Scot didn't waste any more time wondering why. He skidded out of the alcove and ran as fast as his shuffling feet would carry him in the other direction.

Slipping, he cracked his knee against one of the steps carved out of the ice on his way to the elevator. He regained his footing and allowed himself to slide down the rest of the passageway. He pressed the call button and after two seconds decided it might not be such a good idea to hang around and wait. He turned to his left and ran down the hallway toward the restaurants and the exhibition hall, thankful to be off the ice.

When he reached the other end of the corridor, another set of elevator doors was just closing and he shoved his arm inside to stop them. They opened back up, and aside from a few startled tourists, it looked safe. Harvath rode down one level and exited. He sneaked into the Kino Audiovisual show and took a seat off to the side, where it would be difficult to spot him. He glanced at his watch. The next train out wasn't for forty minutes.

Being careful that no one would see him transferring the Glock back to his waistband beneath his sweater, he took his jacket off, rolled it up, and placed it beneath his seat. He put his wool cap on again and pulled it down low. He also put on his wraparound sunglasses and slipped out of the Kino.

In the hall, he checked both ways and then ran for the stairs. He descended three levels and walked quickly down another hall to the souvenir shop. There he bought a red Top of Europe windbreaker and a purple Jungfraujoch knit ski cap. Neither were his favorite colors, nor were they good for remaining inconspicuous, but he needed to change his appearance fast and this was the best way to do it. The goods in hand, he climbed the stairs one level and ducked into a men's room. Picking an empty stall, he went in and locked the door.

Scot took off the hat he was wearing and shoved it into his pocket. He put on the red windbreaker and purple hat and was about to unlatch the stall door when he heard someone enter the washroom. Quickly, he sat on the toilet and raised his legs off the floor. Withdrawing the Glock, he readied himself. The sound of heavy boots thudding along the floor echoed throughout the bathroom. A grunt was followed by someone farting and then a chorus of laughter. Scot relaxed. These weren't his killers.

Peering through the crack in the door to make sure the coast was clear, he flushed the toilet and exited the stall. The appearance of the young men at the urinal was pure snowboarder, and in Scot they thought they saw a kindred spirit and nodded in his direction. He made small talk with them, and they told him that they had finished lunch and were headed back out. Scot joined them. Whoever was looking for him was looking for a lone male in different clothing, not the person he was now and certainly not someone traveling with a group.

Keeping his head down and laughing with the group, Harvath made his way to the Glacier exit. His new friends hopped on their boards, said good-bye, and shot off down the mountain. He was alone and once again a target.

The thing to do was to keep moving. As far as he knew, there were at least three people with guns who were after him. Standing in one spot for too long was not going to pay off. Timing how long it would take him to get back for the one o'clock train, Harvath struck off on the Glacier Trek trail, praying he would figure a way out of all this.

CHAPTER 54

Harvath walked as long as the cold and the time would allow. Although the idea crossed his mind, he knew he couldn't stay up here all night; he'd freeze to death. As he turned to walk back to the main complex, he was joined by one of the many groups of hikers who had passed him along the trail. A plan began to form in his mind. It wasn't a very good plan, but it was better than nothing.

When he was shot at, it had been in a relatively deserted part of the Jungfraujoch. He had chosen the Ice Palace because he thought the tourists would give him good cover. With practically no one in sight, the men had fired indiscriminately, almost taking out their female partner, whom Scot had now come to accept was Aunt Jane herself. He had counted on the fact that whoever he was meeting wouldn't try anything stupid in a group of people. There was no reason to think that didn't still apply.

With a two-and-a-half-hour train ride back to Interlaken, there would probably be a lot of people catching the one o'clock. Whoever was looking for him would undoubtedly be at the station, but the longer he waited up here, the thinner the tourist crowd and his cover would get. Even if he was able to get on the train without incident, surely they were going to follow him. That hadn't been part of his original plan. He had expected to control the situation. At this point, though, that didn't matter. He would think of something.

Blending in casually with the group of hikers, he asked them if they were on their way down. No luck, they were going in for lunch. Dejected, Scot scanned the entrance of the complex as they neared it, hoping to find three or more people he could blend in with. Up ahead, two families were readying their children, and Scot caught snatches of conversation that told him they were on their way down.

Kids . . . The last thing he wanted was for any children to be hurt. He hung close enough to the family to blend in, but far enough to one side that if someone really wanted to take a shot at him, the children wouldn't be in the way.

Subconsciously, Scot felt crosshairs pointing at him from every angle. He had a strange desire to rub his forehead and the base of his skull to somehow wipe them away. As he entered the Sphinx hall, he heard the chime of the elevator and watched as a large group of tourists clamored out. They milled around and waited for the elevator to go back up and bring down the rest of their group. Scot abandoned his previous cover and waited with them. When they were joined by the second half, the group made their way to the train with Harvath nestled snugly in the middle.

As they approached the tracks, he noticed several passengers had already boarded the train and more still were standing on the platform having a final cigarette. Harvath realized that the only person he would be able to ID was the woman. He had no idea what the two male shooters looked like, or if there were any others he hadn't seen.

Toward the end of the platform Scot noticed two solidly built men with wide frames who resembled a couple of bulldogs. His back tensed, but quickly relaxed again when the men were joined by their wives, who had gone back to the gift shop to buy one last thing. Harvath kept scanning the crowd as his group moved closer and closer to the train.

There! In the side passage. Those two fit the bill. Step a little farther into the light so I can see your eyes.

It was too late. Scot's group pushed onto the train, and he allowed himself to be swept along with them. So far, his new plan was working. No one had fired. As far as he knew, no one had even seen him, but that was a sucker's bet and he didn't like the odds. He needed to assume that he had been spotted and the gunmen were waiting for their exact moment to take their shot. It would happen quickly, and they would have to be close. Most likely, they would create a diversion to distract people's attention from what was really happening. The only insurance Scot Harvath had came from staying as close to this group as he could. He began committing each and every face to memory. In nineteen minutes they would be back at Kleine Scheidegg and he would have to change trains.

• • •

At Kleine Scheidegg, Harvath discovered he was lucky enough to be with another crowd of smokers. He'd never thought he would ever call being surrounded by smokers lucky, but today it was. The nineteen-minute no-smoking ride from the top of the Jungfrau had been more than they could bear, and as they crossed the platform to catch the next train, they all lit up, forgoing the gift shop. Harvath was able to stay right in the middle of them.

Even though the transfer time was only four minutes, it was the longest four minutes of his life. He could feel the shooters close by. He knew they were waiting for their opportunity. Harvath's group was descending via Lauterbrunnen, and that was fine by him. Being such a large group, they had automatically accepted him as part of their tour. The bad hat and tacky windbreaker allowed him to fit right in. All he was missing was a camera.

The train whistle blew and the group boarded. This compartment was larger and they had been joined by faces that Scot didn't recognize, but none had the eyes of a killer. Nevertheless, he had to expect that they had seen him and that the attack would come at any time. If it did, what would he do? He had only his plastic Glock. He needed to be preemptive. There was only a half hour until the next stop, which was Wengen. That's where Scot would make his move. Another plan was beginning to form in his mind.

CHAPTER 55

Half an hour gave Harvath plenty of time to become cozy with the members of the tour group sitting around him. A healthy dose of charm made him the darling of the conversation while the train slowly descended from the Jungfraujoch.

As the overhead speaker began announcing the stop for Wengen, Scot could feel the train slowing down. Timing would be everything.

He looked at his watch and then out the window to judge how much distance was left.

". . . It'd be great to have you. We'll take you out on the boat and show you nothing but whales, seals, and beautiful Washington State scenery. Camano Island is like no other vacation you've ever taken," Scot said as he wrote down a fictional address with a pen he borrowed from one of the group members. On vacation, people were so willing to give strangers personal information that they never would at home: names, addresses, phone numbers . . . it was a phenomenon unique to traveling.

As Scot was about to hand the ballpoint pen back to the man he'd borrowed it from, he made it appear as if he had accidentally dropped it.

"What butterfingers I've got. Sorry about that," he said, bending down to pick it up. The train came to a stop in the Wengen station, and Harvath kicked his plan into action.

From where he was fishing beneath the seats for the dropped pen, he screamed, "Oh, my God! There's a bomb underneath the seats! Everybody out!"

A murmur of shock floated across the train compartment, but only a couple of people moved. He didn't have time for this. They were getting out whether they liked it or not. A little added influence was needed. Scot drew the fake Glock from his waistband and began yelling once again as he waved the pistol in the air where everyone could see it, "A bomb! A bomb! A bomb! We're all going to die! Everybody get out! Run for your lives!"

Whether it was the added urgency in his voice or the gun he would never know, but it didn't matter. Passengers were screaming and trampling each other to get out of the compartment and as far away from the train as possible. This only helped Harvath as passengers began streaming out of the other compartments, shouting for help and running for their lives. It was sheer chaos.

Using the fleeing passengers for concealment, Harvath hopped out of the train and began running with the herd's forward direction. Tentatively, he shot a glance backward and his stomach immediately cramped at what he saw—three very large, broad-shouldered men standing alongside the train scanning the crowd and not moving. Trouble in paradise.

Harvath turned around, but not quickly enough to see that a woman in front of him had stumbled, and he fell right down on top of her. She was panicked, hyperventilating, and clawing at the snow-covered ground to get back up and away from the soon-to-be-exploding train. Next, a man ran straight over the top of Harvath, unknowingly digging the toe of his boot into the small of his back. Scot let out a groan of pain. Maybe his ruse had been a little *too* effective.

Knowing he had to move fast, he saw a break in the people running to his right and rolled off the woman, who was up and away in an instant. Scrambling to his feet, Harvath dug his boots in and shot forward out of his crouch, just in time to see two explosions in the snow where he had been lying. The killers had seen him too and were now firing. Harvath took off as fast as his legs would carry him.

There wasn't enough time to try to do another quick change to throw the men off his path. His only hope was to outrun them, or lose them somehow in the village.

Wengen played host every year to the world's longest downhill ski race, the Lauberhorn. Although downhill had not been Scot's area of expertise, he had come to Wengen to see the race twice and cheer on the American team, as well as competitors he knew from other countries.

The village hadn't changed much since he'd last been here. Completely devoid of cars, it seemed frozen in time. Were Goethe to come back to revisit the nine-hundred-foot-high Staubach waterfall, only the fashions would seem out of place.

Harvath's breath came in quick, short gasps as he ran uphill deeper into the village. Dodging the brightly attired skiers that crowded the narrow lanes, he didn't dare venture a look back. He knew his pursuers were right on his tail.

He took a quick right turn, and wood splintered as an ornate balustrade on a low-lying balcony exploded just above his head. Running hard, Harvath removed his purple cap and threw it to his left into a narrow alley between two chalets. He then dove right, behind a wall of hay stacked only a few feet high.

Focusing on his breathing, he willed his body to calm down or at least to quiet down. He strained his ears for sounds of the men coming down the small street. Fifteen feet in front of him, a herd of mountain goats, realizing Harvath was not here to distribute any of the hay he was hiding behind, went back to rubbing their heads against the rough posts of the tiny paddock, their bells ringing in a disjointed chorus.

Scot continued to listen, and slowly, he began to hear the telltale sounds of heavy boots crunching upon the snow. The shooters were close, but they weren't stupid. Taking their time, they moved cautiously down the street, ever watchful for an ambush.

When they were almost even with the bales of hay, Harvath held his breath, his hands tight around the toy Glock, for all the good it would do him. He heard one of the men speak. "Look. On the ground. Ten o'clock. That's the hat he was wearing. He went this way."

"We'll check it out. You go the other way and radio if you see anything. We don't want any more screwups. Get moving, and remember, he has a gun," said another voice. This one was obviously in charge.

These men were speaking English . . . American English. They weren't the same voices he had heard in the Ice Palace. They were different, but the second man sounded familiar. He knew that voice. It was the same one Harvath had heard yell the word *gun* days before outside his bank. These were the men in the ghettomobile with the automatic weapons who had tried to kill him. What were they doing here? How could they possibly have followed him all this way? Harvath was sure that his trail stopped dead in Zurich, even if someone had been sharp enough to have been looking for Hans Brauner. Switzerland was a small country, but not that small. He couldn't figure out how in the world they had tracked him.

He quickly did the math—the woman and at least two men at the Ice Palace and now these three here. What was the connection? Were they all working together? Were the woman and the two men from the Ice Palace also searching for him in the village? There wasn't any time to figure things out; he needed to get moving again.

Peering over the bales of hay, he saw that two of the men had taken the bait and had headed off down the passage between the two chalets, back toward the village. The other man continued down the street in the direction his group had been heading before they split up. There was only one option open to Harvath, and that was to go through the paddock.

It would allow him to put a lot of distance between him and his pursuers quickly, and that was all that mattered. Taking one more look over the bale of hay, he decided to make his move. Tucking the

Glock back into his waistband, he covered the fifteen feet to the paddock in seconds. In hindsight, he probably should have brought some of the hay with him.

The minute he jumped into the enclosure, the animals started going crazy. The neighing and jangling of their bells grew as the animals converged on Harvath. Some of their horns were long and sharp, and undoubtedly could do a lot of damage. The goats didn't look happy, and Scot didn't want to hang around and see if they were friendly. This wasn't a day at the petting zoo.

The animals converged on him almost at once as he tore across the territory they were so vigorously trying to defend. When he got to the far rail and placed his hands on top, ready to vault over, he felt something tear through the upper part of his left arm. He was sure one of the goats had gotten him with its horns, but looking back, he saw it wasn't that at all.

The commotion from the goats had caught the attention of the lone shooter, who'd raced toward the paddock and was able to get off one silenced round before Scot got over the fence. It connected with Scot's arm, tearing through the windbreaker, as well as the clothes and flesh beneath. Harvath could already feel the warm spread of blood running down his arm. He didn't want to give the guy a chance at a second shot.

With only his right arm for support, Harvath vaulted the fence and rolled when he hit the ground on the other side, wincing from the pain. He ran alongside a decaying shed that looked as if it were three hundred years old and then headed to where he could see crowds of people on a more populated thoroughfare.

He heard the muffled spits being fired from behind as the bullets tore up everything around him. Scot ran faster.

Hitting the thoroughfare, he ran across it and saw that he was parallel with a café that must have been popular with skiers, because there were rows and rows of skis and poles resting on racks outside. Quickly, he grabbed a pair that were entangled with ski poles and headed for an alley about twenty feet down.

The alley actually passed beneath an old chalet and therefore was relatively dark compared with the bright sunshine outside. As he hurriedly unlocked the skis, Scot glanced out the far end of the passageway and could see the peak of the Schilthorn off in the distance.

His back flat up against the wall, he looked at his left arm and saw that it was completely covered in blood. The blood had even run down to his hand. There was nothing he could do about it now.

Bottom of the ninth, bases loaded . . . Harvath wrapped both of his hands around one of the skis as tight as he could, the tip resting against the wall above his right shoulder. Time seemed to creep at a snail's pace. *Where is he? He had to have seen me come this way.*

His left arm was killing him, and holding it in this position wasn't doing it any good. He didn't know how much longer he could keep it up.

Then, he heard footsteps from the other side of the wall. *Careful . . . wait for it.*

The gun preceded the shooter through the entrance to the passageway. Scot fought against every impulse in his body that told him to swing and run. *Wait,* he told himself, *not yet.*

Whoever the shooter was, he seemed to sense Harvath was near and chose his steps very carefully. It almost appeared as if he weren't moving at all, but he was. Scot could now see the hand, wrist, and forearm of the gunman. *Soon.*

The upper arm appeared, then the shoulders, a torso . . . *Now!* Swinging with all of his might, Harvath nailed the gunman square in the chest with the ski, and the man went down, dropping his gun. He went for it, but Scot kicked him hard in the ribs. The man grunted, and instead of clutching his side where he'd been kicked, he rolled quickly to his right and grabbed for Scot's leg. The shooter brought his feet quickly around behind him, ready to jump up, and then there was a flash of something in the man's hand . . . *a knife.*

That was the last straw. Harvath's anger raged. He didn't know what the hell was going on, but he'd had enough and he certainly wasn't going to grapple with one bad arm and try to fight this guy for the knife.

The man pointed his knife at Harvath.

"You know what? I really, really don't like it when people point things at me," said Harvath.

The man froze for a moment, confused that Scot would address him, rather than attack, but the confusion was only temporary.

"If it's not a gun, then it's a knife. Here's the deal. I'm not playing around anymore."

Just as Scot finished, the man lunged and slashed at him with the blade. Harvath turned in time and grabbed one of the ski poles from where it rested against the wall. As the man attacked again, Scot faked left, then spun around hard to his right and plunged the pole deep into the man's chest. The knife fell from his hand, and in seconds, blood gurgled out of his mouth, painting his jacket a deep crimson.

"It looks like you got my point," said Scot as he let go of the pole.

The man, still on his knees, fell forward, but only a foot before the bottom of the pole hit the ground and he was propped up like a human pup tent. Not wasting a moment more, Harvath went for the man's pistol.

A blanket of fire erupted in front of him as bullets ricocheted off the cobblestones of the passageway. The gunman must have radioed his position to his two colleagues. There was no telling how far away they were. The bullets were close enough, and that was all that mattered. Harvath ducked and rolled toward the opposite entrance. Snaking around the outer wall of the chalet, he jumped to his feet and ran.

CHAPTER 56

The first thing Harvath needed to do was to stop his bleeding. The next was to get the hell out of Dodge . . . Wengen . . . whatever.

The village was situated on what the Swiss call the Wengen sun terrace: a long westward-facing plateau that got fabulous sun in the afternoon. That was definitely the case today.

Quickly and carefully, Harvath picked his way from chalet to chalet, trying to stay concealed as best as was possible in the blazing sunshine. He made a makeshift pressure bandage from his windbreaker so he wouldn't leave a trail of blood for the remaining two gunmen to follow.

Seven chalets later, Harvath came upon a restaurant that was blaring techno music. This was definitely a snowboarder hangout. Scot scanned the crowd of young faces, hoping to find his little blond girlfriend with the nose ring and her friends. They would be perfect cover, but they were nowhere to be seen. Scot needed to come up with another plan.

Snowboarding was an interesting sport in that it offered a high probability for wipeouts. And, wiping out in the strong sunshine meant that the snow you picked up melted quickly and even the most waterproof of snowboarding outfits got wet.

A leafless tree on the side of the restaurant had become the snowboarders communal coat rack. Why these kids never took them inside or out onto the terraces with them to dry out was beyond him, but right now Harvath was grateful for it. He found a drab brown-and-gray coat that looked as though it would fit and chose a good-sized black helmet from the pile so neatly arranged at the base of the tree. A couple of people would be very angry to find their gear had been stolen, but at least Harvath might have a better chance at survival. Walking away from the restaurant, he also grabbed the last snowboard in the line leaning against the wall.

He put the jacket on and found there was a pair of goggles in the pocket, which he put on along with the helmet. Quickly, he made his way toward the Männlichen gondola. The pain in his arm was almost unbearable. He didn't think he had any arterial damage, but he needed to get a better look at the wound. If he wasn't careful, he could risk bleeding to death. Spotting a busy pizzeria, he ducked inside and went downstairs to the men's room.

Taking off the coat, he saw the windbreaker pressure bandage was stained with blood. Untying the knotted sleeves, Scot braced himself for a gush of blood. The bullet had nailed him pretty good, but it hadn't penetrated an artery. A fraction more to one side and he would have been in real trouble. He checked the injury over thoroughly and realized it was a serious grazing wound and would definitely need stitches, but that should take care of it.

Harvath's belt was made of woven black leather, the type whose buckle can be placed anywhere. He removed it from his cargo pants and quickly wrapped it around the upper section of his left arm, pulling the belt tight, his eyes pinched shut in response to the pain. He looked at his watch and marked when he would need to release the tourniquet. He covered his arm with the bloody windbreaker, hoping to prevent any blood from seeping outside of the jacket, cleaned his hands as best he could, and left the restaurant.

With a snowboard under his right arm, the jacket zipped all the way up, and the helmet and the goggles on, Harvath had his best disguise yet. He moved as fast as his legs would carry him to the gondola and watched for signs of his attackers.

Before getting on board, he bought a hot dog and a couple of cans of Red Bull energy drink. He needed to build his strength back up. A gondola operator pointed at the no eating/no drinking sign.

"You've got to be kidding me," said an exasperated Harvath.

The operator wasn't kidding.

I've been shot at, trampled, chased by goats, shot at again, and this guy's worried about me eating in his precious gondola? What a day, he thought to himself.

After two fast bites of the hot dog, Scot threw the rest of it out and slid the Red Bull into his pocket.

As the gondola drew up the mountain, Harvath stood facing the back, and watched Wengen slowly recede in front of him. He had made it. He was safe, but for how long?

Once at the top of the Männlichen, it was a short but painful walk to the Grindelwald gondola that took him back into the village he'd been in only hours before. The only way down from Grindelwald was the train to Wilderswil. He watched the station carefully, letting two trains go before he decided to get on board. In the station's bathroom, he had released the tourniquet for a moment of precious relief. The fingers of his left hand had gone numb half an hour ago.

In Wilderswil, he caught the bus to Interlaken's Centralplatz, where he found a pay phone and called Balmer's. He told Jackie where he was, that he was hurt and needed her to pick him up.

The weight of the snowboard helmet threatened to crush his neck. He was light-headed, his legs were like rubber bands, and his stomach was churning. He stayed in the phone booth, leaning against the side until Jackie arrived twenty minutes later.

CHAPTER 57

"You look like shit," was the first thing Jackie said as Scot eased himself into the passenger seat.

"And a gentle *bonsoir* to you as well, fair lady. Hey, I'm not auditioning for the Chippendales here. I'm hurt. Did you bring the things I asked for?"

"Yes, but I don't have any experience in this stuff."

"Didn't you take that wilderness medicine course in Utah when we all used to go backcountry skiing?"

"Yeah, but that was years ago."

"I'll guide you through it step by step."

"Scot, I don't think I—"

"Jackie, if I could go to a doctor, I would, but the doctor would ask questions and would probably want to invite the police to take a look. I can't afford that. You have to do this for me."

He closed his eyes, and they drove the rest of the way in silence.

• • •

In Scot's room, Jackie produced a small bag that contained everything he had asked for. The guys who ran Jackie's adventure-sports desk with canyoning, bungee, and rafting trips in the summer had left behind what they joked was their Rambo first aid kit. One of them, an American named Tony, was a certified EMT, and his partner, Paul, had been a registered nurse. There wasn't much these two couldn't handle out in the field, and the kit reflected that. Inside Jackie's bag, which she had dumped onto the bed, was the first aid kit, a bottle of hydrogen peroxide, gauze, and clean bandages.

Scot groaned as he took off the stolen jacket. Jackie gasped when she saw his entire left side caked with blood.

"What the hell happened to you? And don't tell me you cut yourself shaving."

"I cut myself shaving."

"Do you want my help or not?"

"I was shot."

"Shot? I thought no one knew you were here."

"Either that or it's open season on anyone with a bad dye job."

"But who in Switzerland would want to shoot you?"

"Jackie, I'm a little bit under the weather at the moment. Can we play fifty questions later?"

"Of course. I'm sorry. What do you want me to do?"

"First, let's get this windbreaker off."

As Jackie helped him, Scot continued talking. "Now, take the scissors out of the first aid kit, and starting at my cuff, I need you to cut the sweater all the way up to where the tourniquet is and then do the same with the shirt underneath."

Jackie did as she was told.

"Do me a favor and hand me that towel over there so I can use it as a compress . . . Thanks. Now, when we release the tourniquet, there might be some more blood, so I want you to be ready. Are you going to be okay? You're not going to go south on me, are you?"

She shook her head, a few stray wisps of auburn falling into her eyes, which she quickly brushed away.

"All right. Take the needle that looks like a curved half-moon and the coil of black silk out of the kit."

"I got it. I suppose I thread it the same way I would a regular needle and thread?"

"It should already be threaded."

"It's not."

"Great. Just thread it like a regular needle and go to town. We don't have time to learn how to do surgical knots."

Jackie threaded the needle while Scot continued his directions.

"Now, when I release the tourniquet, I want you to tear my sweater and shirt the rest of the way up to my shoulder. I'll hold the compress on the wound to stop any bleeding. As soon as you have my sleeve out of the way, I'll pull back the compress and you dump the hydrogen peroxide straight into the wound."

"How much should I use?"

"Pour a little on the needle right now, and then pour about half the bottle onto my arm."

"That's going to hurt."

"Naw, you think? Listen, Jack, I don't really have any choice. Are you ready?"

When Jackie nodded, Scot released the tourniquet and let the belt fall to the bed. He placed the clean towel against his arm as Jackie used both hands to tear his sleeves up to the collar. When he saw the peroxide in her hand, he pulled back the compress. The blood flow was not as bad as he'd thought it might be. With a quick look at Jackie to signal he was ready, Scot steeled himself for the pain.

When she poured the peroxide into the gash in his arm, the stew of blood and ripped flesh began to bubble and turn a mucus-looking white. Jackie felt queasy, but didn't stop until half the bottle had been emptied. The peroxide ran down Scot's arm and stomach, covering his pants and dripping onto the bed. It felt like hot acid, and he clenched his jaw with a force that was one foot pound of pressure short of cracking his teeth and sending his fillings flying across the room.

When Jackie set the bottle on the nightstand, Scot relaxed his bite and gave her his next instructions. "Now you need to stitch me up."

"Oh, Scot. I don't know if I can do that."

"You've got to, Jackie. Just grab the needle and start from the top."

"But what if I don't do it right?"

He didn't have the strength or the patience to argue with her. He did his best to stay calm. "You'll do fine. C'mon. Start here and work your way down. We'll make sure you draw the folds together as evenly as possible."

"It's going to hurt."

"You're such a kidder. That's what you said about the peroxide, and I was fine," he lied. "Let's go."

• • •

Fifteen minutes later it was done. The stitches were clean, and although there would probably be a scar, it could have been much worse.

"I think you missed your calling," said Scot.

"What do you mean?"

"You should have been a surgeon. These are very clean. I thought you were gonna leave me looking like Frankenstein."

"Very funny. Now, hold still while I put this bandage on."

This time it was Scot who accepted the orders and did as he was told.

"There, that should do it. I'm sorry I don't have any antibiotic ointment."

"That's okay," said Scot. "The peroxide should kill just about anything that might have gotten in there."

"Is there a high risk of infection?"

"With a bullet wound there always is, but I think we cleaned it out pretty well."

"Good. Are you hungry? Can I get you some soup or something?"

"I would love some soup, but we need to talk first."

She gathered up the equipment and set it on the table. "I'm all ears."

"Jackie, you have been a real sweetheart. You've really helped me out—"

"You don't have to thank me."

"Yes, I do. Not just for sewing me up, but for everything else."

"Don't worry. I told you I would put it all on your bill. By the way, critical care is very expensive in Switzerland."

Scot smiled. "I'm sure it is. Listen, I don't know exactly what's going on, but I'm starting to get a better picture. I need to ask you another favor."

"*Another* favor? Sure, why not? What can I do for you . . . take your appendix out?"

"No," said Scot, laughing, "nothing that serious. I need to borrow your car."

"Okay, but the smoke screen and oil slick have been on the fritz. Every time I take it in to be fixed, the mechanic says he's got it working, and then as soon as I get it home and need to wipe out some bad guys, it doesn't work again. It's also not bulletproof, you know."

"That's okay; I don't intend to get it or myself near any more bullets."

Jackie gave him a stern glance, knowing he was lying. "Why don't I believe you?"

"I just need it for tonight, and—"

"Not a chance."

"Why?"

"Scot, I don't care how much of a macho guy you think you are, you could barely make it up the stairs a short while ago. I practically had to carry you the whole way. You are in no condition to drive."

"I was exhausted. Being shot at has a funny way of doing that to you. It's kinda been a bad day."

"All the more reason you shouldn't be behind the wheel."

"Okay, you're right. I'll make you a deal. Bring up some soup, I'll eat, get a little sleep, and then I'll go."

She sat on the edge of the bed not saying anything. She just gave him the same disbelieving look.

"C'mon, Jack. Scout's honor. I promise. I wouldn't ask you if it wasn't important."

"Okay, I'll do it, but on one condition."

"What is it?"

"I want a straight answer."

"Okay."

"What's happening?"

"Jackie, if I knew, I would tell you. I mean that straight."

"So you have no idea who tried to kill you today or how they found you?"

"None at all." Once again, Scot was lying. He did have the beginnings of an idea, but nothing concrete.

"Scot, someone knows you're here. This is serious. I am worried about you. It was one thing when you told me everything was going on back in the States, but whatever this trouble is, it's followed you here. We should get you help."

"No. No help, Jack. I can handle this."

"Scot, I know someone I think can help you."

"Jackie, I mean it. No help. I can get myself out of this."

"Before or after you get shot at again?"

"What are you talking about? This?" he asked motioning to his bandaged arm. "It's just a flesh wound. I'll bite the legs off of anyone who tries anything else."

"Monty Python, very funny. I mean it. You need help."

"Actually, what I need is some soup and then a short nap. Everything will be fine. You'll see."

"I wish I could believe you."

• • •

Jackie left the room and returned twenty minutes later carrying a tray with rolls, butter, soup, and a dish of ice cream.

"The car will be parked next to the bakery, two blocks down. I'll leave the keys under the mat," she said.

"Thanks."

"Promise me you'll be careful?"

"I promise."

"I'm worried about you, Scot."

"Me too, Jack. Me too."

CHAPTER 58

When Scot awoke several hours later, he was surprised that he had actually fallen asleep. He was also surprised at the depth of his exhaustion. Apparently, Jackie had come to collect his tray and he hadn't even heard her. Sleeping that soundly was dangerous. Scot looked at his watch and realized he needed to get going. He had a long drive ahead of him.

There was no blood seeping through the bandage, but his arm was still in a lot of pain, as was his head. He pulled a couple of Tylenols from his shaving kit and chased them with the last of the mineral water. Next, he got out the glue and applied the bushy brown eyebrows and goatee. With a towel across his lap in case he dropped a lens, he sat on the edge of the bed and put the brown contacts in. Then, he slipped on the thin wire-frame glasses. Harvath looked in the mirror, staring at the contrast between the brown eyebrows and goatee and his stark blond, almost white hair. Thank goodness it was cold and he would be able to wear a hat.

With his good right arm he slowly slid into a pair of khakis, but putting on a button-down shirt was murder. The pain surged through his arm and into his shoulder. *Slowly,* he told himself. *Take it slowly.*

Thirty minutes later, disguised as Hans Brauner, Harvath left Balmer's and made his way toward the bakery. The car was exactly where Jackie had said she would leave it. The keys were under the mat, and there was a Post-it note on the knob of the gearshift that read simply, *"Be Careful."* Harvath chided himself again for ever letting her go.

Despite the cold, the car turned over immediately. Scot signaled and merged into the flow of Saturday evening Interlaken traffic.

• • •

The drive to Munich was long, yet thankfully uneventful. At the border, sleepy guards anxious to get off duty waved him on through when he held up his German passport.

Harvath followed the signs toward München Flughafen. Driving in Europe was so much easier than in America. The routes were perfectly marked with easy to understand signs, and as long as you stayed out of Italy, the drivers were courteous and knew what they were doing.

He parked his car at the Munich Airport long-term lot and caught a train for the short ride to the *Hauptbahnhof.* Even though it was late, the city's main train station was alive with activity. There were the requisite homeless people hitting up passersby for spare change, a heaping helping of drunk students, some with large packs, waiting for their trains, as well as a smattering of locals with the wide smiles and hearty laughter that the people of this city had been known for ever since Augustiner monks introduced *Bier* to the city over six hundred years ago. Not counting Oktoberfest, it was said that the average Münchener consumed at least two hundred twenty liters of beer a year, more than twice the average amount drunk in the rest of Germany. The Bavarians were a hearty bunch, there was no denying that.

Outside the station on Bayerstrasse, Harvath caught a cab and gave the driver the address he wanted on Pfisterstrasse, not far from the Max-Joseph-Platz.

When the cab pulled up, the wooden blinds of the establishment were shut tight. The driver made a comment about the café looking closed, but Harvath paid him and got out.

It was after 1:00 A.M. and the Kuntscafé was indeed closed, or at least that's the message its proprietor wanted to send to anyone casually strolling by hoping to pop in for a quick bite or one last drink. Behind the blinds, the lights were still blazing, and Scot heard a mill of voices. Somewhere inside, a piano sprang to life and a beautiful tenor voice began to belt out a song.

The singing continued as Scot went around to the back of the small café. He peeled off his hat and the pieces of his disguise, then placed all of it in his jacket pocket. Garbage was piled high in the alley, and maneuvering around a stack of bright blue and yellow plastic beer crates filled with empty bottles, Harvath found the back door. He knew that if Herman was entertaining, he probably would still have staff on duty. As Harvath entered the kitchen, he surprised two rather stocky waiters. Before they could say anything, Herman's cook, Fredrik, turned and saw Scot standing in the doorway. Instantly, his eyes lit up in recognition and a broad smile crept across his face.

Harvath put a finger to his lips to silence the cook, who in return gave him the thumbs-up and pointed toward the front of the café. After all, what good was surprising an old friend if you couldn't *really* surprise him?

Herman was still singing and had his back to Scot as he emerged from behind a beaded curtain down the hall from the kitchen. Herman's thick fingers crashed upon the last keys, and the small group collected in the front of the café clapped enthusiastically. When they stopped, one pair of hands was still clapping.

"Lovely. Simply lovely," said Scot.

Herman looked up in the direction of the voice and then roared, "First, I am going to fire the cook, and then I am going to get the lock on that back door fixed!" His guests sat speechless. Who was this man standing at the end of the bar, and why was their host yelling at him in English?

It was amazing how quickly Herman moved his six-foot-four, 240-pound frame around the piano and over to Harvath. The limp from his injured leg didn't slow him down at all. Herman's huge hands reached out, and Scot almost flinched as he saw them close in on his face. The beefy German gave him a kiss on each cheek and then raised Harvath completely off the floor in an enormous bear hug. The pain in his shoulder was written across his face, and Herman noticed. Quickly, he set his friend back on the floor.

"What's wrong with you? Are you hurt?" said Herman. "Did your hairdresser beat you up when you refused to pay for that awful hairstyle?'

"We need to talk. I'm sorry to interrupt your little party."

"Party? This? Don't worry, they'll only stay as long as I keep the bar open, and the bar is now closed!" shouted Herman, who turned to the group and told them in German to settle up their tabs.

After the group left, Herman had the cook make them each up a plate of *Würstel* with potatoes and sauerkraut, then sent the staff home.

Herman set two large bottles of beer on the table and said, "It's great to see you. Why don't I call Diana? She's probably asleep by now, but it doesn't matter. She would love to see you, even with your hair like that."

Scot responded as Herman drew a small cellular telephone from his breast pocket. "You know what? For now, let's not tell Diana I'm here. I need to talk to you alone."

Herman replaced the phone in his pocket. "Does this have anything to do with the face you made when I gave you the hug?"

"Kind of."

"You're getting soft! Look at me," said Herman, flexing his right biceps and then slamming his hands upon his midsection. "I am still in better shape than most men my age, and I run a café now for a living. All this food, all this beer, and I haven't put on more than two kilos . . . three max!"

Scot smiled. "You look great, Herman, and I am sure Diana does too. You will have to tell her that I asked about her."

"What do you mean? You can tell her yourself. After we eat, we'll go back to my place. You can have the guest room."

"I'm sorry. I can't stay that long. I just came because I need some information and a favor."

Herman's jovial expression turned quietly serious. "Are you in some sort of trouble?"

"Actually, my friend, I'm in many sorts of trouble." Harvath brought Herman up to speed on everything that had happened to him. Herman listened intently, only picking at the plate of food in front of him. When Scot finished, Herman took a long swallow from his beer and wiped his mouth with the back of his hand before responding. "So, what is it you need from me?"

"Like I said, information. I thought all of the shooters yesterday were working together until I heard the American voices and realized that there were probably two groups. The first, with the woman, must have been gunning for me because of the note I sent to the post office box in Interlaken, and the second was the hit team from D.C., who somehow managed to pick up my trail."

"Okay, two separate groups, then. But why?"

"I have an idea who is behind the American team, but not the team from the Ice Palace at the Jungfraujoch. That team spoke German—"

"You said that. You also said it didn't sound like German German, right?"

"It sounded like Swiss German, but it was only a couple of words. That's pretty hard to nail an accent with."

"Let's assume for a moment that you're correct on the accent. You said they also spoke Serbian?"

"Yes. That I am certain of."

Herman leaned backward in his chair. He appeared to be staring at the ceiling, studying the wine-colored tiles that ran between the old wooden beams. Harvath knew he was thinking, turning something over in his mind.

"You are absolutely certain that your FBI and the rest of the U.S. government is wrong about Fatah?"

"I don't know. I do know there is no way the Fatah, if they are even involved, could have pulled off something like this on their own. We can be sure they had inside help from people within my government."

"And you're positive you are on the correct path?"

"*Positive?* I don't think anyone can be positive on something like this. All I know is that somebody else thinks I'm on the right path."

"What do you mean, *'somebody else thinks'?"*

"I think the attempts on my life, two of them just yesterday in Switzerland, make for a pretty strong case that I'm on to something."

"I agree. I also agree that this entire situation does not seem to fit the Fatah. Someone is using them as some sort of smoke screen."

"So, if we're on the same page, who do you think would be capable of an attack like this and kidnapping the president?"

"You're right that it would have been undertaken by a group with exceptional mountaineering and military skills. They could have come from Germany or, like you said, France, Italy, Austria, or . . ."

"Or?"

"You are sure that what you heard in the Ice Palace was two men, the same who had been shooting at you, speaking Serbian?"

"It's one of the few things in this whole mess that I am totally positive about."

"Then that narrows the field considerably."

CHAPTER 59

"What the hell happened?" yelled Senator Snyder into the scramble phone in his study as Senator Rolander looked on.

"We acquired the target, but there was another interested party already present," replied the hired killer.

"Another interested party? Who were they?"

"We have no idea. They made their move before we had a chance, so we hung back."

"What happened?" asked Rolander.

Snyder cupped the mouthpiece and addressed Rolander. "The girl led the team right to him, but someone else made a move before they had a chance to take him out."

"Shit. Then they know about him."

"They must know something," said Snyder as he turned his attention back to the phone. "What happened then?"

"The target evaded the shooters, and we followed him. When we tried to close out the contract, he managed to get away."

"He got away? Maybe I haven't been clear. You and your associates are not being paid for him to *get away.* You are being paid to take him out! I can't believe this. That's the third time. Harvath must be eliminated."

"He will be."

"Do you have any idea where he is now?"

"No, but we're working on it."

"What about the girl?"

"She disappeared. We had to stick with our target. She shouldn't be too hard to find, though."

"She'd better not be. And I'd better not hear about any more failed attempts. You get that slippery son of a bitch and you take him out once and for all. Do you understand me?"

The killer didn't have a chance to respond. Snyder had already slammed down the phone.

CHAPTER 60

They rode in silence toward the Munich airport as the long mono-wiper of Herman's Mercedes beat a steady rhythm against the windshield and the steadily falling snow. Scot was processing the information Herman had spent the last hour sharing with him.

When NATO forces had been brought in to keep the peace in Kosovo, it had been divided into several sectors—French, German, Italian, and so forth. Despite the presence of NATO, emotions and tempers on both sides still raged very hot. Serbians had hit lists of Albanians they wanted dead and vice-versa. Much of this involved the ordinary citizenry, but there were also very high ranking military, political, and business people who had extremely nasty bones to pick with their enemies, but who were being watched so closely that they didn't dare act.

Realizing there was a need for their services, a band of highly trained killers put themselves on the market in Yugoslavia. Nothing was beneath them. They had no problem killing, raping, torturing, or maiming men, women, or children . . . *anyone* was fair game as long as the price was right. What's more, they specialized in assignments that were considered impossible. There was no security system they could not breach. No hiding place that couldn't be uncovered. Once they had your scent, it was said, it was time to make your peace with God.

"You're sure the killers were Swiss?" said Harvath, breaking their silence. "And the NATO soldiers acted as go-betweens?"

"That's what my contact told me. Remember that much like Berlin after World War Two, Kosovo was divided into sectors controlled by troops from specific countries. As Swiss, the assassins were fluent in French, German, Italian, and English. They only interacted with the people right below the top of the different military commands. The 'seconds.' These soldiers were hungry for profit, and the killers took very good care of them. If there was an Albanian, a Serb . . . anyone in their sector that needed a job done, these soldiers arranged it."

Scot had seen it before, and it made him sick. "Those soldiers were there to keep the peace, not to facilitate murders for hire."

"What are you Americans so fond of saying, *'War is hell'?* Most of the NATO soldiers were risking their lives daily in a country that they hadn't even heard of or thought about since geography class in primary school. Lots of people were getting rich. Why not them? And if a couple of bad guys want to rub each other out, who cares?"

"I understand the mentality, Herman; I just never agreed with it."

"No, but that's not what we're talking about."

"You're right. I'm getting away from the point. So, we know that the hired killers were a group of Swiss. Do we know where they were from in Switzerland? Were they military? Police of some sort?"

Herman pulled at his large nose. "My contact stated that no one seemed to know where in Switzerland these men were from or what they looked like. No one knew what their background was, only that they were extremely qualified."

"How were they contacted when a hit was to be ordered?"

"Through a series of dead drops."

"What else did your contact tell you?"

"Apparently, the killers were known as the Lions."

"The Lions? Why *Lions?*"

"I thought maybe the NATO soldiers gave the name to them to put more of a 'face' on the people they were dealing with, but my contact made it very clear that it was how the killers identified themselves. Just a whisper of the word was enough to send people into hiding."

"Can you get any more information about them for me?"

"I don't think so. The Lions supposedly stopped operating in Yugoslavia and could be dead for all we know."

"Dead? They might be, but I doubt it. One thing is for certain, though, if they are alive and if these are the people I'm looking for, I promise you, they will be dead very soon."

CHAPTER 61

The drive back from Munich was grueling. Twenty minutes after Herman dropped Scot at the airport parking lot to retrieve his car and he was on the autobahn, a deep fatigue had set in. The psychological stress from the past several days and the physical damage to his body both came calling at once. The two cans of Red Bull he had with him and coffees at every other truck stop along his route kept him going until he got back to Interlaken and could finally drop onto his bed and slide into a deep sleep.

It felt as though only five minutes had passed before he drifted into a dream about Jackie. He could hear her concern for him in her voice, but for some reason he could not see her face. She was worried. Should she call a doctor? Was he all right? *There was blood,* she said. *Not as much as before, but a little. Are you sure?* she asked. *I didn't know what to do. Yes, I do care about him.*

Her voice grew louder, but Scot still could not see her. A light shone and it, too, grew brighter. As he got closer to Jackie's voice, the light grew in intensity. He found his eyelids opening of their own free will, even though all he wanted to do was sleep. Soon, he was able to see through the light and make out shapes. Jackie's voice was still with him, but where was she? He blinked his eyes through the mist, trying to focus. There was a figure at the end of his bed. The voice continued, but the figure wasn't speaking. The voice was coming from somewhere else. Harvath shut his eyes tightly, trying to clear his vision. When he opened them, he was terrified by what he saw.

It was her! The woman from the Ice Palace. She was sitting at the foot of his bed. *Was this a dream? Some sort of hallucination?* Out of sheer instinct, he reacted.

He rolled to his right and reached for the nine-millimeter Beretta that Herman had given him before saying good-bye last night. His hand fumbled clumsily along the nightstand. It was gone. But how? He had placed it right there before he went—

"Looking for this?" said the woman, holding up the pistol. "Or maybe, this?" she said as she raised the replica Glock. Now Harvath knew he wasn't dreaming. "Please tell me you didn't carry a toy to the Jungfraujoch yesterday. It will only make me think less of you," said the woman.

Scot was trapped. There was no way he could spring from where he was and get to her before she got a shot off. The situation seemed hopeless.

From out of the corner of his left eye he saw a hand approach his face, and automatically he reached out and grabbed it by the wrist. He twisted it hard.

"Scot! Stop it. You're hurting me. It's me, Jackie. It's okay. Calm down."

"Jackie?" he said, confused. "I don't understand. Are you okay? She didn't try to hurt you, did she? If she did, I'll—"

"No, Scot, of course she didn't try to hurt me. I'm okay."

"I was so careful. I thought I made sure no one was following me. I must have led them here. Jackie, I'm sorry. I never intended to get you this involved."

"Scot, relax. This is Claudia Mueller. She's a friend of ours."

"What do you mean, she's a friend?" asked Scot warily.

"Rolf and I know her from Bern."

"What's she doing here?"

"I've been worried about you," Jackie said as she tried again, this time without meeting resistance, to apply a cold compress to Scot's forehead. "I knew you didn't want me to call a doctor, but I didn't know what to do. You have been asleep for so long."

"Jackie, you're not answering my question."

"Remember when I said I thought I knew someone who could help you?"

"Yes, and I told you I didn't need any help."

"But she can help you. She helped me and Rolf, and it was the same kind of help you need now."

"What are you talking about? She's a killer."

"Scot, listen to me. During the last election there were some threats against Rolf. Claudia works with the Federal Attorney's Office. She was part of the investigation into the threats and helped arrange security for us. We spent a lot of time together. You *can* trust her."

Scot stared at Claudia. "Jackie, I want *you* to trust me. There is absolutely no way this woman is on our side."

"Scot, you're delirious. You haven't moved since last night when I came in to pick up your tray."

"Jack, I'm okay," Harvath said as he pushed himself up into a sitting position with two pillows propped behind his back. "I was gone all night. I got back early this morning and was exhausted. I guess I was so out of it I didn't hear you come into the room."

"And wherever you were," began Claudia, "I assume that's where you got this," referring to Herman's gun.

"Hold it just a second," said Scot as Jackie offered him a glass of juice. "I'm going to be the one asking questions here, okay? Being held at gunpoint by the same person twice in less than twenty-four hours allows me that privilege. So, first, who the hell are you?"

"You have already been told that. I'm Claudia Mueller of the Federal Attorney's Office."

"And you just happened to be up at the Ice Palace yesterday at the same time I was, and just happened to stick a gun in my back, and just happened to have two men with you who tried to kill me?"

"I had nothing to do with the men who were shooting at us in the Ice Palace."

"*'Us'?* What do you mean?"

"You do understand English, don't you?"

"Enough to get by," he replied smugly.

"I mean," said Claudia, who ignored Scot's sarcasm, "they were shooting at us. You and me. I have no idea who they were."

"And you probably have no idea about who was then shooting at me in Wengen only an hour later?"

"I know one thing: it wasn't the men from the Ice Palace."

"How can you be so sure?"

"Because those two were still at the Jungfraujoch an hour later."

"How do you know?" Scot asked as he continued to look her over. She was gorgeous, but he couldn't shake his first impression of her. Funny how a gun jammed in your back could do that.

"I know because I was there too. I was trying to find you while avoiding them. It wasn't easy. I don't know how you managed to slip away. You must be quite clever."

"I have my days, but yesterday sure wasn't one of them. Someone else managed to find me, and they turned Wengen into a shooting gallery. I was lucky to get away with only this." Harvath pointed to his left arm and noticed that a small amount of blood had seeped through the bandage. He started to unravel it, but Jackie quickly sat down next to him and took over.

"Do you have any idea who it was that tried to shoot at you in Wengen?"

"They weren't *trying* to shoot at me; they actually *were* shooting at me; and besides, I said I would ask the questions here. What were you doing at the Ice Palace in the first place, and why did you pull a gun on me?"

"You know what, guys? I have got a ton of stuff to get done," said Jackie. "I think I am going to leave you two alone." Catching the look in Scot's eye, she added, "Don't worry. You'll be perfectly safe with Claudia. She's extremely tough. She climbs mountains in her spare time for fun. Did you know that?" Beckoning to Claudia, she said, "Why don't you finish changing this dressing for me. There's only been a little bleeding, but the stitches are all still intact. It looks like he'll mend. Another toughie. You two'll get along fine."

Getting up, Jackie patted the place on the bed where she'd been sitting next to Scot. Claudia stood up and set the guns from her lap onto the chair and made her way to the bed. She took a roll of clean gauze from Jackie and began wrapping Scot's arm. Jackie closed the door behind her.

"As I said, I work for the Federal Attorney's Office in Bern, which is called the Bundesanwaltschaft. I was following a suspect in an ongoing investigation who had been using a post office box in Interlaken—"

"Wait a second, are you or are you not 'Aunt Jane'?"

"I am not."

"Then what the hell were you doing at the Ice Palace?"

"I think I can make the situation somewhat clearer if you'll allow me."

"Be my guest."

"Once a week, my suspect travels to the post office to check for mail. He is a creature of habit, typical Swiss, very methodical and always comes on the same day at normally the same time, so I have a certain window in which I know I can check the box to see if he has received anything that might help me in tying him to my case."

"*Tying* him to your case? Is he a suspect or not?"

"I haven't been able to gather enough evidence yet, but I know he is somehow involved. I have what you Americans refer to, I believe, as a *hunch.*"

"Yes, *hunch* is the correct word. But that's legal in Switzerland? Reading someone's mail? Please, not so tight on the bandage."

"I know what I am doing, Agent Harvath."

"How do you know who I am?"

"Which question should I answer first?" she said, giving Scot a little slack in his dressing before taping the gauze in place.

"Lady's choice."

"Pardon me?"

"It means you choose, lady."

"I see. Like my suspect, I am also somewhat methodical and of course am Swiss, so I'll take your questions in order. As far as the legality of investigating the suspect's mail, it depends upon the severity of the charge and the investigator. And as for knowing who you are, Jackie told me everything."

"Everything?"

"She cares about you a great deal and is very worried about you. Don't be upset with her. She did the right thing in calling me. I was just as shocked to see you lying in that bed as you were to see me. I thought you had brought those two men to the Ice Palace to kill *me.*"

"You? Why would I do that?"

"Why does anyone commit murder? I'm sure the motivations are no different in Switzerland than they are in America. All I know is that after I picked up what I think I can correctly assume was your letter from the post box, I noticed I was being followed. I engaged in an evasive tactic—"

"Crossing to the bakery."

"Yes, and then I secluded myself in a doorway and waited. As it turns out, I was more patient than you were."

"In the Ice Palace, you called me by the name I had used in the post office and by my real name. How did you figure those out? Wait . . . the Sampras one is the easiest. You went back to the post office and asked if anyone had seen someone matching my description?"

"You are quite charming, Agent Harvath. The woman at the *poste restante* window remembered you perfectly. She also had your alias written down on a piece of paper to check for your envelope, which still hasn't come, by the way."

"I'll have to tell her not to hold her breath."

"I already did. She was quite disappointed she wouldn't be seeing you again. Now, as far as getting your real name, that was a little more difficult. I had seen you on the street, but was able to get a better look at your face from the post office surveillance tape. The female clerk told me you were American, so I went back to my office and started doing some searches on the computer, starting with our watch list.

"Two names had recently been added—a German and an American. The description of the American sounded like it could fit you. I E-mailed a request to the authoring agency and not long after received a picture of you. The hair is quite different, of course, but that only made it more obvious."

"Authoring agency? What do you mean by you *E-mailed them a request?"*

"They are the people who put your name on our watch list. Sometimes it's an Interpol request; sometimes it's a local or federal Swiss agency; sometimes it's another country . . . There is often a wide array of agencies who add to a watch list for a wide variety of reasons."

"I know about watch lists, thank you very much. What I want to know is who put me on yours? It was an American agency of course."

"Yes. It was your State Department. The man who called me mentioned—"

"Called you? Who called you?"

"After I requested the picture, I received a phone call. A man identified himself as being from a particular division of the State Department and said that he was responding to my E-mail request for your photo. He asked me a lot of questions and was frankly not very polite."

"What did you tell him?"

"Basically, I told him nothing. I said we had a lot of ongoing investigations involving tourist crimes, and I wondered if you might somehow be involved. I wanted your picture so I could compare it against some recent witness descriptions we had received in several resort areas."

"And you didn't tell them you had seen me, or thought you had seen me?"

"No. I told them exactly what I just told you. Of course he reminded me several times about informing them immediately if I even thought I had seen you, and not to try and intercept you."

"But you had seen me. Why didn't you say something?"

"I didn't say anything because if the U.S. State Department wanted you that bad and you were somehow associated with the case I was investigating, then I wanted you as well. I have been waiting for a break in this case. I'm certainly not going to sit back and turn it over to the Americans. No offense."

"None taken, but I think you did turn it over."

"What do you mean?"

"Was the German added to your watch list at the same time?"

"It was listed in the same update, which meant they had both been added in the same time period, yes."

"Do you remember the name of the German?"

"I think it was something like *Brunner,* but I don't remember exactly. At the time it wasn't important. I'm normally pretty good with names, but I was so focused on you and what your involvement was and is—"

"Could it have been *Brauner?*"

"It could have been. Yes, it was. Hans. Hans Brauner. I knew I would remember it."

Harvath put his head in his hands and massaged his temples. "Can you be absolutely certain you were not followed here today?"

"Followed, why?"

"Just answer me, please," said Scot.

"After I finally evaded the two men from the Jungfraujoch, I was extremely cautious, even paranoid. I am positive no one followed me here. Why?"

"I think I finally know how the shooters in Wengen picked up my trail."

"Picked up your trail? Who are they?"

"They're an American hit team that tried twice to kill me in Washington several days ago."

"How did they track you here? Have you been using your real name to travel?"

"What am I, new? Please, Ms. Mueller, I don't know how the Swiss do things, but trust me, we Americans are a lot more thorough than that."

"So are we Swiss, Agent Harvath, but the only way someone who doesn't want to be found gets found is if they make some sort of mistake."

"Or if someone tips off the people looking for you, which is what I'm afraid you did quite unknowingly."

"Me?"

"Yes, when you sent that E-mail asking for my picture, it started a whole chain of events. When I left the U.S., I was traveling as *Hans Brauner,* so the people who were after me had enough pull to get both my real name and my false one put on your watch list in case I turned up. Just asking for the picture was enough to make someone suspect that you knew more than you were telling. My guess is that as soon as they had figured out I was Brauner and had come to Switzerland, they sent a hit team over here. They got both the names on the watch list, and then it was just a waiting game.

"When you sent your E-mail, it got people thinking, and they decided to tail you. Either they didn't see me follow you from the post office, or they hadn't begun to tail you until you went to the Jungfraujoch the next day."

"But what about your letter? After I resealed it, I put it back in the post office box. Maybe I am not being followed at all. Maybe your letter drew the shooters. That was your intent, wasn't it? Someone was supposed to read that letter and be sufficiently interested to show up, right? Why were you setting up a meeting at the Ice Palace in the first place, and what do you know about 'Aunt Jane'?"

"At this point, not enough. I do know, though, that our paths have crossed for a reason, and I intend to figure out why. We need to talk more—you and me—but not here."

"Then where?"

"Someplace else. Anywhere else. Having you here has made me realize how much danger I've already put Jackie in. She's too much of a good friend. We need to find someplace safe where we can sort this all out."

"I think I have just the place."

CHAPTER 62

"Just the place" turned out to be the nearby elegant yet vacant summer residence of Claudia's boss, Urs Schnell, which they unceremoniously gained entrance to when Claudia kicked in one of the small windows in back.

"Okay," said Scot, taking a pen and pad from the ornate desk in the far corner of the living room and walking back to Claudia at the fireplace, "let's get started. Why don't we begin with your investigation. What's it all about, who were you following, et cetera . . ."

"That would be fine, except that is classified information and I am bound by my oath to—"

"What? Are you saying you don't trust me?"

"I hardly know you—"

"Hold it. A little over twenty-four hours ago you had a gun jammed into my spine; yet here I am alone and defenseless with you."

Claudia gave him a look that said, *You, defenseless?*

"Okay, I'm not defenseless, but I am here and you did have a gun on me yesterday. I mean, why else would I come to a deserted love nest with you and lock myself inside for the evening?"

Again Claudia shot him a look.

"Okay, you're not that bad looking, but I am not going to let that get in the way of some other mildly important things—like saving my life and the president's."

"You're right. I'm sorry," said Claudia, becoming more business-like. "We need to work together. Our two cases seem to merge based upon who sends and receives letters via the post box in Interlaken."

As Claudia shared the details of her case with Scot, he took copious notes that would be tossed into the fire once they both had looked them over and digested the information.

Hours passed, and they ate from the bags of food they had purchased on the way to the house. When the bottle of mineral water was finished, they moved to a bottle of wine. It was a nice white, a Côtes de Russin from just outside Geneva. Claudia bent her own rule about drinking while she was working.

Scot liked the wine and laughed when Claudia explained that the reason he couldn't find any Swiss wines back home was that Switzerland didn't export wines, it imported drinkers. That reminded him of something, but he couldn't remember what. His mind was still not firing on every cylinder. He let it go, figuring if it was important, it would come back. He drank his wine slowly and looked down at the pages of notes spread out on the floor before them.

"So, let's go over what we know. Senator Snyder, according to the documents I received from André Martin, wrote a letter to someone he called Aunt Jane, signed it with the name Edwin, and mailed it to the post office box in Interlaken. The box is owned or at least used by this man Gerhard Miner, whom you have been trying to link to your investigation of the weapons theft from a depot outside of Basel. How am I doing?"

"So far so good," she said.

"Because of Miner's involvement with this group, Der . . ."

"Nebel. It means 'fog' in German."

"Right, fog. So Miner, many years ago, after cross-training with U.S. Special Operations Forces, returns to Switzerland and establishes this unit which is designed to test the security of Swiss military installations. He's so successful with breaching security at the bases that he quickly earns a lot of enemies and his unit is shut down for fear of embarrassing the military establishment and he is moved higher in your intelligence sector."

"Yes."

Scot paused, tapping the pen against his chin. "I can see why you suspected him. He certainly has the credentials. What about the weapons? What can you tell me about those?"

"It depends. Which weapons in particular do you want to know about?"

He looked at the notes he'd taken. "A lot of what you've described is standard military hardware. Because the Swiss never had in their possession a jamming device, that item isn't part of the theft you're investigating. The kidnappers I'm looking for could have purchased it on the black market or directly from the North Koreans. What stands out on your list are the glare guns. Tell me about those."

"They were Russian issue. Dostov was the name of the company that created them. There were two in the Basel depot. They were brand-new, and the army hadn't even had a chance to fully test them yet. The manufacturer had only produced a limited number and was loaning them to different governments in hopes that they could create large-scale orders for the device. These were prototypes in a sense, so even if an individual wanted to buy them, they weren't available for sale."

"What were you planning to use them for?"

"At this stage, I don't think we planned on using them for anything. My government had acquired them strictly to test their effectiveness."

"Effectiveness against what?"

"Switzerland is a relatively peaceful country, despite your experiences in the Jungfrau," Claudia said with a smile. "As such, we have been looking into a series of nonlethal weapons. Over the next two years we will be hosting several high-profile economic and diplomatic summits. After the WTO and World Bank disturbances the U.S.A. experienced, we decided we needed to be better prepared to handle civil unrest."

"But why the Russians? Why buy equipment from them when we have a very strong alliance with your country and are developing similar technology?"

"From what I understand, your testing of nonlethal laser weapons has not been very successful. The Russians seem to have it more finely tuned. Also, I have no idea if this is a technology that the Americans are sharing. Besides, we were only going to test it. We had not yet decided if we were going to buy it."

"So, this shipment of weapons arrives at the Basel depot, and before your people get a chance to use it, it's stolen. How did the thieves know it was coming and where it would be?"

"We suspect there was a leak."

"Could Miner have had access to this information?"

"Yes, and knowing this, I had both a motive and the means. Motive was easy—money. I tried to check his alibi, but he claims he was working on a classified assignment at the time of the theft."

"What about his superiors? This guy has to answer to someone."

"He's very clever. Whatever he was up to, he had his tracks well covered."

"It looks that way."

"What is it about the glare guns that interests you so much?"

"You know, for the longest time I have been wondering how one of the finest protective details in the world could be ambushed and killed with only one man getting a shot off."

"You are referring to your president's team?"

"Yes. It didn't make sense to me until I began thinking about the glare guns. If Miner is connected to the president's kidnapping and he brought the glare guns with him, I can see how the Secret Service agents were taken out. Blinded and disoriented, they wouldn't have been able to safely evacuate the president or take any shots. But . . ."

"But what?"

"How did one of the agents get a shot off and manage with that one shot to kill a bad guy?"

"Maybe he wasn't as affected as the other agents."

"Or maybe that's just what somebody wanted us to think."

"What do you mean by that?"

"It never sat well with me that the kidnappers would leave one of their own behind. I also never liked it that this guy was found holding a gun that directly tied him to where he was from. For such a carefully planned assault, it seems very careless, and therefore very suspicious."

"If the one body was left at the scene on purpose, what does that say?"

"It says that somebody really wanted us to believe that a Middle Eastern group was behind the kidnapping."

"And what about the demands of the FRC?" said Claudia.

What about them? Scot thought. Today was Sunday, a week since the avalanche. He had been on the run since Wednesday. Just four days, but it felt like a lifetime. America might have already caved in by now, or a whole new set of demands could have been made. All he knew he got from looking at an occasional newspaper—the vice president was refusing to deal, and the president had not yet been returned.

"That's a big question mark. Everything points away from a Mideastern organization, except the demands," said Harvath.

"Maybe who committed the kidnapping and who paid for it are two separate groups."

"That's the direction I am taking, and it's the only thing that could explain the Fatah's involvement. So, if you find one of the groups, you should be able to find the other."

"What else do we have?"

"Well, we have the two shooters in the Ice Palace speaking Serbian and my source's confirmation of a Swiss assassination team working in Yugoslavia in recent years."

"And they called themselves the Lions, right?"

"Yes. Does that mean anything to you?"

"Kind of, but it's really just a feeling."

"Coming to Switzerland was *just a feeling* for me, but with every gun that gets jabbed in my back or bullet that whizzes past my head, I'm learning to trust my feelings even more, so, please, share."

"Well, when you first mentioned the Lions, it made me think of words like 'proud' and 'arrogant.' Those words remind me of Gerhard Miner—"

"The lunch you had with him."

"Yes, which seems silly, but there was another picture that came to mind when you talked about the assassination team being Swiss and being named the Lions. There is a very famous monument in Lucerne of a dying lion. It was carved out of a rock ledge as a tribute to the men of the Swiss Guard who died defending King Louis and Marie Antoinette during the revolution."

"You think there might be some sort of symbolic connection?"

"Why not? Switzerland has always been proud of its neutrality, but also very proud of the ferocity and courage of its mercenaries. Ferocity and courageousness, just like a lion."

"This monument is in Lucerne?"

"Yes."

"And where does—"

"Miner live?"

"Yes."

"He has an apartment in Bern, but his main home is in Lucerne."

"The Lions of Lucerne. You might not have been reaching very far at all."

CHAPTER 63

The next morning, Scot used the color kit Claudia had bought with their groceries and dyed his hair once again. He wanted to return to his sandy brown, but he needed two applications to cover up the white blond and subsequently ended up with a much darker shade than he'd hoped for. At least it didn't all fall out, which had been a definite possibility with all of the chemicals it had been subjected to in the last couple of days. With his hair short, yet conservatively colored, hopefully no one would bother to give him a second look.

After straightening up the house and boarding up the broken window as best they could, Scot and Claudia left to pursue the only other lead they had, a package mailed from a small village north of Lucerne called Hochdorf.

"Do you think he'll tell us anything?" asked Scot.

"We won't know until we try, will we?" Claudia responded.

"And you're sure he's somehow connected?"

"Of course, I'm sure. When Miner had refused to meet and answer my questions, I began following him. That's how I learned about the post office box in Interlaken. I also found he had one in Lucerne. After he and I had lunch, I thought there was little chance I would be able to get anything on him. He went on vacation, but I kept watching both of his post boxes hoping to get lucky. A few days ago, a package arrived for him in Lucerne."

"Which of course you borrowed, steamed open, copied the contents of, and then replaced."

"You're very smart. Yes, I made copies of the contents. It held his passport, canceled train tickets, and credit card receipts. They showed that he had been in Greece, Italy, and France before returning home."

"Was he out of the country during the time of President Rutledge's kidnapping?"

"Yes, but according to the stamps in his passport, he was in Europe, not America."

"Of course not. That would be too obvious. What's the connection with the cousin in Hochdorf?"

"I don't know. I'm hoping he will tell us. Who else would send Miner a package from Hochdorf if not his cousin? My files show he's the only relative Miner has there. It has to be the cousin. Miner wouldn't go up to Hochdorf just to mail himself a package."

"What if he left it there while visiting and the cousin just mailed it back to him?"

"And what were you saying about going with your gut? At this point, this is all we have to go on."

• • •

An hour outside Lucerne, Claudia pulled into a rest area.

"I need to call the office and let them know I won't be in."

"Don't forget to see if you can get someone to look a bit deeper into Miner's file to see if there are any links between him and Yugoslavia."

"I'll see what I can do."

Scot got out of the car and stretched his legs while Claudia went inside to use the phone.

At a pay phone by the washrooms, she inserted her telephone card and dialed her office.

"Christina, hello. It's Claudia. I'm not going to be in today; I have some outside work to do. Do I have any messages, please?"

"Herr Schnell has been looking everywhere for you. Hold a moment. I will connect you."

Schnell? What could he possibly want? she wondered.

Ten seconds later a gruff voice roughened from years of cigarette smoke was on the line. "Where are you?"

"Good morning, Herr Schnell," Claudia politely replied.

"Don't *good morning* me. Where are you?"

"Why, what's going on?"

"Where were you on Saturday?"

"I was pursuing leads in my case."

"Where was that?"

"The Jungfrau area."

"And did you stay at your parents' farm in Grindelwald?"

"Yes, but—"

He cut her off. "And where were you all day Sunday and Sunday evening until now?"

Claudia was getting very suspicious. He couldn't possibly know already that she had been in his house. She wanted to explain things to him, but decided she wouldn't give out any more information until she had some of her own. "I was with a friend." Quickly, before Herr Schnell could fire off another question, she asked one of her own. "What is this all about?"

"What this is all about is that for the longest time I couldn't understand why you were not making any progress on the weapons case."

"It has been extremely difficult. There are not many leads."

"I spoke with Arianne Küess in the Hague. She had some very interesting things to say about you."

"About me?" Claudia had no idea where this was going.

"She says you volunteered for this case."

"That is correct, but I don't understand—"

"So, you don't deny it?"

"No, of course not. Herr Schnell, I must respectfully insist that you get to the point."

He did. They had a brief exchange of words, and when Schnell was finished speaking, all Claudia could do was set the phone down and walk back out to the car stunned.

Scot sensed something was wrong right away. "Are you okay? What happened?"

Claudia started the car and backed out of their parking space faster than safe driving dictated.

"Claudia, hold it a second. What's wrong?"

She gripped the steering wheel with all of her might as if somehow it could purge the anger from her body. "Yesterday, the police raided my parents' farm in Grindelwald."

"Raided? What happened? Are they okay?"

"Physically, I'm sure they're fine, but they are probably very shaken. They are much too old for this."

"For what? Why were the police there?"

"They had an anonymous tip."

"Tip about what?"

"After a thorough search of the barn, the police found two ADATS."

"ADATS? As in Swiss antitank missiles?"

"Yes."

"Let me guess. The serial numbers on the missiles—"

"Match the ones that were stolen from the weapons depot outside Basel."

"Claudia, I don't know what to say."

"I do. Someone is going to pay."

CHAPTER 64

Even though she was stunned, Claudia had still been able to think on her feet. If Deputy Federal Attorney Urs Schnell hoped to have any sort of future with the Bundesanwaltshaft, the last thing he needed was a scandal that would engulf his entire office on his very first big case. Seeing the logic of Claudia's argument and trusting her promise that she would not go to the press, Schnell agreed to give her forty-eight hours before turning herself in. She assured him she would have answers by then. If only she could assure herself of the same thing.

"I never did like anonymous tips. They always smell bad," said Scot.

"From what I can tell, I don't think my boss likes them either and that's why he agreed to hold everything for forty-eight hours."

"That and the fact that he doesn't want a scandal on his hands."

"There'll be a scandal, all right, but it won't involve me or my office. It's going to have to do with Swiss intelligence and Gerhard Miner."

"Well, you better do some fast thinking. You've only got forty-eight hours."

"And what about you?"

"Me? I have no idea how much time I have left. You forget, there are people with guns looking for me."

"I'm not convinced the shooters in the Ice Palace weren't there for me as well. Someone might have seen me putting your letter back into the post office box after I made a copy of it."

"Don't tell me we're actually going to fight over who's going to die first?"

"No. We need to be serious. Why were the weapons planted in my family's barn?"

"That one's easy. You're getting too close to the truth."

"We both are, and the closer we get the less time we have."

• • •

Before driving into the village of Hochdorf, Claudia explained to Scot that she would need to question Miner's cousin in German. Harvath would not be able to open his mouth, but his silence would make him very intimidating. Kind of a Swiss spin on good cop, bad cop.

Wilhelm Schroeppel Carpentry was not hard to find. Claudia parked her Volkswagen across the street, and they entered the small shop. A set of diminutive cowbells rang above the door, announcing their presence. They looked around the showroom as they waited for the shopkeeper to come up front. Harvath traced his finger across one of the shelves and lifted it up to show Claudia the dust.

"Not much of a housekeeper, I'm afraid," came a voice in German. Harvath and Claudia looked up to see a tall, handsome man with gray hair and a fading tan appear from the back wearing an apron. Claudia was immediately struck by how much he looked like Miner.

“I have just returned from vacation and haven’t gotten caught up with my housework,” he said.

“Vacation?” said Claudia. “That sounds nice. Where did you go?”

“Southern Europe.”

“Really? Where exactly? I love southern Europe.”

“I was in Greece for a bit.”

“Greece. Now, that’s a nice spot. How long were you gone?”

“A little bit. I’m sorry, but can I help you with something? I’m quite busy today.”

“I hope you can,” said Claudia presenting her credentials. “I’m Claudia Mueller, and this is Hans Peter Sampras. We’re from the Bundesanwaltschaft, the investigative affairs division, the Bundespolizei.”

“The Bundespolizei? What do you want with me? I haven’t done anything.”

The man was obviously nervous.

“Let’s talk about your recent vacation,” said Claudia. “Did you go anywhere else besides Greece?”

Schroeppel might have been nervous, but he wasn’t stupid. Why hadn’t Gerhard warned him about the possibility that this might happen? Was it his fault? He had done everything his cousin had told him to, right down to the very last detail except . . . the package. Miner had told him to mail it when he changed trains in Bern, but Schroeppel had desperately wanted a coffee and to buy some cigarettes. It wasn’t until he had boarded his new train that he realized he had forgotten to mail the package, so he sent it from Hochdorf when he got home.

He’d talk to the Bundespolizei and then call Gerhard and let him know what took place. Gerhard would be able to fix it. He could do anything. There was nothing he needed to worry about; after all, he had been on an official state mission helping his cousin and, in his own small way, his country. The Bundespolizei were just too stupid to know it. They were messing with the wrong family. When he called Gerhard, though, he would conveniently forget to mention that he had not mailed the package from Bern as he was instructed.

"No, just Greece," he said. "Everything else is too expensive."

"I see," replied Claudia. "So, just Greece."

"Yes." The man eyed the woman's silent partner nervously.

"And of course, your passport will show the appropriate stamps for this vacation?"

"May I ask what this is regarding?"

"This is just a routine investigation, Herr Schroeppel. It's nothing for you to be concerned about. Would you be so kind as to show us your passport?"

"I would be happy to, but first I would like to see your warrant."

"Surely, Herr Schroeppel, you don't have anything to hide and don't wish to complicate our investigation. If you would be so kind as to show us the passport, we will be on our way."

"I think maybe I would like to call my attorney first."

"Why would you need an attorney?"

"If the Bundespolizei came to your place of business and asked for your passport without an explanation, wouldn't you want to call your attorney? I work hard and mind my own affairs. The last time I checked the federal constitution, Switzerland was still a democracy. I don't much care for you, or your questions. Until such time as you obtain a warrant, I suggest you leave me alone. Good day."

Claudia was stumped. He had her. What could she do, put a gun to his head and demand to see his passport? She had nothing, but felt the need to leave him with something that would diminish his superior attitude.

"Herr Schroeppel, one more question before I go. You look quite similar to your cousin, Herr Miner. I know him. The resemblance is uncanny. I will be back and I will have a warrant for your passport. While I am at it, I will get one for his too. You were both on vacation lately, and something tells me comparing your two passports is going to be quite interesting. Have a good day."

She turned and walked out of the shop followed by Harvath, who didn't take his eyes off the man until they were on the street.

"What was all the passport stuff about?" asked Scot.

"Remember when I said I hoped he would be able to tell us something?"

"Yes."

"Well, just seeing his face told me a lot. He's a dead ringer for Miner."

"What's that got to do with his passport?"

"Everything. Think about it. How closely do busy passport control officers study passports?"

Scot remembered how he had been able to breeze through two different passport controls with his Hans Brauner papers. "I don't know. It must vary."

"Well, think about a nicely dressed, middle-aged man on holiday."

"I guess it wouldn't warrant too much scrutiny."

"Even if it did, Schroeppel so resembles Miner, I think he could pass the test."

"Let's say you're right. What does it mean?"

"I think Miner bought his cousin a nice vacation, and all he had to do for it was be seen, get a passport stamped, and charge things on a credit card, all under the name of Gerhard Miner."

"But what does Miner get for all of this generosity?"

"The most priceless thing of all, an almost airtight alibi."

"You're right!" Scot finally grasped what Claudia was saying. "And Miner's got one big problem now."

"Yes. The airtight alibi is starting to leak."

"A leak can be so drawn out and painful. Why don't we see if we can help tear it open?"

CHAPTER 65

Forty-five minutes after she left a message on his voice mail, Claudia's cell phone rang.

"Mueller," she said.

"Fräulein Mueller, what a delightful surprise it was to get your message," said Gerhard Miner.

"I doubt that."

"Why would you doubt that? I'm flattered to have the ardent attentions of such an attractive young woman."

"Well, then you won't mind meeting me for lunch today."

"I'm sorry. I'm much too busy. We'll do it soon, though."

"I think that would be a mistake."

"And why is that?"

"I have some very special information I think you might be interested in."

"That's hard to imagine."

"I can tell you, or the deputy federal attorney, or maybe even the press."

"Fräulein Mueller, I'm surprised you're even free to walk the streets. Are you not being brought up on charges by the deputy federal attorney?"

"Well, he's funny like that. He doesn't much care for anonymous tips. He says they"—Claudia shot a sideways glance at Scot—"he says they stink."

"Stink?" The Americanism was lost briefly on Miner.

"Yes, he much prefers firsthand accounts of things. Eyewitness testimony is so much more powerful, especially in court. An anonymous tip versus, say, the testimony of a carpenter from Hochdorf, is so much more effective. Wouldn't you agree?"

There was absolute silence over the phone.

"Herr Miner? Are you still there?"

Quietly, Miner responded, "Yes. I'm still here."

"You haven't called him back yet, have you? You figured his message wasn't important enough. You'd wait until you felt like it to call him back. It's funny, but I could almost hear his fingers dialing your number the minute I left his shop."

"What time?"

"What time did I leave his shop?"

"No, lunch. What time do you want to meet for lunch?"

"I'm quite busy today. Being framed for a major weapons theft creates all sorts of demands. Let me look at my book. Can you hold?"

Claudia held her hand over the mouthpiece and waited several moments. She hoped he was good and pissed off. She enjoyed being in control for once.

"Yes, Herr Miner. Sorry to keep you waiting. Let's say three o'clock where we had our lovely lunch last time, the Hotel des Balances. I'll see you at three."

Claudia punched the *end* button and severed the connection.

CHAPTER 66

Setting the lunch appointment for three allowed Claudia and Scot plenty of time to surveil the Hotel des Balances and check for anything out of the ordinary. So far, it was clean.

Claudia went in to get a table, and Scot stayed concealed in a shop across the courtyard from the hotel. From his vantage point, he would know if Miner came alone. Having already met the ringer of a cousin and knowing what kind of car Miner drove, it wasn't hard to spot him when he pulled up.

Miner got out of the black Audi and went into the hotel. Scot waited and, satisfied that he was alone, followed him inside. The hostess showed Scot to the table he had reserved earlier—not too close, but not too far away from the action if he was needed. Claudia and Miner were already deep in conversation when he passed.

". . . as lovely as ever, Fräulein Mueller."

"You'll forgive me if I dispose of the pleasantries and get right to the point."

"Of course I will not forgive you. It isn't every day I get to enjoy lunch with a woman as beautiful as you, and I intend to do just that," said Miner as he called the waiter over. "Are you serving the roast duck today?"

"Yes, sir," said the waiter.

"Good, that's what I will have," said Miner. "How about for you, Fräulein Mueller? Do you like duck? It's quite good here."

"I'm more of a fish person."

"Excellent, then I highly recommend the lake trout caught right here in our very own lake. What do you say?"

"Sounds fine to me," said Claudia.

"Wonderful. Now, what do Americans like to eat?"

"Americans?" asked a startled Claudia. "What do you mean, what do they like to—"

"Steak! That's what they like," said Miner, snapping his fingers, very pleased with himself. "And we'll have a nice filet, medium-rare, for our friend."

"For your friend?" said the waiter.

"Yes, he'll be joining us in a minute. How about some wine, Fräulein Mueller?"

It was their first lunch all over again. "I'll be fine with a bottle of mineral water."

"Well, I hope I'm not being rude—you did after all invite me to lunch—but there's nothing that complements a good meal better than a good bottle of wine. Let's see, I'm having duck and certainly our American friend is a drinker—they all are, you know—and he's having steak. Why don't you bring us a nice Saint Emilion wine. The Chateau Quercy is quite good. I'm sure Fräulein Mueller is on an expense account, and I don't want to get her in any more trouble with her superiors, so make it something at least seven years old, but not much more than that. Thank you." The waiter smiled, took their menus, and walked off for the kitchen.

If nothing else, Miner was consistent. Even when the chips were stacked against him, as he must have known they were now, he still was bold enough to try and assume control of the situation.

"By the way, Herr Miner. I meant to ask you how you knew I was in any trouble in the first place."

"You know what? I would hate to start this conversation without your colleague. That's him, isn't it? The one dining alone, pretending to read the paper on the upper level. Not exactly the table I would have chosen, but it provides a good view of the action. Why don't you wave him over, and then we can start."

The fact that Miner had spotted Scot shouldn't have surprised her. He was good. Reluctantly, she gave in and kept waving until Scot understood his cover had been blown and he made his way toward them.

"Mr. Peter Sampras, I would like you to meet Gerhard Miner," Claudia said in English as Harvath reached the table.

"Come, come now. That hardly seems fair. Let's use one of Mr. Sampras's more endearing names like Hans Brauner or better yet, Agent Scot Harvath of the United States Secret Service."

Claudia's eyes showed her surprise, something Miner never missed in his adversaries. "Why so shocked, my dear? Our office receives the same updates to the watch list that yours does." Turning back to Scot, he said, "Please, Agent Harvath, have a seat. I have taken the liberty of ordering a nice steak for you. You do like steak, don't you?"

"I do indeed. Thank you."

"So, before I begin any conversation, there is a little formality . . . well, more like a habit really, that I like to indulge." Miner reached inside the right side of his blazer, but Scot was faster reaching into his.

"Not so fast, Gerry," said Scot, ready to draw his Beretta.

Miner laughed. "You Americans are so, how do you say it? Quick on the trigger? I can assure you it's nothing. Completely harmless. May I?"

"Slowly," Scot said, watching the man for any hint he was going to pull a gun.

Miner withdrew a small silver box that looked like a fancy holder for a pack of cigarettes and put it on the table between them. He depressed a button, and a row of tiny colored lights flashed along the top. He then pushed the right-hand side of the box flush with his palm, and a piece of the silver plate popped out, which he raised like the antenna on a portable GPS system.

"Sometimes it gets some stares, and I explain it away as a designer cell phone. Technology is changing so quickly these days. People will believe just about any answer you give them.

"Actually," continued Miner, pointing as he spoke, "this device is quite ingenious. Right now it is telling me via the green light here that neither of you are carrying any active recorders or transmitters. The yellow and blue lights here indicate that the device itself is currently emitting both a high- and low-frequency signal that will disrupt any eavesdropping equipment that might be placed within the restaurant or outside, such as a long-range parabolic microphone. It allows me to speak with a certain measure of confidence."

"That's funny, Gerry. I wouldn't have figured you for a man who needed any help with his confidence."

Miner laughed again. "You have a good sense of humor, Agent Harvath. I like that."

"And I like your little gadget. Where would someone find something like that?"

"Actually, these are quite difficult to lay your hands on. I don't think you would have much luck, even if you tried."

"Well, I'll tell you what. I have something quite similar, except it wouldn't fit in your coat pocket. It's snow white and about this big," said Harvath, making a show with his hands. "About the size of a subwoofer. Made by the North Koreans. I don't like carrying it in my pocket because it ruins the line of my suits, being so big and all. Maybe we could trade?"

"I doubt it," said Miner.

"Ever been to North Korea, Gerry?"

"No, I haven't had the pleasure. I hear their women are quite subservient. Very much into seeing to the needs and the pleasures of their men. Much like the Japanese or the Chinese. What wonderful cultures the Asians have, but that's not why you asked me to lunch, is it?"

"It's part of it. You see, I'm very interested in your travel habits. There are some other destinations I wonder if you've visited lately. How about Greece?"

"Of course, I was just there on vacation."

"Along with Italy and France as well?" asked Claudia.

"You've done your homework. Yes, along with Italy and France as well. I took a lovely cruise from Greece to Venice and then—"

"Rode the train up through France and back home. First class all the way," interrupted Claudia. "Of course you have all of the appropriate stamps in your passport to prove it, as well as canceled train and boat tickets and credit card receipts."

Miner was surprised by what they knew, but he didn't let on. He forced himself to smile. "Yes, I do. I'm curious, Fräulein Mueller, are you contemplating a job change? Maybe employment as a travel agent?"

"That depends, Gerry. I think arms dealer might be a better job for her. You keep supplying her with the stolen goods; we'll sell them and cut you in. How does that sound?" offered Scot.

"It was most unfortunate to hear that part of the same cache of missing armaments turned up in the family barn of the case's lead investigator. It must not look very good."

"If you want to talk about something that won't look very good, it's you and your cousin," said Scot. "Somehow, I don't think prison uniforms will flatter either of your figures. The fall of the cloth is all wrong these days, and prison tailors just never can keep up with the latest trends from Milan."

Miner's smile became very strained. "Agent Harvath, one phone call and I can have you immediately taken into custody. Your government is very anxious to have you back. I'm not sure what for, but it must be serious."

"Do you want to talk *serious,* Gerry? Serious is you using your cousin to pose as you around Europe while you're actually in my country kidnapping our president. How much did you make? A million? Five million? Ten maybe?"

"Kidnapping your president? Agent Harvath, don't be ridiculous. I was nowhere near America when the kidnapping happened. As a matter of fact, I haven't been there for several years."

"Not since cross-training at Little Creek?" asked Scot. A slight pulling back of Miner's head told Scot that he had surprised him. He pressed on. "Oh, yeah. I know a lot about you too, Gerry. I know, for example, that they won't put you and your cousin in the same cell. No, two handsome guys like you—they'll want to make sure you both have a chance to share your love. You seem pretty tough, though. My guess is that you'll get to be the husband, but you never know. They put a big enough guy in there with you and you might have to be the wife."

"Agent Harvath, this is hardly the kind of talk that we as gentlemen should be exposing Fräulein Mueller to."

"You see, that's where you and I are going to have to agree to disagree, Gerry. My career and my life are basically through. It's funny how being a gentleman doesn't seem so important when that happens. I have nothing to lose, and that makes me very, very dangerous. Not to mention, unstable. I've got you and your friends in the States to thank for that. Now let's talk some more about you."

"Agent Harvath, there is no question in my mind that you are a disturbed individual. I think the best thing for us to do—"

"Chutee!" hissed Scot. The command stopped Miner in midsentence. "That's right, you slimy son of a bitch. You know, you are one dumb motherfucker. Who do you think you've been playing with? Did you actually think we weren't going to nail you and the rest of your little pussycats? Whoops, I'm sorry, it's *Lions,* isn't it?

"Your men are a disgrace. What kind of a sorry-ass unit are you running? If they're not leaving clues at the farmhouse you used as a staging ground for the kidnapping, they're running their mouths off at the Jungfraujoch in Serbian while their bullets were hitting everything but the intended targets. You might want to work with them on that. And while you're at it, I'd seriously think about how long Senator Snyder will hold out before he rolls over on you. You think you have him over the barrel as an accessory, but if he asks to cut a deal before you do, you're out of luck, my fine Swiss brother. How's all that sit with you? Or do you want to hear about the photographs and evidence we have relating to your little assignments in Kosovo and thereabouts, as well as how my country is going to have every PLO whacko on your ass for the murder of Hassan Useff? You really know how to bury yourself, don't you?"

Miner was absolutely silent. For once in his life, he had nothing to say. Every single element had been planned . . . each and every piece of the equation calculated, weighed, and anticipated. Everything had been thought out, except this free-floating rogue Secret Service agent that had somehow managed to connect with Claudia Mueller. *How in a million, trillion years did these two ever find each other?* he wondered.

"What's wrong, Gerry? Cat, I mean, Lion got your tongue?"

Miner composed himself. "You know, Agent Harvath, Fräulein Mueller has been a little too quiet and you have been a little too vocal. Do you know what this tells me?"

"No, what does it tell you? I'm dying to know."

"It tells me you have nothing. You have no concrete evidence at all. You dragged my poor cousin into this to try to intimidate me. I came here to meet with you and you have nothing but spurious accusations grounded in fantasy. If you really had something, you would have used it. Why bother coming to me?

"I also think Fräulein Mueller is in very serious trouble and will undoubtedly be facing an inquiry and most likely a trial. Somehow in all of this, she got connected with you, which is not going to help her career. I think you are a deeply disturbed individual and she would do well to get as far away from you as possible."

Miner reached across the white-linen-covered table and retrieved the silver box. Turning it off, he retracted the antenna and put it back in his blazer pocket. Looking at Claudia, he said, "Fräulein Mueller, I am very sorry for your circumstances. I am also sorry that this man was able to cloud what I had thought was sound investigative judgment on your part. A word of advice. Enjoy your lunch together. It will be my treat, but walk out of this restaurant and never see this man again. You are in enough trouble already. Good-bye." Miner placed his napkin on the table, slid his chair back, and stood up.

"You know, Gerry, there's one thing that bothers me . . . humor me for a moment. How is it that you can kidnap, smuggle out of the country, and then hide one of the most recognizable men in the world?"

"Well, Agent Harvath, I once again maintain my innocence and can only say that in my life I have learned that under God all things are possible. It is my sincere hope that we do not meet again."

CHAPTER 67

"It appears as if we are no further along than we were when we started," said Claudia.

"C'mon, Claudia. You don't believe that. Of course we are. We aren't exactly where we want to be, but we certainly have made progress. We talked to the cousin, and we know he's involved. We can be sure Miner used him as cover so he could be out of the country with a perfect alibi. Why else would he have to come to meet us for lunch if he didn't want to find out exactly what we know?"

"Well, now he knows. I think it did him more good than us."

"Maybe, maybe not."

"Why do you say that?"

"Say what?"

"'*Maybe, maybe not.*' Why don't you just say what you are thinking?" Claudia sounded irritated.

"What's bothering you?"

"The way you talked to him."

"He was taunting us."

"What were you thinking? You sounded crazy. And the language you used was awful. Is that standard law enforcement practice in America?"

"It can be. I didn't mean to offend you. Miner is used to being in control and having people follow his orders. We needed to send him a message."

"If the message was that you are unstable, I think he got it."

"Actually, that was the message. I wanted him to know what he's up against. He needs to understand that I'm convinced he's responsible and that I'll stop at nothing to nail him. He knows we're on to him and it's just a matter of time before we have enough to get him."

"So we sent him a message. Are you happy?"

"No, not completely."

"Why not?"

"It was the last thing Miner said. It didn't make sense to me. I don't know. Maybe it was just the translation."

"What thing?"

"When he said '*under God* all things are possible.' In English, we say with God, not under him, except in our Pledge of Allegiance. In Spanish I know they say *vaya con Dios,* 'go with God.' It's normally *with* not *under.* Is it different in Swiss German?"

"No, we say 'with' as well. Maybe he made a mistake."

"Miner's act is a little too polished for me. But anything's possible." Scot started to laugh.

"What's so funny?" asked Claudia.

"Look who's grasping at straws now."

Claudia smiled, more out of a feeling of defeat than anything else.

At that moment, the waiter reappeared at the table and presented Scot with a bottle of Saint Emilion Grand Cru. Scot waved him off, saying, "We've changed our minds. We won't be having lunch."

"But," said the waiter in halting English, "you are Herr Miner's guests. He has invited you. It is all paid for."

"Then I'll tell you what. Are you married?"

"No, sir."

"Girlfriend?"

"Yes."

"That's a nice bottle of wine. Take it home tonight and share it with her; she'll love it."

"And the meals?"

"You and the staff can have them. We'll be leaving shortly."

The waiter removed the bottle and retreated to the kitchen.

"You know, I'm beginning to associate wine with unpleasant moments in my life," said Claudia.

"Why?"

"Well, at the end of the first lunch I had with Miner, he ordered dessert for me, a sweet wine that he made a very big deal about. It was foreign, but not from France. He said an American friend of his had introduced him to it. It was supposedly very famous and very hard to get. This hotel keeps a private reserve for him. He was unbelievably pompous about it and practically insisted that I drink it. The whole experience made me extremely angry."

"Wait a second. Back up."

"Back up?"

"A dessert wine! Now I remember. Last night there was something about what André Martin had told me, something connected with Switzerland that I couldn't remember. It was a small piece of information that I had let go of as inconsequential, but it might not be. You said an American friend turned Miner on to the wine?"

"That's what he said."

Scot racked his brain for everything André told him about the wine. *It was a gift from Snyder, who had lied to him about being in France when he really was in Switzerland. The wine couldn't have come from France because . . . because why? Because the sugar content and therefore the alcohol level were too high for EU standards. It wasn't made in the EU. It was made in—*

"Claudia, was the dessert wine from South Africa?"

"Yes. How did you know?"

"When Senator Snyder returned from his trip to Switzerland, he brought André Martin a bottle of wine. Snyder said he had been in France, but André found out that this type of wine wasn't available in the EU. Snyder was obviously lying to cover his tracks. We've got to be talking about the same wine. Let's get the waiter to bring us a bottle so we can check it out. After all, we are Herr Miner's guests."

"I have a better idea. Follow me."

• • •

A front desk clerk pointed Claudia and Scot toward the office of the Hotel des Balances' food and beverage manager, Johanus Schepp. After a short walk down the cream-colored marble hallway, they arrived at a door marked "Schepp." Claudia knocked, and a small voice from inside told them to enter.

Schepp was about the same size as his voice, balding with bifocals, and looked around sixty years old.

"How may I help you?" said Schepp, looking up from a pile of papers on his neatly arranged desk.

Claudia replied in English, signaling to Schepp that the conversation would not be continued in German. "Herr Schepp, I am Claudia Mueller of the Federal Attorney's Office, and this is my colleague Peter Boa of the South African Bureau of International Fraud." Claudia flashed her credentials, and Harvath stood still with his hands at his side, but tilted ever so slightly so Schepp could see the butt of his Beretta protruding from inside his jacket.

"We have reason to believe," continued Claudia, "that your hotel has been trafficking in illegal goods smuggled from South Africa."

"Illegal goods? This is a most serious accusation. I must call the manager about this."

Scot stopped the man as he reached for the phone. His South African accent was pitifully off, but he figured it would be enough to fool Schepp. "I don't need to speak with your manager. If I did, I would have gone to see him first. Instead, I came to see you. Just because I come from South Africa doesn't make me stupid. Okay?"

"Yes, sir. Of course. I didn't mean to suggest—"

"Enough yammering. If you cooperate, there's a chance you can get yourself out of this, and neither the hotel nor your manager need suffer any embarrassment."

"But, why would I hide something from them?"

"Mr. Schepp, if you only knew how many times your name has come up in our investigation."

"My name? But, I have not done anything illegal."

"That's what you think," said Scot as he pulled a piece of paper from his inside pocket, completely revealing the gun this time, and pretending to read from it, "Have you ever heard of Tommy the Torch also known as Top Shelf Tommy?"

"No, I have not."

"How about, Patrick the Ace?"

"Once again, no."

"Jeff the Matchmaker?"

"Herr Boa, these names sound more like they come from an American gangster movie," said Schepp, whose upper lip was beading with sweat.

"They might sound funny to you, but my government takes them very seriously." They actually sounded funny to Harvath too. Sometimes his ad-libs were spectacular, and sometimes his warped sense of humor got the better of him. Harvath had always been the type of person who would laugh in church and, knowing he was not supposed to, couldn't help laughing harder.

Claudia saw the need to draw the interrogation back into the realm of not only respectability but believability and took back control. "Herr Schepp, each of these men have mentioned you when questioned in South Africa. They work at a rather exclusive winery that, among other things, has been violating international customs regulations with their shipments. Is any of this sounding familiar?"

"Well, we do have several South African wines in our cellar, but we purchase those through a Swiss distributor."

"No, these men specifically stated that the wine was delivered here to the hotel in the name of a certain individual." Turning to Harvath, she said, "Mr. Boa, do you have the name on your notes there?"

"Yes, the name is Gerhard Miner. Ring any bells, Schepp?"

"Yes, I do know Herr Miner. He is a regular customer. We keep a case of dessert wine for him, Vin de Constance. Has the hotel done something wrong?"

"That depends," said Claudia. "Why does the winery name you as their contact in Switzerland?"

"I would imagine because the wine was shipped here for Herr Miner, but to my attention. Had I known the transaction was illegal, I would have politely refused Herr Miner's request."

"Ignorance of the law, Mr. Schepp, is no excuse. This could reflect quite poorly on the hotel and your career," said Harvath.

"Herr Schepp," said Claudia, easing comfortably into the good cop role, "I think your participation in this affair can be minimized, if not forgotten, if you would be willing to offer us a few moments of cooperation."

The man was definitely eager, and his head nodded up and down so quickly that Claudia was afraid it would snap right off his neck.

"Now, you state that you only received the wine. You didn't order it?"

"Yes, that is correct. From what Herr Miner explained, a friend of his arranged it as a gift. It is extremely difficult to get. The estate only sells this wine in a limited quantity."

"Herr Schepp, we would need something to corroborate your story. A receipt, a bill of lading. Do you have any paperwork that came with the wine?"

"I have a file for Herr Miner," said Schepp as he moved from behind his desk to a row of file cabinets. "Sometimes the wineries will include special handling or storage directions with the shipments. I always keep all of this information together."

Claudia looked over at Scot, who rolled his eyes.

It took Schepp no time at all to find what he was looking for. "Here it is. This is the shipping and order information that came with the delivery. I don't know if this would be helpful for you, but some tasting notes and a small promotional piece about the wine was included as well."

Schepp showed Claudia and Scot the paperwork.

"Herr Schepp," said Claudia, "this may prove to be very helpful. We will need to take this with us, but you are free to make a copy of it if you like, to retain for your records."

"That is very kind of you. I would hate for my records to be inaccurate. I don't need the promotional piece, but the other things I should copy. The machine is at the front desk. Do you mind waiting a moment while I make the copies? I'll do it very quickly."

"Very well, Herr Schepp. We appreciate your cooperation."

In a flash, the man was out the door, and Scot was half scanning, half reading the promotional piece out loud. "'In the eighteenth and nineteenth centuries, Vin de Constance was the most celebrated wine to come out of the southern hemisphere. . . . Napoleon Bonaparte had thirty bottles a month shipped to the island of Elba to ease his confinement. . . .' It seems the king of Prussia used to knock back a few glasses every night after dinner, as did Louis XVI, Frederick the Great, Bismarck, and a busload of Russian czars."

"Now I know why Miner's lecture to me about the wine seemed so knowledgeable; he memorized the tasting notes," said Claudia.

"Wait a second," said Scot.

"What?" she asked, drawing closer to try and read over his shoulder. "What is it?"

"In *Sense and Sensibility,* Jane Austen apparently recommended Vin de Constance as a cure for a broken heart."

"So?"

"Guess who else wrote about it? Charles Dickens in *Edwin Drood."*

"Dear Aunt Jane; Yours, Edwin," said Claudia. "The code between Miner and Senator Snyder."

"Bingo!"

When Schepp reappeared, Claudia accepted the originals of the documents and told him that if he didn't hear from either her or Herr Boa again, it would mean they had decided to let him off the hook. They thanked him and quickly left the hotel.

CHAPTER 68

"When they come out, kill them both! And this time, no mistakes," commanded Miner over the radio once he was in his car and had driven away from the hotel.

Klaus Dryer and Anton Schebel were both waiting outside the Hotel des Balances for Scot and Claudia to appear. Klaus carried a nine-millimeter Walther P4 pistol with a sound suppresser, and Schebel carried his favorite H&K MP5 SD1 submachine gun, which was also silenced. Both weapons were compact and easily hidden beneath a jacket. Schebel and Dryer made a decidedly deadly duo.

Miner had indicated to his men that the wait might be at least an hour, as he had purchased a last meal for the condemned couple. The shooters were taken by surprise when Claudia and Scot exited the hotel less than twenty minutes later. They turned right and walked along a narrow, relatively deserted passageway that hugged the hotel's service entrance. Scot had thought it best to leave Claudia's car in the parking lot by the Matthäuskirche and walk the five minutes to their rendezvous with Miner.

The passageway turned to the right, and as they began to follow it, a hail of sharp plaster rained down on top of them while a small utility window in the building in front of them shattered in an explosion of glass.

"Move!" yelled Scot, grabbing Claudia's arm.

The shots came from behind, and instinctively, Scot steered them in the opposite direction. When he came to the Rathausquai, the pedestrianized area bordering the Reuss River, Harvath pulled up and looked around the corner before pulling Claudia out with him. They ran as far as the Hotel Schiff and then ducked into its old stone colonnade.

"Who's after us?" Claudia demanded while she panted for air.

"I'll give you two guesses. Either it's the American hit team or Miner's men. My money's on Miner's guys, but they're both equally capable. I don't want to wait to find out. Let's keep moving, shall we?"

They walked quickly forward, and Scot glanced behind him to see if he could spot the shooter or shooters.

"Claudia, look behind us. See the two women with the baby carriages? To their left is a tall guy in a long, dark coat. That's our man."

Another quick tug on her arm and Claudia turned back around and moved faster. They were out of the colonnade and getting ready to cross the bridge when a series of spits came from uphill to their left. Scot whirled and pulled his Beretta. A man dressed in a blue ski parka was making his way toward them from the direction of the Kornmarkt. He melded into a group of people and prevented Scot from getting a clean shot.

"There's a second one! Run!" he said to Claudia, and the two of them took off down the quay.

They ran past the Rathaus, the Zum Weissen Kreuz, the Pickwick, the Hotel des Alpes, and at St.-Peters-Kirche, steered a hard right and ran up the creaky stairs of the covered wooden bridge known as the Kapellbrücke. Scot looked over his right shoulder as they ran across the bridge and saw Blue Coat coming down the quay. The man in the long coat was nowhere to be seen, but Scot knew he couldn't be too far behind.

The man in the blue coat looked around and quickly drew the pistol from his parka. The suppresser looked as if it was a foot long.

Reflexively, Scot pushed his hand down hard on Claudia's head while yelling, "Gun! Get down! Get down!"

Claudia dropped to her stomach on the damp wood. Because the side of the bridge was about three feet high, they were now completely hidden from view, but they were far from safe. Scot yelled, "Keep your head down and move!" just as splinters of wood began flying, only inches behind them. The man in the blue coat had seen where they'd ducked and was firing blindly into the sides of the bridge, hoping to get lucky. Had the man been using a machine gun, he could have cut a much wider swath. Harvath had caught one break; he didn't expect to catch another.

It was only a matter of moments before the man in the blue coat would be on the bridge, closing in on them from behind. Scot urged Claudia on, and the two ran as fast as they could, crouched beneath the shield of the bridge's outer wooden wall.

Halfway across the river, the bridge edged to the left. They had put enough distance between them and the man behind. What they needed now was speed to increase the gap. Scot stood up, and Claudia did the same. They were both breathing heavily, yet they pressed on, their feet thumping along the wooden planks as they raced for the other bank.

When they drew alongside a small series of gift shops and the bridge's tower, Scot's heart seized. Coming around a bend from the other direction, the direction of their hoped escape, was Long Coat. Harvath saw him pull out a piece of weaponry he knew very well, an H&K MP5.

"Shooter at eleven o'clock! Down! Down!" yelled Scot. Both he and Claudia literally hit the deck. Startled shopkeepers had no idea what was happening until they saw the pair draw their weapons. Scot's was first out, and he let loose with a booming volley of three rounds.

Long Coat disappeared somewhere where Scot couldn't see him.

"Check our six!" he now yelled to Claudia.

"Six?"

"Behind us! Six o'clock. Check for the man with the pistol!"

Claudia spun just in time to see the man in the blue coat coming around the turn in the bridge. She fired four shots from her nine-millimeter SIG-Sauer P220, which sent the man running back in the direction he had come.

"Are you okay?" Scot asked.

"Yes. He took off, but I don't know for how long."

"I don't know either. I think they thought they'd surprise us. I doubt they were expecting such a fight. They're probably in radio contact, so it won't take them long to regroup and come back."

"If they're going to, they'll have to do it soon. The police will be here any minute."

"Yell to the shopkeepers in German and ask if we can get out through the tower."

Claudia did, and then responded to Scot. "No, the only way out is by either end of the bridge."

"Can you see the man in the blue coat from where you are?"

"No, I can't. Do you see the other man?"

"I don't see him, but they're close."

The roof of the Kapellbrücke was a series of posts and rafters covered with wooden shingles. He wasn't going to win any awards from the Lucerne Historical Society, but he didn't care.

What I wouldn't give for a nice sawed-off shotgun right about now, thought Harvath. Rolling onto his back, Scot raised his pistol and aimed at the roof, trying to avoid the overhanging paintings the bridge was famous for. He squeezed off five rounds. Half of his magazine was now empty.

The bullets ripped through the brittle wood shingles, filling the moist air with dust and exposing small bits of sky. The pigeons and white seagulls that had remained on the roof were now flapping their wings as hard as they could to get away.

Scot and Claudia had the slight advantage of being in a crook in the bridge where neither of the shooters could see them very well.

"When I count to three, I want you to hop up on the sidewall there and hoist yourself into the rafters toward where I shot those holes in the roof. It shouldn't be too hard to peel those shingles away. Start making a bigger opening the minute you get up there. I'll cover you."

Claudia squinted up. "Okay, I understand," she said.

"Do you have an extra magazine?"

"No, I don't. Had I known I would be doing so much shooting when I left my house on Saturday, I would have stolen a crate of bullets to go with those missiles in my parents' barn."

"Very funny. We need to conserve our ammunition. If you see the man in the blue coat, I only want you to take two shots at him, no more. Do you understand?"

"Two shots. I've got it. Ready when you are."

Scot rolled back onto his stomach, facing where he had last seen Long Coat coming up the stairs. There was still no sign of him. He took a deep breath and then began, "One . . . two . . . three!" He swept his pistol from side to side expecting Long Coat to show his face, but there was nothing. He glanced quickly over his shoulder and saw that Claudia was already hoisting herself up onto the lower rafter.

He knew she could no longer be his eyes for the man in the blue parka, so he rolled sideways against the wall and looked behind him. While the bend in the bridge was an advantage, it was also a disadvantage. Without standing up, he couldn't tell how close or how far away either of the shooters might be. Above, Claudia was beginning to tear at the latticework, pulling away loose shingles and opening a wider hole.

With his back against the wall, Scot ejected the magazine from his Beretta partway and verified how many shots he had left. Slowly, he slid himself over to the place where Claudia had been. He pulled the slide back just a fraction to make sure there was a round chambered and got ready to make his move. Glancing overhead, Scot saw that Claudia had opened the hole wide enough and was now beginning to wiggle through. It was his turn.

Using the wall to support his weight, he pushed himself upward. His head was almost at the level where it could be seen. In the distance, he heard the braying of European police sirens. Time was running out, and the shooters would be emboldened to make one final push. Scot was sure of it, because that's exactly what he would do. He took a couple of deep breaths and raised the Beretta.

He fired in quick succession; two shots toward where he'd last seen Long Coat and in the direction of the man in the blue parka. Tucking the pistol into his waistband, Harvath vaulted onto the edge of the wall and prepared to grab hold of the rafter when muffled spits started coming at him from both directions. Long Coat and Blue Coat were returning fire.

From their positions, they hadn't been able to see him when he was on the bridge floor, but now that he was standing on the wall, he was completely exposed. A bullet missed his forehead by a whisper and crashed into the rafter he was reaching for. Without thinking, Scot jerked his hand away and, before he could steady himself, lost his balance and began to fall backward.

If he landed on one of the pilings below, he knew the result would be fatal, so he used his powerful leg muscles to give himself one big push outward. Sailing over the water, he saw the look of horror on Claudia's face as she stood on the sloped roof of the Kapellbrücke. Pulling his knees into his chest like a child cannonballing into a swimming pool, Harvath braced himself for impact.

CHAPTER 69

The shock of the frigid water stunned him into immobility as the swift current grabbed him and rapidly pulled him beneath the bridge.

After the first few seconds, his body's natural instinct was to struggle to the surface, but Harvath fought it. He needed to stay as deep as possible. The men on the bridge would be waiting for him to appear on the other side, their side, when they would begin firing.

As he looked up, Scot could see on the surface of the water the shadow where the bridge ended and open sky began. Just as he suspected, as soon as he was out from beneath the bridge, the men started shooting.

He heard the *ploonk, ploonk, ploonk* of bullets hitting the water all around him. He saw the rippled air-bubble tunnels as the shots drilled their way toward him from above. He swept water past him with his arms in a desperate attempt to get closer to the bottom. Suddenly, the bullets stopped, but there was no time to try and figure out why. The current was sweeping him along even faster now.

Glancing skyward again, Harvath saw the shadow of another bridge as he passed beneath it. Knowing it was important to preserve as much of his core body heat as possible, he slowly pulled himself upward. His lungs took in huge burning gasps of air as he broke the surface. He saw that he had passed the second bridge and was a sitting duck in the middle of the river. Taking another large gulp of air, he submerged himself. Kicking his feet and pulling himself forward with a breaststroke, Scot steered himself underwater toward the north bank.

When he came back up for air, he noticed that he had passed the Hotel des Balances. The river was too fast. He needed to grab hold of something . . . anything. The cold was numbing, his fingers refused to move, and it was all he could do to ball his hands into fists. His head pounded both from the shock of the cold and the exertion.

Another bridge was coming up fast. It was anchored in concrete islands, and there were what looked like iron rings attached in places close to the water level. If he could get ahold of one of those rings, he could at least rest for a moment and figure out what to do. He set his sights on a ring and allowed the current to carry him toward it. It was only a few yards away. He stretched his right arm out of the freezing cold water, willing his fingers to obey and grab hold when his hand made contact. He knew his fingers wouldn't know when they were touching the iron, he would need to watch and tell them when to close around it. He was closer now, only a yard away, maybe less.

Ploonk, ploonk, ploonk. The shots were wildly inaccurate, but they came in rapid bursts, tearing up the water in all directions around him. The shooters were back. Their inaccuracy told Scot they must be firing from the other side of the river. He heard the roar of two shots being fired from a nonsilenced weapon somewhere behind him, and he prayed it was Claudia. Bullets kept splashing around him, and he knew he had no choice but to forget the ring and submerge himself once again. His strength was ebbing at an alarming rate, and he felt that despite his awesome training in deep cold, there was only so much more he could take. Scot sucked in another huge breath and once again swam for the bottom.

He knew that in cold water, the key to survival was to move as little as possible, as swimming took desperately needed heat away from the center of the body and radiated it out to the limbs. The body cooled four times faster in water than in air of the same temperature. The effects of extreme cold could take over very quickly.

The river continued to sweep Scot along at an awesome rate of speed. He counted to five and, not seeing any rips of bullets carving into the water around him, decided to surface. He needed to find someplace to get out. He swam slowly upward, ready to dive again if anyone began shooting. Strangely, the water seemed to have an even stronger pull on him now. His arms felt like limp noodles, and he was worried that the cold was beginning to adversely affect his mind. *I have to get out,* he told himself.

As Harvath once again broke the surface, he quickly scanned the opposite bank. There was no sign of the shooters, but at this moment, that was the least of his problems. His mind had not been playing tricks on him. The river was pulling him with much greater force. It was picking up speed as the water was sucked into a small pumping-and-generator station next to Lucerne's other covered bridge, the Spreuerbrücke.

The speed at which he was traveling doubled, and then in an instant tripled. Half of the river's force was being funneled into a set of iron grates fifty yards ahead. Harvath didn't care about the shooters any-more and focused all of his concentration on the grates that were rushing up to meet him. The white froth and level of the water told him that there was a drop-off right before the metalwork. If he didn't find a way to break free from the river's hold, he would be pulled under and pinned against the grates, where his lungs would fill with the icy water and he would drown.

Summoning every last ounce of strength he had, Harvath began to try to paddle across the current, closer to the north bank and safety. His muscled arms pumped like giant pistons, and he didn't give a single thought to the stitches or the pain radiating from his left arm. Again and again, he pulled and stroked, trying to break free of the frigid grasp that hurtled him toward certain death. For a moment, he thought he was making progress, then came to the crushing realization that the current had only adjusted itself to the right as it entered a directional chute of concrete. The chute narrowed, and the water picked up even more speed.

Harvath pulled with all of his might and kicked his legs frantically. Suddenly, a new pain shot through his body. Something had come racing down the river and slammed into his hip. Before Scot could take stock of what had happened, he felt the pressure of the river growing on him. It was bending him almost as if he were a twig. *Bending instead of pushing? The only way you can bend something is if there's resistance!* As the river swirled and pushed against him, sending sheets of water shooting up and over his head, he realized what had happened. He'd come to a stop.

Twenty yards before the pumping station was another grate submerged just below the water line. Its function was to keep large objects such as trees, oars, and other waterborne debris from being sucked in. Thankfully for Harvath, it had worked. The pain he'd felt had not been something hitting him, but rather his hip and the rest of him crashing into the grate. For the moment, he was safe, but the water was crushing his chest. The cold already made it so hard to breathe that the added pressure from the water was now making it impossible. He wouldn't die from drowning, but suffocation was an all-too-new and all-too-likely possibility.

Ten feet away was a concrete embankment that jutted out from the pumping station like a finger into the river. Scot tried to shuffle toward it, but in his weakened state, he was pinned too tightly to move. He fought to breathe in slow steady breaths. He couldn't see a way out. *But there must be.* He closed his eyes and tried to think. A splash nearby startled him, and he opened his eyes just in time to see a huge, neon-yellow object racing toward his head. Instinctively, he threw up his hands to protect his face.

"Don't let it go by! Grab it! Scot, do you hear me? Grab onto it, and I will pull you in. Hurry, they're coming. We don't have much time!"

It was Claudia's voice. The object was a life ring with a line attached. Claudia was standing on the embankment holding the other end. He wrapped an arm around it.

"Good. Listen to me. I need you to put your right arm and shoulder through and then your head. The water is moving very fast, and I don't want to lose you. Do you understand?"

Scot fought to regain control of his body. His arm didn't seem to want to cooperate. Finally it did, followed by his shoulder and then his head. Half his body was now safely in the life ring, and he found he could move against the current with Claudia pulling from the embankment. She guided him to a short ladder he hadn't seen before and kept the rope taut as he climbed up.

"Are you okay?" she asked.

Was he okay? Sure, a swim was just what today needed to make it perfect. Scot could only shake his head. He was too cold to speak. He had lost all of his color, unless you counted the blue in his lips, and his teeth were chattering.

"Here, put this on," said Claudia as she removed the life ring and draped her coat over his shoulders. "I hate to do this to you, but can you move? We have to get going."

Scot nodded, and they made their way up the embankment.

As they reached the top, the ground in front of them erupted in a volley of muffled pops. The shooters were charging down the Spreuerbrücke right at them.

Claudia shoved Harvath down and reached for her SIG. She faked left and then jumped and rolled hard to her right, trying to draw their fire away from Scot. The trick worked, and the shooters turned their attention in her direction.

The bullets tore up the ground around her, and Claudia continued to roll, aiming as best she could at the figures closing in on her. She had long ago lost count of how many shots she had fired and had no idea how many she had left. Only two thoughts raced through her mind: stop these two men and protect Scot. Over and over she pulled the trigger and finally she saw one of the men drop his weapon and fall forward. It was the man in the long coat. Claudia had managed to hit him square in the chest. He dropped his H&K and fell forward, his momentum causing him to slide across the frozen ground like a runner stealing third. *Only one left.*

Claudia turned her sights on the man in the blue parka and pulled the trigger. She heard a sickening click. *Nothing.* She was out of ammunition. Not only that, but she had rolled as far to her right as she could. Claudia was trapped against the wall of the embankment. The man knew it and closed the gap fast.

As he moved in for the kill, there was a smile on his face. Claudia wondered if it would hurt to die or if it would be instantaneous, like turning out a light. She saw a muzzle flash and closed her eyes waiting for the projectile to shatter her skull and tear through her brain, but it didn't happen. Slowly, she opened her eyes.

Three feet away, the man in the blue coat was on his knees with both hands clutching his throat, trying to stem the gurgling tide of blood. Ten feet farther, she saw Scot drop the heavy Beretta from his hands and fall back onto the ground.

Claudia ran over to the man in the blue parka and kicked his pistol away. She then ran to Harvath. "I thought for sure he was going to kill me," she said.

"Not on my watch. I hear sirens, the police are getting closer. We've got to move."

"You're right. I have to get you out of here and into some dry clothes."

"Wait," said Scot. "Search both of the bodies. Don't bother looking at anything, just shove everything you find into your pockets. Hurry up; it's a bit nippy out here." Scot managed a grin for a fraction of a second before his teeth began chattering violently again.

Claudia went right to work. Neither of the men had a wallet or very much else on them. She put everything she found in her pockets and then rushed back to Scot.

Her car was on the other side of the old town. *How would she get him back to it?* Any minute now the police would be swarming all over. Then she saw it. About two blocks up the St. Karli-Quai from where they were was a sign for the Tourist Hotel. Claudia got Scot on his feet and urged him forward. She hoped the exercise wouldn't do him any further harm.

When they reached the hotel, a group of people were standing in front. They had heard the gunshots and come outside to investigate. They had no idea from which direction they were fired. There was a line of three taxicabs, and Claudia rushed with Scot up to the driver of the first one.

"Please, sir," she said in German, "I need to get my brother to a hospital. We heard something that sounded like gunshots, and he lost his balance and fell into the river. I think he has hypothermia."

Before the cabdriver could answer, the manager of the hotel, who was standing in the doorway, said to the cabdriver, "Heinrick, wait!" and he disappeared inside. Claudia had no idea what was going on. All eyes, including the cabdriver's, were turned to where the manager had stood just a moment before. As quickly as he vanished, he reappeared with a thick wool blanket, which he wrapped around Scot. "Now you go!"

Claudia thanked him and climbed into the back of the cab with Scot as the driver peeled away from the curb. She spoke softly with Scot for a few moments and then addressed the driver. "My brother says it's not as bad as I thought. He says I'm overreacting. My car is parked at the Matthäuskirche parking. Please turn right here and take Diebold-Schilling Strasse along the Musegg Wall to Brambergstrasse."

"But he is soaked through. Are you sure?" asked the driver.

"He was only in the water for a few moments before I helped him out. I think the most important thing is to get him home to a warm bath and some *nudelsuppe.* Our mother is a nurse. I'll call her and have her come over straightaway to look at him."

"I can take you to the hospital. It's no problem."

Harvath managed a feeble, but believable, *"Nein, danke,"* from the backseat.

"As you wish," replied the driver, who turned right at the Geissmattbrücke bridge and headed along the Musegg Wall toward the Old Town section of Lucerne, where Claudia and Scot had parked her car.

"Please turn up the heat," Claudia asked the driver.

Scot smiled to himself as two police cars sped past. *Could it possibly get any hotter?*

CHAPTER 70

Claudia got them out of town and onto the auto route for Bern as fast as she could. The heater was turned up as high as it would go. Scot stripped out of his wet clothes and remained huddled in the wool blanket until Claudia found a roadside café, where she bought containers of piping hot soup and coffee. Scot drank down everything she gave him and, when he was finally feeling up to it, reached into the backseat and pulled some clothes from his suitcase. Although Claudia should have been watching the road, every once in a while she sneaked a guilty peek at him getting dressed.

The color began to return to Scot's face, and his shivering lessened.

"How are you feeling?" Claudia asked.

Even though he was fully dressed in new clothes with heavy wool socks, Harvath wrapped the blanket back tightly around his body. "Very pissed off."

"Good. The way you were shivering, I thought we had made the wrong decision."

"No, we made the right one. If we'd gone to the hospital, there could have been police, questions, and who knows what. Miner probably would have found us, and that would have been the end of the story."

"I guess so, but if we had been wrong about the severity of your condition, that could have been the end of the story as well."

"I know my limits. You don't ever need to worry about me."

"Thanks, Scot. I'll remind myself of that next time I see you looking like a flipped turtle."

There was a touch of hurt in her voice.

"Thank you," said Scot.

"For what?"

"For saving my life."

"You mean when I drew the fire of Miner's men and pulled you from the river? That? That was nothing. Sorry I didn't have a towel ready when you got out."

Scot thought about what a gift she had for pissing him off while at the same time making him want to laugh out loud. They made quite a pair.

"How do you know the men were Miner's?" asked Scot as he brought his mind back.

"They weren't wearing any American brand-name clothes, and the man you shot in the throat was mumbling in German as he was dying. I just assumed Miner had sent them."

"Seems like it."

"You were also right about something."

"What was that?"

"They were in radio contact. They each had an earpiece and a sleeve mike. The radio was a German brand."

"Was there anything in their pockets?"

"No wallets, which doesn't surprise me. These men would not be carrying ID around with them. That's not the way it's done."

"I agree. Anything else?"

"Cash, cigarettes, and each had one of these," said Claudia, who pulled out what looked like two playing cards from her pocket and handed them to Scot. He was getting warm now, and with his free hand he turned down the VW's heater.

Harvath examined the cards. They had a magnetic strip on the back and a red dragon on the front, under which were the words *Mt. Pilatus* and some other lines written in German.

"What are these?" said Harvath.

"They are kind of like lift tickets for Mount Pilatus."

"What is it?"

"Pilatus is a mountain not too far from Lucerne. Normally, on clear days, you can see it from the city. According to legend, the body of the Roman governor Pontius Pilate is buried in the lake near the top, and supposedly this was the only place his soul could rest. Every year on Good Friday, he is said to rise from the water to wash the blood from his hands. The mountain is named after him."

"That's just charming. What about this dragon on here? What's that all about?"

"That is the logo for Mount Pilatus. It comes from something different. Starting in the fourteen hundreds, the people of Lucerne began to think they saw dragons around the mountain, and the image stuck."

"Tell me more about the mountain."

"There are two hotels on the top. One is called the Bellevue, and it is completely round like the Schilthorn in the Jungfrau region. The other is a more traditional hotel called the Hotel Pilatus Kulm."

"What's the attraction up there?" asked Scot.

"The views mostly. Although some people come for hiking, rock climbing, and paragliding as well."

"So it's kind of like the Jungfraujoch?"

"I guess that would be a fair comparison, but the Jungfraujoch is actually carved into the glacier and the mountain, while the hotels at Pilatus are basically built on top of it."

"But, why would these two guys be carrying lift tickets for Pilatus?"

"Maybe they were hikers," said Claudia.

"C'mon, Claudia, think. They don't carry wallets with them, but they do carry these lift tickets? Why would they need them?"

Claudia focused on the road in front of her while she toyed with Scot's question in her mind.

"Do you suppose," Scot continued, "that they were going to kill us and then go off for a nice little hike?"

"Don't be stupid."

"Then why have the tickets?"

"To get up to the top of Pilatus."

"Right. And if they were carrying the tickets with them when they attacked us, that probably means they were going to be using them afterward, right?"

"I guess you could be right."

"How many ways are there to get up Pilatus?"

"Well, you can hike it. That takes about five hours. Then there is a series of two gondolas and a cable car from the town of Kriens, or you can take the cogwheel railway from the town of Alpnachstad."

Scot opened Claudia's glove compartment and started rummaging around.

"What are you looking for?" she asked.

"Do you have a map of the area around Lucerne?"

"Yes, it's in my Swiss atlas, underneath your seat."

Scot fished out the atlas and found the pages he was looking for.

"Okay, I've got the towns," said Scot. "So the cogwheel train is direct, no transfers?"

"Right. Why? What are you thinking?"

"Would it be possible to hide someone in one of the hotels up at the top of Pilatus? Let's say maybe Miner knows the owner or is blackmailing him? Could he do it?"

"I suppose he could, but it's not very likely."

"Why not?"

"The staff of those hotels are much like others all over the country. They're very chummy and they talk. They all know each other's business and everything that goes on in the hotels. It is hardly likely Miner could hide your president there."

"Good point. What about someplace else, maybe only halfway up the mountain?"

"From what I could see on the tickets, they are good for travel all the way to the top. Why would they pay for full trips and not use them?"

"To throw anybody off if they ever came across the tickets?" Scot speculated.

"If they ever thought anyone would find the tickets, why not leave them at home in their wallets? Or better yet in their car?"

"I was thinking about that. If for some reason the two men got separated or couldn't get back to their car, they would need to know they could still get up the mountain, so they would have to keep their passes on them at all times."

"Why not just carry enough cash to be able to buy a new ticket?"

"That means dealing with a cashier . . . maybe standing in a line. There's too much chance of being remembered or seen on a security camera. If Pilatus is where they're staying, they'd need to get up and down as easily as possible. Hence the need for keeping the passes on them at all times. Now, if they aren't using the hotel, where else might they be?"

Claudia twisted her lip and frowned. "Aside from the gondola and cable car stations, the mountain only has scattered cowsheds and yurts that are used for hikers. . . . What are you thinking?"

"There is a small airfield on the map here at Alpnachstad. It would be a piece of cake for Miner to get in and out from here with relatively little interference. Do you know if it's a private airfield?"

"From what I remember, it's mainly for civilian aircraft, but there are one or two military hangars. . . . That's it!" cried Claudia, thumping her palms against the VW's steering wheel.

"What?" said Scot. "What's it?"

"I was wrong," said Claudia.

"About what?"

"About Pilatus."

"How so?"

"I was wrong when I said the attraction, the tourism infrastructure such as the hotels, was built on top of the mountain, unlike the Jungfraujoch."

"So, either it is or it isn't."

"Actually, it is and it isn't. All of the things the tourists see are pretty much sitting on top of Pilatus. The final cable car ride up and the cogwheel railway each approach the summit from different sides of the mountain. Normally the tourists go up one side and come down the other. The marketing people at Pilatus call it the Golden Round Trip. The cable car and the cogwheel railway arrive and depart beneath the Hotel Bellevue, which is partly recessed within the mountain."

"So?"

"So, when I first started climbing in competitions, I did some around Pilatus. My grandfather was a climber and he was my coach. He had done a lot of climbing on Pilatus itself. Do you know what my grandfather did for a living before he retired?"

"No, but I hope it has something to do with what we're talking about."

Claudia ignored Scot's crack. "He was an engineer with the army." She looked at Scot as if where this was leading should be obvious. Scot looked right back at her with a blank stare.

"Scot, have you ever seen a Swiss military base in all your visits to Switzerland? Ever seen any piece of military hardware except for a jet that might have flown overhead?"

"No, I never have. I always heard that despite their continuing stance of neutrality, the Swiss had a pretty good army. Nobody ever saw it, though, because . . ." His voice trailed off.

Claudia finished the sentence for him. "Because everything is hidden away in the mountains. When I was accepted into the Federal Attorney's Office, my grandfather was very proud of me. I was his only grandchild. With my security clearance and role with the Bundespolizei, he began opening up to me more, telling me about what he did with the army. Do you know now what he did?"

"He was involved with the construction of the military mountain fortresses."

"Very good, Agent Harvath. Yes, he was one of the engineers on the primary design team. From what he told me, they were involved with constructing these incredible fortresses throughout Switzerland. Oftentimes they used the development of ski resorts or other tourist attractions as a cover for all of the military activity. If you were building some sort of resort or something to boost tourism, who would suspect the real reason for gondolas, cable cars, or—"

"Cogwheel railways!" Scot broke in.

"Yes, again," replied Claudia. "How can someone so smart not have the good sense to stay out of the water until spring?"

"A good swim relaxes me and helps me to think. Much like a well-placed gun in the back. So Pilatus is one of these Swiss military fortresses?"

"No."

Scot's heart sank. The pieces had all seemed to finally be coming together.

Then Claudia spoke again. "It isn't one now. It used to be, but my grandfather said it had been decommissioned."

Scot's hopes began to rise. "Decommissioned, meaning it was abandoned?"

"Sort of. It was sealed off and put on the inactive list."

"But it wasn't destroyed?"

"No, nothing like that. The Swiss are pragmatists. You never know when we might need something like that again. It was just sealed off and left alone."

"So theoretically, if Miner knew about this place, which in his position with the military there is a good chance he did, all he would have to do is figure out a way to unseal it?"

"It might not even be that difficult. According to my grandfather, there were several ways to access these fortresses. They needed to circulate air, so there were ventilation shafts. There were also escape passages. Cargo bays for delivering materials and supplies . . ."

"I'm liking your grandfather more and more. Do you think there's any chance he might be able to help us? A person with that much knowledge could be very useful."

"I think my grandfather would have liked nothing better. But, he passed away two years ago."

"I'm sorry," said Scot, and he really was—sorry for Claudia, sorry for himself, and most of all, sorry for the president.

Claudia seemed not to hear him. "He told me that every structure you saw on Pilatus served a purpose."

"What do you mean?"

"For example, Pilatus already had the very large Hotel Pilatus Kulm, but they then built the little Hotel Bellevue."

"What was the Bellevue's purpose?" asked Scot.

"That he couldn't share, even with me, but he said nothing happens by accident. Every structure serves a purpose. There's the purpose the tourist appreciates and then the purpose the military appreciates. Those engineers were some of the greatest minds Switzerland has ever known."

"Claudia, from what you've told me, it seems reasonable that Miner might be using this inactive fortress as his base. The question is, though, which way did he get in? You said there are many ways in, and all of the structures serve a purpose, right?"

"Right."

"So there are the two hotels, and the cable car and cogwheel railway come and go from just beneath the Hotel Bellevue. Are there any other important structures on top of Mount Pilatus?"

"Let me think. The hotels, a small weather station, a radar station, and a . . ." Claudia's voice trailed off.

"And a what, Claudia? What is it? What else is up there?"

"A church," she said, looking at him with wide eyes.

Harvath repeated the words that Miner had said when they last saw him, which at that point seemed to make no sense at all, "Under God, all things are possible."

Claudia pressed down hard on the accelerator, and the pair sped toward Bern.

CHAPTER 71

Harvath saw pictures and symbols of bears everywhere as they entered Bern. Claudia explained that the bear was the emblem of the city and the canton. They passed signs and coats of arms with bears, bakeries with bear-shaped cookies, and even a bear pit with a couple of live frolicking bears.

Claudia was careful to make sure that they weren't being followed. She crossed back and forth across the Aare River several times and chose small out-of-the-way streets where it would be obvious if someone was behind them. This was Scot's first time in Bern, and he marveled at the ancient sandstone-and-mahogany buildings, the covered arcades of the Old Town, the brightly colored fountains, and the spire of the Münster church, which Claudia told him was the highest in Switzerland.

Far below the Münster, at the foot of an enormous retaining wall, was Claudia's neighborhood. It was called the Matte. Once a workers and artisans' quarter, it was now very popular with the young Bernese in the city's various creative fields. While Claudia couldn't exactly classify what she did for a living as creative, it did demand certain amounts of creativity from time to time, and besides, she really liked the area's energy.

They agreed that since Scot needed to make a phone call and use a fax, she would drop him at her friend Fabia's travel agency, which was only a couple of blocks from her flat. Claudia's apartment was on the fifth floor of a typical European walk-up. As much as Scot protested to the contrary, he needed to rest and five flights of stairs would have been murder on him after everything he had been through today. The thing Scot didn't like was that there was no doubt the American hit team had followed Claudia from Bern to the Jungfrau and they probably had her apartment under surveillance right now. She was convinced, though, that she could get in and out without being seen.

After getting Scot set up in Fabia's private office, Claudia told him she would be back as soon as she ran a couple of errands and got the rest of what they needed from her apartment.

One of Fabia's staff was sent to a small restaurant on the corner to get Scot something to eat. She returned with typical Bernese favorites, fried veal and sauerkraut. To top it off, there was a little bar of Toblerone chocolate.

Scot thanked the woman. Once she had closed the door, he took a couple bites of his food and spread his paperwork in front of him. He picked up the phone and dialed a number by heart.

"Lawlor," came the clear, curt voice over the line. The connection made it sound as if he were only across the street, rather than thousands of miles away.

"Gary, it's Scot."

"Harvath? Where the hell are you?"

"All in good time. What's going on at your end? Any luck getting the president back?"

"Why should I tell you?"

"I guess that answers my other question. I'm still persona non grata, correct?"

"You are much worse than that, my friend."

"Gary, I think I may be able to help you out, but you have to share with me what you have first."

"Jesus, Harvath. I don't know why I bother with you."

"Because we've got a history together and you know I wasn't involved with the president's kidnapping and I had nothing to do with Natalie Sperando and her friend being murdered."

"History or not, I'll tell you what I know, but after that, you tell me where you are."

"Deal."

"We're maxed out. The FBI, CIA, DOD . . . we've got every agent from every possible law enforcement agency working on this, and we still haven't come up with anything. The kidnappers cut off the president's finger and sent it to Vice President Marshfield with a ransom demand of fifty million dollars. We're convinced they will kill the president if we don't give in to their demands."

"You're sure the finger was his?"

"DNA and print positive."

"That's barbaric."

"You're telling me. It really shook Marshfield up."

"How's he handling this?"

"He's hanging tough on the no-negotiation-with-terrorists policy. Other than that, he's falling apart. He looks like shit and hasn't slept or eaten in days. He doesn't even consult with DaFina anymore. Every time someone comes to him for a decision on what the next move should be, he kicks them out and presumably hops on the horn to someone outside his office. There's a rumor he's in touch with a psychic."

"I hate to say this, but I could have told you this would happen. The man has no balls."

"Indeed. Now you know what I know. It's your turn. Where are you?"

"Before we start, I want you to record this. I've got a lot to cover and I know there are people you will want to play this back for, so get the tape rolling."

"I didn't ask for your life story. I want to know where you are."

"I'll tell you, but I strongly advise that you do not trace this call."

"Why not?"

"For one, I won't be here after we hang up, and two, if you trace it, the information, as secure as you think your agency is, might fall into the wrong hands. Just trust me. It'll all be clear after I'm finished."

"All right, Scot. Go ahead. It's your dime."

"First of all. Give me your fax number. I'm going to be sending several things through, and I want to know they are going to a secure line."

Lawlor gave Scot a number.

"And you're in your office right now, alone?"

"Yes. What is this all about?"

"I think I know who actually kidnapped the president and where he is being held."

"You what?" Lawlor couldn't believe his ears. "Where the hell are you? What evidence do you have?"

Scot filled Lawlor in on the entire story, starting with how he thought the kidnapping happened, all the way to his swim down the Reuss a couple of hours ago.

"I'm faxing the contents of the envelope that was in André Martin's locker at Union Station. If you send a man to my apartment, you'll find the piece of chocolate I recovered from the Utah farmhouse buried in the planter box outside my bedroom window. I'm also faxing the shipping invoice for Gerhard Miner's wine. I think when we find out who paid for it, we'll have the connection between Miner and Senator Snyder. Can you put one of your people in South Africa on it right away?"

"Of course. I just hope it shakes out in time."

"Then wish me luck."

"Luck? What the hell are you talking about?"

"My job was to protect the president, and I didn't do that properly, so now my job is to get him back."

"Scot, if you're right, you could only make things worse by storming that mountain alone."

"First, I won't be alone. Second, I'm tired of being on the defensive and getting shot at every twelve hours. And third, if the kidnappers intend to make good on their threat, the president doesn't have a whole lot of time left."

"Scot, just take a second and think about the situation. If they kill him, they'll never get the money. They're not going to strangle the golden goose."

"You don't know that for sure. Who knows what they'll do next. The longer we sit around on our asses, the worse his odds are."

"You can't just John Wayne your way through this. Give me time to look into what you've told me."

"So you think I'm right about all of this?"

"If what you've uncovered is true, you've made a hell of a lot more progress than all of our agencies combined. But we're talking *if.*"

"Well, *if* you add up all the bullets that have been fired at me since Wednesday, I'd say this whole thing is as far away from an *if* as you can get."

"I agree, but this is a hostage situation."

"And the clock is ticking. Listen, Gary, no matter what you say, the president was snatched on my watch and a lot of men died. I was responsible for them, and I let them all down. The only way I can make it right is to see to it that the president is returned safely and that the people behind his kidnapping pay. I won't allow my men to have died in vain. Keep playing defense if you want, but the smart money's on the offense."

With that, Harvath hung up the phone.

CHAPTER 72

It took Claudia twenty minutes to run her errands and gather most of the equipment she and Scot would need. As she crept through the back door of her apartment building, his words still echoed in her mind. The fact that her apartment would be watched was a given. There was probably a person or persons watching her office as well.

As she crept quietly up the stairs, she wished she hadn't talked Scot out of coming with her. It was a silly thought and she knew it, but she felt safe around him. When she got to the top landing, she turned and walked toward apartment 5B. As her left hand trailed along the iron railing, her right gripped the butt of her SIG-Sauer. She was grateful that Scot had given her his remaining three nine-millimeter rounds.

At the door, she examined the locks closely for any signs that they had been tampered with. There were none. She pulled her keys from her pocket, selected the correct one, and gently slid it into the lock. Quietly, she turned back the upper lock and then repeated the process on the lower. The door slid open noiselessly on its hinges. Claudia pushed it the rest of the way, to make sure no one was standing behind it. Scot had warned her not to turn on the lights, because it might alert anyone watching the front of the building that she had returned home. She took a moment to let her eyes get accustomed to the darkness that was growing outside her windows and filling the apartment.

Her weight distributed evenly between both legs and her feet in a wide stance, Claudia reached out with her left hand for the brass doorknob of the hall closet. She twisted, but it wouldn't budge. *Piece of junk,* she thought to herself. You always needed to put your weight against the door and lift up on the knob to get it open. Claudia didn't like having to get that close, but she had no choice. She took a deep breath and in one quick movement leaned against the door, twisted the handle, and popped it open.

She immediately jumped back, not quite sure of what she expected to come flying out at her. Nothing did. She saw two of the items she was looking for and, without setting down her pistol, removed them from the closet and placed them on the entryway floor.

Her heart was beating as she prepared to close the door, afraid someone would be standing on the other side when she swung it shut. She knew she was being too cautious, but somehow that didn't seem like a bad thing. Moving backward toward the front door, she raised her pistol to chest level and nudged the closet door closed with her foot. There was nothing behind it except her living room.

Claudia quickly swept the living room and the kitchen. Both were empty. It was the same in the bathroom and the linen closet. She gathered some extra medical supplies so she could change Scot's dressing and, entering the bedroom, tossed them on the bed. She walked along its edge, toward her closet, and let out a scream as a hand reached out for her ankle.

Like an arrow being released from a bow, Claudia sprang away from the bed and the hand beneath it. Her back slammed into the wall, and she pointed her pistol at the figure that any second would emerge from underneath the bed and come for her. She waited, but whatever was under her bed refused to come out. She peered down the barrel of her SIG, the iridescent night sights illuminating the direction the bullet would take when she pulled the trigger.

Slowly, she focused beyond the gunsights to the underside of her bed. There, where she expected to see a sinister gloved hand, was the black nylon handle of one of the many bags she stored beneath the bed. Claudia exhaled in exasperation and laughed at herself for being so keyed up. She got down on her knees, placing her right hand on the mattress and her left on the floor for balance. She and Scot had decided they would each need a midsize backpack, and Claudia had two that would work perfectly. If only she could pull them out.

Claudia left the gun on the mattress and with both hands dug deeper into the tangled mess of bags. As she dug, she brushed against something that didn't feel like it belonged . . . *the hand!*

In the blink of an eye the powerful hands encased in black leather were wrapped in a vise grip around Claudia's wrists, and she was yanked off balance. Without the use of her hands to break her fall, she hit her head on the wooden bed frame and was instantly dizzy.

The stranger quickly kicked away the bags and slid out from beneath the bed. He was dressed completely in black.

Claudia shook her head to escape the fog that had enveloped it. Before the man could get on his feet, Claudia flipped onto her side and lashed out with a strong kick toward his groin. It missed, and she scored only a glancing blow to his upper thigh.

"Fucking little bitch," the man growled.

English. Not one of Miner's. Scot was right. The American hit team is watching my apartment. That means they don't know where Scot is. He's safe—

Before Claudia could finish her thought, the man was on his feet.

He jerked her to a standing position and twisted one arm hard behind her back.

"Where is he?" the man snarled.

"Who?"

Still keeping her arm held high behind her back, the man grabbed a handful of Claudia's long brown hair. Wrapping it around his hand, he whipped her head back and then slammed her face forward into the mirror of her armoire. The glass shuddered, but didn't break. Claudia, though, felt as if her face had been broken into a million pieces. She could feel a warm trickle of blood begin to run from her nose. Then she tasted the coppery essence in her mouth.

"Do you want to play stupid? Or do you want to cooperate?"

"I don't know what you are talking about. Please."

With one hand tangled in her hair and the other pinning her arm behind her, the man dragged Claudia from her bedroom. She tried to resist, but he tightened his grip, causing even more excruciating pain to shoot through her body. Despite the pain, she tried to make it as difficult as possible for him to pull her down the small hallway toward the . . . *Oh, no, please! Not the bathroom.*

Claudia had always harbored a terrible fear of drowning, ever since she'd been a little girl. If they were going toward the bathroom, it could mean only one thing. He was going to torture her with water.

He kicked the door open and flicked on the light switch with his elbow. Releasing Claudia's arm, he punched her hard in the kidney, and she dropped immediately to her knees in front of the toilet. He threw open the lid with such force that it snapped off the hinges and clattered onto the tile floor.

"Last chance. Where is he? Where's Harvath?"

Claudia was paralyzed with fear, but she knew she could not give Scot up.

"Go to hell," she spat.

"Fine, have it your way," said her torturer as he locked her slim neck in his powerful grasp and plunged her face into the bowl.

Claudia struggled wildly, her arms flailing in all directions. *What a horrible way to die.* The man was showing no mercy. She felt as if she had been held under for five minutes, even though she knew that was impossible. Finally, he pulled her face from the water. Claudia breathed as deeply as she could and then began coughing and sputtering.

"Feel like talking now? Tell me what I want to know and I'll let you go."

"Like hell you will," said Claudia. "Fuck off. I'm not telling you anything."

With a sigh the man said, "Women," and shoved her head back down into the water.

Claudia tried desperately not to struggle this time. She needed every ounce of strength she had. She let her arms go limp next to the bowl. When the man had pulled her out the first time, he had pulled her head so far back she thought her neck would surely snap. He had placed his face so close to hers that she could smell his fetid breath.

Not struggling seemed to make the time she was under water drag on for twice as long. He was not going to let her up this time until she was dead. The plan she had begun to formulate was all for nothing. She might as well try struggling again. At least she would go out fighting. Then she felt the pressure on her neck let up ever so slightly and her head was yanked violently from the toilet. Now was her chance.

"Are you done playing games, you stupid little bitch, or do you really want to be drowned? Is that what you want? Huh? Huh?" With each *Huh?* the man emphasized his point by jerking her head back even farther and harder. Claudia was seeing spots. The man's face was pressed right against hers. She could taste the rotten onions on his breath and feel the stubble of his whiskers against her cheeks. Her fingers kept groping forward. *Where was it?*

"It would be a shame to kill you, you know. You are one nice-looking woman. I'd much rather you and I have a little fun, but you're not making it easy on yourself. Tell me what I need to know and we'll have a party. If you don't, I'll simply have to drown you, but—"

Claudia had found what she was looking for. Behind the toilet was a stainless steel toilet brush that had a decorative plastic ruby on top.

The point of the plastic gem was sharp enough that she was able to drive it right into her assailant's left eye.

The man roared in pain. He let go of Claudia to free his hands, which shot directly up to his face. She slid away across the tile as quickly as she could. He pulled the long-handled brush from his eye and grabbed for a towel to try to stem the flow of blood.

"You fucking bitch! Now you're going to pay! Do you hear me?! Do you hear me?!" he raged.

Claudia certainly did hear him. She was already on her feet running for her bedroom. *The gun? Where is my gun?* Frantically she searched for it. It wasn't on the edge of the bed where she had left it. Somehow during their struggle it must have gotten knocked off. She could hear the man's incessant screaming as he came out of the bathroom down the hallway, "Where are you, you little bitch? I'm going to make you wish you were never born!"

Come on, where is it? Claudia scrambled wildly under the bed, her arms sweeping out in all directions. She had only a few more seconds before the man would be right in the bedroom with her. Her mind shuddered at the possibilities of what he might do to her, and she searched with an even greater frenzy. *It isn't here! Could he have taken it? He didn't have enough time. His hands were busy holding me. Where could it have gone? Why can't I find it?*

Then Claudia realized maybe it hadn't fallen off the bed at all. She swept the remaining few bags out of her path and shot for the other side. Crawling out from under the bed, she almost froze as she heard the sound of the man's voice in the doorway. "There you are. Trying to hide from me? Well, it's too late. Time to die, lady!"

The man began firing wildly with a silenced Russian PM, Pistole Makarov. Claudia's bedside lamp shattered, as did a picture on the wall behind her. The damage to the man's left eye had ruined his aim. Claudia ducked her head. *The gun? How do I get my gun? It must still be on the bed. It has to be.*

Grabbing the comforter with both hands, Claudia pulled down hard, stretching it taut. Preferring a hand be shot rather than her head, she raised one above the level of the mattress and swept it from right to left. She felt something cold and hard. *The gun!* She grabbed it and quickly removed her hand from the bed.

"You know what, bitch? I've got a nice little knife here," said the man.

The shooting had stopped for the moment, and Claudia heard the unmistakable click of a blade locking into place.

"I think you and I are going to have that party first, and then I'm going to let you watch while I cut you up. And then, you know what I'm going to do? I'm going to let you watch as I pluck each of your eyes from your head. Now get out here and take your medicine!"

Claudia pulled the slide back on her SIG and saw that there was already a round chambered.

"I told you to go to hell!" she shouted as she rose from behind the bed and put two slugs into the man's chest.

He dropped the knife from his hand and slumped to the floor.

From the corner of her eye, Claudia saw the barrel of another gun in the doorframe of her bedroom. She whirled and fired, sending splintering pieces of wood flying. That was her last shot. She vaulted over the bed and landed on the corpse of the man who had intended to kill her. She grabbed for his pistol and fell back on her haunches ready to fire at the figure in the hallway.

"Claudia? Claudia? It's me, Scot. Hold your fire. Don't shoot. It's only me. I'm going to come into the doorway. *Don't* shoot."

As soon as she saw it was him, shock took over and she began to sob uncontrollably.

CHAPTER 73

The first thing Scot did was to pull the comforter off the bed and wrap it around Claudia, whom he'd moved into the living room. Next, he went to the bathroom and retrieved a towel to dry her hair.

"He didn't hurt you, Claudia, did he?" Scot asked as he held her close and began drying her off.

"Oh, Scot," she said, breathing in short gasps. "It was . . . It was horrible. He was trying to . . . to kill me. He was trying to drown me in the . . . the bathroom. He told me if I didn't . . . didn't tell him where to find you, he'd kill me."

Harvath wrapped his arms around her. "You're going to be okay. You killed him. He's gone."

"I can't stop shaking," she stammered.

"You're in shock, but it'll pass."

Scot hated to do it, but he had to let her go. He moved quickly around the apartment, gathering up the things Claudia had set out for them.

"How about the backpacks, Claudia? Where are they?"

Her eyes moved toward the bedroom and that told Scot everything he needed to know. Inside, he found two that looked as though they would do the job. While there, he went through the dead man's pockets, but didn't find much. The man did have a radio, which now sported a nice hole from one of Claudia's shots. It had passed through the radio and into the man's chest. The radio told Scot what he already knew—the man wasn't working alone.

Scot picked up the nine-millimeter Russian Makarov pistol and checked the magazine. There was one round left in the mag and one up the pipe. The assassin wasn't carrying any extra ammo and the nine-millimeter round used in the Makarov was an intermediate, falling somewhere between the nine-millimeter Parabellum and the nine-millimeter Short. None of Claudia's ammunition would work in this weapon, but at least two silenced shots were better than none. Scot dropped it into one of the backpacks.

Harvath returned to the living room and saw that Claudia was still shaking.

"Do you have any brandy?" he asked.

She nodded her head yes, and he went into the kitchen in search of it. He returned a moment later with a small bottle and a coffee cup.

Scot poured some into the cup and handed it to her. "This will help steady your nerves a little bit. I'm almost done packing things up, and then we need to go. The police will be here soon."

Claudia nodded.

On the floor in the entry hall, Scot had everything laid out. He quickly fieldstripped Claudia's civil defense force assault rifle. The difference between Claudia and most of the rest of the standing Swiss citizen army was that she was authorized to have ammunition for the weapon. Scot loaded the triple magazine into the pack and followed it with a box of nine-millimeter rounds for their pistols, as well as two extra magazines for Claudia's SIG.

Carefully, Scot wrapped the Swiss SG551 SWAT assault rifle's telescopic night-vision scope in a towel and placed it at the top of the pack.

He helped Claudia to the door, where he got her into a warm coat and then slung the two packs over his shoulders.

When they reached the alley, he was very careful to check things out before exiting. The man upstairs would have partners, any or all of whom could be lying in wait for them.

The distant wail of police sirens grew louder, and Scot had no choice but to pick up his pace. With his left arm around Claudia's waist and his right hand holding his Beretta, Scot made it through the alley without incident. On the street, he tucked the Beretta away beneath his sweater and began the two-block walk to where Claudia had parked her car.

Scot forced himself to walk at a casual pace, so as not to draw any undue attention. Claudia's VW was now only a half a block away. The ruse had almost worked.

Leaving the Federal Attorney's Office, where he had been waiting for Claudia Mueller to return to work, the leader and last remaining member of the American hit team was now speeding toward Claudia's. The final transmission he'd had was that someone was entering her apartment. There had been no further transmissions since then, and his man in the apartment had not responded to his repeated hailings. Something was wrong.

When he saw Claudia Mueller and Agent Harvath trying to appear casual while walking down the street two blocks from her apartment, he knew what had happened.

Instinctively, the man reached under the newspaper on the passenger seat for his weapon. He slowed his car to a crawl, as if looking for a parking space, to make sure he hadn't been noticed by Harvath and the girl. So far, so good. It would only be a matter of moments and he could complete his assignment, collect the rest of his money, and get Senator Snyder off his back.

If Harvath was on to him, he gave no indication of it. The couple maintained their forced leisurely pace. It was only a matter of meters now. The black Opel rolled forward and he was so close that if he'd known German, he would have been able to decipher the writing on the two backpacks Harvath had slung over his shoulder.

It would all be over in less than a minute. The assassin removed the gun from beneath the newspaper and cradled it in his lap.

Despite his request to the contrary, the car rental agency had given him a vehicle with manually operated windows, not power. Harvath and the girl were on his right side, which meant he would need to lower that window. He didn't want to risk the potential problems that could come from shooting through the glass. He let go of the weapon and leaned over to roll the passenger side window down. He grunted from the pain in his bandaged ribs and wondered how long it would take for him to fully recover from the shots he had taken in DC.

His eyes were off them for only a second, but when he straightened back up, two Bern police cars were careening down the street toward him at full speed, with lights and sirens blaring. Harvath and the girl had disappeared. There was no sign of them. A side street loomed only feet away. *Did they go this way? Maybe they're behind a parked car?* The gun in his lap, the assassin had no choice but to make the quick right turn and get out of the way of the oncoming police cars.

• • •

Scot threw the backpacks on the backseat of the VW, slid the driver's seat back, started the car, and eased out of the parking space.

Claudia told Scot where and when to turn. They were taking the fastest route out of Bern. Harvath checked his mirrors occasionally, but as he didn't know the city that well and didn't want to get caught in any possible police dragnets, he forwent his usual evasive driving procedures. He was confident there hadn't been anyone else at the building from the assassin's team. If there had been, the man would have come to investigate the shots. Whoever was in contact with the assassin via radio was most likely watching Claudia's office and was therefore nowhere nearby. He was sure they were not being followed.

CHAPTER 74

Scot chose to drive around Lucerne rather than through it to get to Mount Pilatus. By now, all of the city's policemen would be carrying descriptions of him and Claudia, courtesy of the shopkeepers on the Kapellbrücke. The way they were going took more time, but it gave Claudia a chance to get some sleep. She had finally nodded off a while ago, and Scot had no desire to wake her. He needed her to be as fresh as possible for what lay ahead.

It was pitch black outside. Headlights blurred from one set into the next, indistinguishable as they zoomed past in the opposite direction. The VW's dash lights glowed an eerie green. Scot was tempted to turn on the radio, but decided against it. The heater was turned up high, and he glanced over at Claudia, who was wrapped in the same wool blanket he had been in only this afternoon. It was funny how quickly roles could change. It also made Scot aware again of how painfully alone he was in life. Claudia stirred, and he was happy to find that she was awake.

"Hey there," he said. "How are you feeling?"

"Pissed off."

Scot laughed. "That's good. Now I know I don't have to worry about you."

"How did you know I was in trouble at my apartment?"

"I made my call and used the fax at Fabia's, then waited around for you for about an hour. When you didn't show, I started to get a bad feeling."

"That man. He wasn't one of Miner's men."

"No?"

"No, he was an American."

Scot had guessed as much when he'd retrieved the shattered Motorola radio from the man's pocket.

"You should have told him where I was," he said.

"What, and let him kill you? Besides, he was going to kill me anyway. That I'm sure of. Why would I want to make things any easier on him?"

"You're right. Here," said Scot, pulling the Toblerone chocolate from his pocket, "one of Fabia's staff gave this to me. I thought you might like it."

"Thanks," she said as she unwrapped the chocolate and began to eat.

A light snow had started falling outside, and Scot turned on the windshield wipers.

"This ought to make things fun," he said.

"If it keeps up, it will give us added cover. Don't complain," replied Claudia, who finished the chocolate and leaned over into the backseat.

"What are you doing?" asked Scot.

"Taking inventory and deciding how we'll pack the gear so the weight is evenly distributed."

"Don't you want to do that when we get there?"

"I'm just getting organized. I don't want us to be out in the open any longer than we have to."

CHAPTER 75

Forty minutes later, Harvath began seeing signs for Alpnachstad. Claudia showed him where to pull off. The snow was falling harder now, and she made Scot drive through the village twice before she found the road they were looking for. It led back toward the lake and the cogwheel railway station. Fifty meters before the entrance to the station, the road branched off into a clearing beyond a large grove of pine trees. Claudia instructed him to park all the way at the end of the clearing, as far away from the road as possible.

"The cogwheel station is normally jammed with tour buses and they use this lot for the overflow. The hikers use it because it provides better access to the trailhead," she said.

Scot just nodded. His mind was on what lay ahead of them at the seven-thousand-foot summit of Mount Pilatus.

Claudia raised the VW's hatchback and worked with extraordinary speed. Items were packed in the order they would most likely be used. The later it would be used, the farther down in the pack it was stowed. Claudia had already loaded the three magazines of her SIG-Sauer before Scot had maneuvered into his snowsuit. He had given Claudia his sizes, and she had done a good job of finding something that fit him. The snowsuit was warm and, judging from the fabric, relatively waterproof. It was made by a commercial ski manufacturer, and he didn't much care for the brightly colored stripes around the wrists and pockets, but overall it was predominantly white, and that was the most important thing.

As if reading his mind Claudia said, "Catch," and threw him a large roll of white tape. "I'm sure you know the proper way to wrap the weapons as well?"

Winter camouflage wasn't something Scot Harvath, formerly of SEAL Team Two, needed help with.

They had agreed he, as the more skilled marksman, would carry the two-shot, silenced Makarov along with his Beretta. When they were close enough to their objective, he would remove and assemble the assault rifle from his pack. Claudia carried thirty-six rounds of ammunition in the mags of her SIG-Sauer, plus one in the chamber. Her role was strictly support, and Scot would be the point man. If things went well, Claudia would never even have to fire a shot, but they knew things seldom went exactly as planned.

Scot pulled on the climbing boots Claudia had purchased for him during one of her errands. They were snug, but hopefully wouldn't be the cause of any blisters. Claudia had purchased the Swiss equivalent of moleskin and would have it ready at the first sign their boots were causing either of them any discomfort. They had a long trek in front of them, and they could not afford to compromise their feet in any way.

The weapons and gear packed up, they put on their headsets and tried the link between their commercial walkie-talkies. A-okay. Claudia gave the thumbs-up, and they zipped up their suits. Normally, now would be the time to tape over the zippers, but with such a strenuous climb in front of them, they would need to vent their body heat often. Once they reached the top, they would finish taping up. They slipped on their white gloves, white balaclavas, goggles, and looking like a pair of phantoms, headed off into the woods toward the trailhead.

• • •

Two hours into the climb, Scot and Claudia stopped to take a rest. They each ate a PowerBar and polished off a liter of water between them. Scot applied moleskin to the inside of his right foot, which had been rubbed slightly raw by the new climbing boots. He leaned back on his elbows and breathed the cold air deep into his lungs. The snow had picked up in the last half hour. Judging by the altimeter on Claudia's sport watch, they were making good time. Scot was carefully searching for any early warning devices Miner might have planted along the trail to alert him of an assault, but so far he hadn't seen anything. He also frequently withdrew the assault rifle's nightscope from his backpack to scan the terrain above them. He never felt compelled to look behind.

After their break, the pair got back on the trail and continued their hike toward the summit. The winds were fierce and bit at any exposed pieces of flesh. The snow blew from almost every direction, cutting visibility and forcing Scot and Claudia to move more slowly, choosing their steps with more care. One wrong move and they could tumble down the mountain. Scot took a length of rope from his pack and tied it between the two of them, so neither lost the other.

They stopped to rest two more times, finishing off their water and two more PowerBars. Because of the frigid conditions, they were happier when walking, their bodies burning more calories for warmth. Despite the high-quality suits, gloves, and boots, the cold found its way in everywhere, and each of them was feeling numb. Not a good situation, considering they hadn't even faced the hardest part of the ascent yet.

• • •

Half an hour after their last rest stop, Claudia gave a tug on the rope and Scot stopped. When he turned to face her, she was pointing up. He removed the nightscope and peered through the green light to see what she was pointing at.

Between gusts of snowy wind he could make out two buildings, which he knew from Claudia's diagram would be Pilatus's two hotels. Several hundred feet above the larger hotel, he made out the faint lights on top of the Pilatus radar station.

It had taken them over five hours to hike to this height. They came to a ridge hidden from above by a wide plateau. Had they been normal hikers, the plateau would have signaled the final part of their journey with plenty of cold beer and *Würstel* to be had only twenty minutes away in one of the hotel bars. But, Scot Harvath and Claudia Mueller were anything but normal hikers.

The plateau allowed Scot and Claudia to maneuver their way around the mountain without risk of being seen by any sentries above. The idea, which had been Claudia's, was to come from a direction Miner would never suspect—right up the icy face below the church. To have attempted to infiltrate the perimeter by one of the typical tourist routes would surely have been to invite early detection and probably more than a few bullets. Scot had had enough of those.

Because of Miner's comments, Scot and Claudia believed the church was the most logical point of entry into the fortress. Any other choice might have meant days of searching for entrances that were either impossible to find or impossible to access.

It took them over an hour to round the ridge and arrive at the base of their climb. Looking up, Scot saw only snow, rock, and ice. There wasn't any sign of the church, but he trusted Claudia's judgment.

They slid into harnesses, strapped on crampons, laid out their ropes, and taped each other the rest of the way up. As Claudia was the more experienced climber, it was decided she would lead this part of the ascent. She warned Scot again about the dangers of climbing with the assault rifle fully assembled, but Scot's mind was made up. He had climbed more difficult mountains with bigger weapons before. Besides, the need to be prepared for what might lie waiting for them when they reached the top far outweighed all other considerations.

Scot assembled the rifle while Claudia removed the pickaxes from their packs and finished laying out the rest of the gear.

They checked each other's rigs, and satisfied that they were completely ready, or as close thereto as possible, Claudia started to climb the face.

She moved with extraordinary skill and agility. Climbing was normally viewed as a man's sport, requiring lots of upper-body strength, but Claudia was obviously very strong. She swung the axes with great force and had no problem hammering in the pitons as she worked her way up.

Scot was sure the climb could have been done in half the time if he hadn't been working with an injured left arm. There was no other way to covertly assault the mountain, so they had decided this would be it, but that they would take it slow.

His left arm throbbed, from both the fatigue of the climb and also the cold. Scot was glad that Claudia was on point, chipping out toeholds and hammering in the pitons. He had no idea if he would have been able to do it. He was breathing heavily and appreciated Claudia's frequent stops to rest. He knew she didn't need to. She was stopping for him.

The climb was slow going, and the wind tormented the pair with every step, threatening to rip them from the face of the mountain and cast them into the valley far below. Scot was growing more tired and started initiating the breaks himself, and with greater frequency. Claudia never said a word. She waited for him to give her the thumbs-up and only then would continue.

Finally, the sound in his ears of his own heavy breathing was replaced by the sound over his headset of Claudia clicking her tongue twice against her teeth. That was their signal that they were approximately twenty meters away from cresting the top. Claudia froze where she was and waited for Scot to join her. When he did, he rested for ten minutes without saying a word. He was exhausted.

He couldn't ask Claudia to go straight to the top and put her life in danger by peering over the edge toward the church. What if there was a guard stationed there, or some sort of motion detector? The fact was that because Scot knew what to look for, he needed to be the first one over. When he felt he had sufficiently regained his strength, he began to lead the climb.

Hammering in the pitons and cutting out the toeholds was excruciating. Scot hadn't realized how much he had demanded of his right arm while he favored the left. He wasn't a quitter, though, and they were so close now. Just a few more meters. Claudia hung back, monitoring his progress and giving him plenty of space, as he had requested. She was to have her weapon drawn when he went over the top, just in case he was taken by surprise and one of Miner's men should happen to peer over the edge to see if anyone was behind him.

Scot didn't want Claudia to be easy pickings, unprepared on the face all by herself.

Harvath continued to cut his toeholds and hammer the pitons. Reaching above his head, he readied to hammer another home, and the unthinkable happened. An enormous gust of wind peeled him right off the face and sent him shooting downward. Although he knew he had set his pitons properly, this was the moment in which every climber fears he will discover his safety measures hadn't been set as well as he thought.

Scot kept falling, his hands flailing, knowing there was nothing to grab on to, but trying nonetheless. Then came the snap of being jerked to a slapping halt, but instead of feeling it in his harness, where he should have, he felt it hard along the left side of his ribs and dangerously across his windpipe. It took a few moments for him to realize what had happened.

He had not been stopped by his rope and safety harness, but rather by the shoulder strap of the assault rifle. Somehow it had gotten caught on a piton and, with the downward weight of his body, was threatening to cut off all of his oxygen and strangle him. Scot clawed at the strap, trying to free himself, but it wouldn't budge. His legs were completely out of energy, and he couldn't muster enough strength to even push himself away from the frozen wall of rock behind him. Harvath's eyes drifted out over the dark valley below, and he wondered if this was how it would end.

CHAPTER 76

Claudia scrambled up the icy face to where Scot hung choking. In a flash, she had unsheathed her blade and was preparing to cut away the strap of the assault rifle pinned against his throat. As she brought the blade down toward the strap, what she saw amazed her; Harvath was shaking his head *no.*

He didn't want her to do it. Choking was okay, but God forbid the soldier should lose his assault rifle. *Men!*

Claudia frantically assessed the situation. If Scot didn't want her to cut away the strap, maybe there was another alternative. She raced up to just about his shoulder level and tried with all her might to lift the strap and untangle him from where he was caught. As strong as she was, Scot was too heavy. It didn't work. Time was running out.

She thought about trying to wedge herself between Harvath and the face, using her legs to push him out and off the piton, but there was too great a danger of them both becoming entangled and then falling with a combined weight that their equipment couldn't handle. No, there was only one solution. Scot had to be lifted up, and that could only happen with Claudia off the face and anchored on the crest.

After wrapping an extra length of rope around Scot's chest and under his arms, Claudia shot upward. There was no time to dig proper toeholds or hammer pitons; safety was forgotten as she focused on the man slowly choking to death below her.

The wind continued to buffet her body as she climbed. Twice the gusts threatened to rip her from the face, but she dug in deeper and refused to be beaten. Claudia's axes swung and cracked into the ice, delivering bone jarring *pings* through her arms as she scrambled up the mountain. With each swing of the ax came a synchronized kick of the foot; her crampons sending shards of ice and rock flying in all directions, until she was just below the snow-covered crest of the face. From here, it would be two to three more ax holds, and then Claudia could swing herself over the top. This was the spot where Scot had said they would most likely encounter the first signs of danger—an intrusion-detection system or worse . . . a sentry.

Claudia thought about unholstering her SIG, but realized that her death-defying free climb had left her with no nearby pitons to snag her if she should fall. She would have to go without.

The wind howled with a ferocious intensity. It was so loud that even if someone was standing directly above her, they probably would not be able to hear the sound of her axes digging into the last of the ice. Claudia held her breath and tried to concentrate on what she was about to do. Traversing the last two meters as if it were only two feet, she prepared to hoist herself over the lip. Digging in her crampons, she gave herself a count of three and then swung her body with dangerous abandon over the top.

Unbeknownst to her, the other side of the crest sloped at an extremely steep incline, and Claudia lost control as she began rolling down the slick snow-covered surface. She dug in her heels as hard as she could and was able to stop rolling. The last thing she had expected was that the crest would give way to such a steep hill.

Claudia's mind raced with more pressing concerns. *Had there been any intrusion detectors?* There was no way of knowing. The incline took her by such surprise that she didn't have time to look. *Scot could be on his last breath,* she reminded herself. *I have to get to him. But what about sentries?* Claudia took a quick look around and saw nothing. *Time to get Scot.*

Hammering with a vengeance, she placed two pitons a few feet back from the lip of the crest and anchored herself in. Scot had insisted on total radio silence, but Claudia decided to break it, if only briefly, to let him know she was about to pull on the rope. She didn't want him to give up.

"On belay," she said into her microphone.

There was no response.

What if I'm already too late? Once again, Claudia dug in her heels, leaned back into her harness, and began pulling hand over hand with all of her might.

The rope instantly became taut, but wouldn't move. *He's more tangled than I thought.* Claudia leaned farther back and pulled harder. She willed Scot Harvath to live, and to move. Her arms ached, her back and shoulders burned, but she wouldn't give up. Slowly, she felt herself making progress. *He's free!*

She kept pulling, hand over hand, an inch at a time. The pace and strain were excruciating, though Claudia didn't care. Scot was free. She continued pulling him toward her. The rope piled in a twisted coil as she fed the slack off her waist. *Not too much longer . . . almost there.*

"Halt, stehen bleiben!" (Stop, don't move!)

The voice came from behind her right shoulder and took Claudia completely off guard. She was so frightened by it that she almost let go of the rope.

"Stehen bleiben!" the voice commanded again.

The man was dressed in all white, much like them, and carried an automatic weapon, which was pointed right at her. Claudia stopped pulling on the rope, but held it taut with her left hand.

"Was machen Sie hier?" (What are you doing here?)

"Auf halber Höhe wurden wir von einem Sturm überrascht. Wir haben auf besseres Wetter gewartet und uns entschlossen, den Absteig nicht mehr zu machen." (We are climbers. We were stuck by the storm halfway down. We waited for it to get better, and when it did, we decided to finish the climb.)

"Mitten in der Nacht? Das glaube ich nicht. Komment Sie mit!" (In the middle of the night? I don't think so. Come with me!)

The man had been steadily closing in on her. She wrapped the rope twice around her left hand for security.

"Ich habe die richtige Ausrüstung. Schau!" (I have the right equipment, look!)

With that, Claudia grabbed one of the ice axes with her right hand, spun to her left, and with a *snap,* let it fly. The ax hit the man square in the chest. His throat let out a dry rasp of a death rattle as his winter white combat fatigues went red with the gush of blood pouring from his body.

"I don't know if you can hear me," said Claudia over her headset as she began pulling furiously on the rope, "but I'm not alone up here. We've got to get moving."

Claudia was able to pull in several more meters of rope and thought surely he was almost there when the snow around her exploded in a hail of gunfire. There wasn't time to warn Scot. If she stayed where she was, she was a dead woman. She reacted with the speed of a cat who'd stepped onto a hot stove.

Tying off the rope on one of the anchor pitons, Claudia rolled hard to her left toward the shelter of a small snowbank. The bullets fell like a hailstorm as the second sentry ran toward her with his weapon blazing. Claudia fought to pull the gloves from her hands. She needed to remove the pistol from inside her suit. The gloves came free and next was the tape that covered her zipper.

The sentry was getting closer. She could hear his boots crunching in the snow as he rushed in her direction, continuing to fire. Claudia pulled part of the tape away and then yanked down on the zipper. It opened a couple of inches and then stopped. *What's the problem?* Looking down, Claudia saw the tape had become caught inside the zipper. *Damn it!* The opening wasn't large enough for her to get her hand in and retrieve her gun. She pulled frantically. *Come on . . . come on!*

The man was almost all the way up the slope and in only a matter of seconds would have her perfectly in his sights. Claudia kept pulling on the zipper, then remembered her knife. She could cut a hole in the suit and pull her pistol out that way. She unsheathed the blade, pulled the material away from her body, and plunged it in. She ripped in a downward stroke and was about to reach in for her gun when she saw the sentry appear at the top of the slope. She was too late.

As the man stood in front of her, his weapon rising to fire, it was preceded by a little red dot. *Laser sight.* Claudia watched helplessly as the dot traced up her leg, then her chest, where she lost track of it before it flashed once in her eyes and then came to rest on her forehead.

Suddenly, the sentry's body tensed and a red dot appeared on his own forehead. For a moment, Claudia didn't understand, then the sentry's dot darkened and began to drip. *Blood!*

Looking to her right, she saw Scot precariously perched half over the lip of the crest. He was still aiming the silenced Makarov at the sentry, who slumped to his knees and fell face first into the snow, a lake of blood forming beneath his head.

Claudia ran to Harvath as he hoisted himself onto the crest and unslung the assault rifle. For several moments he didn't move and didn't speak. He just lay in the snow, staring upward.

Finally, as Claudia leaned over him, he spoke. "Wow, talk about a cliff-hanger, eh?"

"Are you okay?"

Scot rubbed his throat and continued to breathe heavily. "I'll probably be wearing turtlenecks for a while, but I'll live. How about you?"

"Scared, but I'll live too. You know that's the second time you've done that?"

"Done what?"

"Saved my life."

"You pulled me out of the water and off this mountain, so I'd say we're even," said Scot.

"Speaking of mountains, I thought you said you were a *good* climber."

"I used to be. I don't know what's happened. Maybe I'm getting old."

In most other circumstances, Claudia would have laughed at that. Instead, she just looked down at him, so happy he was alive.

"What happened to your suit?" said Scot referring to the slash Claudia had torn with her knife. "Were you hit?"

"No. I did it myself."

"What were you going to do? Distract the guy by flashing him?"

"Very funny. I guess I can stop worrying about you now. You're one hundred percent intact, bad sense of humor and all. Should we check the bodies?"

"Yeah, I guess my little nap time's over. Where there's two sentries, there's bound to be more. We've gotta get moving before they figure out we're here."

"If you want to rest a few moments more, I'll check them."

"No, you take the one I just shot. I think I'd better take the other guy. He looks like he might have an ax to grind with you. Look for anything that might tell us how to get inside."

They searched the sentries, patting down all of their pockets.

"Anything?" Scot asked.

"No. Just cigarettes. Nothing else useful."

"My guy's still warm, like he hasn't been outside for that long. How about yours?"

"Same thing, I think."

"Good, they probably just came on duty. Hopefully no one will be expecting them to check in for a while."

"But this one has a radio. What if he called in?"

"There's nothing we can do about it anyway. Let's get going. Grab his weapon. You know how to use it?"

"H&K MP5. It's a common weapon for the Swiss police. We don't normally use silencers, but I can handle it."

"Good, let's move."

Claudia pulled the weapon from the dead sentry and rolled him to the edge of the crest. Harvath counted to three, and they pushed both sentries over and threw the climbing gear along with them. They kicked up as much snow as they could to cover the blood and headed down the slope.

CHAPTER 77

The trail was well marked, even in winter. It twisted and turned as it wove upward around high outcroppings of rock. After a final bend, Scot and Claudia came upon a small ridge that sloped downward, and in the distance she could just make out the church.

"That's it," she whispered into her headset.

"Excellent. Let's see if anyone's expecting us."

The pair lay down in the snow, and Scot affixed the nightscope to the assault rifle. He scanned the ridge and the area surrounding the little church. While Scot did that, Claudia emptied the nine-millimeter Parabellum rounds from two of her SIG mags and loaded up the H&K submachine gun.

"It looks quiet. Doesn't seem like anyone's raised the alarm," said Harvath, rising to a crouch. "Follow me."

He picked a careful path, off the trail, down to the small plateau that held the church. Several times he raised the SG551 to his shoulder and peered through the scope, scanning the area to make sure they were not walking into a trap. *So far, so good.*

They reached the back of the church, and Harvath tried to look in through the stained-glass windows. It was completely dark inside. He signaled Claudia to stay low, creep around the other side, and meet him in front. He slung the rifle over his shoulder and removed the Makarov from inside his snowsuit. Cautiously, he crept around his side of the building. By the time he got to the front, Claudia was already waiting for him.

"Anybody home?" he whispered.

"Some footprints in the snow. They look new."

Claudia shined her small Mag-Lite on the ground, illuminating the prints. After examining the door of the church for any wiring or alarms, Scot tried it. It was locked. He signaled Claudia what he wanted her to do and then got into a crouched position. His eye against the nightscope and his finger on the trigger, he nodded. Claudia flipped the firing selector on the MP5 to single shot and positioned the weapon where Scot had indicated on the lock. Scot nodded again, and she fired, shattering the lock into a mass of hot, broken metal. Claudia gave the door a kick and quickly jumped back as Scot ran into the dark room, scanning every corner with the night-vision device mounted on the rifle.

Harvath signaled Claudia to join him as he continued to sweep the room. This time she understood what it meant to cover someone's six and she did just that. The church was very small. There were about ten wooden pews on each side of a narrow aisle. The whole room took only moments to clear.

Suddenly and without warning, Scot put his right hand up in a fist and Claudia came to a halt where she stood. He had taped his Mag-Lite to the underside of the assault rifle and now twisted it into the on position. He scanned the floor all around them. Claudia wanted to know what he was looking for, but she remained deathly quiet and didn't move a muscle.

Confident no one was within earshot, Harvath finally broke the silence. "Do you see the floor?"

Claudia nodded *yes*.

"We dragged a lot of snow in here, and it's already starting to melt. You see there and there?"

She nodded again.

"Now look over there."

Claudia looked in the direction Scot was pointing, and on the gray flagstones she could make out the imprints of two pairs of stocking feet. "What is it?" she asked.

"I think our friends don't want to make the same mistake we did and track in tons of snow, especially if this is one of the ways into the underground fortress. They take their boots off at the door and carry them in. But after standing around during a watch rotation, your feet get pretty sweaty. Believe me, I know."

"So they walked through the church in their socks, not knowing they were leaving a trail?"

"Yup. Time to follow the yellow brick road."

Claudia fell in step behind him.

The footprints led across the floor to a raised stone platform that held the altar. Harvath scanned the flagstones for any sign of pressure plates, making sure to follow the prints step for step. They ended at an enormous stone baptismal font, above which hung a statue of the crucified Christ.

"A lot of folks come up here for baptisms?" asked Scot.

"Marriages mostly."

"Seems kind of a pain in the butt to haul the kids and everyone up here to baptize a baby."

"You would bring all the same people for a wedding, wouldn't you?"

"I guess, but it seems awfully out of place."

"Remember, everything has a purpose."

"Your grandfather's words, right?"

"Right."

"Well, the footprints end right here, so there must be a door of some sort. We just need to find it. But first, let's get out of these suits. I'm burning up."

Scot and Claudia removed their snowsuits and hid their gear as well as they could at the far end of the church. Harvath then traded Claudia her assault rifle for the H&K submachine gun. It was a weapon he knew extremely well, and it felt good in his hands. While the SG551 with its night-vision scope was excellent for taking out targets at a distance, for close quarters' work in tight spaces, nothing beat an MP5. Scot also gave Claudia the silenced Makarov pistol with its one remaining shot.

Back at the baptismal font, they looked for hinges or any indication of where a door might be concealed. Almost an hour had passed since they'd entered the church.

Finally Claudia whispered, "Scot, look at this."

Harvath came over to Claudia's side, where she was using her Mag-Lite to examine a series of stone reliefs above the font. "What is it?"

"See these?"

"Yeah, what about them?"

"They represent the original cantons of Switzerland, but there's something wrong."

"What's wrong?"

"There's an extra. It doesn't belong," said Claudia.

"What is it?"

She moved her hand over the worn stone. "It looks very old, but it isn't. It's been made to look that way, to match the rest of the church."

"Great, but *what* is it?"

"It's the crest for the army corps of engineers. It was on a ring my grandfather used to wear."

"Are you positive?"

"It's hard to tell exactly, but I think that's the point. If you were looking specifically for their crest, you would eventually find it, even though it's been worn down. But, if you didn't know what you were looking for or didn't know enough to make the connection, you would pass it right by."

"So what do we do now?"

"Let me move over here and stand where the footprints end. . . ." Claudia moved as she spoke. "From here, my arms are too short to reach the emblem, but a taller person, like those sentries, would have no problem."

"Do you think the crest springs a door?"

"There's only one way to find out."

"You're right," said Scot. "Stand back over there and have the Makarov ready."

Claudia stepped backward and used the altar for cover. Scot transferred the MP5 to his left hand and reached up with his right for the emblem. The stone was cold and rough beneath his fingers. He took a deep breath and tried to push it in. Nothing happened. He then tried pulling it out—nothing. *Think,* he told himself. He tried turning the crest clockwise, and it began to give.

There was a heavy grating sound of stone scraping against stone as the entire baptismal font slid back to reveal a narrow spiral staircase leading straight down.

Open sesame, said Scot to himself.

Small flickers were followed by a series of lights beginning to illuminate. Scot flinched, and his finger tightened around the trigger, ready to fire. After nothing further happened, he realized that there must be an automatic mechanism that turned on the lights when the hatch was sprung. Whoever designed the stairway was quite ingenious. The first fixture was far enough down so that it wouldn't cast any light whatsoever into the church. Scot signaled Claudia, who slung the assault rifle and followed him into the stairwell.

CHAPTER 78

Scot quietly descended the metal stairs with Claudia directly behind him. He delicately placed one foot in front of the other, careful not to make any sound. They were inside the Lions' den now, and there was no telling when or where the first one would appear.

When they reached the bottom, Claudia could see that the energy it took to move with such stealth was depleting what fragile reserves Scot had left. She gave him that same *you are going to be okay* look he himself had given wounded colleagues and kidnap victims he had been tasked with rescuing over the years as a SEAL. In response to her glance, Harvath simply flashed back a thumbs-up.

He knew there was probably a mechanism to trigger the closing of the secret door above, but he didn't have any time to waste looking for it. A small hatchway led from the bottom of the stairs into a deserted corridor. The whole scene was eerily familiar.

He remembered visiting one of the last remaining Nazi bunkers in Berlin. Everything he now saw was exactly the same—vintage World War II. The walls, which had been painted a utilitarian gray, were amazingly smooth considering they had been carved right out of the rough stone of the mountain itself. With it located this far below the surface, there was no doubt how solid the compound was. Even the hatchway they had just passed through was made from thick sheets of steel capable of withstanding an incredible blast. The bare bulbs that lined the walls and lit the corridors were enclosed in rusty wire cages, which only added to the feeling of total isolation that the Swiss bunker exuded at every turn.

"Where do we start?" whispered Claudia.

A series of three different hallways branched off from where they now stood. Squares of lighter-colored paint with holes in the corners were on the wall at the beginning of each hallway and probably marked where evacuation plaques had once been. It would have been extremely helpful to look at one of those right now and ascertain the bunker's layout.

"Eenie, meenie, miney . . . We'll take this one."

"What about more sentries?"

"The way I figure it, Miner doesn't have a lot of men he can spare."

"Why not?"

"We killed two of his men in Lucerne and two more outside. That makes four. There's a finite number of men he would have risked bringing in on this assignment. They would have to be men he could trust, men he had worked with before, and just enough to do the job. More men means more people to split the money with and more chances of word leaking out and getting caught.

"We'll take this tunnel first."

The entire structure looked deserted. The only noise came from the overhead ventilation system, which creaked and moaned as it circulated air. Someone was here, somewhere. It was just a matter of finding them.

Scot and Claudia passed room after room . . . all empty. There were barracks, a mess, and even a communications room with its equipment covered by locked metal panels. No Smoking signs were posted every three feet, and the tunnel seemed to go on forever. When they finally reached the end, they had the choice of going right or left.

"What do you think?" whispered Claudia.

"I think someone around here doesn't much care for smokers."

"What?"

"Never mind. All the other tunnels turned left, so I say left."

"I agree."

Carefully, the two moved forward, checking each and every room for signs of life. The fact that they had yet to see any gave them both the chills, though neither would ever have admitted it.

They came upon another room. This one appeared to be an infirmary or operating room of some sort, and it didn't look deserted. It had been used recently. They entered and swept the room with their weapons, Scot on point and Claudia watching his blind spots. She was quickly getting the hang of this.

Medical instruments, saline IV bags, empty vials, and surgical equipment were scattered everywhere. A stainless steel table stood in the middle of the room. Scot depressed the foot pedal of a nearby garbage can and found a mass of bloody gauze, gloves, and paper wrappers.

"Well, now we know someone's been here for sure," said Scot, beckoning Claudia to come see what he had found.

Claudia looked inside as Scot dug around the can with the muzzle of his H&K. She never learned whether he was looking for something in particular or just out of curiosity, because a stocky man with a military flattop strode into the room at that very moment.

The man's first reaction was surprise. The last thing he expected to see standing in his surgery room was an armed couple going through his trash.

In one smoothly executed move, Claudia let go of the assault rifle and drew the Makarov from her waistband. She had only one shot and she used it perfectly. The bullet entered the nurse's brain, just above his left eye. He was killed instantly and dropped straight to the cold tile floor.

Harvath was on the man in a heartbeat, dragging him inside, where his body couldn't be seen from the hall.

"Where'd you learn to shoot like that?" he asked.

"Growing up on a farm in Grindelwald, you find lots of ways to amuse yourself."

"I doubt you learned that kind of shooting on a farm. Help me get him all the way inside."

Claudia was just as amazed as Scot at her own deadly accuracy because, in fact, she hadn't aimed at the man's head; she had been aiming at his chest. Either he moved or she moved, or they both did just at the last second. It really didn't matter. What mattered was that the man had been neutralized before he could sound an alarm.

"We must be getting close. They wouldn't have spread themselves too thin. There are probably three or four rooms that they're using. They will be as close together as possible. Let's get moving before anyone comes looking for this guy."

Harvath checked the hallway, twice, before signaling to Claudia that it was safe to come out. They continued in the same direction, hugging a flat wall with no further doors. A group of crates were pushed up against the left-hand side, and they had to swing out to the right to get around them.

As soon as they stepped into the middle of the hallway, a yell broke out behind them. *"Eindringlinge! Eindringlinge!"* (Intruders!), followed by a spray of automatic weapon fire.

Scot grabbed Claudia and threw her behind the crates for cover and then landed right on top of her.

"I guess they know we're here," she said.

"You think so? Listen, I'll take care of the guy with the big mouth, and you make sure nobody comes from the other direction."

Harvath flipped on the laser sight, swung the MP5 around the side of the crates, and rolled out onto his stomach. The man at the other end of the corridor was on full auto, and the bullets sent pieces of gray-painted rock everywhere. Despite how close the shots were falling, Harvath focused his concentration, gently squeezed the trigger, and fired. The spray from the other end of the corridor came to an abrupt halt, and the man fell to the floor, dead.

That's one down, he thought, *but how many more to go?*

"Scot, I think you'd better get back here," said Claudia, immediately answering his question.

He rolled behind the crates and began hearing what Claudia had heard—footsteps, and lots of them, coming fast from the opposite direction. Claudia had the assault rifle ready to go. When the first of the men appeared around the corner, she let loose with a deafening round of fire. Everyone's weapons to this point had been silenced, so the unsilenced SG551 Swiss SWAT assault rifle sounded like a rapidly booming cannon. The men retreated back around the corner.

"Now's our chance. Let's go."

Harvath jumped up and pushed Claudia around the crates, in the direction they had originally come. Scot ran as best he could backward, guarding their six, as Claudia ran as fast as her legs would carry her forward. They came upon and passed right through the T intersection where they had been five minutes ago. Now they were running down the corridor to the right, opposite of all the other tunnels.

Only sporadic doors were visible along this passageway, and they were all locked. This hallway was carved much rougher than the others and seemed to be some sort of access or service tunnel. Eventually, it began to curve back around to the left. Scot and Claudia kept running.

Fifty meters later, the tunnel opened up onto a large cargo bay complete with overhead winches. Huge pallets stacked with food and bottled water sat in the middle of the otherwise empty room. Scot walked over to examine the pallets.

"Evian," he said.

"There's also French wine and Italian pastas," said Claudia.

"Somebody's got good taste."

"But, how'd they get it in here?"

"That way," said Scot, pointing to a set of railway tracks on the far side of the bay that led into a dark tunnel. "I'll bet you a year's worth of water that those tracks link up somehow with the cogwheel railway."

At the far end of the pallets was a smaller pallet covered with a green canvas tarp. Scot walked over to it and drew it back. Underneath were crates of ammunition and wooden boxes filled with various weapons. The look on Claudia's face said it all as she stepped closer.

"Let me guess," said Harvath. "Your stolen weapons."

"Yes. I don't know why I'm going to say this, but I can't believe it."

"Well, that takes care of everything on your Christmas list. Now for mine. Where's that U.S. president I asked for?"

From behind the pallet closest to Claudia, the groundsman sprang up and placed the point of his pistol against her temple. "That is not part of the tour, I'm afraid," he said.

Harvath's eyes bored into the man, and he tightened the grip on his MP5.

"I suggest you drop your weapons," said the groundsman.

Claudia hesitated until he grabbed her left arm and gave it a good, strong jerk. She let her assault rifle clatter to the floor.

Scot also hesitated, but then set the H&K down gently.

"Very good," the groundsman said, as he ran his hands along Claudia's body. He found her holster and removed the SIG-Sauer. "And what about you?" said the killer, indicating he was speaking to Harvath. "You American cowboys never only have one weapon. I should expect at least five or six, no? Let's go. Out with the rest of them!" He kept a firm grip on Claudia's arm as he pointed his pistol at Scot to emphasize the seriousness of his point.

"You know," began Harvath, "I really hate it when people point things at me. It doesn't matter whether it's guns, knives, or . . . now, Claudia!"

Harvath dove for the deck on the off chance an involuntary spasm might cause the pistol the killer had trained on him to go off. Claudia clumsily drove the blade of her knife deep into the side of her captor's throat and stepped back. He clutched ineffectively at the blade, falling to his knees in agony. As the blood gushed from his neck, all that was visible of the knife was the bone handle.

Claudia rushed to Scot, who pulled her into his arms. "You okay?" he asked.

"I think so."

"Not bad, but remind me to teach you sometime the correct way to use one of those things."

Claudia stared at the man, who had killed so many in his lifetime, lying on the floor dying. "My grandfather gave me that knife. I never climbed without it."

Scot was about to say that he liked Claudia's grandfather more and more with each passing minute, but he didn't get the chance. A group of men emerged from the access tunnel and began shooting.

Claudia tried to reach for her assault rifle, but Scot pulled her away.

"There's no time. Let's move!" he yelled, grabbing her hand and running toward the opposite end of the cargo bay. The pallets provided some cover at first, but the bullets got closer and closer as they broke into the open and ran for the nearest hallway.

CHAPTER 79

Between the two of them, the only weapon they had left was Scot's Beretta. Out of habit, he examined the magazine and drew back the slide to check the chamber. He had sixteen shots, semiautomatic. Not much against a group of men carrying submachine guns, but it was better than nothing. He and Claudia kept running.

They came to another intersection, and before they knew what was happening, two men with H&Ks appeared from around a corner. Scot dropped to one knee, and Claudia hid behind him. He fired three shots at each man, taking them both down in a roar of gunfire that echoed throughout the tunnel. Scot and Claudia were deafened by the blasts from the Beretta and couldn't hear the men from the cargo bay coming down the hall behind them, but Scot sensed it.

He whirled, and managed to keep Claudia protected as he fired again from his crouched position. The bullets didn't find their targets as quickly this time, and he pulled the trigger repeatedly until, finally, one man fell and then another. Scot yanked Claudia to her feet and pushed her down the corridor. They came to another intersection.

"Which way?" she yelled.

Scot pointed left and they ran. Thirty meters later they hit another intersection. Scot glanced quickly behind them and motioned for Claudia to go right. They did, and Claudia stopped dead in her tracks.

She wasn't sure what she noticed first, the man or the smell. Fifteen feet in front of them was a man dressed in desert fatigues with an Arabian-style headdress. Only his eyes were visible, but even then, they were shaded by the fabric. In his right hand, he held a model 61 Skorpion machine pistol, and it was pointed right at them.

Scot, who was right behind Claudia and had almost bumped into her when she stopped so suddenly, reached his left hand out for her waistband, knowing the man in front of them couldn't see it.

"Drop your pistol on the floor!" Scot yelled.

Harvath hoped Claudia understood what he was going to do, or they were both dead for sure. He gave her waistband the first tug as if to say, *one.* Then came another tug, *two.* Claudia nodded her head ever so slightly as if to say she understood, and on tug three she let her legs go limp, and the two of them dropped.

Scot's first shot went off just as he was hitting the floor and missed the man's head by a fraction of a centimeter. His next shot was dead-on, right between the eyes, and the man went down. Scot's pistol was empty, and he let it fall where he lay.

The man had been sitting at a small wooden desk across the hall from a large metal door. On the desk was a ring of keys. Harvath stepped over the man to grab the keys and almost had to pinch his nose from the stench of body odor. *Fucking Middle Easterners. Why hadn't some of them ever heard of showers?*

Scot had been convinced that neither Abu Nidal, nor his FRC was involved with this whole mess, but now it looked as though he might have been wrong. Or had he? Harvath reached down and yanked off the headdress. Underneath was the head of a man with blue eyes and blond hair who looked more Swiss than Heidi of the mountains herself. Scot glanced at Claudia, whose face was registering the same bewilderment as his own. *Why pose as a Middle Easterner? What's the point?*

With the keys in his hand, Scot motioned to Claudia to pick up the Skorpion.

"Cover me," he said.

Claudia nodded and looked both ways up and down the hallway.

Approaching the door, he noticed a shelf had been built directly to the left and on it sat a box. Wires ran from the box up the wall and above the door. *Booby trap?* Very gently, Harvath opened the box and looked inside. What he saw made absolutely no sense at all—a tape recorder. He pushed the *play* button and he heard a faint wailing sound coming from the unit's built-in speaker. It was a Muslim call to worship. Even more bizarre.

Above the door, was another box with some sort of fan unit pointing toward whatever lay on the other side. Scot dragged the creaky wooden desk chair around the body and beneath the box so he could check out this other mysterious item.

Once again, he eased off the lid. Immediately he was sorry. It was like being punched in the face. The stench was horrible. There was only one thing in the world that smelled like that—camel shit.

The two boxes were not booby traps. They were meant to annoy the hell out of whoever was on the other side of that door, and Scot was finally sure of one thing. He knew exactly whom he'd find inside.

He gave the door a last once-over and also checked beneath the desk for any hidden wiring or switches. There were none. Claudia stood ready with the machine pistol as Scot found the correct key and turned it in the lock.

As the door opened, Harvath was greeted with a hot gust of air and the terrible smell of camel feces. The temperature had to be at least thirty degrees higher than in the hallway. The room was dark, and it took his eyes a moment to adjust. The walls had been treated to look like sandstone, the floor was covered with straw, and there, sitting in the corner, his hand in a dirty bandage, was the president.

He was dressed in the simple robes Harvath had seen on so many Arab peasants during missions in the Mideast. The same type of robes the members of operation Rapid Return had been wearing when they were all killed. The light from the open door hurt the president's eyes, and Scot maneuvered himself in front of it to help shield the glare.

"What do you want? If you've got my food, then leave it. If you're going to take another finger, then get it over with!" said the president. His voice reflected how drained he was.

"Nobody's going to hurt you anymore, Mr. President," said Scot.

Rutledge lifted his hand to his forehead and tried to peer into the light. "Who is it? Who's there?" he asked feebly, too forlorn to even hope that a rescue had been achieved.

"It's Secret Service Agent Harvath, sir. You're going home."

"I seriously doubt that," said a voice as Claudia was struck in the back of the head and thrown in a heap across the floor, landing next to the president.

Scot spun just in time to see Gerhard Miner bring the machine pistol down hard across the top of his head.

Harvath's knees buckled and gave out. He fell to the ground and before he could catch his breath, Miner kicked him hard in the jaw, sending him reeling backward.

"Do you know how many of my men you have killed? Do you have any idea what an incredible inconvenience you have been?"

While he ranted, Miner kicked Harvath repeatedly in the ribs. "Some of the finest men I assembled for this mission are dead. I worked tirelessly, thinking of everything, and then you come along and ruin it all."

The blows fell again and again. Scot was unable to breathe. The man was going to kill him, and then Claudia, even Rutledge. Scot was seeing stars, the blow to his head had been incredibly painful. He needed to do something now, or it would be too late.

As Miner drew his foot back and came forward for the next kick, Scot was ready for him and grabbed at his ankle in mid-strike.

"Do you honestly think I am that stupid, Agent Harvath?" said Miner, who'd anticipated the move, avoided it, and now pointed the Skorpion right at him. "You seem to have more lives than a cat, yet this is how it is going to end for you, and your president will be able to watch you fail him yet again. I would like to say it has been nice knowing you, but it hasn't. As I said last time, I hope never to see you again. Now I will make sure that happens."

Harvath started laughing.

"What's so funny, Agent Harvath?"

"Ah, Gerry. If you only knew how much I hate having things pointed at me."

Miner's smug look of satisfaction was quickly replaced by fear as he was barreled sideways into the wall of the makeshift cell. Claudia had taken advantage of the fact that Miner was distracted and thought her unconscious to surprise him. He fell to the floor with the machine pistol in his hand, rolled, and struck Claudia full across the face. Once again, she fell in a heap along the floor, and this time Harvath knew she wasn't faking.

Without wasting a moment more, Harvath fought back his dizziness to pounce on Miner. As Scot fought to subdue him, Miner struck him repeatedly with the gun. Harvath returned the favor with a knee to Miner's groin, an elbow to his face, and an uppercut to his jaw. Harvath hammered at the man's shoulder and reached for the hand that held the gun, which was once again swinging dangerously toward him.

Scot caught Miner by the wrist and drove it with incredible force into the area where the wall met the floor. He heard a snap as Miner let out a scream and his finger squeezed the trigger. The twenty-round magazine emptied in the blink of an eye. Bullets showered the room. Scot could only pray that neither Claudia nor the president had been hit. As he continued his assault Miner began to weaken, and Scot knew he had hurt him . . . badly.

He pounded the man relentlessly, the blows falling faster and with more ferocity. He pounded him for Agents Maxwell and Ahern and Houchins. He pounded him for the betrayal he had suffered at the hands of William Shaw and for the lives of his friend Natalie Sperando and her friend André Martin. He pounded Gerhard Miner for all of the innocent lives that had been lost, especially that of his best friend, Sam Harper. Miner was going to die, and Harvath was going to send him to hell on an express train, all expenses paid.

Scot's hands were covered in blood. He heard bone shatter as he landed his blows. His rage, guilt, and remorse drove him on like a madman. In the middle of it all, something called out to him, urged him back toward the shores of sanity. There was a hand on his shoulder, the president's. He was speaking to him.

"Agent Harvath, that's enough," he rasped. "We need him alive. Come on now. He can't hurt us anymore. Let up on him."

The president was right. Scot slowly rolled off Miner and looked at the badly beaten body lying before him. He couldn't tell if the man was breathing or not, and frankly, he didn't care.

The president had begun to regain his equilibrium. Despite his haggard appearance, some of the stately confidence was back in his eyes.

"Are you okay, Mr. President? Can you make it on your own?"

"I'll be okay. Let's get her up."

To Scot's relief, Claudia was coming around. Her lip was split and bleeding, but at least she was responding. He put his arm around Claudia's waist and struggled with her to the door. He was beyond the point of exhaustion. *We're almost there. Don't give up,* he told himself. *Don't give up.*

"Mr. President," said Scot, motioning toward Miner, "unless you've got an idea on how to get him out of here, we're going to have to leave him. My mission is your safe evac, period."

"You called the man Gerry. Do you know who he is?"

"Yes, sir, Mr. President. He is a high-ranking member of Swiss intelligence."

"Swiss intelligence? What's he doing over here in the middle of the godforsaken desert?"

"Actually, sir. You are in a mountain in Switzerland."

"Switzerland?"

"Yes, sir. For some reason—I don't know why—they wanted you to believe you were being held by a Mideast terrorist group."

"Fine. We're in Switzerland; we'll let the Swiss handle him. Let's get out of here."

"Yes, sir!"

Scot steered Claudia out the door and to the right. The president followed behind. Harvath had no idea if any of Miner's men would be in front of them, but he knew they had to chance it. Going back the way they came didn't seem like the best idea.

Not even five feet down the hallway, they discovered the direction Scot had chosen wasn't such a hot idea either.

A tall man, with the build of a linebacker, stood blocking their way with a submachine gun. Unlike Miner's men, he was dressed in street clothes. The minute he spoke, Harvath knew exactly who he was.

"No gun, eh? What a shame."

It was the hired killer who had been after him since D.C.

"You know what?" the man continued. "You are the biggest pain in the fucking ass I have ever encountered. I'm going to charge double for you and waste your girlfriend for free. Good men, talented men, died trying to nail you, and I guess that makes me the best because I finally got you." The hit man raised his gun for a better firing angle. "I took two rounds from you in D.C., and my ribs are so fucked up, I can hardly breathe. If I'd had a clean shot, I would have nailed your ass before you led me up this godforsaken mountain. You know, you actually lost me for a bit. You almost got away. While you were climbing up the side, I took the easy way up and eventually saw you going into the church. That's when I knew I had you. It's been fun, but now it's time to meet your maker!"

The assassin's finger had just begun to apply pressure to the trigger when his head exploded. His lifeless body lurched toward the wall and then fell to the ground.

Standing behind him was his killer. He was quickly joined by a group of similarly dressed figures in black Nomex fatigues with goggles and black balaclavas. *My God, how many men does Miner have?* Harvath thought desperately.

He had no idea what to do. His mind raced for options. He knew he had to protect the president at all costs, but what could he do against a group of six heavily armed men when he had nothing? He and Claudia had almost made it. Almost.

The man who had killed the assassin reached across his weapon and pulled a piece of black material from his arm. Underneath was a red, white, and blue flag along with the symbol for the army's elite Special Forces. He then removed his balaclava, revealing the face of Dr. Skip Trawick.

Using his favorite mock Scottish accent, the first words out of his mouth were, "Surprise, surprise."

"You guys sure took your time," deadpanned Harvath.

"We were on our way for a pint and heard ya needed a wee bitta help," said Trawick still in character. "Where's the president?"

"Right here," he said as Claudia and Scot parted to let him pass.

Trawick dropped the accent immediately and identified himself.

"Glad to see you. Hell, I'm glad to see all of you. Is the area secure?" asked the president.

"Yes, sir. It is now."

"Thank God you got here in time."

"If you don't mind, sir, I would like to check you out before we evac."

"Absolutely not. First you check on the young lady, and next it's Agent Harvath. Then I want your men to—"

"I'm sorry, sir, but these are not my men. I just happened to be first down the hall and got a clean shot. This is a JSOC op. These men are from SEAL Team Two."

As the men started removing their balaclavas, Scot recognized almost every one of them. Their commander shot Harvath a thumbs-up and several others followed suit.

It was finally over.

CHAPTER 80

GENEVA, SWITZERLAND—TWO DAYS LATER

Scot Harvath awoke slowly. The room took a few moments to come into focus. Looking down at his arm, he saw that he was on an IV. The sunshine streaming in through the window bothered his eyes. A shadowy figure loomed at the edge of his bed.

"How ya feeling, buddy?" a voice said.

Scot recognized the voice, but it took him a few moments to focus in and clearly see the face.

"Dr. John Paulos. Well, I'll be. This is getting to be like old home week around here," said Scot, struggling to sit up. John helped him adjust the bed.

"Yeah, the kid told me he found you," said John.

"Who, young Dr. T? Skip knows better than to share classified information. I'm sure this mission has big red stamps all over it."

"He only told me he was part of the team that picked you guys up. He wouldn't say anything he's not supposed to."

"Well, why don't you tell me what the hell you're doing here?"

"First, tell me what you remember."

Scot closed his eyes and thought back over what had happened and what he'd be able to tell without revealing too much. "You're doing a diagnostic and checking my memory, right?"

"Yeah, that's all I'm doing. I've been cleared to a certain extent, but why don't we start from when Skip gathered you all up."

"Is that how he's putting it? He gathered us all up?"

"The kid's a cowboy. You know how those guys from Texas are."

"Okay, so Skip gathered us up. We took the cogwheel to Alpnachstad, where a couple of jets were waiting to bring us to Geneva. I assume the president is still here?"

"Nope, they brought him in for the complete once-over and then zipped him back to D.C. They want to do the hand surgery back there. You've made a lot of people very happy and very proud of you."

"Thanks, John, but what the hell are you doing here? Last time I saw you, you were back in Park City."

"There was a lot of concern about what condition the president might be in, if and when they found him. You know about the finger?"

Scot nodded his head. The fact that they'd done that to the president still made him sick.

"Well," continued his friend John, "there were big-time fears that these guys might go even further and that he might be in pretty bad shape once they found him."

"So, they had the world's greatest orthopedic surgeon standing by, right?"

"I don't know about the greatest. One of the top ten, how about that?"

"Plus, you already had security clearance, so that didn't hurt. But if they were flying Skip over, why not let him do it?"

"Like I said, the kid's a cowboy. He's good, but don't forget who discovered him. He still has a way to go before he can take the old man."

"I don't doubt it," Scot said, chuckling. "What confuses me, though, is how you all knew the president would be here in Switzerland."

"That is information that I am not on a need-to-know basis on. You'd have to ask your buddy Lawlor at the FBI; he put this thing together from what I hear."

"So if the president's gone, why are you still hanging around?"

"Scot, just because you're not on the ski team and don't live in Park City anymore doesn't mean I don't still care about you."

"You've gotten friendly with one of the nurses, haven't you?"

"Maybe."

"John, some things never change."

"As far as you're concerned, you were suffering from exhaustion and got beat up pretty good. They'll want to run some more tests here and at home, but I think you'll make it."

"Thanks."

"Don't mention it. Is there anything I can get for you?"

"Yes, as a matter of fact."

"Whoops, I forgot. I left something outside. Can you hold that thought for a second?"

"I guess," said Scot, who watched as John jogged out of the room.

A minute later he heard the door open and John say, "Here we are." He entered pushing Claudia in a wheelchair. Her faced was bruised, and Scot could see that she had received some stitches to her swollen lip, but she was as beautiful as ever.

Scot didn't even hear John say, "I'll leave you two alone," as he graciously slid out of the room.

She stood and walked to the side of Scot's bed. Wordlessly, she reached out and took his hand. Scot pulled her to him, and as carefully as he could, so as not to hurt her injured lip, he kissed her. Claudia wrapped her arms around him, holding him tightly. They both ignored their pain, happy it was all over and that they were together.

CHAPTER 81

LAKE GENEVA, WISCONSIN—04:30, NEXT DAY

Two pairs of white Mercury Villager minivans pulled into the driveways of the houses bordering Donald Fawcett's palatial estate. A fifth van waited out on Snake Drive, ready to apprehend any vehicles that might try to escape. At precisely the same moment, a Boston Whaler with quieted outboards was waiting for the *go* code to beach in front of Fawcett's home and assault the house from the lawn.

Gary Lawlor watched the seconds tick by on his watch. The team of heavily armed FBI HRT and support agents had practiced the raid over and over again until Lawlor was confident they could do it in their sleep. Only then did he okay the actual assault. Based on what he had gleaned about Donald Fawcett and his involvement with the president's kidnapping, he didn't expect him to come willingly.

Lawlor had been provided with the details of a Swiss intelligence officer's confession, given from his hospital bed in Geneva. Despite the Chinese wall that served to hide who took the confession and how it was obtained, Lawlor knew it had been done by the CIA. Supposedly, Gerhard Miner had willingly provided the confession and named names in exchange for a reduction in the charges. Whether certain methods had been used to extract the confession was anybody's guess, but they probably had.

Despite Lawlor's leads and a quickly closing net on Donald Fawcett, the White House wanted a quick end to the situation and had agreed to the deal. Gerhard Miner would probably show up somewhere with a bullet in the back of his head within a month anyway. Just as long as whoever did it wasn't dumb enough to use one that said, "Made in the U.S.A."

The information delivered to Lawlor also came with a special FYEO—For Your Eyes Only. The reason Gerhard Miner was in the hospital was because Scot Harvath had beaten the shit out of him, almost killed him with his bare hands. Lawlor couldn't help but smile.

He looked once again at his watch. Thirty seconds. He told his teams to stand by. "Five . . . four . . . three . . . two . . . one. Go!"

Fifty-five agents moved in from their assigned positions. All of the utilities were cut, and the security system disabled. Within a minute, agents had breached the front doors and were sweeping the house. There was no sign of Fawcett.

A call came over the radio that agents clearing the study had found two bodies. Lawlor got to their position as soon as he could. What he saw turned his stomach, even after all these years. The bodies of two men, shot execution style, lay in a pool of congealing blood on the hardwood floor. Retrieving their wallets and seeing the names on their IDs made him even sicker. The bodies appeared to be those of Senators Russell Rolander and David Snyder.

After a thorough search of the property, Donald Fawcett was still nowhere to be found.

CHAPTER 82

WASHINGTON, D.C.—ONE WEEK LATER

After five days in the Swiss hospital, Harvath was flown home to the United States, ostensibly to recuperate and undergo further tests. In reality, a whole host of people including the Justice Department, the CIA, the FBI, and the Secret Service wanted him back for debriefing. After a while, the questions grew to be monotonous and repetitive, but it was all part of the job.

Director Jameson had an authorized agent transcribe Scot's debriefing and only asked him to read it over and sign it if it was correct. Mercifully, Scot had no typing to do.

He attended a private ceremony at the White House after the funeral of the vice president. The story in the press was that the cause of death had been injuries suffered in a freak accident at home, while in reality Marshfield had finally cracked under the pressure of what he had done. Knowing he would soon be caught, he'd realized he couldn't face the music and took his own life.

Harvath was shown into the Oval Office and was soon joined by the president, who was accompanied by the attorney general, Gary Lawlor, and Secret Service director Jameson. Scot stood as they entered.

"Here is the man I've been waiting to see," said the president as he strode across the blue carpeting.

Seeing the president's right arm in a sling, Harvath immediately offered his left hand. The president grasped it warmly.

"I cannot thank you enough," the president said. "Once the full story of what you went through was relayed to me, I couldn't believe it. You risked everything."

"That's my job, sir," said Harvath.

"Well, I don't know how to repay you."

"It's not necessary, sir."

"Sir, if I may interrupt?" broke in the attorney general.

"Of course."

"I know your time is limited, and I also know you requested that this meeting with Agent Harvath function as a wrap-up."

"A wrap-up?" asked Scot.

Director Jameson cleared his throat. "Kind of a final debriefing. We know the overall facts are a bit fuzzy for you, and the president felt you had earned the right to the full story."

"I see," said Scot.

"Why don't we all take a seat?" said the president. The guests divided themselves among the couches and assembled chairs.

"Since Deputy Director Lawlor was responsible for such a large part of the investigation," said the attorney general, "I think he should be the one to fill you in. Agent Lawlor?"

"Thank you, Attorney General. Agent Harvath . . . Scot. On behalf of all of us, I would like to apologize for the way in which we treated you," Lawlor said.

"That's not necessary," said Scot.

"No," continued Lawlor, "it is. Your instincts were right on the money every step of the way. It's because of you that we have the president back in one piece."

"Well, maybe not exactly one piece," the president said, holding up his sling. Everyone in the room laughed politely. Lawlor waited for the laughter to die down before continuing.

"To a certain degree, the real linchpin was the wine invoice you sent me. The Vin De Constance that Miner had cellared at the Hotel des Balances was actually paid for by Donald Fawcett."

"The industrialist?" Scot was amazed. Yet another twist. "What does he have to do with all of this?"

"The president had put together—and you will excuse me for saying so, sir—a rather shaky coalition to pass a new piece of legislation. It is an alternative-energy bill that would cut our dependence upon fossil fuels dramatically over the next twenty years. Do you know how Fawcett Industries makes most of their money?"

"Lemme guess. It has something to do with fossil fuels?" asked Scot.

"Right, their mining, extraction, refinement, distribution, and sale, to be exact. His commercial empire is based on it. Even passage of part of the president's bill would have cost him hundreds of millions of dollars. If the act passed in full, it would cost billions."

The president broke in. "There were strong lobbying efforts for and against this bill. There were lots of jobs and related issues at stake. It's no secret that I am not seeking another term. This bill was going to be my legacy, and I was bound and determined to get it passed. As Deputy Director Lawlor noted—and no offense taken, by the way—the coalition of votes I had established was shaky at best. Without me there to cajole and handhold, the whole thing would have fallen apart."

"So—if I may?" asked Scot.

"Certainly," replied the president.

"Fawcett's goal was to get you out of the picture long enough to have the bill stall and fall apart?"

"The deputy director is the best one to fill in all the details."

"Thank you, Mr. President. Apparently, that was the plan," said Lawlor. "But it went bad. I'll remind you, Scot, that nothing we talk about can ever leave this room."

"Yes, sir. I understand completely."

"Star Gazer turned out to be the vice president."

"Vice President Marshfield?" Scot was sickened by it, but not completely surprised.

"Yes. Unfortunately, the vice president, being of weak character, was drawn into this mess along with Senators Snyder and Rolander."

"What was in it for them?"

"It was the same across the board for all of them—money. Rolander and Fawcett had been pals since their college days, and I think Rolander had always been envious of Fawcett's wealth. Rolander got in his pocket early on, and then at some point in this process, when and how we may never know, he brought Snyder in. They wooed Vice President Marshfield with promises of a huge campaign war chest filled with untraceable contributions."

"And," said Scot, "with the president not running for reelection next year, this scenario gave Marshfield a chance to get out in front of the cameras and show American voters how he could operate in a tough situation."

"That's right. The thing he wasn't expecting was for the situation to get tougher. From what we've been able to uncover, the deal had been that the kidnappers would hold on to the president long enough for the bill to collapse, and then he would be sent home."

"So the FRC angle was just a front all along, wasn't it?"

"Exactly. The kidnappers knew Marshfield would never authorize the release of the Disneyland bombers, nor would he put pressure on any other countries like Egypt to release any funds or other prisoners the kidnappers might ask for. It was all one big ruse."

"Just like the president's cell in Switzerland. When he was returned home and debriefed, everything he would describe would be consistent with having been kidnapped by the Fatah. Right down to the lousy smells, desert heat, and calls to worship."

"That was the plan, but then the kidnappers got greedy. They already had the president, why not demand more money? Fawcett didn't care what happened, so he wasn't going to pay up. He'd already paid them enough and even if they did kill the president, Marshfield would take his place and Fawcett would own the new president lock, stock, and two smoking barrels. When the kidnappers turned their sights on Marshfield for more money, that's when he began to fall apart."

"How did Bill Shaw fit into all of this?"

"Marshfield recruited him. Shaw had been involved in a couple of small things he shouldn't have been. He was helping to rig security contracts for old friends, and when Senator Snyder gave this information to the vice president, it was pretty easy bringing Shaw on board. He was offered money and a good chance at the directorship of the Secret Service once Marshfield took office."

"But you didn't put all this together from the wine invoice, did you?" asked Harvath.

"No. A lot of this was the result of Miner's and Shaw's confessions. The wine invoice led us to Fawcett, which led us to the refinery fire in Magna, Utah, just outside of Salt Lake. When we realized the president had been kidnapped, we checked and triple-checked every flight that left the Salt Lake area. There had been a MediJet flight supposedly repatriating one of Fawcett's British chemists terribly burned in the fire back home to England to die. The problem was, the deeper we looked into it the harder the chemist was to find. He was a ghost. He never existed.

"We got ahold of the plane and had our forensics people go over it for everything. The MediJet people said that because of an oxygen tent that was needed to transport the terribly burned patient, the patient used his own stretcher. We found small pieces of mud that must have been on the wheels of the stretcher that matched the mud from the farm where the Mormon couple had been murdered."

Scot remembered how badly Lawlor had chewed him out at that farm and let it pass. That was behind them now. "So, the farm *was* a staging ground and they loaded the president into an ambulance there and simulated the burns before leaving on the MediJet flight?"

"Yes, and all of this has been confirmed in Gerhard Miner's confession."

"That's why I needed you to let him live, Scot," said the president. "We needed to know who was behind all this."

"So, what now? I understand Fawcett is still at large," said Scot.

"With his kind of money, it's easy to disappear," said Lawlor, "but we'll find him. We already have a couple of leads. By the way, I have a message for you from my boss, FBI director Sorce."

Scot's eyebrows raised.

"He was needed at the office and was sorry he couldn't be here to give it to you in person. You can imagine how busy all of us still are."

"Of course I can."

"Director Sorce wanted me to tell you how proud he is of you. He says you are a credit to the Secret Service and to your country."

"Hear, hear," said Director Jameson.

"Secondly, he knew the tremendous burden you felt losing so many men. He wants you to know his thoughts are with you."

"That's very kind of him. Please tell him I said thank you."

"But, that's not all."

"No?"

"No. He is very aware of how William Shaw betrayed you and the rest of the Secret Service. He wants you to know that Shaw will be standing trial and that he apparently 'slipped' several times as agents took him into custody. The director knew you would appreciate this last bit of information."

Scot looked at the president and the attorney general, who acted as if they didn't comprehend the reference, and then let a small smile creep across his lips. "Thank you."

"You're welcome," said Lawlor. "So, that's about it. Any questions?"

"I have one for the president."

"Go ahead," he said.

"How's Amanda?"

"She's wonderful and is mending quite well. That's another thanks I owe you. You saved my daughter's life."

"I'm just glad she's going to be okay."

"If you have time after this meeting, she's recuperating in the residence and would love to see you."

"That would be nice. I'll make sure I stop by."

"Director Jameson, I believe you have something else to say?" said the president.

"Yes, sir. Scot, the Secret Service is extremely proud of you. We know what has happened over the last almost two weeks has not been easy for you at all. It also goes without saying that you have been cleared of all allegations of wrongdoing, and we apologize that you were ever placed in this situation to begin with. We know you'll probably need a little more time off for R and R, but the president has authorized me to offer you the position of chief of White House Security. We have a lot of rebuilding to do, and none of us can think of a better man to do it."

"I don't know what to say."

"Say *yes,"* said Lawlor, and the room broke out in another polite round of laughter.

"Yes, I'll take it."

Everyone in the room stood and applauded, and Scot rose to shake their hands.

"Before you go," said the president as a hush fell over the room, "I would like to ask you, Agent Harvath, if there's anything else I can do. You saved my life and my daughter's. I've given you a new job, but that's hardly enough. If there's anything else I can do for you, say the word and it's yours."

"Well, Mr. President, there is one thing."

EPILOGUE

Caspian Sea—one month later

"*Dahling,* if you don't hurry, you will miss sunset," drawled the beautiful blond woman in her thick Russian accent. Her tan body was a stark contrast to the white cotton hammock in which she lay. Their sleek sailing yacht sat peacefully at anchor off the Russian coast, with only an occasional ripple across the warm, dark water to disturb yet another otherwise perfect day. "*Dahling,* are you bringing drinks?" she said in that voice that had captivated him when he first met her in Minsk.

"*Da.* A little more tequila and I'm going to show you the best margarita you've ever had. Even the fucking Mexicans don't make 'em this good," shouted a man's voice from below deck.

"Well, hurry. Light is going!"

"Yeah, yeah, yeah. Keep your perestroikas on. If you knew how to do anything else but lie around, I'd be up there enjoying it instead of down here!"

From the quiet water, eight wet-suited men with rebreathers broke the surface. Four swam forward to the bow of the vessel, while the remaining men boarded from the stern.

With his MP5 at the ready, Scot Harvath crept quietly into the bowels of the yacht and searched for his target. As he rounded on the galley, he could hear the sound of a blender working on crushed ice.

Ten feet away, his target was dressed in madras Bermudas and a white linen shirt. Harvath conspicuously cleared his throat, and Donald Fawcett spun to see the MP5 pointed right at his forehead.

"Who the fuck are you? What do you want on my boat? I paid some pretty big people a lot of money for protection. If you don't want to have the Russian Mafia crawling up your ass, I suggest you turn around and get off my yacht immediately," said Fawcett, incredulous even in the face of death.

"I'm operating on a little higher authority than the Russian Mob," said Harvath.

Fawcett hadn't expected to hear English. Whoever this was, he was American, and that could mean only one thing.

"I have a special delivery for you from the president," Harvath continued. He lowered his weapon, took aim, and shot the finger of Fawcett's right hand that still rested on the blender's *pulse* button. The blender exploded, sending margarita mix all over the galley as Fawcett reeled back in pain. He staggered and moved backward toward a row of drawers. Shock and disbelief was written across his face as he clutched his bleeding hand.

"You have no authority here. These are Russian waters," cried Fawcett. "There is no extradition deal here. You can't just come and take me."

Fawcett let go of his bleeding hand and reached for something behind him.

"You see, that's where we have a problem due to lack of communication. I didn't come to take you back," said Harvath. He saw the fear in Fawcett's eyes quickly turn to hate as he pulled a gun from behind his back and pointed it at Harvath.

Reflexively, Scot squeezed the trigger and sent a volley of bullets into Fawcett's head.

Before the lifeless body had slid to the floor, Scot engaged the throat mike beneath his wet suit and spoke the four words he knew the president, Gary Lawlor, and everyone else watching and listening in the White House situation room were waiting to hear. "Tango down. Mission accomplished."

He then disengaged the microphone and said into the quiet space, "That was for you, Sam. I'll miss you."

Harvath looked at his watch and figured he would be able to make the morning flight to Zurich. He knew Claudia would be more than happy to pick him up. It was finally time for that vacation.

ACKNOWLEDGMENTS

Seven years ago, my good friend Jill Thevenin and her family opened their small flat to me in Paris and let me live with them while I started work on my first thriller. I wrote about three or four chapters of a promising novel (that I may still finish and have published) before I decided writing was too solitary a life for me. I shelved the manuscript and shipped my "slab" top back home to the States so I could travel "lite" throughout Europe. To be honest, writing a book was one of the most difficult challenges I had ever faced.

I eventually made it back to the Greek island of Paros, where I had lived and worked two summers before. I was having a good old time until I met someone, not far in age from me, who was writing a book of his own. The encounter made me realize how deeply I wanted to be a writer. So, what did I do? Did I grab pen and paper and get back to it? Nope. I had another idea. The writing could continue to wait. I wanted to create my own television travel series. Whether that was avoidance behavior or not, I don't know.

In a five-year odyssey that saw me bloodied, battered, and bruised, I made my television dream a reality. *Traveling Lite* now numbers twenty-three episodes and is seen across more than eighty-five percent of the United States, as well as in Canada, Europe, South America, Asia, and the Middle East.

Even though that was a wonderful feeling of accomplishment, I still felt something was missing. That something was writing. I knew it was the one thing I would regret on my deathbed not having done. So, with my wife spouting Arnold Schwarzenegger's words of advice to his author-spouse, "Don't talk about it, do it!" I plunged into what I have always wanted to do since I was a child—write books.

That being said, I want to thank the people who have shown me that an author's life is anything but solitary and who, through their extreme generosity of time, wisdom, and hard-won experience, have made this book and the Scot Harvath character possible.

Gary Penrith, FBI (retired), a great family friend, a sharp dresser, and my guide through the myriad levels of local, federal, and international law enforcement. **Peter A. Cavicchia II,** Secret Service (retired), who never took the "secret" out of Secret Service, but trusted me enough to let me peek behind the curtain. **Harry Humphries,** Navy SEAL (retired), a man who, despite having everyone and their brother knocking on his door for his expertise, not only found time to answer my questions about the lives of some of America's most honorable warriors, but also paid attention to what I was trying to do and gave me suggestions on how to make it even better. **Bart Berry** and **John Krambo,** the master networkers, for helping introduce me to Harry Humphries.

John Clair, FBI (retired), an incredible font of tactical information and someone to whom I still owe a drink the next time I'm in Wisconsin. To my D.C. contacts **Joan Harvath** and **Patrick Doak,** as far as where they work, let's just say their backgrounds were extremely helpful and I greatly appreciate their assistance with the novel. **Chad Norberg,** for always being available and always having the right answer. My team in Switzerland—**Simon Dryer, Phil Boesiger,** and **Sebastian Ritscher**—thanks for trying to make sure I got everything right. **Richard Levy,** my good friend, who not only guided my wife and me through the streets of Munich and the tents of Oktoberfest, but who also aided in the novel's German translations. **Sam Perocevic,** who helped with the Serbian translations and is the main reason I hope to visit Montenegro some day. **John Morris,** of the *London Telegraph,* whose wonderful series, *The Grail Trail,* exposed me to Vin de Constance.

Sharon Maddux and **David Sinkkonen,** my good friends, who know a good time and a good idea when they see one and are ready with constructive criticism on how to make either better. Their attentive reading of the manuscript early on is much appreciated.

Emily Bestler, my editor at Pocket Books, who really is the best in the business, and **Heide Lange,** of Sanford J. Greenburger Associates, my Lion of an agent—I will always be grateful for everything they have done. The assistants of these two ladies, **Sarah Branham** and **Esther Sung.** The L.A. Dream Team—my film agent, **Angela Cheng,** of Writers and Artists, and my entertainment attorney, **Scott Schwimer**—for their friendship, unfailing commitment, great advice, and knowledge of the proper weapon to bring to a gunfight.

T. C. Boyle, Steve Binder, Stanley Ralph-Ross, David Cosnett, and **Gloria Russo,** for all the things they taught me, which are too numerous to list. **Scot Thor** and **Joseph P. Fawcett,** two of the nicest "landlords," whose hospitality and couches I relied upon heavily in the early days and who are two of my biggest heroes. To that list I have to add my father and mother, **Brad Thor, Sr.,** and **Judy Thor,** without whom I wouldn't be here today. In all seriousness, it is their love of reading and strong belief in education that has helped me reach my goals.

Finally, I want to thank two wonderful ladies. The first is my wife, **Trish,** who always encouraged and supported me in my dream of writing. Trish also gets a big thanks for her help with the medical sections of the novel and her willingness to read chapters over and over again until they were just right. The second wonderful lady is our dear friend **Cynthia Jackson,** of Pocket Books, whom Trish and I met on an overnight train from Munich to Amsterdam. Cindy was one of the first people to read and believe in my manuscript. It is because of Cindy that I found my place in the Pocket family. I can't imagine how things might have turned out if Trish and I hadn't taken that train. It just goes to show you that everything happens for a reason and it all works out for the best. That being said, Trish and I are pretty heavy sleepers, and I am still missing a pair of hiking boots and a couple hundred Deutsche Marks.

Turn the page to enjoy special bonus material from Brad Thor's instant *New York Times* bestselling thriller

BACKLASH